YESTERYEAR

by

STEPHEN G.
EOANNOU

sfwp.com

Library of Congress Cataloging-in-Publication Data

Names: Eoannou, Stephen G., author.
Title: Yesteryear / by Stephen G. Eoannou.
Description: Santa Fe, NM : SFWP, [2023] | Summary: "It's 1930s Buffalo, and the Great Depression rages. Playwright Fran Striker needs to write the pilot for a new radio show but, to do so, he must overcome writer's block, defeat a Gypsy curse, foil a plot to assassinate FDR, and recover stolen diamond rings belonging to an alcoholic boxing champion. Who was that masked man? Based on the controversial true-life story of Lone Ranger creator Fran Striker, Yesteryear takes us on a magical journey leading to an icon's debut, a show that provided hope to Americans during the country's darkest days"—Provided by publisher.
Identifiers: LCCN 2022042014 (print) | LCCN 2022042015 (ebook) | ISBN 9781951631192 (trade paperback) | ISBN 9781951631208 (ebook)
Subjects: LCSH: Striker, Fran, 1903-1962--Fiction. | LCGFT: Biographical fiction. | Novels.
Classification: LCC PS3605.O16 Y47 2023 (print) | LCC PS3605.O16 (ebook) | DDC 813/.6—dc23/eng/20221121
LC record available at https://lccn.loc.gov/2022042014
LC ebook record available at https://lccn.loc.gov/2022042015

Published by SFWP
369 Montezuma Ave. #350
Santa Fe, NM 87501
www.sfwp.com

For Fran

The universe is full of magic things,
patiently waiting for our wits to grow sharper.

—Eden Phillpotts

Men should live by the rule of what is
best for the greatest number.

—Fran Striker, "The Lone Ranger Creed"

Contents

(MUSIC UP)

Announcer:

Striker is dead.

Barrett read the article on page fifty-three of The Buffalo Evening News, *not on the front page where it belonged. The newspaper shook in his hands, the headline blurred by tears. He'd been killed in a late-afternoon car crash, a head-on collision that sent the other driver and his granddaughter to the hospital. Barrett was certain the accident had been Striker's fault.*

He could picture the crash as if he were reading one of his radio scripts: Striker behind the wheel, a Lucky dangling between his lips, the window cracked to let smoke coil into the autumn air. As his mind drifted from the highway to storylines, from storylines to characters, and finally from characters to scenes—the things that always cluttered Striker's mind— his car had drifted across the double-yellow lines and into the path of the oncoming station wagon. He didn't die on impact. He had time to be surprised by this final plot twist. Barrett was sure that as Striker sat pinned behind the steering wheel, his vision tunneling, he must have been thinking of the many ways he could describe the details surrounding the accident— the blood streaming from his scalp, laboring lungs about to quit, the cold spreading to his limbs—so his readers or listening audience would feel as if they were beside him, watching and hearing him die.

The article listed all that Striker had accomplished in chronological order, but Barrett had known him before all that, before the radio and T.V. shows, before the books and comics, before his characters had become cultural phenomena. Barrett knew him when they were both young and

Buffalo, New York was brimming with gangsters and bootleggers, dames and dolls, and there were not many heroes to be found, except for the two of them. They were best friends back when bathtub gin blinded, when magic shimmered on Buffalo sidewalks like lost silver waiting to be found, back when Barrett was the original Lone Ranger.

Striker is dead, that much was certain, and Barrett hadn't spoken to him in thirty years.

Return with us now to those thrilling days...

EPISODE 1

Slattery's Rings

The magic didn't always occur at the typewriter. Sometimes it appeared after midnight, swirling over Buffalo's cobblestone streets like Christmas snow, accumulating on shoulders and hat brims, the pregnant flakes never melting. Tonight was such a night.

When the clock struck twelve, the bell in St. John's steeple rang across Colonial Circle, echoed off General Bidwell's bronze statue, and reached Fran Striker's house at 26 Granger Place. He looked up from his Remington Sixteen typewriter, his slender fingers poised above the keyboard, and cocked his head. The clapper striking the hour returned him from his world of heroes and villains to his attic writing studio where his desk was tucked under a sloping eave. He checked his watch, certain a mistake had occurred, that time had accelerated, that he had somehow been transported into the future. It couldn't be midnight already.

This was his witching hour, the moment his neighbors and extended family insisted that he stop his relentless typing, complaining that the hammer's continuous striking, the single bell announcing each margin end, the sliding carriage being returned and returned and returned were keeping them awake, preventing them from rising early to search for jobs that didn't exist.

He leaned back in his chair and stretched his arms toward heaven. A forgotten Lucky Strike smoldered in a littered ashtray. He reached for it, his fingertips nicotine golden, and took a final drag before stubbing it out.

The house settled around him. The joists and load-bearing walls creaked and sighed as if relieved that the typing had finally ceased. On the floor below, his grandparents extinguished their nightstand lamps, thankful the clattering in the attic had ended. Across the hall from them, his brother-in-law, Jerry, lay smoking in bed, an ashtray balanced on his chest, praying for work. In the smallest bedroom, the boys, Bobby and Donny, ages four and two, slept curled in the same bed, unaware of their father's radio scripts or the late hour. In Striker's bed, his wife Janet waited for him.

He rose from his desk and rolled his neck, popping vertebrae. Moonbeams streamed through the attic window and gleamed off his Conn silver-plated saxophone propped in the corner. His eyes, reddened by too many cigarettes and too little sleep, took in his office—his desk stacked with scripts, paper scraps scrawled with story ideas, and his Kodak Brownie holding the pile of overdue bills in place. The wooden file cabinets were crammed with radio scripts he'd written; the drawers would not close. A chemistry lab was set up in the corner, but the beakers and test tubes were dusty, both untouched since he'd dropped out of the University of Buffalo. His neglected sax had once carried him to a different world where growing bills and dwindling cash did not exist, but he no longer had time to play. He fought the urge to pick up the horn and to try to blow like Joey Hodges or King Carter. If he closed his eyes, he could feel the reed between his lips, his fingers on the keys, hear the notes bouncing through the attic walls to be heard by those who wandered the streets in threadbare coats. The silver sax would have to wait.

He remembered the last time he'd succumbed to the urge to play at midnight when his writing day had ended: how the boys awoke screaming, startled from their dreams, how Jerry had grabbed a broom and pounded on the ceiling yelling for him to knock it off, and how Janet had raced up the attic steps in her nightgown wanting to know what was wrong with him and didn't he know people were trying to sleep?

Striker switched off the gooseneck lamp and plodded downstairs, his legs heavy and stiff from sitting. Each riser creaked under him as if complaining. Before heading to his room, he checked the children. He stood by their bed watching them sleep. What do little boys dream of? The last story he'd read to them? Playing in the snow earlier in the day? Juice? He pulled the quilt to their chins, smoothed their hair into place, then shut the door behind him.

Janet was awake, propped on pillows, reading. Her hair, the color of chestnuts, was cut to the bottom of her ears and parted on the side. She lowered the book when he entered. "How'd it go?"

He patted his shirt for cigarettes. "Good. I worked on a couple *Dr. Dragonette* scripts and finished adapting *Tom Sawyer*. Have you seen my smokes?"

"On the dresser." She slid a bookmark between the pages and set the novel on her lap. "You finished *Tom*? I'll have time to edit tomorrow."

Striker crossed the room, moving like a much older man. He shook a Lucky from the pack. "Old Sam Clemens had Olivia as his editor, and I have you."

"That's right. And don't you forget it. Now come to bed. You look exhausted."

"I'll toss and turn and keep you awake like last night. I can't stop thinking about Dragonette."

"Is the evil doctor up to no good again?"

"He's not evil enough, I'm afraid. I need to come up with something better, dastardlier." He lit the wooden match with his thumbnail then lit his cigarette.

"You will. You always do. Come to bed."

Striker held the smoke in the back of his throat. His mouth formed an 'O' as he puffed one ring after another toward the ceiling. They swirled higher, breaking into bluish haze. The winter wind rattled the windowpanes as if vying for his attention.

"I think I might take a walk," he said, squinting through the fogged window at what might await him in the night. "Get some fresh air and try to unwind. Maybe work out the Dragonette problem."

Janet pressed her lips into a thin line before speaking. "It's late, Fran, and cold. You'll freeze. Listen to that wind."

He tilted his ear toward the window. The wind whispered through bare branches. He wondered what stories those voices were telling, if his hearing would be keen enough to translate.

"I won't be long," he said, when the whispers faded. "A few blocks up and back and I'll be home."

"With a stopover at a speakeasy."

"Just for a drink or two."

"We need to watch our money, Fran. The mortgage is due on the fifteenth. We need every dime."

"I need to walk. To think."

Janet opened her novel to the bookmarked page without looking at him, not wanting to argue again. "Go then. The sooner you leave, the sooner you'll be back. But even you need sleep, Fran."

He stopped to kiss her before he left. She turned, offering her cheek.

The wind had faded as quickly as it'd started. The moon ducked in and out of clouds, bringing and taking light as Striker walked down Elmwood Avenue. The fresh-fallen snow robbed the world of sound, muffling his footsteps and the narrow tires of passing cars as if both he and the Model A's were floating inches above the earth. He passed Bidwell Flowers, Kaplan's Delicatessen, Flickenger's Grocery and other shop windows covered by yellowed newspaper or soaped swirls. Some windows were left uncovered, revealing emptied stores, casualties of the crash. Shadows shifted in these doorways. Cigarette tips glowed in the gloom. He inched closer to the curb, away from the men on the bum who waited for the train whistle, the signal that it was slowing and for them to dash to boxcars heading west towards hope, towards jobs, towards California.

He'd told Janet that it was Dr. Dragonette keeping him up at night, but it was the fear of failing everyone that made him toss and turn until it was time to get up and write again. He heard the lonesome train whistle and for a flashing moment envied the men who ran from the entranceways in patched overcoats and sprinted for the tracks, leaving their responsibilities behind.

Along a near building's roofline, neon spelled B-O-W-L-I-N-G a letter at a time. He headed toward it and heard commotion from the tracks—the bull's shrill whistle, men shouting, cries of pain. He imagined the scene: railroad guards swinging billy clubs like Gehrig swinging for the fences; hungry men slipping on ice trying to get away; blood dappling the snow like fallen berries.

A Silver Arrow was parked in front of Voelker's All-Night Bowling Emporium. Striker stopped to admire the car, the blood-red pin striping that matched the rims, to peer through the driver-side window at the oaken dash. Snow had accumulated on the fenders and hood ornament, covering the archer's drawn bow. He fought the urge to brush off the car to see the uninterrupted lines. He wanted to touch the steel with an ungloved hand. Striker had sold his car—a Nash Roadster he and Janet had called *Black Beauty* after his favorite childhood story—to his friend John Barrett to help with the mortgage. As he circled the silver car, admiring it from every side, electricity hummed through the green neon above him like buzzing hornets.

Striker left the car weighed down by all the things he could never afford, a feeling as heavy as a lingering dream. He made his way down the side of the brick building to a gray door. A smaller neon sign hung above the side entrance showing an orange ball moving towards white pins until it struck them. Janet had been right. He couldn't afford the luxury of a speakeasy. A car crept forward, snow crunching under tires, the entire building suddenly illuminating in blazing light. Striker raised an arm to shield his eyes.

"Keep your hands where I can see them," a voice commanded over the megaphone. "Approach the squad car slowly."

"Jesus, Pops. Turn the spotlight off already. You're blinding me."

The light was doused, leaving only neon brightening the alleyway. Striker walked to the idling cruiser and leaned into the open window. His father, known to everyone as The Lieutenant, sat behind the wheel grinning. "I never get tired of that."

"You're going to give me a heart attack."

"That's because you smoke too much. What are you doing out so late? Nothing good happens after midnight."

"I finished writing and needed some air."

"Speakeasy air it looks like."

"How's Ma?"

The Lieutenant's smile dissolved. Skin around his eyes loosened, leaving the tired face of a man who'd seen too much. Bags under his eyes attested to sleepless nights spent applying cool compresses, administering medicine, holding his wife when her pain grew unbearable. "No better, no worse. I'm heading home now."

"I'll stop by tomorrow and sit with her."

"I moved the radio into the bedroom, so she can hear your shows."

"I'll tell her all about Dr. Dragonette."

"She'd like that. She talks about your characters like they're real, like they're friends of hers."

"They are real, Pops."

"Say, Janet came over today with the boys. She tells me her parents are moving in."

"The bank foreclosed. I'm setting up a bed in the library for them."

"That's tough. First, Grandma and Papi move in with you, then Jerry. Now your in-laws."

"It's okay. I've got room."

"You have a lot of mouths to feed now, Francis. A lot of responsibilities. Wish I could help, but I got my hands full with your mother. Hell, we may be moving in with you soon."

"My job's safe for now, Pops. We'll get through this."

"You're staying at WEBR?"

"Why would I quit? I love the radio station."

"You've never stuck with anything long. I figure you're about due to make a move. First it was photography, then chemistry, then that silly band."

"The Domino Six wasn't silly. We played a regular gig on WGR. We got paid."

"How long were you at Woolworth's? A month?"

"Three weeks."

"You should've stuck with it. You'd be in management by now. Think of the security you'd have."

"Why you bringing this up tonight, Pops? It's old news."

"I've been worrying ever since Janet told me about her parents. So many people depend on you now, Fran. Can you afford more mouths to feed?"

"I'll be fine, Pops. Stop worrying. And I'm not quitting anything either. Writing's what I'm supposed to be doing."

"That's what you said about the saxophone. And photography. If you do quit, make sure you have something lined up first. Something that pays better. You have to do what's best for everybody. You have to do what's best for the greatest number. It's hard, sacrificing all the time. I don't know what's going to happen to this family if you're out of work. I'd give you money, but the damn doctor bills are bleeding me."

"It's going to be okay. I'm going to take care of everyone."

"I hope so."

"You're tired, Pops. Go home. Stop worrying."

The Lieutenant looked at his watch. "You should go home, too. Janet's probably worried."

"I'm just going to have one drink."

"That's what they all say." He put the police car in gear. "I'll let you know if I hear about any better-paying jobs."

"Okay, Pops, but there's no better job."

After his father drove off, Striker needed a drink more than ever. For months he'd watched his mother wither. Each new treatment failed. Hope was dwindling as her illness remained a mystery. Maybe his parents *should* move in with him. A bed could be set up in the living room. They could all take turns caring for his mother. Tomorrow he'd bring up the subject again with his father. This time, he was certain, he could convince him.

He walked to the gray door and rapped three times, paused, then rapped again. A peephole the size of a mail slot flipped and two eyes dull as stones peered at him.

"What do you want?"

"To bowl a few frames," he answered.

The peephole snapped shut and deadbolts slid free. The door opened enough for him to turn sideways and enter the speakeasy before slamming shut behind him. Striker unbuttoned his overcoat and stretched out his arms to be patted down. He felt small next to the bouncer, Little John Liddle, whose shoulders were as broad as the door he guarded. His thick neck strained at his shirt collar, threatening to shoot the top button across the room like a bullet. A deep scar cleaved his sloping forehead, a visible reminder of the Great Railroad Strike of '22 when a New York Central detective had struck him with a railroad spike, splitting his skull and leaving him bleeding in the July heat. Little John Liddle still suffered from blinding headaches, fits of rage, and hearing a purring woman's voice that often led him astray. He never worked the trains again.

"How you doing tonight, Little John?" Striker asked, as the bouncer's hands roamed over his arms, back, and down his sides, searching for a gat.

"Aces. Always aces," Little John Liddle said, straightening. He stood a foot taller than Striker.

Striker pulled a pack of Luckies from his coat pocket and shook one free. "Say, whose Pierce Arrow is that out front? Can't be Roosevelt's. He isn't supposed to be here for a couple more days. It's gotta be Rockefeller's."

Little John Liddle rubbed his scar as if massaging the answer from his damaged brain. "No, I never seen no Rockefeller come in here. That's Mr. Magaddino's new car."

Striker lit a match, pausing before touching the flame to tobacco. "The Undertaker's here?"

Little John Liddle shook his massive head from side-to-side, the scar moving like a thunderbolt. "You shouldn't call him that. He don't like being called undertaker. And don't make no coffin jokes. It's bad luck. You might end up in one."

Striker flicked his wrist until the match quit. "Don't worry," he said, the Lucky bobbing between his lips. "Not even The Undertaker can hear us out here."

"Stop calling him that," Little John Liddle said, lumbering past him to unlock another door. He yanked it open to the sound of laughter and music. Life grabbed Striker by the lapels, lifted him off the ground, and pulled him deep into the heart of it.

The speakeasy was hazy with smoke from hand-rolled cigarettes and Lucky Strikes; from Stefano Magaddino's Havana cigars; from ladies' cigarette holders held by painted lips. A jazz band played "Stardust". The clarinetist stepped into the spotlight. He wailed, twisting and bending notes, telling the story of loss and heartbreak, making the audience forget about Artie Shaw's rendition. When he'd finished his solo, he stepped back in the shadows and let the piano and bass bring the audience home, reeling them back as the drummer kept time.

Striker made his way toward the bar nodding at regulars, shaking hands with those he knew well, smiling hello to a table of girls who worked at the radio station. The speakeasy was already working its magic. His worries were fading. He climbed on the stool next to Pando the Pinsetter, the alcoholic midget who they said once killed a man. Striker sat shoulder-level with him. Old Man Voelker, whose passion was woodworking and not running a bowling alley or a saloon, had built a barstool for his long-time pinsetter that stood higher than the rest. Only he and the prettiest short girls were allowed to sit on the stool.

"What do you know, Pando?" Striker asked, without looking and signaled Hans, Voelker's son, for a beer. He could afford one beer.

Pando didn't answer.

"What do you know, Pando?" he repeated, louder, and faced him. Pando was dead asleep balanced on his stool, still holding an empty glass of Don Stefano's Canadian whisky. Hans placed a beer in front of Striker, the white foam running down the mug.

"He's going to fall again," Striker said, taking the glass from Pando and passing it to Hans. He pressed the pinsetter's back to steady him.

"Some of The Undertaker's men have a pool going on how long he stays upright. You want in?"

Striker shook his head, taking his hand away. "What's The Don doing here anyway? I saw his Arrow out front."

"Talking business with my old man."

Striker studied the bartender—the ginger hair, freckles that dappled cheeks and arms, the stipples disappearing under gartered sleeves. "Your old man building something for him?"

Hans moved down the bar to wait on another customer. "I don't ask questions, and neither should you."

Striker had always liked Voelker, going back to when he was a child and Voelker, an old man even then, would let him bowl for free if he didn't have money. It seemed as if he'd been poor his entire life, struggling day-to-day, meal-to-meal. Now the entire nation was in the same sinking economic boat unless Mr. Roosevelt could ride in on his wheelchair and somehow save them. He didn't like the old man building things for The Undertaker.

Striker reached for his beer but a man wearing a double-breasted suit the same shade as his slicked black hair, grabbed his arm, squeezed hard, and stopped him.

"You touched him," the man said.

Striker recognized Maranto, Don Stefano's driver. He pulled his arm away. "What are you talking about, friend?"

"You touched the midget. You steadied him."

"I what?"

Maranto leaned closer, his face freshly shaved and smelling of Bay Rum. "You steadied him. I was standing over there watching with my friend and you steadied him."

Striker glanced at Pando then back to the gunsel. "So?"

"So, I had money on him falling before the quarter hour and you propped him up. You owe me a sawbuck, *friend*. He would've fallen for sure if you hadn't touched him."

"I don't owe you anything," Striker said, meeting his gaze. "Not a damn thing."

Striker didn't have a sawbuck.

"Oh, you're wrong there," Maranto said, grabbing his sleeve again. "Dead wrong."

Striker jerked his arm away. Before he could rise from his barstool, he felt a heavy arm thrown over his shoulder keeping him seated. Maranto took a step back.

"Shakespeare! I've been looking for you!"

"Hello, Slats," Striker said, to Jimmy Slattery, the pride of Irish South Buffalo, the former light heavyweight champion of the world, the guy who was supposed to take Jack Dempsey's crown until Scotch and all-night parties caught up with him.

"I know you," Slattery said, squinting bloodshot eyes at Maranto. "Little Joey Maranto, fought out of the west side, am I right?"

"That's right," Maranto said, hitching his shoulders. "I trained with Lou Scozza."

Pando listed and Slattery straightened him. Maranto frowned.

"You remember this guy, Shakespeare? Fought under a funny name. Joey Maranto, The Buffalo Mosquito."

"Torpedo. It was Joey Maranto, The Buffalo Torpedo."

"He was a flyweight but fought like a mosquito. An annoying little fuck buzzing around on hairy little legs. You ever smack a mosquito when it's biting you and it bleeds, Shakespeare? That's Maranto here. Soon as he got smacked, he'd bleed. Never seen nothing like it. It's like if you looked at him hard enough, he'd start hemorrhaging."

Slattery stared at Maranto, his gaze trying to break the flyweight's skin, and Striker thought of Dr. Dragonette inventing a death ray.

Slattery's best days in the ring might have passed, but he was still dangerous. Striker and Maranto had both seen Slats in too many drunken brawls, beating men bloody with bare fists, the frustration of losing the light heavyweight crown to Maxie Rosenbloom after one hundred thirty-five days as champ evident in each blow. When he was sober, he was the same old Slats from the First Ward, who liked to dance with pretty girls and sing Irish songs with his arm draped over a friend's shoulder, the way it was thrown over Striker's. But when he was drunk, and his mood swung, the man who may or may not have insulted him—or his mother, or Ireland—would transform before his drunken eyes. The man's visage would rearrange, his features expanding and contracting, twisting here, elongating there until Slattery saw Maxie Rosenbloom's grinning face. Punches would then come in flurries, without mercy, and without a referee to step in and end it.

"Some guys," Slats continued, blinking once more, "their eyebrows always open, or blood gushes from their nose like firehoses. Some are mouth bleeders. But The Mosquito here? He bled from *everywhere*, even his ears. His fights looked like murder scenes. One time, Father Brejski from Our Lady of Black Rock climbed in the ring and stopped the fight. The old padre thought he needed to administer last rites. Like I said, Shakespeare, I ain't never seen nothing like it."

Slats smiled his crooked smile, light dancing in his dark eyes the way he had once danced in the ring, up on his toes, elusive as a ghost, before Dewars robbed his bounce and his middle grew soft.

Pando fell forward, and Slats caught him by the collar and held him upright. Maranto's upper lip curled above his teeth before he spoke, the words caught in his throat, coming out in a rasp.

"You stupid Mick. You'll be falling down drunk like that dwarf in an hour."

Striker held his breath, wondering if Slattery would start swinging, if Little John Liddle had patted down Maranto at the door, if he and Pando were about to be caught in the middle of something inescapable. But Slats wasn't drunk enough to fight.

"He's a midget, not a dwarf. There's a difference. Now fly away little mosquito. Buzz away before I swat you." Slats shooed him with his free hand, Pando's collar still clutched in the other.

Maranto nodded and started to back away. "I'll be seeing you, Slattery. One of these days, I'll be seeing you."

"You don't see me now? I'm standing right here holding up a goddamn midget. You can't see that? How could you miss me? Am I a ghost? Am I invisible? Say, Shakespeare, you should write about that. Write a story about an invisible ghost that takes care of bleeders like The Mosquito here."

"I might do that," Striker answered, certain Dr. Dragonette could concoct an invisibility-inducing elixir. What evil acts could he perform if he went unseen?

Maranto pointed at Striker. "You watch yourself, too, *friend*. You still owe me. Watch yourself."

Maranto rejoined another double-breasted mobster at the end of the bar, this one younger, sadder, and dressed like a pall bearer. They stared at Slattery balancing Pando on the stool. The Mosquito talked to the pall bearer out of the side of his mouth like a bad vaudeville ventriloquist. The younger gangster never spoke, only nodded as if struck dumb.

"I wouldn't have minded seeing that mosquito get squashed. I would've liked to have done it myself," Striker said.

"Your hands were made for writing not brawling. You want another beer?"

"Sure."

Slattery ordered drinks. "I wasn't kidding before, Shakespeare. I was hoping you'd come in tonight."

Striker studied the ex-champ. His face, though still handsome, hung slack from drink; his eyes were bloodshot, unfocused. He was breathing heavy through his mouth, each exhale a puff of Scotch. "Whatever you need, Slats."

"I feel another one coming on, Shakespeare. Another bender. I think it's going to be a doozy," he said, reaching for the fresh Dewars Hans had set in front of him, his hand trembling.

"Ah, Slats. Are you sure you want to do that? Don't you have a fight coming up?"

Slattery took his hand off Pando to wave Striker's words away, dismissing them as if they were mosquitos or hornets buzzing around. The pinsetter leaned, and Slats re-grabbed his shoulder. The gunsels glared, their wager long ruined.

"I got no choice, Shakespeare. I can't control these things. Least this time I feel the toot coming on."

"What can I do? You want me to call somebody? Your mother? Father Brejski?"

Slattery shook his head, a black forelock falling free. He set down his Scotch. "Hold the midget a minute, will ya?"

Striker held Pando upright. Slattery tugged at his pinky ring, the diamonds catching the speakeasy's light. "I don't want to lose these when I'm drinking," he said, struggling to get the ring off his swollen finger. "Last time I went on a bender, I ended up in Muncie."

"That was right before the Levinsky fight."

Striker had lost money on that bout, certain his friend couldn't lose, that the bet was an easy way to make extra money to pay bills, not knowing that Slats had gone on a ten-day drunk before the fight.

The ring popped from his left pinky, and he set it on the bar next to his Scotch and went to work on the matching ring on his other hand. "I beat that bum two months later in Chicago Stadium."

Striker nodded. He hadn't bet on the second fight. He'd never bet on Slattery again.

The second ring slid off. Slats set it next to its twin, then pushed the pair toward Striker. "Here."

"I can't accept those, Slats."

"Jesus, Shakespeare. I'm feeling a brannigan coming on, but I ain't stupid. They're not yours to keep. Keep them safe for me. I don't want to lose them playing cards or in The Gypsy's brothel when I'm blotto. You're the only one I can trust. The rest of these bums," he said, sweeping his arm as if including the sleeping city itself, "they'd hock these as soon as the pawn shops opened."

Striker picked up the matching rings and felt their weight and worth. Seven circular diamonds were set in white gold. He remembered when Slattery had bought them back in the Twenties when he couldn't lose, when the money was rolling in like an endless cloud, back when he owned a closet's worth of suits and two-toned shoes. Slats would roar through the streets in his butter-yellow Bugatti, releasing dollar bills into the wind as children shrieked behind with outstretched hands, as if angels had let the money slip from their fingers and the bills were floating from heaven itself. The convertible had ended up in Cazenovia Creek and Slattery was found sleeping under an ash tree, his suit soaked and clinging, but not a single mark on him. Luck of the Irish, he'd told the police when they rousted him.

"These must be worth a fortune," Striker said, and thought of mortgage payments, his in-laws about to move in, and the growing number of Depression mouths he had to feed. Rings like these only come with a success that Striker had never tasted.

Slats gulped his Scotch. "That's why I need you to hold them until I'm right again. You're the only honest Joe around."

Striker dropped the rings in his pants pocket.

Pando snored.

Slattery ordered another round.

The wind howled not only on Lake Erie's shores but across the entire country. Gusts swirled over the barren east Colorado plains, kicking up dust and coloring the night a deeper shade. A tempest battered the Texas Panhandle. Old-timers whispered banshee stories to horrified children by candlelight. Dust found its way under doors and through loose-fitting windows, coating everything—chairs, counters, children. The Texas and Colorado winds married in Oklahoma, their mating stripping the once rich topsoil. Layers of rust-colored earth were peeled away, sucked skyward, and moved east in a shifting reddish curtain like a swarm of locusts. A portion broke from the curtain and was sucked higher, spiraling upward towards the clouds, then captured in an air stream that raced towards the Atlantic.

The wind that whipped across Lake Erie stung Striker's face as he made his way home from Voelker's. Canadian gusts drove the temperature down, the fallen snow golden in the streetlamp's yellow light. He'd bought one beer at the speakeasy and Slattery had treated him to four more. As he'd sat drinking and laughing with his friends, his worries about finances and family were forgotten. Half-written scripts did not haunt him. When he had thought of his mother, he pictured her younger, smiling, healthy. The closer he got to home, however, the faster his problems and doubts returned. Perhaps his stories didn't matter. He'd written so many radio series—*Crimson Fang, Betty and Jack, The Sky Boat*—and none of them had landed a major sponsor or garnered network interest. They were written, performed, and forgotten. Striker wished he could write something that mattered, something memorable, something that would save them all.

He hunched to the relentless wind and ran through every script he'd ever created. Maybe one of them could be reworked into something that'd win the attention of New York or Hollywood producers, men with money who'd pay for a good story. The western series, *Covered Wagon Days*, was one he always returned to. He'd written twenty-four episodes plus the *Adventureland* and *Way Out West* spinoffs and he still felt as if he hadn't gotten the story right. He remembered Episode 10, "Danger at the Gold Mine," about the assayer who'd tried to cheat a prospector out of his claim, and how he always felt that something was missing from that script, certain that episode could have been special if he'd only been more talented or inspired.

Then, as if a radio had been switched on, he heard John Barrett's voice. The actor's tone dripped with want and need, like a broken man on the verge of losing everything—his gold mine, his wife, his sanity. The voice came from nowhere and everywhere, startling Striker. He searched for the source but the homes on Elmwood Avenue and the apartments above the closed shops were all darkened at this hour, the windows shut tight to keep out the cold. The broadcast grew louder, as if someone had turned the volume knob. Dialogue rang across snow. "Danger at the Gold Mine" had aired two years ago, but it was as if it had never ended, traveling across the universe on radio waves long after WEBR had signed off that long-ago night.

Striker mouthed the dialogue he'd written, moving his shivering lips but hearing actors' voices. He was so caught up in reliving the broadcast that he didn't hear the footsteps behind him, moving faster, catching up, their sound muffled by snow. The back of his skull exploded. Light flashed like shattering gold ore, and he plunged face first into a dark mineshaft, his arms and legs flailing, the air growing colder and blacker the deeper he dropped.

EPISODE 2

Mystery of The Phantom Voices

Barrett stood in front of the dead microphone performing the *Covered Wagon Days* script. His voice, rich and resonant, boomed across the deserted studio as he delivered his lines. The words rang like struck notes. It was the sonorous voice of a man with broad shoulders, a cleft chin, someone strapping who stood over six feet bootless.

Barrett was none of these.

He was shorter than most men, although taller than Pando, with delicate features—pronounced cheekbones, a slender nose, pale, graceful hands that floated when he gestured. Even his mustache was delicate, trimmed precisely like the silver screen actors he idolized. He developed a habit of smoothing the whiskers into place, first the right side and then the left. His hair, the color of Arabian sand, had begun to recede and was pomaded into place.

When Barrett entered a restaurant or party, people didn't notice his pencil mustache, or retreating hairline, or floating hands. They didn't notice him at all—until he spoke. Then heads would turn. Necks would crane to see who belonged to that voice that bordered between baritone and bass, whose words filled every corner before they pushed at walls, overturned furniture, and demanded to be heard. Surely a voice like that belonged to a talking picture star, a New York Yankee, a hero from The Great War. Barrett had a voice made for radio, so smooth and rich it was destined to be heard by millions. He was certain of it.

Buffalo families huddled around their Crosleys and RCA Victors and Zenith Stratospheres each night tuned to WEBR to hear him read the news, or introduce the next program, or star in the comedies and dramas written by Striker. His voice was his instrument, like Striker and his Remington or Artie Shaw with his clarinet. He'd mastered it, learning to modulate volume and timbre, to color tone, to extract emotions from Striker's words and send them over airwaves to the kitchens and living rooms and into the ears of his audience. He tugged tear ducts and pressed passions with mere inflection. His voice made hearts gallop.

When he delivered his lines, people would turn to their wooden or Bakelite radios and stare as if expecting him to stride from the speaker and perform in front of them. He could voice any role—villain, foil, young, old—but was best when he played the hero, and his wondrous phrasing was matched with his character's remarkable deeds. The taller the tale, the deeper his register.

The head turners and neck craners who'd heard him speak at a restaurant or a party would burn with disappointment when they realized that the Olympian voice that had seized their attention belonged to a slender whisper of a man sporting a slender whisper of a mustache. They would return to their meals or resume conversations feeling cheated, as if Barrett had somehow swindled them. Some would scowl or glare, their expressions shouting *How dare he*? He grew sensitive to this and learned to rein his voice in public, to speak softly, to save the full beauty of his vocalizations for the microphone, the way a stallion waits for open fields before running unrestrained.

Barrett had no intention of performing the old *Covered Wagon Days* script in front of a lifeless microphone in an empty radio studio on a blustery winter night. He'd gone to the cluttered desk he shared with

Striker searching for a box of Pine Brothers Glycerin Throat Drops. He worried about sore throats, laryngitis, and somehow damaging his voice. Papers—old scripts, new scripts, half-finished scripts—covered the desk like mounded snow. Even Striker's Remington Sixteen, the same model he had at home, was buried in radio plays. As Barrett approached the desk, certain he felt a tickle or scratching somewhere between his pharynx and larynx, an indication of an oncoming cold, or strep, or influenza, *Covered Wagon Days*, Episode 10, "Danger at the Gold Mine," tumbled from the pile and landed at his feet opened to the first page.

He picked up the radio play, dog-eared and ringed with two-year-old coffee stains. He was about to return it to the pile when the dialogue stopped him. Barrett had read the script before, of course, back when Episode 10 had aired. The words were familiar but now seemed richer with meaning and heavier with importance. He smoothed his mustache, first the right side and then the left, while he held the script in one hand and read the opening. His lips moved as he grew more excited. By the second page, he was reading aloud, the scratchiness in his throat forgotten, his free hand gesturing like a dove. When he reached the bottom of page three, the walls of the tiny office, once a storage closet, compressed around him, the space too small to contain Striker's words. Reading the episode wasn't enough. He wanted to perform it again.

He hurried down the deserted hall to the broadcast studio, called The Gold Room because of the golden draperies hung to absorb sound. Everyone else—the director, the orchestra, the other actors—had left the station after midnight when Barrett signed WEBR off the air until morning. He was quite alone in the building.

He pushed open the door not bothering to turn on the lights; he could see more clearly than he ever remembered and crossed to the floor microphone. His eyes shut. He heard the swell of Charles Armbrewster and The WEBR Players all around him. The music played by the invisible orchestra chilled him, raising the hair on his arms. Of course, the orchestra would play. Striker's stage direction *Music Up* was on top of page one. Barrett waited for his musical cue to begin the announcer's introduction:

Old Ezra Holton was a prospector and with his wife had given the best years of his life in the endless search for gold in the west. Nothing but defeat had met him at every turn...

Barrett's voice thundered as he read, so powerful it startled him; it didn't matter that his microphone wasn't live. He'd planned on performing all the roles but as he opened his mouth to deliver the wife's first line, he heard Darcy Menifee cut in on cue, her voice so close he expected their shoulders to brush. Then he heard other voices—Jonathan Bliss as the sheriff, James Connolly performing the assayer's part—both sounding as if they were gathered around the microphone, leaning in to deliver their dialogue as they had two autumns ago. Barrett was too caught up in the performance to question the presence of disembodied actors, soon forgetting that only their voices were present. Their exchanges had never been crisper, their rendition never as clear. The words they spoke, Striker's words, wove such a vivid dream that Barrett was transported back in time and could smell sawdust on the saloon floor and feel the angles and points of gold nuggets in his hand. Even the orchestra, bridging scenes and setting moods, was performing at a higher level, rivaling any orchestra that played on the NBC Blue Network or on the Columbia Broadcasting System.

Barrett thought he knew everything about his voice—the strengths and weaknesses, the limits, the power—but his performance startled even himself as he raced from the lowest sonorities to the highest and back again. Like a gifted musician, he pushed the octave range in both directions. His dramatic pauses, the dead air left in his voice's wake, deepened the tension and would have crackled and sizzled like snapped electrical lines if pauses could've mustered sound. The other actors—

Menifee, Bliss, Connolly—delivering the performances of their careers, sounded like amateurs compared to the maestro.

After the last dialogue had been spoken and the musical finale had faded, Barrett, intoxicated by his performance, the type of performance that could catch the attention of a Hollywood mogul, turned to congratulate his fellow cast members. Only then did he remember that he was standing alone in front of a lifeless microphone in an empty radio studio on a blustery winter night. He hurried to the light switch, praying to see Connolly, Bliss, and Menifee smiling and patting each other's backs, or The WEBR Players slipping their instruments into plush-lined cases and arguing where they could hear the best jazz at this hour—The Colored Musicians Club or The Little Harlem Hotel? Light flooded the empty studio.

The tickle in his throat returned and he felt his forehead, hoping he was feverish and had been hallucinating. His skin was cool to the touch. He shivered and remembered his mother standing in Forest Lawn Cemetery years ago, a candle burning on a nearby tombstone, explaining how you only shiver when someone steps on your future grave. Barrett dropped the script, the pages scattering across the floor, and ran from The Gold Room, leaving the lights blazing.

The winds were now blowing over the entire world. Moist air churned from the Pacific Ocean, intensifying as it swirled toward British Columbia's rugged shore. Gusts crossed above coastal islands, straits, and mountainous fjords, pulling more moisture into the growing system. The air current collided with the Canadian Rockies and grew stronger by the steep, upward climb to the peaks, then barreled leeward down the mountains. During its descent, it was baptized the Alberta Clipper and began its race across Canada, moving fast and sure as the ship it was named after. The Clipper roared toward the Saskatchewan and Manitoba prairies, towards Regina and Saskatoon, oblivious to borders. To its south, an airstream swollen with rust-colored Oklahoma dust, angled northward.

Black Beauty fishtailed down Main Street, the back end sliding from side to side as Barrett fought to straighten the roadster. His teeth chattered. He'd left his mackinaw on the coat tree in his cramped office, his fedora on top, giving the appearance of a slouched sentry guarding Striker's scripts.

The ice beneath the snow again stole the tires' grip and he almost lost control. He was driving too fast for the wintry conditions, distracted by the fear that voices would fill the car at any moment, that apparitions would appear at the window, riding the running boards and mouthing Striker's words. He worried about his sanity. This was a legitimate concern.

His mother, Delores, was a long-time resident of the Buffalo State Asylum for the Insane on Forest Avenue, a block off Elmwood and walking distance from Striker's home. Barrett sometimes wondered if the sounds from Striker's typewriter would drift from his Granger Place attic, float above Elmwood Avenue, and slip between the asylum's bars to his vacant-eyed mother.

Delores' parents, Noni, a devout Catholic who wished she'd joined the Religious Sisters of Charity instead of marrying, and Timothy, a superstitious man who believed in curses, fate, and omens, had both emigrated from Cork and were both afraid of Delores, the product of their lone attempt at marital relations. Noni feared her child because she never cried—not when she was born, not when she was wet or hungry, not even when she was fevered. What child of God doesn't cry? Noni would ask any priest who would listen. Even Jesus wept, she would argue.

Timothy was afraid of Delores because she was born en caul, perhaps a sign of luck but most certainly a sign she possessed powers and gifts he didn't understand. After the membrane covering her head had been worked off, he was terrified to discover she had one blue eye and one brown, convinced this was some manifestation of an ancient Druid curse. Because of their fear, Timothy and Noni spent little time with Delores. Holding or playing with her was a rarity. Cuddling her was never considered. Since she never cried to remind them of her existence, they often forgot about her, leaving her alone in her room for days, or at the market swaddled in the vegetable bin amongst the cucumbers, or rolling in the back of a trolley car until someone noticed and would bring the silent baby to the closest police precinct or parish priest.

Delores' childhood friends were invisible. There was never laughter when she played with these visitors, just hours of quiet conversation over nonexistent tea, an activity that would drive Timothy from the house in panic and cause Noni to cross herself with such rapidity it was as if she was fanning flames. When she turned thirteen, Delores became a candle lighter and grave keeper. She was often seen kneeling in Forest Lawn Cemetery washing headstones with a wet rag and speaking unrecognizable words. A candle would burn atop the marker she was scrubbing, the flame's light lost in hazy sunshine.

Barrett never knew the identity of his father, but there was speculation that it might've been Danek, Forest Lawn's Polish gravedigger. There was wilder speculation between Delores' parents on whether Danek had forced himself on the girl or if Delores had been going to the cemetery to do more than clean headstones. Delores never said a word on the subject and would pick at cemetery dirt under her fingernails while Noni and Timothy asked her again and again.

After a long, painful delivery, Barrett was pushed into the world weeks before he was due. Unlike his mother, Baby Barrett wailed. The power of his premature lungs startled nurses and confounded doctors. Delores, exhausted and weak from hours of active labor and blood loss, never shed a tear but began to see things no one else could see and hear things no one else could hear. On Barrett's tenth birthday, she was taken to the asylum, babbling of a masked man and a green hornet.

Barrett grew up with the fear that one day he would wake with different colored eyes and see visions, hear voices. As he sat shivering in the Nash, thinking of his mother and people tap dancing on his future grave, he worried that day had arrived. If he wasn't losing his mind, then where had those voices in the studio come from? Did he imagine the whole radio production? Had he been sleepwalking and dreamed the entire performance, music and all, of *Covered Wagon Days*, Episode 10, "Danger at the Gold Mine"? And of all the radio plays that he had performed—the small parts, the starring roles, the hits and flops—why *that* script?

Barrett skidded through a stop sign, sure of nothing except that he didn't want to be alone. At first, he'd thought he'd never tell anyone of what had occurred this night, convinced that such a confession would punch his one-way ticket to Forest Avenue, and he'd again share an address with his mother. But the secret was percolating inside him, bubbling higher, bursting to make a break for it. Then, more certain than the snow that had begun to fall or the wind that had begun to blow, Barrett felt he should tell Striker every detail of the broadcast, that somehow Striker would understand.

"Yes," he said, as he downshifted, hoping for traction. "I'll tell Fran."

Barrett veered west on Amherst Street, toward Voelker's, hoping Striker was having a nightcap. The Nash's engine had never run so sure. Sparkplugs sparked and pistons pistoned better than in any Pierce Arrow or Lincoln Zephyr ever built. The engine purred then hummed then made no noise at all as if it had been lifted from the ground and was being carried on the broad shoulders of gentle currents.

The warmth in the car grew from an unknown source. Barrett loosened his tie and unbuttoned his collar. He grew drowsy and his eyelids fought to remain open. He pressed the clutch and shifted gears without thinking, moving his foot and arm by memory. In the distance, Voelker's neon sign was visible and haloed the bowling alley in green. There was little traffic on the road, but wide headlights approached and somewhere in the back of Barrett's sleepy brain he acknowledged that it was another car gliding toward him at too great a speed for this inclement night. The silver automobile was squeezing in front of Barrett before he knew it, their door handles and side mirrors almost grazing.

"Slow down, Joey," Don Stefano said, from the back of the Silver Arrow, turning his bull neck to watch the Nash pass inches from his car. His voice was quiet for a heavyset man; the gulf breezes of his hometown, Castellammare del Golfo, Sicily, still wafted in his accent. "It's too cold to die outside tonight."

"Sorry, boss," Maranto said. "I'm not used to this car. It wants to race. I look at the gas pedal and it takes off."

"They tell me it has the power of one hundred and seventy-five horses. One hundred and seventy-five! That's an entire herd. An entire posse!"

"Like I said, it wants to race."

"No racing tonight, Joey. They only made five of these. I don't want to wreck mine in the snow."

Maranto eased down on the brake so the silver sedan wouldn't skid. "Where to, boss? Home?"

"Not yet. One more stop. We need to see The Lieutenant."

"At the station house?"

"No," The Don said, settling back. "His house."

In his black hat and coat, Don Stefano was lost in the backseat shadows, a hulking figure riding in a ten-thousand-dollar automobile, smoking an imported cigar. He rode passed hungry, homeless men who'd retaken shelter in shop doorways, some still hemorrhaging from their earlier railroad thrashing. One of the hobos might, if they were hovering outside the Pierce Arrow and peering through the windows, observe that the round-faced man in the backseat was dressed like an undertaker. They would not be mistaken. The Don, a licensed mortician, owned Magaddino's Memorial Chapel, a funeral parlor on Niagara Street. Business was brisk.

When someone disappeared—a rival, an old enemy from Castellammare del Golfo, an overeager Prohibition Officer—gossipers joked that the only thing working during this depression was Magaddino's crematorium. Pall bearers complained about the weight of caskets, suspecting that they were horsing a special coffin, one handmade by Old Man Voelker, one that could hold two bodies—the deceased, whom everyone had come to bury, and another, often bullet-riddled one. The pall bearers called such a coffin The Voelker Coupe and no one wanted to hitch a ride in one. Even Danek the Polish Gravedigger, when told that a coffin was coming from Magaddino's, would refer to the casket as a 'bunk bed' as he spaded the rich Forest Lawn earth. A candle, lit in memory of his lost true love, would burn atop a nearby headstone while he worked.

There were two offices at Magaddino's Memorial Chapel. One upstairs, adjacent to the viewing rooms, where the bereaved finalized plans for the departed. The second in the basement near the crematorium furnace. It was here that the Don ran his main businesses—bootlegging, gambling, loan sharking. It was not uncommon for someone indebted to The Undertaker to be whisked from Buffalo streets and into the back of a black sedan. Witnesses, who always saw nothing, never expected to see the indebted again and, if they did, they were spotted days later, bandaged or splinted, sometimes missing a digit, an earlobe, an eye.

Often these laggards were taken to The Don's basement office. He liked to have the furnace roaring and the oven door open when he entertained these visitors. The Don, with an arm around their shoulder, would remind them of their business arrangement—the amount owed, the expected payments, deadlines—and how he, a simple immigrant from Trapani Province, had entered into their business arrangement with a blessed saint's devout faith, expecting to be paid, on time, and in full. The Undertaker would then walk the debtor to the oven's mouth, the heat robbing moisture from eyes and melting courage, and change the subject, explaining the effects of cremation—how the body immediately dries when placed inside the oven, how the skin and hair burn, how the muscles have no choice but to contract and char, how bones calcify then crumble.

"It's best," Don Stefano would point out, "if the poor soul is deceased before he's shoved in there. But sometimes..."

The Undertaker would let his voice trail off like a fading Sicilian breeze then clasp the abducted man's shoulder, his fingers pressing in until he felt the man wince, the shoulder drop.

Perhaps the only thing more intimidating than a welsher visiting The Undertaker at his funeral parlor was if The Undertaker visited the welsher. He'd appear unannounced like a dark angel on the next barstool, or beside him at the horse track, or in his living room, smiling at the man's wife and daughter, perhaps touching the little girl's hair. If The Don went out of his way to visit a person, to track them down, the trouble they were in was inescapable.

Maranto killed the headlights as the Silver Arrow crept down The Lieutenant's street. The homes were older and without driveways, built before automobiles. Cars humped with snow were parked by curbs. The houses, mostly duplexes, were dark except for burning porch lights. The Pierce Arrow stopped in front of the lone house with a shoveled walk, as if the occupants were expecting The Don's arrival. The wind, that coquette, came and went as she pleased. When Maranto shut off the ignition, the V-12 engine pinged as it cooled.

Don Stefano swung from the backseat and flipped up his overcoat's velvet collar. He'd been in this country since 1919, first in Brooklyn then Buffalo, but his Sicilian blood never thickened; he felt the cold to his marrow. His footsteps were light for a heavy man and soundless. He strode up the walk and porch steps as if he owned them already. Maranto, well-heeled, stayed a pace behind. The Don smiled when he tried the front door and it opened. Why would a police lieutenant lock his door? What could he fear?

Maranto paused to allow his eyes to adjust to the darkness when he stepped inside, but The Undertaker climbed the stairs to the second-floor flat without hesitation. The apartment door was also unlocked, and Don Stefano stepped inside. Here he did pause, his eyes sweeping the living room, taking in the matching wood-carved couch and love seat, the framed needlepoint—*Bless This Home*—, and an upright Kurtzmann piano, Buffalo-made at the factory on Niagara Street not far from The Don's funeral parlor. The wife must be the pianist, he decided, unable to picture The Lieutenant's thick fingers stumbling across the ivories. A framed photograph of Striker and his family was set on top of the piano.

The Undertaker passed through the living room into the small dining room, noting the silver tea set on the sideboard and the Rose Point china in the cabinet. He proceeded down the narrow hall to the bedroom. No floorboard creaked, nothing was bumped in the dark. The bedroom door was open; hinges never had the opportunity to squeak and warn. The Lieutenant was lying on his back next to a concave of blankets shrouding his wife. His body jerked and twitched beneath the covers as he again relived the terror of running into the burning Ingleside Home for Reclaiming the Erring, Buffalo's home for wayward and fallen women. The unwed mothers' and illegitimate babies' shrieks filled his dreams. From the living room, the mantel clock chimed the late hour.

Don Stefano stood next to the bed. The Lieutenant's service revolver rested on the nightstand. The matching table on the other side was covered in pill bottles and ointments. Maranto picked up the .38 and cocked the hammer, the sound awakening The Lieutenant, who reached for the Colt. When he realized there was nothing on the nightstand but his alarm clock, The Lieutenant pulled back his hand. He sucked in his breath as he became aware of the shadowy figure by his bed. His eyes wandered up the black coat to the unsmiling face.

"Don Stefano," he said.

The Don nodded.

"You're in my bedroom. You're in my house."

The Don nodded again.

The Lieutenant pulled the comforter higher. "What are you doing here? What do you want?"

"How much money does The Lieutenant owe us, Joey?" The Don asked.

"Too much."

"How many payments has he missed?"

"Too many."

"And that's why we are in your bedroom, Lieutenant," The Undertaker said. "That's why we are in your house."

"I don't have the money," The Lieutenant answered. "If I had it, I would've paid you. You know that. But my wife, she's still sick. They can't figure out what's wrong. It's a mystery. There are doctor bills. Specialists in Albany. They say she might need an operation. That's why I came to you in the first place. To help with all that."

Something rattled in his wife's throat when she breathed as if an important anatomical piece had loosened.

"That, of course, is unfortunate," The Don said, shaking his head as if familiar with empathy. "So many are sick during these hard times. But you see, Lieutenant, you still have to *pay* me. On time. In full. That was the business arrangement we made."

"I understand," The Lieutenant said, sitting up, his back against the headboard, "but you can't get blood from stone."

"No," The Undertaker agreed, then leaned closer to his ear. "But stones can be broken."

Maranto aimed the .38 at The Lieutenant's scrotum.

"And the wives of stones can be broken," The Undertaker added.

Maranto swung the barrel at The Lieutenant's wife, who moaned in her sleep. The Lieutenant shifted his body between her and the gun.

"Your son and grandsons can be broken. Everything can be broken," The Undertaker said.

"I can…"

"What is money used for?"

"What?"

"Money," The Undertaker repeated. "What's it used for?"

"To buy things? To pay for things?"

"That is correct. To buy things. And I've just bought you, Lieutenant. I paid with the money I lent in good faith that you never repaid. You will do what I say now. You will tell me things. Police things. Things I need to know. You will do me favors. You belong to me. Do we understand each other?"

"No, I won't. I'm a good man. I'm an honest copper. I saved those women and children from burning at Ingleside."

Maranto stepped forward and pressed The Lieutenant's service revolver into his ear.

"Ingleside was a long time ago. I will either buy you or bury you," The Undertaker said. "And if I bury you, who will take care of your wife?"

The Lieutenant's wife coughed, the sound thick with phlegm and misery.

The Nash struck another pothole and jarred Barrett awake. He swerved back on the road just before jumping the curb and striking an elm. As he approached Voelker's All-Night Bowling Emporium, its neon sign cast a green hue over the streetscape. He squinted through his splattered windshield, the wipers smearing the glass making it difficult to see. On the sidewalk, a mound was covered with lush snow.

"What the devil?" Barrett said, his voice filling the car.

The mound had feet.

He pulled to the curb and hurried to the sidewalk. He rolled the shivering body on its back, his eyes drawn to Striker's blue-tinged lips.

"Fran!" he yelled, his voice full volume. Icicles broke free from nearby overhangs and fell to the ground, shattering to diamonds.

He felt Striker's neck for a pulse and found a butterfly's weak flutter. Striker had an average build, but he was half-frozen and unconscious, his weight as dead as anything Danek had ever buried. Still Barrett, a mere splinter, found the strength to grab his friend by the lapels and pull him to his feet, as if all that strength that resided in his vocal cords had been diverted to his biceps, triceps, and latissimus dorsi. He slung Striker over his shoulder and trudged his way to Voelker's. Striker stopped shivering and grew still.

Barrett kicked the speakeasy door three times, paused, then kicked again.

Striker was pulled from the mineshaft, soaring upward toward the light. He was flying then, not flapping like a bird but propelled forward by some unseen force, like Lucky Lindy crossing the Atlantic or the fighter planes in Howard Hughes' *Hells' Angels* crisscrossing the skies, spiraling downward in deep dives and then climbing heavenward, a movie he had seen with Barrett at the Allendale Theater. His thick black hair was blown back as he cut through the stratosphere, his tie trailing over his shoulder like a kite tail. He felt as if he'd fly forever, like radio signals sent into space, and would never walk on solid ground with mortals again. As soon as that thought entered his concussed brain, he descended, not in a cut engine's freefall but controlled and measured, like Lindy's *Spirit of St. Louis* landing at Le Bourget or Hughes' biplanes rolling to safe stops in grassy French fields.

Striker did not wake up in France. He awoke stretched atop Voelker's bar, his head touching Pando the Pinsetter's head, their feet facing opposite directions. Spilled beer soaked through his pant leg.

Pando snored. Striker groaned.

"Thank God," Barrett said, fingering his mustache.

Striker tried to sit up, but lightening flashed in his brain. Pain rippled through his spine. He tipped to the side and Barrett held him in place until he was ready to swing his legs around and sit on the bar.

"Jesus, Fran," Barrett said. "Are you all right?"

"Yes," he said, and reached around and felt the growing lump where he'd been struck. "No."

Striker took in the speakeasy as if he had never seen it before. Hans had yelled Last Call before he'd regained consciousness and the crowd was thinner than when he had left. The band had packed their instruments. Those who remained were finishing their drinks or putting on coats, already complaining about the wind that awaited them. The house lights glared. Striker shielded his eyes.

"What the hell happened, Fran?" Barrett asked, and Striker winced, the actor's voice shattering his cranium.

"Public voice, John."

Barrett reduced volume. "What happened?"

Striker shook his head and light bulbs flashed behind his eyes. His stomach pitched. He searched for a cigarette.

"I thought you were dead," Barrett said.

"He would've been," Hans said, offering Striker a Lucky, "if you hadn't saved him. He would've froze to death out there."

Striker took the cigarette and leaned toward Hans for the light. He sucked in the smoke and held it until his stomach settled. Old Man Voelker shuffled from the backroom carrying a green and red tartan blanket. He had been a tall man when younger, over six feet, but was now stooped with age. His nose and jawline were still straight and pronounced, as if his face had been carved from hardwood, the edges sanded true and smooth. His vertebrae and shoulders must have been formed from lesser timber and had warped over time. Sawdust clung to his hair like dandruff.

"I found this in my woodshop," he said, throwing the blanket over Striker's shoulders. "I'll look for another."

Striker pulled the blanket around him. It smelled of varnish. Voelker patted his shoulder and set off for the backroom.

"What happened?" Barrett asked a third time, always impatient for one of Striker's stories.

Striker shut his eyes and tried to pluck the memory from the gauzy film that clouded his mind. The images returned to him one at a time, as if flipping through photographs. "I was walking home. It was cold. I was walking fast. Then I heard…"

"What?" Barrett asked. "What did you hear?"

"You," he said. "I heard you."

"Me? I didn't get there until later. I was at the station. I found you on the ground."

Striker rubbed his forehead with two fingers, the cigarette glowing between them. "It was your voice. Your radio voice. I heard it. It was coming from…somewhere. Everywhere. Like every tree and lamppost was a radio speaker. It was all around me."

"You heard his voice coming from trees?" Hans asked, pouring a shot of bootlegged Canadian Club. He offered it to Striker.

Striker shook his head, turning down the whisky. Fewer flashbulbs popped in his brain this time. "I guess so. It seemed that way. It was a radio broadcast. An old one that we did."

Barrett felt his throat close and had to force out the words. "*Covered Wagon Days.*"

Striker nodded. "Episode Ten."

"Danger at the Gold Mine," Barrett said.

"That's right," Striker said. "From a couple years ago."

"I was broadcasting it."

"No," Striker said, shutting his eyes and rubbing the base of his neck, the cigarette still between his fingers. Ash fell on his collar like gray snow. "I didn't leave the house until after midnight. You'd already signed off by then."

"I know," Barrett said, not quite sure how to explain. He'd been much more certain in the Nash. "But I was in The Gold Room reading the script. Well, performing it. In front of a dead microphone. In the dark."

Hans downed the shot of whisky.

"Why?" Striker asked, pulling the blanket tighter.

It was Barrett's turn to shake his head. "I don't know, Fran. I guess I wanted to hear myself perform it again."

The snoring pinsetter passed flatus in his sleep, the duration and intensity of which caused Striker to check for levitation. He, Barrett, and Hans moved farther down the bar.

"I can't explain it," Barrett said, once they'd settled a few feet away. He took a deep breath, summoning his courage, and smoothed his mustache, right then left, before speaking. "There were other voices in the studio."

"Bliss, Connolly, Darcy. All the actors who originally performed the script."

"You heard them, too?"

"Why was everyone there so late?"

"They *weren't* there, Fran. Only their *voices*. Performing their parts like they did the first time but better. A lot better. And the orchestra was there, too. Well, not the whole orchestra, not Armbrewster or the guys, no instruments even. Just their *music* playing on cue."

Hans poured another shot and pushed it to Barrett, who didn't drink hard liquor, fearing it would somehow damage his vocal cords. He drained the glass without thinking.

"That's crazy, John," Striker said.

"Jesus, don't say that," Barrett said. "Please don't say that."

Old Man Voelker came shuffling into the bar again, this time carrying a steaming cup of coffee. "I couldn't find another blanket, but this is better," he said, handing Striker the mug. "Drink it. It will thaw you from the inside."

"Thanks," he said, cradling the cup in both hands, feeling the warmth spread from fingers to wrists.

"Say, Fran," Hans said. "You want me to call the cops about you getting jumped? They get your watch and wallet?"

Striker set his coffee on the bar and pushed back his shirt cuff; the Bulova still ticked on his wrist. He felt his wallet's slim outline inside his suit coat and then remembered Slattery's rings. He partially jumped, partially fell from the bar and shoved his hands in his empty pants pockets.

The diamond rings were gone.

Pando sat straight up, eyes wild and searching, hair pointing at angles. Panic washed over him as if he'd awoken in a different world. He studied Hans' face, then Barrett's, and then Old Man Voelker, their features foreign to him. His gaze settled on Striker, and the pinsetter sighed, his muscles relaxed, relieved to have found somebody he recognized. He greeted Striker as he always did.

"Hi-yo, Striker."

EPISODE 3

The Gypsy's Curse

The morning skies above the Great Plains darkened. Topsoil transformed to coppery dust and was sucked into The Airstream. Farmers watched from their windows as the dark blizzard barreled toward their barren fields and ripped at the earth, scraping what it could take, filling the air with churning grit. Farmers stepped from their homes for a closer look at the intensifying storm. They covered their faces with kerchiefs like outlaws, but grime found its way into nostrils, mouths, and ears. They took shelter back in their farmhouses, their faces streaked with dirty tears, telling their wives and children their eyes were watering from the wind.

In Detroit, inside the studio of the Maccabees Building, home of WXYZ, *The Last Word in Radio*, station owner George Washington Trendle paced his oak-paneled office, oblivious to the gusts that painted his windows with a fine brush; snowflakes' points and branches were distinct against the glass.

Everything about Trendle was round. His head was almost a perfect sphere and so bald it was difficult to imagine hair had once grown on such a desolate spot. Black pince-nez pinched his nose. His stomach ballooned his vest, drawing his watch chain taut across the expanse. He pressed his abdomen as he paced, his insides aflame. His other hand gripped a bottle of Doctor Foley's Pain Relief Medicine, guaranteed by Foley & Company of Chicago, Illinois to cure colic, diarrhea, bowel complaints, rheumatic and neuralgic pains, lame back, lumbago, swellings, bruises, sprains, chilblains, frost bites, sore throats, and toothaches. Trendle suffered from none of these.

The concoction, made mostly of alcohol and chloroform, helped his simmering stomach or at least helped him forget how much his stomach boiled. He pulled his hand from his vest, unscrewed the cap, and took a healthy swig. A soothing warmth spread through him followed by a fuzzy numbness. Trendle stopped his pacing in front of the snow-painted window and surveyed Woodward Avenue. He glanced at the line of hungry men that stretched from the soup kitchen across the street then ignored them. Trendle had his own problems. He was losing money.

He stared out at the world with telescopic vision, the kind of power a radio superhero might possess. He could see all his dreams floating out of reach on the darkening horizon: WXYZ dominating the Detroit airwaves allowing him to buy other stations in cities like Grand Rapids, Ann Arbor, Lansing, Flint, and Kalamazoo until he controlled all of Michigan's programming. A Niagara of advertising dollars would follow. With that kind of financial clout, it would be easy to expand outside of Michigan, into Ohio, Indiana, and Wisconsin. He knew he could steal the troubled WHBL in Sheboygan for pennies. Trendle was a big man and dreamed big dreams that were bigger than Sheboygan itself.

Why stop at Wisconsin? Why not become a *national* network like the National Broadcasting Company or the Columbia Broadcasting System, WXYZ' parent? Why not the *Trendle* Broadcasting Company?

"TBC," he said aloud, his breath fogging the window with avarice. The money he could make!

Trendle, a heavy mouth breather, inhaled and exhaled faster and harder at the thought of these millions. The window fogged and his dreams became impossible to see. The problem with his vision was that

WXYZ, the keystone of his planned empire, the launching point to the immense wealth he craved, was a lame dog, a nag dreaming of becoming a thoroughbred, a radio station that was losing four thousand dollars a week.

His stomach roiled at the thought of his mounting losses. He had never failed at anything before, making his reputation and money in theaters then banking it all on radio, convinced this new medium could triple his fortune and open doors he didn't even know existed. He took a deep, thoughtful swig of Doctor Foley's cure-all. He'd been mulling his options for weeks. It was time to act.

"Campbell!" he barked, without facing his closed office door. "Get in here!"

He turned when he heard the door open. Allan Campbell stood in the doorway still holding the knob in case he had to shut the door quickly to block flung ashtrays or paperweights, a common occurrence as the gouged door attested. Campbell, a slender man with wiry hair that refused to stay combed, held many positions at WXYZ—Sales Manager, Business Manager, Trendle's assistant. Why pay three people when Campbell could do everything on one small salary?

"Come in, Allan," Trendle said, looking past him to a man sitting in the waiting area who was all limbs with jutting elbows and protruding knees. He wore an ill-fitting coat and his hollowed cheeks hinted that he needed a good meal, perhaps several. "Shut the door," he said, as the man wiped his nose with a black neckerchief.

Trendle nodded to the chair in front of his desk but remained standing by the window, the wind swirling outside as if eavesdropping. "Who's that in the lobby?" he asked, as Campbell took a seat and tried to smooth his hair into place.

"Ted Sutton, a sound man. Did a lot of work in Chicago before moving here. He seems perfect for the job."

Trendle took another sip of Doctor Foley's then nodded as if he and Campbell had agreed on something without the need for discussion. "Hire him but don't pay him."

Campbell blinked several times and smoothed his hair twice before speaking. "You want him to work for free, boss? To volunteer?"

"Tell him he's a good man and you're impressed with his experience, but times are tough, and we can't offer him a salary right away. Tell him to start tomorrow, and we'll pay him as soon as things get better. Show him the books if you have to."

"Which set?"

"The real one. There's plenty of red in it. He'll jump at the opportunity to work."

Campbell patted his cowlick. "Why? Why would he work for free?"

"Hope. Hope is a powerful thing, Allan, especially during these times. Tell him better days are coming, and he'll be rewarded handsomely when they arrive. Let's see how many weeks we can squeeze out of him before we have to pay him. Wait until he threatens to quit then start his salary low, maybe seven dollars a week. No, make it six. He'll be happy with that. Being paid something is always better than being paid nothing. He'll be grateful. He'll thank you. He'll think he's rich."

Campbell pulled a small notebook from his suit pocket and a pencil nub from behind his ear and scratched a note.

"After you take care of that, I want you to draft a letter to CBS. Tell them that WXYZ is ending our relationship with the Columbia Broadcasting System. As of the first of the month, we will no longer be their Detroit affiliate."

"What?" He reached for the bottle of Doctor Foley's.

Trendle handed him the medicine. "We're going independent, Allan. To hell with CBS. What have they done for us? We'll make more money without them."

"How?" Campbell asked, taking a pull of pain relief. "What will we broadcast?"

Trendle grinned, taking the bottle back. "Local programming with local sponsors. That's our new motto—until we go national. We'll write and produce everything in-house. The listeners will love it and we won't have to pay CBS another nickel. I have it all worked out," he said, tapping his hairless dome with his forefinger.

"We'll have to hire writers and actors, boss. Musicians."

"Hell, they're easy to find. That soup kitchen across the street is probably lousy with pencil pushers and horn players."

"Can we afford to do this? How do we pay all these people?"

Trendle grinned again, wider, breathing hard through his smile. "I already told you. Hope. Offer them hope and security, Allan. Offer them a lot of it, and we'll get them for close to nothing."

Campbell scribbled in his notebook.

"Hope," Trendle repeated, turning to the window. He wiped the fogged glass with his tie and looked down on the growing soup line. "That's what this radio station needs. Hell, that's what this country needs. We need to keep that in mind when we decide on programming."

Campbell glanced up from his notebook, his pencil poised above the page, hair flopping out of place. "I'm not sure I understand, boss."

"We need to give the people a reason to listen to us, Allan. We need them to turn the dial away from WXYT and WJR and tune to *us*. We need to offer them something different. We need a program that everyone wants to hear, one they'll talk about every day until we broadcast the next episode. We need a show that gives all the out-of-work shmucks and their dirty-faced brats *hope*. A program like that can save this station. It could build an empire. It could make millions."

"I don't think I've ever heard of a show like that, boss. Not on any station. Not even on the ones out of New York."

Trendle resumed pacing, holding the Doctor Foley's by the bottle's neck and gesturing with it as he talked. He breathed through his mouth like a New York Central locomotive working up steam. "No one has. A show like that has never aired before. We have to come up with it. We have to be smart about it, Allan."

"Maybe we should hire writers. They're good thinkers."

"This country is in trouble, Allan. Men out of work. Businesses folding. People losing their farms. Wall Street failed us. Our government failed us. The banks sure as hell failed us. We need to be saved, Allan. We *want* to be saved. All of us. That's what binds us—our need for salvation. We need *someone* to rescue us, to give us hope."

"A hero," Allan offered.

"Exactly. Someone good, pure. Someone kids can look up to. Someone they'll crowd around their radios to listen to."

"Someone," Allan agreed.

The wind shrieked, startling both men. Trendle crossed to the window, and Campbell joined him. They passed the bottle of medicine back and forth and stared out on Woodward Avenue as if the hero was out there, somewhere, struggling against the wind or, perhaps, still lying in bed.

The wind had blown the clouds east to Rochester, Syracuse, and Schenectady, draping them in gray, but in Buffalo, the morning sun reflected off the snow in a blinding glare. Elmwood merchants—Mr. Flickenger in front of his grocery, Mr. Kaplan at his deli—cleared their front walks, their shovels scraping pavement. A flatbed rattled past, its engine struggling in the morning cold. The truck stopped at Bidwell Parkway where men scampered aboard. When the truck was filled, the driver skidded his way to The Central Terminal. Shovels, dull and chipped, were handed out. Railroad guards who'd swung their clubs at some of these men hours earlier, squinted at them in the sunshine, making sure no one snuck on boxcars.

The day workers, several bruised and bandaged, spread along the tracks, half working their way east and the other half west, clearing the rails and ties. Their visible breath created the illusion of smoke, of heat, of small fires burning within. Shoveled snow was tossed in every direction as if flurries were swirling from cloudless skies.

On Granger Place, Striker woke with a groan, the back of his head screaming. He heard a ringing in his left ear as if a tuning fork was vibrating inside his pillowcase. Sunlight streamed through the curtain's gap and burned through his closed lids, searing its way through cornea and pupil. He covered his face with a forearm. A trail of suit pants, jacket, shirt and tie marked the crooked path he'd staggered from hallway to bed.

"I thought you were just walking a block or two last night," Janet said, from the doorway, her hands on her hips, her mouth curling downward revealing fine lines.

Striker opened his eyes, but they wouldn't focus.

"I was up for hours editing *Tom Sawyer* and worrying about you."

He swallowed a few times, forcing his voice to work. "How far did you get?"

"Never mind that. Where did you go? The Rendezvous Room? Ulrich's? I know you can't afford The Hotel Lafayette. Actually, you can't afford any of those places."

He tried to sit up, but it felt like his head would halve. "Voelker's."

"You really tied one on, didn't you?" she asked, bending to pick up his suit coat, her voice a blade.

"No."

"No? Look how hungover you are. Did they repeal Prohibition last night?"

Striker rolled on his side, showing her his swollen head.

"What happened?" she asked, rushing to him. "Did you slip on the ice?"

"Somebody sapped me. They got me good."

"Who?" she asked, touching the lump with fingertips then pulling them away when Striker winced. "Why?"

He told her about Slattery's rings. "Somebody saw me pocket them, I guess."

"You have to find them, Fran. You have to get those rings back. There's no telling what Jimmy will do when he finds out."

"Slats is a friend."

"You know how he gets when he drinks."

Striker groaned, not from his throbbing skull but because he knew she was right. He swung his feet to the floor, remembering the time Slats had told him that he resembled Maxie Rosenbloom and he had to leave the speakeasy, fearing a beating was coming.

"Barrett will help you. You know he will. Call him."

"Okay," he said, hoping he could make it downstairs to the phone.

"I'll make you some coffee." She rose and left the room, stopping in the hallway. "Don't forget mom and dad are arriving today. You need to clear out your library and help carry in their things."

Striker bent forward, his elbows on his thighs, and pressed his hands against his eyes as if holding them in place. "How much are they bringing?"

"I'm not sure. They've sold a lot. Some things were repossessed."

"Can Jerry help?"

"He's working."

"Where?"

"Shoveling railroad tracks," she said. "I'll get your coffee."

Striker lowered his hands and stared at the window as if he could see through the curtains to the railroad yard. How long would his brother-in-law be bent over clearing track—eight hours? Ten? And for how little pay? Even working in Woolworth's was better than that.

He imagined Jerry shoveling his way west to Erie, Chicago, Saint Louis, never raising his head from his work, becoming a shoveling legend mentioned in the same breath as John Henry and Paul Bunyan. He'd shovel to Jefferson City, to Topeka, to Denver, his arms never failing, his back never straightening. Newspapers from *The Arkansas Gazette* to *The New York Herald* would report on this snow-tossing marvel, more machine than man, who worked around the clock fighting snow and chipping ice for the good of the company. Some clever reporter would name Jerry's shovel "Old Hickory" or "The Silver

Scoop" and the name would stick, and their legend would grow as they battled the elements together.

The New York Central would name Jerry their *Shoveler of the Month, of The Year, of The Thirties* as he cleared track through the Rockies, unfazed by high altitude and thin air. The railroad would proclaim Jerry the ideal worker, an example to all their employees, someone they should all emulate. Look how his whole life is dedicated to the company! He doesn't care about eating or sleeping or getting paid! Only the work matters. Companies need more men like him, not those selfish, loud-mouthed union thugs always demanding wages.

Children would follow him and point, wanting to reach out and touch him the way the South Buffalo kids had followed and pointed at a younger Slattery when he had danced in the ring, beating every opponent like the victories would never end.

Wholesome farmer's daughters and sinewy Colorado cowgirls would offer Jerry warm soup, fresh coffee, and good luck kisses, but he wouldn't stop for food or drink or rest. He'd shovel his way through Utah as if pretty girls and warmth were unaffordable during these Depression days. He wouldn't even stop when he hit the Nevada desert. He'd shovel sand next to the track like a dervish until he crossed into California. Then he'd lay Old Hickory down, straighten his crooked back, and fall in with the other pilgrims looking for work.

Striker thought of jotting down that passing daydream in his notebook. Perhaps he'd write a bedtime story for his sons, a tall tale about a man shoveling his way across America, something his boys and other children would enjoy and one day tell their own children. Maybe a New York publisher would be interested in a children's book about a shoveler. How much would they pay?

He reached for the notebook on his nightstand, opened it, and tried to read his last entry. His eyes failed, refusing to remain focused. One paragraph dripped into the next. Words seceded from sentences and scattered. Periods pinballed off margins. Commas swam across the page as if searching for ovum. He shut his notebook and touched the back of his head.

Striker felt chilled. He couldn't find his robe, so he pulled his wrinkled suit coat over his shoulders and tried to stand. The room didn't spin, he did. He gripped the nightstand until vertigo passed and nausea subsided. He shuffled to the banister and rested before taking careful steps down the stairs. His head throbbed every time it moved. At the bottom, he held onto the newel post as another wave of dizziness overcame him. When the spinning stopped, he staggered to his library, grabbing anything solid for support as he passed.

His library was a converted sunroom off the dining room. Old Man Voelker had built him bookshelves, and Striker had bought a pair of secondhand oxblood leather chairs and a brass floor lamp and declared the space a library. The shelves were filled with Twain, Dickens, and Zane Grey novels—*Riders of the Purple Sage*, *The Rainbow Trail*, and *The Lone Star Ranger*. A candlestick telephone and an ashtray sat on a small marble-topped table between the chairs. Empty cartons were stacked in front of the bookshelves waiting to be filled. His in-laws had sold their dressers and armoires. He needed to pack his novels to make room for their clothes. The leather chairs and books would be relocated to the basement, perhaps the pawn shop, and a bed would take their place. The brass floor lamp, little table, and phone would stay until they, too, needed to be pawned.

One-by-one Striker pulled books from shelves and placed them in boxes, handling them like crystal. He'd stop and open a novel to read a passage, but words still pooled, his head still throbbed. The phone shrilled two long rings then two short, signaling the call was for the Striker household on the party line. The ringing sliced through his damaged skull and he grabbed the phone from the table before the cadence could repeat. Barrett was on the other end of the line.

"I was about to call you," Striker said, remembering Janet had told him to ring Barrett, but he couldn't recall why.

"How you feeling, Fran?" Barrett asked, his voice blasting through the line. Striker pulled the receiver from his ear.

"It feels like my damn head is about to fall off."

"Well, screw it on tight. I've been thinking. We got to go to The Gypsy's."

"Jesus, Barrett. I'm not going to a whorehouse."

"We got to track down Lefty. If anyone knows about Slattery's rings, it's him."

"Janet's not going to like this."

"Don't tell her. Meet me at The Gypsy's house in an hour," Barrett said, "I have to run an errand first."

"All right. See you there," he said and hung up, wishing he had a cigarette, wishing he'd never gone out last night, wishing he'd never agreed to hold Slattery's rings. He heard his father's voice mumble, "There's always a cost that comes with helping people, Francis," a phrase he'd repeated so often since the Ingleside fire that it'd become The Lieutenant's motto.

The last thing Striker wanted to do this morning was track down Leftarios Mavrakis in a whorehouse. But Barrett was right. If anyone was trying to sell Slattery's rings, Lefty would know. He might even be trying to sell them himself.

Leftarios Mavrakis was born in Evia, Greece. His father, Athanasios, was a gambler and not a very good one. He lost money in the *tavernas* and *kafenias*, betting on backgammon, dominos, goat races, and other games of chance. Soon he was in such debt he had to ask his older brother, Spiro, who'd emigrated to America and made his fortune in steak knives, for a loan. After many letters back and forth, Spiro agreed to pay Athanasios' debt. Spiro, however, had never done anything out of the goodness of his heart or for the sake of familial love. Helping others came with a price tag, so arrangements were made.

Leftarios, sixteen at the time, would sail alone to New York, then take a train to Boston where he'd be met by his uncle. He'd live in his uncle's basement between the coal bin and fruit cellar and work in the steak knife factory in Peabody, Massachusetts. Uncle Spiro would keep all his wages until his father's debt was paid, which could take years, perhaps a decade, because Uncle Spiro paid poorly in general and paid family members even worse. Leftarios had fifteen sea-sick days in steerage to consider this plan, to weigh the pros and cons, to decide what was best for him, as no one else seemed concerned for his welfare. As his ship docked in New York, he concluded that this deal stank worse than all the bodies crammed around him in steerage.

After being processed through Ellis Island, Leftarios bought a ticket for the next train heading anyplace other than Boston. He arrived in Buffalo during a late spring snowstorm, the kind of storm that breaks the spirit of those who'd suffered through a long winter or those who'd only known Mediterranean temperatures.

Young Leftarios staggered from the train station into the squalls with little money in his pocket and no destination in mind. He'd never seen snow before and tilted his face to feel the flakes and catch them on his tongue. He grabbed fistfuls from the sidewalk and squeezed them through reddening fingers then tasted it, expecting ambrosia but only feeling cold against his lips. His thin clothes were useless against the wind. He pounded his arms with numb fists in a failed attempt to maintain circulation. Snowflakes accumulated on his head until his black curls whitened. He took tentative steps, fearful of falling on the ice and shattering bone.

Leftarios assumed it was normal for thunder to rumble and lightning to pitchfork when it snowed, oblivious to the Buffalonians who pulled back curtains to marvel at the thunder snow and question its meaning. The wind gusted stronger, and he lost feeling in his feet and hands. His nose burned. Had he made a mistake? Should he have chosen steak knives over freedom? Was Peabody, Massachusetts anything like Athens? He shivered, certain that it must be.

The streetlamps burned above him as he stumbled through the snow. Some snapped off as he passed leaving him in sudden darkness. His body shook, each muscle spasming from the cold. A smudge of red smeared in the distance, a scarlet light whose glow seemed to promise pleasure and respite. Leftarios staggered toward it.

He fought two more blocks until he reached Genesee Street and then climbed the turreted Victorian's front steps. The porch light bathed him in red, baptizing him in color. The oak door swung open as if the lion-head knocker had summoned those inside. Mirela, a young gypsy with flowing black hair and eyes that held years of sorrow, stood in the brothel's doorway. She saw Leftarios encased in snow, unable to move or speak. She led him into the house to thaw.

The virgin Leftarios had never set foot in a bordello before but recognized The Gypsy's house as one immediately, overheard descriptions of such places from Greek sailors passing through Evia burned forever into his adolescent brain. The house smelled of old tobacco and fresh perfume and was heated by blazing fireplaces that crackled and snapped. The walls were painted salmon and the couches, settees, and overstuffed chairs were silk covered in shades of pink and mauve. Heavy fringed drapes curtained windows to foil the curious and gave the rooms the perpetual ambience of midnight, the hour when anything was possible if you had the money to pay for it.

Mirela took Leftarios upstairs and gave him a soapy bath, fellatio, and a bowl of hot gypsy stew made with a tender meat he could not identify. She could not pronounce his name and introduced him as Lefty to the girls who worked for her—Laima, the one-legged Lithuanian, Angelique the Creole from Louisiana who knew dark deviltry, and Simone from Montreal who could whisper obscenities in seventeen different languages into customers' ears, eighteen if he paid extra. Mirela tucked Lefty in her own bed, the sheets and quilts smelling of lilac and wonder, and he fell asleep convinced Buffalo was a magical city where miracles could be found in the unholiest of places.

Mirela had taken in Lefty twenty years ago and they were still together in the brothel on Genesee Street, still sharing the same bed. New girls worked for Mirela: Laima had died during the pandemic of 1919, Simone had run off with a handsome traveling salesman from Foley & Company of Chicago, Illinois, and Angelique, who'd been elevated to full voodoo priestess, had simply disappeared. Mirela, however, hadn't changed. Her hair was still dark and flowing without a single gray strand. Her olive skin remained smooth and unlined. She still had the body of a twenty-year old. Time had forgotten her. Only her eyes had aged with two more decades of sorrow.

Lefty had become a fixture on Genesee Street, the prince of petty crime. Mirela had taught him how to shoplift, pander, pickpocket, deal Three-Card Monte, and cheat at poker, which was how he managed to pay his father's debt to Uncle Spiro. As Lefty grew older, his criminal repertoire expanded to breaking and entering, dognapping (for resale or ransom), jewelry fencing, blackmail (as many of Mirela's high-profiled customers learned), forgery (in both Greek and English), stealing cars, and grifting. If a dog went missing, or a wallet had been lifted, or a washed-up prizefighter's diamond rings had been stolen, the odds were good that either Lefty was involved or knew something about the caper. Like most Greeks in the neighborhood, he called everybody— friends and enemies alike—*Malaka*, 'one who masturbates himself into idiocy,' a term he thought endearing.

Barrett's errand was a scheduled one. He visited his mother at the Buffalo State Asylum for The Insane on Tuesdays and on special occasions: her birthday (March 24, the same as Houdini's), Christmas morning, and All Hallows Eve (her favorite holiday), which marked the beginning of Allhallowtide, the period where the dead are remembered. Before she was committed, Delores would spend all three days of Allhallowtide at Forest Lawn Cemetery fasting, scrubbing headstones, and lighting candles. When the wind, that trickster, would douse the candles, Danek the Polish Gravedigger would relight them with his Bowers' Sure-Fire Lighter. He'd acquired the lighter when he and another gravedigger had dropped an inordinately heavy Voelker Coupe and it split open. The corpses had tumbled free into the cemetery mud, and the brass lighter had fallen from a pocket. Danek was never certain which of the dearly departed the Bowers' had belonged to, but he suspected the owner was the overweight gentlemen with the garrote still wrapped around his neck.

Today, however, was not Delores' birthday nor Christmas nor All Hallows Eve. It was a regular Tuesday, and Barrett pulled into the hospital's circular drive on Forest Avenue with the same sense of foreboding he always felt when he visited his mother.

If there was one place in the city that was haunted, besides WEBR's Gold Room, it was the Buffalo State Asylum for The Insane. The Romanesque complex constructed from red Medina sandstone sprawled over ninety-three acres and was more haunted house than hospital. It was as easy for Barrett to imagine tortured apparitions wandering the grounds as it was to picture his mother there. The sandstone had absorbed the lunatics' howls and held them until it was time to release their cries to the wind.

The Central Administration Building was the eeriest of all the buildings. Its twin towers, positioned in the center of the asylum, were capped in copper washed in patina. They rose one-hundred-eighty feet and narrowed at the top like a pair of ill-sharpened weapons. In summer, bats flittered from the towers at dusk, darkening the sky. Five gloomy wards—the men's wing to the east, the women's to the west— flanked either side of the administration building. It was in the farthest wards where the most afflicted patients were kept—the violent, the suicidal, the ones who visited other worlds.

Delores lived in Building I, second from the end, with the catatonics, the speakers-in-tongues, and women who could see what others couldn't imagine. She shared the ward with former nurses from The Great War who'd witnessed horrors, others who'd heard voices since childhood, and several writers, mostly lyric poets.

Barrett parked the Nash and stood for a moment breathing in air so cold it hurt his narrow chest. The asylum was set back from Forest Avenue, separated from the city by a high wrought-iron fence. The grounds consisted of rolling, snow-covered lawns, a forest of old-growth trees that gave the avenue its name, and ponds and winding paths, leaving patients delusional with the false impression that they were living deep in the country.

Barrett climbed the thirteen steps to the arched loggia leading to the Administration Building's main entry. Mosaic tiles of varying shades of peach and umber were inlaid on the archway's vaulted ceiling. He liked to pause at the top step and give WEBR's top-of-the-hour station identification—*You're listening to WEBR. We Extend Buffalo's Regards*—to hear his radio voice echo in the portico. After that, he had no choice but to go inside.

A fire crackled in the hallway's fireplace. Smoke curled from the ill-drawing flue. Barrett's wet boots squeaked across the marble floor to the front desk. Mrs. Pottebaum, the receptionist, a woman with gray hair and gray skin, who looked as if she'd worked there since 1880 when the asylum had first opened, greeted Barrett by name; he hadn't missed a Tuesday visit since he was ten. She had him sign the guest book and told him she'd fetch a nurse to escort him to Building I. Mrs. Pottebaum did not move. She waited, her gray eyes dancing, forcing Barrett to ask the same question each week. Barrett felt his face burn, certain he was blushing like a schoolboy.

"Is Celestina working today?" he finally asked. "Could she escort me?" Celestina always worked Tuesdays.

Mrs. Pottebaum smiled, showing gray teeth, enjoying the charade. "I will check," she said, cackling as she waddled away. Barrett held his hat with both hands and felt his heart crash around his chest.

Time stopped.

Barrett felt as if he'd been waiting for hours, for days, for a lifetime. Panic seized him as it always did when he waited for Celestina to guide him to his mother. He wanted to flee, to run up the grand staircase to the second floor and dash down the long corridor to Building I, or to race out through the loggia, down the thirteen steps past the old-growth trees, past the ponds and paths, not stopping until he was beyond the wrought-iron fence across Forest Avenue. But he didn't run. He never did and never would. Barrett knew deep in his soul he'd wait for Celestina forever.

Celestina's starched uniform rustled, a sound he'd recognize even in his most fragmented dreams and turned to her. His heart paused mid-crash, quivered, wobbled, then started crashing again like waves breaking over rock. Golden ringlets escaped from under her nurse's cap. Perfect eyebrows arched above emerald eyes. Celestina smiled. Her cheekbones rounded, her red lips curved, revealing dimples and pearls, everything he longed for. Her face made him hopeful for angels.

"Good morning, John," she said, her voice a song.

Barrett swelled in Celestina's presence. In his mind, he grew over six feet tall. Shoulders broadened. Biceps strained against sleeves. Bones transformed, strengthening his jawline and cleaving his chin, turning him into the leading man he wanted to be. It was his voice, that magnificent voice, however, that betrayed him. Thoughts half-formed. Sentences were swallowed. He strained to utter a syllable. Instead, he stared at her heart-shaped face and thought how much he wanted to kiss her lips and caress her cheek. He wanted to take off her nurse's cap and unpin her hair, letting it shimmer to her shoulders. He'd trade his voice to hold her close and breathe her in.

"Hi," he managed.

Celestina glided toward the grand staircase leading to the second-floor hallway. Barrett matched her stride, walking as close as he dared.

Her starched uniform whispered secrets as she walked, the sound mixing with the blood thrumming in his ears.

"Your mother is so excited to see you today," she said, her right hand sliding on the maple railing as they ascended the stairs. "She's been waiting for you all morning."

He stopped on the second riser. "She has? She knows I'm coming?" he asked, the shock loosening his vocal cords.

She paused three steps above and glanced at him over her shoulder. Sunlight streamed through a shallow-arched window and lit across her face. He wanted to photograph her at that moment for a locket he could wear above his heart.

"She's quite present today. She knows it's Tuesday. She knows it's winter."

"Oh," Barrett said, the word gusting out as he exhaled. He felt his vocal cords retighten. They both continued up the stairs.

He tried to remember the radio scripts he'd performed, the ones where he played the dashing main character who said clever things, wooed with ease, and won the girl's love at the end of each episode. Barrett searched for Striker's words but couldn't find them. Only the lines from *Covered Wagon Days*, Episode 10 came to him.

"Sheriff Curry says he dug out some of the bullets and has them in his desk!" he blurted, his radio voice erupting in full force like a long-dormant volcano coming to life. The delivered line ricocheted off the staircase, careened against plaster walls, and rang off the tin ceiling like he had rung the strongman's bell at the Erie County Fair. From down the hall, schizophrenics howled.

Celestina, startled by the unexpected power of Barrett's voice, missed a riser. Her hand slipped from the maple railing. She lost her balance, teetering on the step's edge, fighting gravity and the possibility of toppling. Her mouth formed a perfect oval, but no sound escaped, as if Barrett's voice and the schizophrenics' screams had left no room in the entire asylum for either whimper or prayer. Then Barrett was beside her, not realizing he had climbed two stairs at a time to catch her. His arm wrapped around her waist like it belonged there. He pulled her close. Her body pivoted a quarter turn until she was facing him. Her arms went around his neck to steady herself as his other arm encircled her. They were nearly the same height and her chest, so soft and full even through the starched uniform, pressed against his. Their hearts beat a paired rhythm.

If Striker had written this scene, the radio announcer would have told the listening audience that the two shared their first kiss then strands from lush strings and woodwinds, perhaps a piano, from the WEBR orchestra would have blended and blossomed signaling the end of the episode, leaving the audience to imagine the sweetness of Celestina's lips and the passion of Barrett's embrace.

But this wasn't a radio program and Striker didn't write the scene and Barrett did not kiss Celestina. She blushed, her neck and cheeks turning a shade of rose, her pulse fluttering in her throat's soft hollow like it, too, was anxious to be loved.

"Thank you," she said, her voice shy, breathy.

"Everything all right up there?" Mrs. Pottebaum called from the bottom of the stairs.

"Welcome," Barrett mumbled, his limbs trembling, his voice once again weak.

"Everything's fine," Celestina called down, her gaze never breaking from his. "Mr. Barrett saved me."

"You're crazy!" yelled one of the patients at the top of the stairs as Barrett let Celestina slip from his arms. "Crazy, I say!"

"What's this about bullets?" she asked, over her shoulder, and again he wanted to capture the moment and carry it with him forever. "Who's Sheriff Curry?"

"Rehearsing," Barrett said, squeezing out the word. "Radio."

"Your voice startled me. It's so...powerful. Do you sing? I bet you have a beautiful singing voice."

Her compliment warmed him to his core. At that moment Barrett felt like he could sing better than Al Jolson, better than Maurice Chevalier, even better than that new crooner, Bing Crosby, the talk of the radio station these days. Barrett wanted to stand on the top step of the Buffalo State Asylum for The Insane and sing Celestina a love song—something with teardrops, flowers, and springtime in the lyrics—belting it out until his voice rattled barred windows, woke catatonics, and won her heart. He wanted Charles Armbrewster and The WEBR Players to fill the long hallway with orchestral music, their notes floating up to the ceiling then down again. He wanted to take Celestina in his arms and dance with her, twirling her past doctors, droolers, and public masturbators. He wanted to feel his hand on the small of her back and her body against his.

He wanted.

"I can sing a little," he said.

"I bet you can," she said, and smiled a smile that lit his soul.

Celestina moved down the corridor everyone called the Day-Room, and Barrett caught up to her. Light streamed through high windows and reflected off polished wooden floors. Patients sat in rocking chairs and benches that lined either side of the hall as sane looking as anyone Barrett knew from the speakeasies and radio station. Paintings and etchings dotted the wall, and a female patient, about the same age as him, stared at a landscape with her head cocked to the side as if listening to colors.

"Many patients think the paintings are windows and they're looking into another world," Celestina said, noticing his staring. "The scenes come alive for them. Some say the people in the pictures move and they can hear voices or water lapping or leaves rustling."

"Voices?" Barrett managed to say, worrying that a trained psychiatric nurse could tell he'd heard ghostly radio voices by looking at him. "How strange."

"Wouldn't it be nice if it was true?" she asked, stopping in front of a country scene of two young girls walking barefoot down a dusty road.

"Wouldn't you love to hear their conversation and know their hopes and wishes? I'd ask them where they've been and where they're going and if they're sisters or cousins or best friends."

Barrett stared at Celestina's profile and wanted to know her hopes and wishes and where she'd been.

She blushed. "You must think I'm silly."

"Never," he said, fighting the urge to touch her hair.

As they continued towards Delores' ward, a new dread seized Barrett, not because soon he'd face his mother but because soon Celestina would drop him off in Building I and leave. Then he'd count down the time until next Tuesday when he'd see her again. He didn't think he could suffer through another ten thousand and eighty minutes of thinking about her, dreaming about her, of missing her until he heard her whispering uniform and saw that heavenly face again.

"Coffee!" he blurted, catching the attention of another nurse who was certain a Tourette's patient had wandered over from Building H.

"Would you like some coffee?" Celestina's perfect eyebrows bunched in confusion.

Barrett shook his head then closed his eyes and breathed. He *was* a radio actor, damn it. A local star who would be in Hollywood one day. He *had* played the dashing leading man who'd said clever things, who'd wooed with ease, who'd won the girl's love in the end. He *could* play that part again, even without Striker's words to guide him. He'd pretend he was back in The Gold Room, standing in front of his microphone. He'd concentrate on every word.

"Would you like to go for a cup of coffee sometime?" he asked, his radio voice rich and slow like poured mead oozing through a Crosley speaker.

Celestina smiled. "I like jazz better."

Before he could respond, he saw his mother waiting for him in a rocking chair, not at her usual spot by the high window staring beyond the trees to places that only she could see. She was perched on the seat's edge, the rocker dead still. Her muscles tensed as if she was about to pounce. Delores was in her mid-forties, but her hair had turned pure white since being institutionalized. It had also grown thicker and fuller, wreathing her face in a cloud, contrasting her eyes, making the brown eye seem browner and the blue the color of a swirling sea.

She stood and rushed towards them, a strange light smoldering in those eyes.

"Mom?" Barrett asked, stunned to see her lucid.

Delores stopped in front of him and grabbed his upper arms, her fingers clamping around his small biceps and squeezing. She studied his face from forehead to chin, as if inspecting for blackened eyes, split lips, a damaged soul.

"Are you all right, Johnny?" she asked, her voice full of motherly concern, a tone he hadn't heard since he was ten.

"Of course, I am, Mom. But how are *you*? You look wonderful. You look...here."

"Something happened to you. I can feel it."

He shifted his weight from one leg to the other, then his eyes to Celestina, who was standing next to him awaiting his answer. He knew it was never a good idea to admit hearing voices when visiting an insane asylum.

"I'm fine, mother. Nothing's happened."

Delores squeezed his arms tighter until he worried of bruising. "You're lying! You're like me now," she yelled. "I can tell. I can see it in your eyes. You've heard them. The voices! You must be brave, John. You must be careful!"

"You must calm down, Delores," Celestina said. "You must lower your voice."

A fear gripped Barrett stronger than his mother's grasp, which was sinking deeper into his flesh and pressing against bone. He did not want to become like her. He did not want to stay here listening to paintings and hearing voices.

Delores shook her son. "Are you listening? You must be careful!"

"Why don't we rest for a minute, Delores, and compose ourselves," Celestina said. She touched Delores' wrist and her grip was broken.

"Promise me you'll be careful, Johnny! Promise me!"

"I promise," Barrett said, and meant it. He rubbed his arms where she'd squeezed.

"Maybe we should lie down," Celestina said, and led Delores toward Building I.

Delores called over her shoulder, "Danek will help you. He knows things. He knows where the bodies are. Go see Danek when the sky bleeds!"

"That's enough, Delores," Celestina said. "And we were having such a good morning, too."

"Johnny?" Delores cried, grabbing the doorframe leading to her ward, forcing Celestina to stop.

"Yes, mother?"

"Beware the man who wears the ring!"

Jerry was no snow-tossing marvel. Blisters had already formed beneath his gloves. After three hours of shoveling, his arms felt heavy, the soreness giving way to numbness. All he could think about was food.

"The flatbed driver promised me soup," a short, compact man shoveling behind him complained, his voice teetering to anger. The man didn't throw the snow but pushed it off the tracks. "They can't expect a grown man to work on an empty belly."

Jerry didn't respond. He, too, had been promised soup and knew it would be greasy, without a trace of meat, if they ever brought it. His best hope was for a drowned carrot, perhaps a potato that wasn't too spoiled. At least it would be hot, something to defrost him, perhaps return the feeling to his fingers and toes.

"They ain't giving us soup," a pale man with a bandaged eye said, shoveling on the other side of him. "You can bet on that. They'll say anything to get us suckers out here."

"They promised coffee, too," the compact man added, his voice indignant.

"With my luck," the bandaged man said, "the coffee will be like my wife. Thin and bitter."

The wind blew then, stabbing exposed skin like a thousand icy needles. No one laughed at the bandaged man's joke. Jerry's stomach growled like something feral.

"I can't take this!" the compact man said. "I'm starving! They promised me soup!" He threw down his shovel.

Jerry watched the man trudge through knee-high snow to the foreman, a former boxer named Wild Bill Krenshaw, who was a better railroad foreman than he'd been a pugilist. His eyes were hooded with scar tissue, his nose flattened, both ears cauliflowered by glorious defeats.

"I quit," the compact man yelled at Krenshaw. "I didn't get no free soup or no coffee. Plus, I'm freezing out here. How do you expect a man to work when he's froze and hungry? Pay me what you owe me."

"You get a full day's wages for a full day's work," Krenshaw said, his eyes narrowing more. "If you want to get paid, you got to work the whole shift."

"I ain't working three hours for nothing. Pay me what you owe me!"

Two railroad guards gripping billy clubs slogged through snow and stood behind their foreman. Both were thick-necked and eager to swing.

"A full day's wages for a full day's work. That's what you signed up for. Either get back in line or get the hell out of here," Krenshaw said, his left eyelid drooping from long-ago jabs.

The guards slapped batons against gloveless palms—wood against skin, wood against bone. Their truncheons were nicked in spots, the varnish wine-stained with old blood.

"It ain't right," the compact man said. "Promising soup. Promising coffee. Giving us nothing but frostbite."

"Back on the rail or back on the street," Krenshaw said, poking the compact man in the chest with his finger.

The compact man studied Krenshaw and then the two guards before deciding that a bowl of bad soup wasn't worth a beating and spun away. Disappointment passed from one guard's face to the other. The man muttered something lost in the wind as he waded through the snow to where he'd tossed his shovel. He grabbed it and returned to his place behind Jerry, not meeting anyone's gaze.

Jerry wanted to quit, too, but he couldn't let the family down. He knew his brother-in-law was struggling to pay bills and needed his shoveling money. If they just gave him something to eat, he was certain he could shovel the entire shift, earning that full day's pay. Tomorrow he'd bring something from home—an apple, a sandwich, anything his sister could spare to keep him going.

The emptiness in Jerry's stomach spread to his brain. He felt light-headed as if the numbness of his arms was metastasizing through his shoulders, then seeping to his cerebral cortex. The world seemed to teeter from left to right then back again, as if something had gone wrong with the planet's axis. He concentrated on the mechanics of his shoveling as he searched for equilibrium. He developed a rhythm to his work, murmuring *Dig-and-toss, Dig-and-toss* to keep him focused and upright. The sun blinded as it reflected off snow. He shut his eyes and shoveled by feel, the earth roiling under him as if he was standing on something awakening.

Dig-and-toss. Dig-and-toss.

The wind intensified, lifting the snow off the tracks. A white funnel swirled around the men, starting at their ankles and rising above their heads, trapping them inside a winter cyclone that sucked oxygen from lungs.

"Keep shoveling!" he heard Krenshaw yell. "A full day's wages for a full day's work!"

Jerry struggled to regain his breath, wanting nothing more than to find a warm place where he could feel his limbs. But he couldn't. He needed to help his brother-in-law who had taken him in when no one else would.

Dig-and-toss. Dig-and-toss.

Tossed snow was blown back, pelting his face and icing eyelashes. He opened his eyes and through a frozen curtain glazed by sunlight saw Jimmy Slattery running with Pando on his shoulders, the pinsetter's head lolling as if asleep. Jerry marveled at how Pando kept his balance as Slattery, missing his coat and hat, slipped and slued across the railyard. A strong gust blew, and Jerry had to turn away.

"Keep shoveling! A full day's wages for a full day's work!"

When the wind subsided, and the snow veil dropped, he glanced back, but Slattery and Pando had vanished. In their place, a man with a very small chin appeared like a blemish against the snowy backdrop— black hat, black boots, black gun. He pushed another man ahead of him, shoving him hard and jabbing him with his gun barrel. Jerry stared at the man's hint of a chin but had to duck his head from the wind.

"Keep shoveling! A full day's wages for a full day's work!" the foreman cried again, his voice coming as if from another land.

Jerry was coned in white and blinded by snow that seemed electrified by the brilliant sun. He heard a rumbling then, reverberant and powerful, heading straight toward him. The paralysis that had been seeping through his arms and brain spread to his legs. He was unable to move. The sound grew louder, closer. He wanted to run, but his legs ignored him.

"Keep shoveling! A full day's wages for a full day's work!"

Was the foreman insane? Couldn't he hear the quaking that vibrated in Jerry's chest? Jerry was certain rail cars had uncoupled and were accelerating towards him, churning up snow and crushing everything in their path. The wind diminished enough for Jerry to slit his eyes. He expected to see a coal car or caboose, perhaps a Pullman bearing down on him. Squinting through the glare he didn't see a runaway tender or renegade sleeper but horses escaping from stockcars, the doors and side slats splintered by hooves. Equines of all kinds—mares heading to farms, broken-down nags destined for The Cooper Glue Factory, racers put out to stud—churned through the snow, their eyes wild from wind and hours packed in freight cars.

A white stallion led their charge. It raced through the snow like something from a fairytale. Muscles rippled from crest to heel. Contrails shot through the stallion's nostrils as it increased its speed. Drifts reached the horse's hocks, but it galloped through the accumulation without breaking stride, snow kicking behind him like a dust cloud. Jerry knew nothing of horses but could tell by the way it held its head and its effortless power that this horse was a thoroughbred, a champion, a steed worthy of knights and kings.

The stallion covered ground at terrifying speed, shortening the distance to Jerry in seconds. He was too scared to move or scream, certain he was about to be trampled. The great horse stopped three feet from him and reared on its hind legs, revealing its broad barrel. Forelegs pawed the winter air and it neighed nearly to roaring. Its horseshoes, crystalized in ice, sparkled in the sunlight as if forged from silver.

Jerry dropped his shovel and crouched, raising his arms to cover his face as if that would protect him. Another wind blast blinded him. He squeezed his lids shut and waited for hoof to meet skull, fetlock to crack bone, collisions that never occurred. When he was able to reopen his eyes, the horse had sprinted around him and raced toward town.

"Keep shoveling! A full day's wages for a full day's work!"

Jerry, stunned that he was still alive, trembled as the adrenaline-produced heat gave way to winter chill. The other laborers, who had run from the stampede or dove out of their path, wandered back to their shovels, brushing snow from their sleeves. They swore at the horses and waved mittened fists at disappearing flanks and tails.

The compact man complained about soup.

Striker hurried to catch the streetcar, the wind biting through him. He didn't want to be out in the cold. He wanted to be back in bed, his aching head nestled on Janet's lap, but he knew they needed to talk to Lefty. The trolley rattled and shook. He imagined welds breaking and rivets firing off like sprayed bullets. Every jostle sent pain shooting down his neck and upset his stomach.

When he was a photographer, he'd ride the trolleys and surreptitiously take photos of passengers boarding or waiting at the stops. But as he developed the pictures, he found himself imagining the lives of his subjects—the man smoking the pipe was wanted by the police, the woman in the veiled hat had left her husband. Over time, the stories began to matter more than the photographs. One day he set aside his camera and bought his first Remington Sixteen.

His father had been wrong. He hadn't quit photography. It had just evolved into writing, just as leaving Woolworth's to direct stage plays had led to directing radio plays. Everything had led to this moment. But today his head hurt too much to think of the past or imagine his fellow passengers' stories. A forgotten newspaper lay folded on the seat next to him. He tried to read the article on FDR's planned arrival in town but gave up when the words bled together.

The driver called out the Genesee Street stop, and Striker hopped off the trolley. He trudged toward The Gypsy's house with his hat pulled to his brow and his hands buried deep in his pockets. The wind intensified as soon as he stepped on the sidewalk. It blew the fallen snow as if storming anew. He pulled his black scarf up from his neck until it covered his face like a mask. Sunlight reflecting off snow hurt his eyes. He wished he'd remembered sunglasses. His old black Nash drove past and Barrett tooted the horn, the sound an icepick in his ear. Striker raised an arm in more of a surrender than a wave. Barrett parked in front of The Gypsy's house and got out of the car and waited for him.

"You look frozen still," Barrett said, as Striker approached.

"It's like the Yukon out here. Only Mounties and sled dogs should be out in this weather."

"It's not that cold, Fran."

"I haven't been right since I got conked on the noggin. I'm freezing all the time. Lights are too bright. Sounds are too loud. I can't even write. Say," he shielded the sun to get a better look at Barrett. "Are you sick, too? You're paler than I am."

"I visited my mother this morning."

"Today's Tuesday? How is she?"

"I'll tell you later. Let's talk to Lefty first."

They walked single file to the Victorian, Barrett leading the way and Striker shivering as much as Leftarios had when he'd first found this house. The sun offered no relief from the cold as the pair climbed the front steps, but it illuminated the porch in soft yellow. The red lightbulb had been extinguished after the last client had bounded out earlier that morning, satiated and smiling, both his wallet and step lighter. Striker raised the lion-head knocker and thought of Jacob Marley before hitting the plate.

There was no answer.

"Knock again," Barrett said. "Harder."

Striker did, and the door flung open.

Mirela stood in the doorway, hair flowing in every direction as if her locks and tresses had been caught in a whirlwind. Her eyes brimmed with more sorrow than Striker had ever seen.

"We're closed," she said, her voice wavering. "It's morning, for God's sake. What are you, Greek sailors? Come back when the red light's on." She started to close the door, but Striker stiff-armed it open.

"We're looking for Lefty," he said, his voice muffled by the scarf.

Mirela stepped over the threshold. She was a stray hair above five-feet tall and tilted her head to lock on Striker's eyes. He was unable to move or divert his gaze. He had to concentrate to breathe. She yanked his scarf to his throat and pressed her forefinger against him. "How do you know Lefty?"

"Everyone knows Lefty," Barrett said. "But we mostly know him from The New Genesee Restaurant up the street. We're in radio and sometimes after we sign off for the night, we'll go there…"

"What do you want with him?"

"We want to ask him about a pair of rings," Striker answered. "Gold ones with diamonds"

Her pupils dilated until her irises were black pools then constricted to pinpoints. This repeated three times. Striker swayed with vertigo as if only her fingertip, still pressing his chest, was keeping him upright. "How do you know about the rings?"

"They were stolen from me. I want them back."

"They were *your* rings?"

"Well, no," Barrett cut in. "Fran was holding them. You see…"

"Your rings got him killed!"

"Lefty's dead? When?" Barrett asked. "How?"

"I do not know," she whispered.

"What did the police tell you?" Barrett asked.

"I never talk to the police. Not even when they line up for free girls."

"Maybe Lefty's not dead then. Maybe he's…delayed."

Mirela glanced at Barrett, lifting her finger off Striker's chest, who felt as if he'd been released from shackles. He reeled backward to the porch railing.

Mirela clutched her left bosom. "I know he's dead. I felt it in my heart the moment he died. A gypsy's heart never lies. Lefty is dead and this one," she said turning back to Striker, "killed him."

"I didn't kill anyone," Striker managed, looking past The Gypsy to the door knocker, afraid of what may happen if they locked eyes again.

"Your rings got him killed."

"They weren't my rings."

"They were taken from you. That makes them yours. And my Lefty, an honest man trying to make a dishonest dollar, went to The Colored Musicians Club to meet a man with a very small chin about the rings. And now he's dead. Because of you and your rings."

"Who was selling them? Lefty or this chinless man?" Striker asked.

"My Lefty, of course."

"Who is this man with a small chin?" Barrett asked.

The Gypsy ignored him and stomped toward Striker who was already against the balustrades and could retreat no further. "If I had the power to kill you, I would, but I can only curse you. I can only kill your dreams and fill your life with constant struggle and disappointment."

"I didn't do anything."

Mirela, a southpaw, pointed forefinger and pinky of her left hand at Striker and jabbed at him three times. "You want money. I can see that. Money for your family. To feed them. To save your mother. But you will never have money. Not ever. You will work yourself into an early grave and for nothing. No one will remember your name when you're dead. Others will take credit for your work. Millions of dollars will slip through your fingers."

Striker laughed. "Millions? I'd settle for ten bucks."

"Millions," The Gypsy repeated, and spat in Striker's face. Her spittle burned. His laughter stopped.

EPISODE 4

A Mysterious Letter Arrives

Striker counted those sitting around the dinner table to make sure—himself, Janet, her parents, his grandparents, the boys, Jerry. Nine. Enough for a baseball team, he thought, touching the tender spot where The Gypsy had spat.

He counted again—nine servings of turkey, of potatoes, of corn, of bread. Two glasses of milk, six glasses of wine, and one steaming cup of coffee for Jerry, who sat wrapped in an eiderdown, his teeth chattering, his fingers still stiff from shoveling. It was a feast, Striker decided, like Thanksgiving without dressing or Easter dinner without colored eggs. A feast they couldn't afford.

Who was paying for it all?

Striker gulped his wine. He knew the answer. He was. And tomorrow he'd pay for nine breakfasts, nine lunches, then for another nine dinners and the cycle would repeat until this depression ended. If it ended.

He'd pay for doctor and dentist visits, for coal and electric bills. He'd pay for shoes and clothes and the Christmas bills when they arrived—how he dreaded that day. He'd pay the mortgage to The Buffalo Savings and Loan, so they all had a place to live. He'd pay his mother's medical bills if he could. He'd never stop paying.

Striker swirled the wine in his glass. How could he support nine people on his WEBR salary? He needed to make more money. But how? Maybe he could sell short stories to magazines or a novel to a New York publisher. The country needed to lose itself in pages and chapters and forget about market crashes and bank holidays, shuttered factories and closed mills, at least for a while. He was certain Americans were hungry for escape, for Zane Grey adventures and Horatio Alger happy endings, realizing that *Covered Wagon Days*, Episode 10, was a combination of both.

Hell, *he* wanted to escape, and did when he sat at his typewriter and created worlds so vivid it was like taking a holiday from responsibilities. His rising debt might drive him to the attic to write, but once there, the stack of bills and deepening depression were forgotten, at least until St. John's bell tolled midnight and the writing stopped. He'd return then to his attic, to his debts, and know that, sooner or later, he'd have to settle up.

He fingered the back of his head. How could he work? The swelling had subsided, the bump less painful to touch, but he still couldn't concentrate enough to sit at his Remington. His vision remained blurred and typed words continued to backstroke across the page. He worried that The Gypsy had cursed his writing, too. What if his vision and concentration never returned? What if words eluded him and story ideas vanished? Who would pay for everything then? The room tilted at this thought. He expected turkey and potatoes to slide from him, crashing from table to floor, shattering glasses and plates, splattering gravy and wine.

"Everything okay, Fran?" Janet asked, from across the room.

Striker gripped his chair and managed a smile, the skin where The Gypsy had spat pulled taut as the room spun. "Sure. Quite a feast."

"It's a celebration. Our first meal with all of us living together. Don't get used to feasts," she said. "We won't be eating like this every night."

"I'm sure we won't," he answered, almost tasting the Salvation Army chipped beef the nine of them would be sharing if he didn't make more money.

Janet turned to say something to her mother. Striker's face felt aflame. He pressed his napkin against his new blister. Maybe he should have stayed at Woolworth's.

The dining room was filled with noise: simultaneous conversations, the boys' giggling, cutlery clinking against china, each sound hitting his brain like striking typewriter hammers. Jerry sat holding the coffee mug with two hands, his food untouched in front of him, speaking to no one. He was gazing across the room like across an endless snowy field.

"You warming up, Jerry?" Striker had to ask three times before his brother-in-law broke his stare.

"What?"

"I asked if you were warming up."

Jerry sipped his coffee, considering the question. "I don't think I'll ever get warm."

"It must have been tough out there."

Jerry set his cup on its saucer and leaned toward Striker. "It was awful, Fran. So cold. So windy. I wasn't thinking right. I started seeing things."

He then told Striker about Slattery and Pando and The Man with the Very Small Chin.

"Was Lefty with him?"

"Maybe. He was shoving another guy ahead of him, but I couldn't see who it was. It could've been Lefty. And this Man with the Very Small Chin was carrying a gun. A big one with a long barrel. The kind cowboys used to carry. And right out in the open, too, like he was about to fire it. I thought he was going to shoot the other guy, but then they were gone."

"Gone?" Striker asked, leaning back in his chair. How would he get Slattery's rings back if Lefty was dead like The Gypsy insisted? He pushed some turkey and corn around his plate with his fork.

"I turned my head for a minute, and when I looked back, he'd vanished. I think maybe I imagined it."

"Strange."

"It gets stranger," Jerry said, and told him about the white stallion.

Striker stared at his dish while Jerry described the horse in such detail it was as if the turkey, potatoes, and corn had disappeared, and he was watching the running steed on a miniature motion picture screen. He could see the streaming mane and tail, the legs corded with muscle, the royal way it held its head. The stallion was a winter horse, sired from snow, hooves silvered in ice, running like the frigid wind that had brought him. Yet Striker thought of him as fiery. As Jerry told how the stallion drew closer, Striker could have sworn his dinner plate was vibrating from thundering hooves.

"He was about to crush me, Fran. I'm sure of it. He was so close, I could smell him. I shut my eyes, certain I was about to be trampled, and then," Jerry snapped his fingers, "he raced by and was gone."

But the white stallion wasn't gone. He raced around Striker's mind like he'd found a home in his imagination. He galloped and pranced and bucked, thankful to be there. Striker's concentration returned, and he thought of all the ways he could describe this wonder horse, certain he had no choice but to write about him. The clearer his mind and vision became, the stronger the urge to write grew inside him, expanding like an inflating balloon, shoving aside the desire to eat, to find Lefty, or find Slattery's rings.

He pushed his chair away from the table, scraping the legs against the hardwood, the noise so loud all the other sounds in the room ceased and everyone watched him rise.

"Fran?" Janet asked. "What's wrong?"

"I need to write."

"Now? You haven't eaten a thing."

"I'll eat later."

"But this is our first time all together."

"There will be other meals. I'll see everyone at breakfast."

"There won't be one like this for a long time, Fran. You know that. Mr. Flickenger cut off our credit at the grocery yesterday."

Her parents exchanged glances. His grandparents studied their plates. The boys poked each other with potato-covered fingers.

"I've got this idea…"

"You always have ideas. Finish eating with us."

"I don't want to lose it. I need to get it down on paper."

"Can't it wait twenty minutes until we're done?"

"I need to write."

"You're being selfish. Please finish eating with us."

"Just stop typing at midnight," Jerry said, before resuming his stare across imagined tundra. "I need to sleep tonight. I have to shovel in the morning."

Striker didn't want to write in the attic office, certain the ideas gestating in his mind were too big to be contained under the eaves. He wanted to walk outside, in the open, letting the wind and night fertilize his sprouting thoughts. He wanted to write not in the solitude of his attic surrounded by his dusty chemistry set and tarnished saxophone but down at the radio station where he could feed off the energy of Barrett and the other actors, where Charles Armbrewster and The WEBR Players would provide the musical backdrop to his forming ideas, where old scripts that cluttered his shared desk could inspire him. Most of all, he didn't want to stop writing at midnight.

"I think I'll work at the station tonight."

"You're going out? After what happened last night? And why do you keep touching your face? Tell me what happened to it," Janet asked.

More looks were exchanged, more eyes were downcast, more fingers poked.

"I'll tell you all about it later, but now I have to go."

"Stay home, Fran. I edited more of *Tom Sawyer* for you. It's up on your desk. Let's go over it after dinner."

"I'm sorry."

"Fran!" But Striker was already moving. He grabbed his coat and hat from the hall tree, checked to make sure he had enough Luckies to see him through, and stepped into the night.

No matter how much the wind whispered or how hard it blew, it couldn't get Striker's attention as he caught the trolley. The single digit temperature went ignored. Even the shaking and rattling streetcar couldn't jar him from his thoughts. When an idea gripped him the way this white stallion had hold of him now, he had no choice but to write about it. The need took over as strongly as when Slattery needed a drink. Nothing could stop it—not the boys, not Janet, not training for the Levinsky fight. It was a compulsion he could not explain, a compulsion that came with a cost.

The only way he knew to make more money was to write more stories, but that meant locking himself away in the attic until midnight or wandering the streets alone hoping ideas would find him. It meant working late at the radio station, missing meals with the family and playtime with the boys. It meant being away from Janet. His absence put a weight on them, but he needed to create something that would change all their lives. That was the only way he knew how to save his family.

He hopped off the cable car in front of the WEBR studios on Main Street, a few blocks from Woolworth's in The Brisbane building. There were occasions when he wrote at the station not because of a need that overtook him, but from necessity when Barrett and the other actors were on the air performing an unfinished episode. His typing sounded like a Gatling gun as he raced time. He'd yank a finished page and its carbons from the Remington and pass it to a secretary. She'd run to The Gold Room as he fed another sheet into the typewriter, trying to stay ahead of the live broadcast. When the final scene was handed off, when it was certain there would be no dead air or improvising actors, Striker would lean back in his chair, enjoy a smoke, already thinking about the next episode.

He entered the building and hurried to his desk. A manila envelope addressed to him sat on his Remington Sixteen, but he pushed it aside without noticing the sender's name. He tossed his hat on a pile of scripts but didn't remove his coat, leaving it unbuttoned as he rolled paper into the typewriter. He tucked a Lucky between his lips but forgot to light it. The white stallion cantered in front of him.

Who would own such a horse? A king? A knight? A prince? No, America needed an *American* hero, someone raised here with values shared by WEBR's listening audience, not some royalty from a distant land. Out-of-work, hungry people didn't want stories about those born to privilege. This American hero needed to be as noble as the horse he rode. The white stallion snorted in approval. Striker typed:

1. I believe to have a friend, a man must be one.

He didn't know where that line came from. Forming characters began with something concrete like an occupation—detective, gangster, spy—or a physical description—shifty eyes, a lame leg, a dueling scar ridged across cheekbone—but what was more noble than friendship and all the love and loyalty it implied? The white stallion whinnied and neighed. Striker concentrated. He was creating an *American* hero. What else would he believe?

2. That all men are created equal and that everyone has within himself the power to make this a better world.

He re-read the line, the unlit Lucky hanging between his lips, questioning if he had written a true sentence. He was struggling to make his family's life better. How could *he* improve the entire world? Would it be through his writing, the stories he had yet to tell? Had Slattery made the world a better place in the ring, bringing joy to his fans, at least for a hundred and thirty-five days? Or does a simple act of kindness—taking someone in from the cold, tending a forgotten grave, preventing a drunk from falling—count far more? Striker left the sentence and wrote another.

3. He believes in being prepared physically, mentally,
and morally to fight when necessary for that which is right.

The white stallion reared on his hind legs, transforming into a warhorse ready for battle, waiting for Striker to create its rider.

The broadcast of this week's episode of *Dr. Dragonette* ended. Barrett barged in their little office. "Fran," he said. "What are you doing here?"

"Working," Striker answered, his eyes not leaving the page, searching for a worthy rider.

"You must be feeling better then," Barrett said, rummaging through the desk for that still missing box of Pine Brothers Glycerin Throat Drops. "I think I'm getting a cold." Scripts skidded from piles.

Other actors came out of The Gold Room and stopped in the doorway to say hello, to ask Striker if his head was okay, to bum a cigarette. Some crammed into the former broom closet and leaned over his shoulder to see what he was working on, asking if it was next week's episode of *Dr. Dragonette*.

"I'm working," Striker said, now wishing he was back in his attic, snug under the eaves, with no one bothering him until he broke his midnight curfew.

Charles Armbrewster, the lanky band leader with thinning hair and limbs that moved like trombone slides, stuck his head in the doorway and said everyone was going to The Colored Musicians Club, his Adam's apple genuflecting as he spoke.

"Working here," Striker said.

"Say, what's this?" Barrett asked, reaching in front of Striker for the manila envelope. "It's addressed to you, Fran."

"Open it," Striker said, hoping that would keep him quiet, and typed:

4.

He waited for a sentence to form, for the fourth point of this new character's creed to come to him, but the page remained as white as the stallion.

Barrett ripped open the envelope and pulled out a sheaf of papers. "It's a radio script from...Phillips Lord."

"Who's Phillips Lord?" Striker mumbled, still staring at the page.

"Someone offering us the opportunity to buy his script," Barrett said.

"Why? Let me see that."

Barrett handed Striker the cover letter, then skimmed the script. "Say, this is pretty good. Not as good as your stuff but still pretty good."

Striker straightened in his chair. His eyes widened as he read then re-read the letter. "His *idea* is better than pretty good. His idea is genius. Why didn't *I* think of this?"

"Think of what?" Barrett asked, lowering the script and peering over Striker's shoulder.

"He wrote this script and is offering it to WEBR for a royalty fee."

"How much is the fee?"

"Two to six dollars. I guess it's negotiable."

Barrett picked up the envelope. "He's from New York City. Why's he offering it to us?"

"That's the genius part. He's not just offering it to *us*. He's offering the same script to independent stations across the country. Think of it, John. If he has fifty radio stations broadcast this script for six dollars each…"

"That's three hundred dollars!" Barrett exclaimed, his voice bursting like a cannon shot.

"For one script!"

"If you write two a week…"

"Six hundred dollars!"

"And if they buy episode one…"

"They have to buy episode two!"

"Guaranteed income."

"I could recycle scripts as other stations come on board. I could sell the same script a hundred times!" he said, the Lucky flopping as he yelled.

"Two hundred times!" Barrett yelled back, his voice causing scripts to fall to the floor revealing the long-lost box of Pine Brothers Glycerin Throat Drops.

"I can sell them in Canada too!"

"You could be a rich man, Fran Striker. A very rich man," Barrett said, grabbing the Pine Brothers and popping a lozenge in his mouth.

Striker took the envelope from Barrett and studied it. "Phillips Lord. I know that name, don't I? Doesn't he write the *Seth Parker* series about that backwoods preacher and philosopher? The guy who plays all the old-time songs and tells corny jokes as part of the show?"

"It's not *Covered Wagon Days* or *Dr. Dragonette*, is it?"

"No, but if he's selling it all over the country, who cares? This guy must be loaded."

Striker found a pencil, lit his cigarette, and worked out the math on the back of the manila envelope: six hundred a week multiplied by four weeks equals twenty-four hundred a month. Twenty-four hundred times twelve months equals…twenty-eight thousand eight hundred dollars a year. An astonishing number! Striker was sure he could write more than two scripts each week. His pencil scratched against the envelope. Royalties on three scripts a week could earn him forty-three thousand, two hundred dollars a year! Four scripts, fifty-seven thousand, six hundred! If he could write and sell five scripts, writing a new one each day, he could make…

"Seventy-two thousand dollars a year," Barrett said, his breath piney.

Striker laid down his pencil. "Roosevelt will make seventy-five when he takes office." He inhaled a lungful of smoke, held it, then exhaled, filling the small office with a mystical haze. "I could make as much as the president. Wait 'til I tell Janet."

Barrett slapped Striker's shoulder. "What are you going to do with all your money, Mr. Rockefeller?"

Striker leaned far back in his chair and thought of the mortgage he wouldn't have to worry about, a new car he could buy, the nine mouths he could feed. He could afford the best doctors for his mother. They could have turkey and potatoes every night if they wanted. Maybe they could have another child. He knew Janet longed for a daughter. But an uneasiness crept over him. The spot where The Gypsy spat tingled.

"It's risky," he said, rubbing his cheek. "I'd have to quit this place. WEBR. They wouldn't let me stay if they knew I was writing for other stations."

"They're paying you peanuts. You'll make more on royalties."

"There's no guarantee I'll make *anything* on royalties, John. My salary here may be small, but I can count on it. What if nobody buys my scripts? What if I get writer's block? What happens then? What happens to my family? It's a gamble. If this royalty scheme doesn't work, I'll be like all the other guys in this country without a job."

Barrett smoothed his moustache. "Hell, you're a better writer than this Phillips Lord. Radio stations across the country will be begging for your stuff."

"You don't know that."

"So, find out. Send out some scripts and see what happens. You don't have to tell WEBR anything, not at first. Think of it as moonlighting. You have to do what's best for Janet and your boys, Fran. You have to do what's best for everybody."

"You sound like my dad." He took one last drag off his Lucky before stubbing it out in an overflowing ashtray. He leaned forward and typed:

Men should live by the rule of what is best for the greatest number.

EPISODE 5

The Man with the Very Small Chin

Don Stefano sat at his desk near the crematorium oven, drinking homemade grappa and cursing Franklin Roosevelt. That damn downstater would ruin everything with his campaign promise of repealing the Volstead Act. The end of Prohibition would mean the end of speakeasies and the money that flowed faster than cross-border booze. These Buffalonians would drink anything—watered-down beer, bathtub gin, hair tonic, even the good stuff from Scotland, Russia, and Canada when they could afford it. The Don could sell them anything and hadn't been able to count his cash fast enough since he'd pulled on his bootlegging boots. Soon it would all end because of Roosevelt. Happy days are here again my eye, he thought, knocking back another grappa.

He'd need to concentrate more on the old standbys—gambling, loansharking, prostitution—to make up the pending rum-running loss. He nodded and sipped some more. The Lieutenant will help with that. He'll provide a list of all known brothels and gambling parlors and together they will take them over and bring them into the family. He won't like it, but he'll do it. Roosevelt will take office in March. That gave them time.

Still.

He swore in Sicilian and swept the unread editions of *The Courier Express* and *The Evening Times* from his desk. If he had his way, he'd nail FDR inside a Voelker Coupe and bury him in Forest Lawn Cemetery next to Millard Fillmore's grave. He'd never be found. No one visits Fillmore.

He poured another grappa. Something other than the twenty-first amendment was bothering him. Stefano Magaddino, The Undertaker, The Don, the bone breaker, the widow maker, the whisky peddler, the shylock, the man they said had no heart was...lonely. He needed something more than homemade brandy to warm him. What he needed, he decided, was a wife. It'd be easy to have a bride sent from Castellammare del Golfo. He could mail a single letter and the town beauty, or the local Don's daughter, or a buxom first cousin would be put on the next steamer to America for him. The Undertaker, however, had always been partial to northern Italian women, especially from Carrara with their fair skin and delicate features. Artists sculpted goddesses in their likeness from Carrara-quarried marble. Old men prayed that the angels in heaven would look as lovely.

Yes, The Don thought. He needed a Carrara woman, someone to bear him broad-shouldered sons and thin-waisted daughters, someone to come home to after a long day of undertaking and racketeering, a wife who enjoyed the simpler things like a quiet evening in front of a fire. His head grew heavy from the liquor and nodded to his chest. A smile wormed across his face as he dreamed of blonde hair, green eyes, Carrara passion.

He didn't doze long. Joey Maranto was shaking his shoulder. His eyelids fluttered open as he was pulled from his dream's soft arms. "We've got a problem, boss."

The Undertaker shook his head and slapped his cheeks to rouse himself. He sipped some grappa to melt sleep's fingers that clung to him.

"What kind of problem?" he asked, his voice thick from slumber and brandy. "A problem that The Lieutenant can take care of or a problem that needs Tommy guns?"

"An in-between problem. Slattery's missing."

"We saw him last night at Voelker's."

"He's on a bender, boss, bigger than the one before the Levinsky fight they're saying."

"Christ. What do we know?"

"Not much. We know he left Voelker's and went to The Kitty Kat and bought a round for the house and sang Irish songs until he cried. Then he went to The Colored Musicians Club and threw a piano player down the stairs because he thought he was Maxie Rosenbloom. That poor *mulignan* is all busted up in Sisters Hospital. They say he may never play the ivories again. Who picks a fight with a pianist?"

"The colored piano player looked like a Jewish boxer from Connecticut?"

"To that drunken Mick he did. I don't see the resemblance myself."

The Undertaker stroked his jaw. His black whiskers whispered against his palm. "Is that the last place anyone saw him?"

Maranto shook his head. "He went to The New Genesee after that, but The Greek threw him out because Slats kept trying to eat the waitress' hair. He was shoving handfuls of strawberry-blond curls in his mouth like he couldn't get enough. He thought it was cotton candy. He's always had a sweet tooth."

"Tamis threw out Slattery? *Physically*? That's hard to believe."

"It's true, boss. That Mick could hardly stand by then. The Greek gave him the bum's rush by the collar and belt, tossed him out on the sidewalk, and Slats belly-slid across the ice into Genesee Street. He almost got run over by a cabby, but the taxi swerved and hit an old lady. Which was lucky for Slats but not so good for the old lady. She's all busted up and in Sisters Hospital, too. Luck of the Irish, I guess. Last anyone saw was Slats staggering off into the storm without his hat and coat."

"I have plans for him. Things have been arranged. Money has been paid."

"I know boss. That's the problem. That's why I woke you."

"Find him. Check every speakeasy, flophouse, and whorehouse from here to Erie. Bring me that Mick. Sober him the hell up and thaw him the hell out. I need four more fights out of him, then I don't care what the hell happens to him." The Undertaker stood, nearly knocking over his chair. "Go find Slattery."

Maranto didn't move. "There's something else. Lefty Mavrakis got into a scuffle at The Colored Musicians Club, too."

"Lefty doesn't fight. He's a thief. Who'd he fight? Slattery?"

"No, some chinless gunsel. Nobody recognized him. We think maybe he's from out of state."

"Chinless?"

"A man with a very small chin."

"Why is Lefty's scrape with a man with a very small chin my problem?"

"He forced Lefty into the back of a Packard, boss. He had a gat pressed against his head. A real old one. Lefty wasn't looking too healthy at the time."

Understanding slithered across The Undertaker's face. "I need Lefty alive."

"I know, boss."

He spoke through clenched teeth. "Find Slattery. Find Lefty. Bring them here."

"Yes, boss."

"Tell The Lieutenant to get his men looking for them. Go!"

Maranto scampered toward the stairs.

"Joey!"

Maranto stopped and faced The Don. "Yeah, boss?"

"What was Lefty and this man with a very small chin fighting about?"

"I don't know, boss. Something about rings."

The Undertaker nodded. "Bring me this chinless man, too. I want all three in front of the oven."

"Right, boss," Maranto said, and disappeared up the stairs and into the funeral parlor.

The Undertaker sighed, drained his grappa then threw the glass against the wall where it shattered into a thousand shards. He began pacing. Roosevelt, Slattery, and that damn Lefty Mavrakis would all cost him a lot of money.

The fights had already been fixed for Slats: first that bum Belanger, then Joe "The Calamity Kid" Knight from down south and George Nicholas right after. None'll give Slats a chance against any of them. He's a drunk, they'll say. A washed-up Irish tomato can. Only a fool or someone who had rigged the fights would bet on Slattery. The Undertaker was no fool and planned on betting heavy.

After those victories, Maxie Rosenbloom would have to give Slats another shot at the title. They'd all jump on board then—the speakeasy know-it-all's, the South Buffalo believers, the ones who *knew* Slattery would beat the bottle and become champ again. This time, they'd all say, he'll be champ for more than one hundred thirty-five days. They'd all bet on Slats, scraping together whatever wager they could by stealing their family's bread money or grabbing coins from the collection plate, certain Slattery's twin fists would provide for them again. He, of course, would bet on Maxie, who might kill Slattery in the ring this time around. Maybe he could pick up Slattery's funeral business.

Lefty was a different story. He needed him alive for the foreseeable future. The Gypsy had run the most profitable Buffalo brothel for as long as anyone could remember. He needed Lefty if he hoped to get a piece of it. Lefty was the one who could reason with Mirela, who wasn't afraid of her. The Undertaker was certain he could persuade him it'd be in everyone's best interest if they partnered and shared the profits. Lefty, in turn, would persuade her. The Undertaker had grown up listening to stories of the gypsy caravans that'd rolled into Castellammare del Golfo and the curses the *zingari* had cast—how fishermen had caught nothing but seaweed in their nets and families had starved for a year, the seventy-three straight days of black skies and blacker rain that had flooded streets and homes, how every daughter born in 1891 was struck barren. He had no intention of facing Mirela without Lefty on his side. The usual methods of muscling wouldn't work on a woman who doesn't age.

His plans for The Gypsy's brothel would be ruined if that out-of-stater with the very small chin had already planted a very large bullet in Lefty's very average-sized ear.

"Why are all my troubles coming at once?" The Undertaker said aloud. He kicked the copy of *The Evening Times* that had fallen to the floor earlier, scattering pages like cemetery leaves. Roosevelt.

His picture was staring at him from the front page, the president-elect's thin lips mocking him with a smile. He snatched the paper from the floor intending on wadding it like an angry child but stopped when he noticed the headline:

FDR TO VISIT BUFFALO

He returned to his desk, smoothed the pages, and began to read.

EPISODE 6

A Masked Man Appears

The Airstream crossed into Defiance County, Ohio. Lake Erie wasn't yet frozen. The smell of carp and crappie drifted from its banks. The weather system had travelled miles of Depression despair. It had passed over homeless Okies, Hooverville dwellers, and bankers on holiday. It pulled from the earth moisture, lost faith, rust-colored farm dirt that filled it to bursting. To the north, The Alberta Clipper bore down, growing in size and gathering strength. The two hurtled toward each other like conductor-less trains.

George W. Trendle's hands were folded over his belly as he lay on his office couch, the leather squeaking, the springs protesting each time he shifted his corpulence. An empty bottle of Doctor Foley's Pain Relief Medicine had fallen to the floor and was surrounded by his still-buttoned vest, his inside-out suitcoat, one sock, a shoe, and crumpled sheets of Big Chief tablet paper. Another bottle of Doctor Foley's, this one half full, lay on his chest. The cap wasn't secured, and a growing amber stain spread across his shirt like a bullet wound. The room smelled of alcohol and chloroform. His eyelids were puffy and opened to slits behind his pince-nez.

WXYZ had signed off for the night and was deserted, the only sound filling the studios was Trendle's mouth breathing, a combination of snoring and asthmatic wheezing. He was neither awake nor asleep, but instead bobbed in a Foley fog as hornets swarmed between his ears. The stomach pain that had bothered him earlier had been numbed hours ago.

Wedged between his side and the couch was an open writing tablet, also amber spotted with pain medicine. BIG IDEAS was written across the page in capital letters and possible occupations for his new radio hero were listed: Soldier, Detective, Terry the Crime-Fighting Mailman. 'Prohibition Agent' was crossed out with violent pencil strokes and *NO!!* was written in the margin. 'Cowboy' was listed last, underlined twice, and circled.

The couch cantered beneath him, its legs raising and lowering in three beats, suspending in air after each stride. Trendle closed his eyes, enjoying this unexpected journey. He was certain he was travelling great distances, first circling his office, then down the hallway to the waiting area. A cold blast greeted him as he rose and fell in the leather, certain he'd loped out the front entrance onto Woodward Avenue. He wished he'd put on his sock. It took great effort to force his vision to focus. When he did, he was back in his office, the floor around the couch still littered with his clothes and tablet paper. It was as if the couch hadn't moved at all. Everything was the same except for the masked man standing next to the couch and pointing a gun at Trendle's heart.

Trendle didn't panic. He doubted the man was real, just as he doubted that he'd rode his couch around the studio. Surely, Dr. Foley was playing tricks on him. His fingers felt stiff and clumsy as he adjusted his pince-nez, leaving them crooked on his nose and fingerprints smudging the lenses. He rolled from side to side and pushed with his feet. His bare foot lost traction and slipped on the leather upholstery. His mouth breathing intensified as he struggled to get upright and sounded tubercular. The masked man took a step backward. Trendle floundered to a position somewhere between sitting and lying. He was vertical enough, however, to unscrew the leaking cap and take a sip of Doctor Foley's, but not before losing the cap in the cushions. He angled his head to the left and shifted his eyes to see around the fingerprints on his lenses. He blinked several times to make sure the masked man was still there.

The masked man was still there.

The bandit's mask was made from a black neckerchief that hung below his nose. The eyeholes were ragged and uneven, as if cut with a dull blade. The openings were so misaligned that the robber was forced to tilt his head to return the station owner's stare.

Trendle pursed his lips and swallowed hard to get his larynx operational. It felt as if his tongue had thickened and had been sleeved in winter wool.

"Who are you?" he croaked, taking in the bandit's jutting arms, boney knees, his sunken cheeks. The thief was all angles and sharp points and mask. His shapeless overcoat was a size too large.

"Never you mind," the masked man said.

The gun barrel's opening enlarged until it was wide and yawning and as capable of swallowing Trendle as it was of shooting him. He pressed his puffy eyelids shut, and when he opened them, the barrel had returned to normal size and was again, thankfully, only capable of shooting him.

"What do you want?" he asked.

"What do you think I want? I'm robbing you, you damn fool."

"You're robbing a radio station? I've never heard of such a thing," Trendle said, as he struggled into somewhat of a more upright position. He removed his glasses and cleaned the lenses with his shirttail, noticing the amber stain across his chest for the first time. He imagined the gun discharging, the amber stain turning vermilion.

"There's a reason nobody robs radio stations," Trendle continued. "You see, my masked friend, there's nothing to steal. No cash drawer to clean out, no safe to crack. There's nothing here but 78's and broadcasting equipment. You're better off robbing brothels. That's where the money is."

"But I'm not robbing the radio station," the masked man said, pulling a second pistol from his waistband, a gun now pointed at each ventricle. "I'm robbing *you*."

"Me?"

"Yep. You. George W. Trendle. Michigan's miser. The cheapest man in Detroit. The Ebenezer Scrooge of Woodward Avenue. The fat cat who's getting fatter while the kittens starve."

"I'm none of those things. I'm a businessman."

"Give me those damn cufflinks."

"These were my father's."

"Well, they been in your family long enough then. Give them here."

Trendle set Doctor Foley's Pain Relief Medicine on the floor and removed the ruby cufflinks.

"Put them on the floor, Georgie Boy."

Trendle placed the rings next to the medicine bottle. "Do I know you?"

"Know me? You don't even see people like me when you walk by the soup kitchen. We're invisible. You keep walking."

"Who are you? I've heard your voice before."

"What kind of watch is that?"

"A Dunhill."

"Put it on the pile," the masked man said, pointing to the cufflinks. "Where's your wallet?"

"Suitcoat. Inside pocket." Trendle nodded to the jacket crumpled at the bandit's feet.

The masked man tucked a pistol back in his waistband and squatted, keeping the other Colt trained on Trendle's chest. He pulled a green alligator wallet from Trendle's jacket thick with bills.

The masked man whistled. "All this money and you want a man to work for free." He pulled the bills out and stuffed them in his pocket before throwing the wallet at Trendle. The billfold smacked him in the forehead and fell. "Where's the rest?"

"That's all there is. I told you, we don't keep money here."

"Get dressed."

"What?"

"Your shoe, your sock. Put them on. Vest and coat, too. We're going for a ride."

"Where?" Trendle asked, swinging his legs to the floor.

"Your house. It must be filled with things worth stealing. There must be a safe there. Come on."

Trendle stood and wavered. His bald head felt heavy and enlarged as if it'd grown to something monstrous. The swarm of hornets had multiplied, the buzzing between his ears deafening.

"Don't stand there," the masked man said. "Get dressed."

Trendle bent to pick up his vest and almost pitched forward but regained his balance and straightened. He studied the buttoned waistcoat as if he'd never seen it before, baffled how he had taken it off. He unbuttoned it, wrestled it on, then misbuttoned it.

As Trendle dressed, the masked man pulled a cloth bag from his overcoat pocket. He scooped the ruby cufflinks and Dunhill timepiece and dropped them in the bag. He scanned the room for something else to steal, choosing a sterling silver letter opener, a gold cigarette lighter engraved with the initials *GWT*, and a ruby tie tack that he found lying on the floor that matched the cufflinks.

"Where do you live?" the bandit asked.

"The Whittier, by the river."

"That's some fancy hotel. Who else is there tonight?"

"My wife, Adelaide."

"Let's go see Adelaide."

The masked man pushed Trendle toward the hallway, then to the front door, and finally onto Woodward Avenue. The masked man liked pushing Trendle. Each time Trendle was shoved, he staggered and fought to keep balance. The cold cleared some of the Foley fog, but he still felt unsteady. His mouth breathing crescendoed to coal miner's snort.

"Where's your car?"

Trendle pointed to a maroon Cadillac convertible, the wide whitewalls whiter than the snow.

"Fat wallet, lives at The Whittier, drives a pretty new Cadillac. And all I ate today was yesterday's biscuit." He pushed Trendle again, this time harder. "You drive."

"I shouldn't. I'm having trouble with my eyes. I'm seeing double. Must've been something I ate."

"Your eyes are fine," the robber said, opening the car door and climbing in, the soft seat cupping him in leather.

Trendle poured himself behind the wheel and took several deep breaths through his mouth, hoping that would improve his steering. He drove over the curb as he pulled away.

"Try keeping her straight for a while," the bandit suggested, as Trendle wove down the street.

"You should be driving," Trendle said, covering his right eye to bring things into focus.

"How can I drive and keep my gun pointed at you?"

"You could skip the latter," Trendle suggested, running a stop sign. "I won't mind."

"Stay on this side of the road, Georgie Boy."

It took about twenty minutes of weaving and skidding before Trendle pulled in front of The Whittier. He parked with two tires on the curb, uncovered his eye, and leaned his forehead against the steering wheel.

"What floor are you on?"

"Fifteen," Trendle mumbled, certain he could sleep through the night propped against the steering wheel, hypothermia notwithstanding.

"Top floor. Should've figured." He jabbed at Trendle's gut with his gun. "Come on. Your apartment isn't going to rob itself."

He kept prodding the gun barrel into Trendle's stomach until the station owner lifted his forehead from the steering wheel, opened the car door, and fell onto Burns Drive.

Trendle lived in the Whittier Hotel's South Tower, an Italian Renaissance building made of buff brick and terra cotta trim. The arched windows on the ground floor were large and expansive but no one was up to see the masked man and Trendle walk past the Corinthian pilasters and through the main entrance. The lobby was deserted—even the night manager's desk was abandoned—but the interior was bright. Sconces and crystal chandeliers were all illuminated, the light reflecting off each facet. Their footsteps echoed off marble floors and reverberated against columns as they made their way to the elevator. They rode in silence to the top floor. The masked man pulled the cloth bag from his pocket holding the items he'd already stolen and worried the bag wouldn't be large enough for the treasures he was about to steal. He stuffed the bag back in his pocket.

"Which one's yours?" the masked man asked, as brass doors parted.

"1502," Trendle said, pointing to the door across from the elevator.

The masked man shoved Trendle towards it. "Open it."

Trendle searched for the key first in his right pants pocket then his left. He checked his topcoat, finding a single lambskin glove, a gift from Adelaide, and wondered what had happened to its mate. He unbuttoned his overcoat then patted his suitcoat, smiling when he felt the key's outline in his misbuttoned vest's pocket. After fishing it out, he raised the golden key in triumph.

"Open it," he repeated.

Trendle thrust the key toward the opening several times, missing with each jab.

"I'm amazed you have children," the masked man said, watching Trendle struggle.

"How do you know about my children?" Trendle asked, the key finding its mark. He turned the knob and the apartment door swung open.

"I been asking around," the robber said, pushing Trendle inside. "You have a boy and a girl but they all growed and gone so I don't have to worry about them."

The pair stepped into a long hallway, the floor tiled in a black-and-white diamond pattern. To the left was the living room. The drapes were open, and the Detroit skyline winked before them. Logs smoldered in the fireplace casting shadows up the walls to the beamed ceilings capped with crown molding. Suspended from the picture rail were still lifes and landscapes, watercolors and oils. A portrait of an unsmiling woman hung above the mantle, her bustline large and threatening.

"I knew I should've bought a bigger bag."

"George?" a woman's voice called from the bedroom. "Is someone with you?"

"Yes, dear. I brought home a masked outlaw. We're being robbed." The desperado jabbed him with his pistol. "At gunpoint," Trendle added.

"*What?*"

There was commotion in the bedroom and then Adelaide Trendle burst through the door, cinching her satin robe around her waist. She was petite, small-boned, with thick brown hair and flashing dark eyes. Her movements were fast and determined, as if she was always running behind schedule. She gasped when she saw the masked man press a gun against her husband's nose. All her quick movements—her stride, her belt cinching, her darting eyes—halted.

"Turn around and get your jewelry box or I'll blow his nose off."

Adelaide didn't move. "Not my jewelry."

"Now!" the masked man yelled. She spun on slippered feet and hurried back to the bedroom.

"Get the money," the robber said, into Trendle's ear.

"What money?"

"From the safe in your bedroom," he said, pushing Trendle after his wife.

"How do you know about that?"

The masked man smiled, his teeth uneven, coffee-stained, pleading to be flossed. "Take me to it."

He led the masked man down the hallway through an arched doorway to the bedroom on the other side of the suite. The drapes here were also opened. The window faced the Detroit River and Windsor's distant lights. The walk-in closet was open, and Adelaide was stretching on her toes to reach her jewelry box. The robber looked past Adelaide, past the hanging suits and designer dresses and Parisian gowns to a safe at the far end of the closet. *George W. Trendle* was written in gold leaf above the safe's door and *The Julius Bing Safe Company* was scripted beneath the handle and dial. The masked man pushed him towards it.

"Open it. And don't give me no bull crap about forgetting the combination."

Trendle brushed shoulders with his wife as she stepped from the closet holding her jewelry box. They exchanged sympathetic expressions, her eyes bright with tears, his dull from a bottle and a half of Doctor Foley's.

"Set it on the bed," the robber told her. "Open it."

Her tiny hands trembled as she lifted the lid revealing silver bracelets, gold necklaces and platinum brooches. There were smaller black boxes of various shapes for rings and earrings and watches.

The masked man made a clucking noise like a satisfied chicken. "Georgie Boy spoils you," he said, pulling the cloth bag from his pocket and tossing it on the bed. "Fill it."

Adelaide emptied her jewelry box into the bag, her tears catching chandelier light. The robber went to the closet to check on Trendle. He was crouched on his haunches, his pudgy fingers working the dial. He lifted the handle and pulled the heavy door open, revealing sheaves of paper, legal documents, and a few stacks of banded money.

"That's it?" the masked man asked.

"Times are tough for everyone. Even I'm running out of cash."

"Put it in the bag."

Trendle grabbed the money then rose, his knee clicking like a second safe had been opened.

"Why are you doing this?" Adelaide whined.

"For food," the masked man said.

"You can call down for a sandwich," Trendle offered, who stood next to his wife and shoved the money in the bulging bag. "Instead of robbing us."

The robber smiled another mustard smile. "I think that bag is better than any sandwich they can make. Pull the strings tight."

Trendle cinched the bag and faced his robber. "There. You're a rich man. How are you going to spend all your ill-gotten gains? I doubt on food like you say. More likely you'll waste it at some speakeasy with bootleg whisky and painted tarts."

"This money isn't for me."

"Who's it for then?"

"All those families out there who are starving to death and standing in line for a free meal. I'll buy food and leave groceries on their doorsteps. When the cash runs out and if I still ain't caught, I'll sell or hock the jewelry and buy more groceries—hams and turkeys and milk for the little ones. Then if I *still* ain't caught, I'll find another George W. Trendle in another city to rob and start all over again. This country is lousy with your kind."

"This money isn't for you?" Trendle asked, a weird light chasing dilation from his eyes.

"You're like Robin Hood," Adelaide said, wiping her tears with an embroidered handkerchief. She eyed the bag of stolen jewels like it contained her kidnapped children.

"A masked man who does good," Trendle said, the gears in his brain grinding. "Everyone thinks he's bad, but he's not. He's helping others. *Saving others.*"

"Yes, sir. Saving them from the likes of you. There's one more thing I got to do before I leave," the masked man said. He cocked his arm as if drawing a bow, then let it fly, punching Trendle square in the nose. The heavens exploded into a million light rays, detonating as they must have at creation. Then everything darkened and Trendle tumbled backward onto the bed.

EPISODE 7

Trouble At The Colored Musicians Club

Pando the Pinsetter was climbing the stairs at The Colored Musicians Union Hall, Local 533, a red-bricked building located on Broadway near Michigan Avenue, when Barrett and Striker arrived. A steep staircase led to the speakeasy above the hall where musicians, both Black and White, wandered in after they had finished their gigs, to drink and laugh and play in improvisational wonder. The saying at Local 533 was that you had to be colored to be in the union, but any color was allowed upstairs in the club.

"Do you need help, Pando?" Barrett asked, his voice rich and lush as a woodwind. The drunken pinsetter was climbing the stairs on all fours, pulling himself up as if scaling Everest.

"No," Pando answered, wiping his face with the back of his hand. "Almost there." He noticed Striker for the first time. "Hi-yo, Striker."

The radiomen stepped over Pando as he searched for a toehold.

"Say, Pando," Striker said. "I heard you were with Slattery this morning. You seen him lately? He's not upstairs, is he?"

"Last I seen of Slats he was running to catch a freight train," Pando slurred. "Well, more like staggering than running. I think he crawled part of the way. He made it, though. Still an athlete, that one."

"Where was the train headed?" Barrett asked.

"I don't know. West? Maybe east. Damned if I know. We'd been drinking for a while. Well, all fucking night. He said something about a prostitute in Poughkeepsie with hair like butter. Or was it Piscataway? I was supposed to go with him. He said the prostitute had a short sister, but I couldn't run through the snow. Too damn deep. He carried me on his shoulders for a while but kept dropping me."

"So, you *were* at the railyard today?" Striker asked.

"I think so. Is today still today?"

"You didn't happen to see a man with a very small chin there, did you?" Striker asked.

"A man with a very small chin?"

"Very small," Barrett confirmed.

"Dressed all in black, carrying an old Colt .45 like Wyatt Earp?" Pando whispered, staring beyond Striker and Barrett as if The Man with the Very Small Chin was standing at the top of the stairs ready to slap leather.

"That's him," Striker said. "You saw him then."

Pando shook his head. "Never seen a guy like that. Not ever. And I hope I never see him again."

"Wait, what? Did you see him or not?" Barrett asked, his voice sharp and impatient like a tough radio gumshoe.

"I'm done talking. You guys ain't coppers. I got climbing to do."

"Can you at least tell us if Lefty was with him?" Striker asked. "It's Lefty we need to find."

Pando rested his forehead against a step. "Poor Lefty."

"Why?" Striker asked. "What happened to him?"

"Nothing. I don't know nothing. I didn't see nothing," he said, squeezing his lips closed as if they'd remain sealed forever.

Striker and Barrett asked again about Lefty and The Man with the Very Small Chin, but Pando refused to answer. After they asked once more and were ignored, they gave up and pushed through the door into the speak.

"Hey," Pando called after them. "Buy me a drink when I get to the top? I drank all my money. All of Slattery's, too."

"Sure," Barrett said, holding open the door to the club. "What are you having?"

"Whisky. A short one."

The Colored Musicians Club was long and narrow with an oak bar that ran the length of the building. The walls were exposed brick and the floor wide planked, giving the impression more of warehouse than social club. Pendant lights, some with loose canopies and missing screws, were attached to the tin ceiling by frayed wires. The black stage, elevated a foot off the ground, stood at the front of the speakeasy. An upright piano, the top ringed from years of sweating lowball glasses and burned from countless cigarettes, sat stage left while a double bass stood opposite in its stand. A drum kit was tucked furthest back, its brass cymbals angled as if they'd recently been struck.

The musicians were easy to spot. Band members wore matching suits or white dinner jackets with loosened bow ties and unbuttoned collars. Some clutched a case—clarinet, saxophone, trumpet—in one hand and Don Stefano's whisky in the other. Larger cases—trombone, guitar—were lined against the brick wall like luggage at The Central Train Terminal. Female singers wore evening gowns that hugged hips and teased cleavage and clavicle. The crowd was a blend of white and brown and ebony. Striker and Barrett stood at ease smack in the middle.

They saw Charles Armbrewster leaning against the bar. His thin leg, bent like an egret's, rested on the foot rail. Drumsticks protruded from his back pocket like a pair of slender fingers. They made their way to him, shouldering through the crowd, smiling their apologies, as musicians greeted each other by their nicknames—Coal Car, Big Dip, Jug-Jug.

"Hello, boys," Armbrewster said, pushing his glasses up on his nose. "Get much writing done, Striker? I didn't think I'd see you so soon. I figured you'd write till dawn."

"I wrote a little," he said, pain flitting across his face. He had written a few more lines, but the white stallion's rider still eluded him.

"What are you drinking?" Armbrewster asked.

"Ginger ale for me and a short whisky for Pando," Barrett said. "He'll be here any minute, unless there's a rockslide."

Armbrewster raised an eyebrow. "Ginger ale?"

Barrett cleared his throat. "I think I'm coming down with something,"

"If you're buying, I'll have a beer. If not, water's fine," Striker said, still trying to see the stallion's rider.

"This might take a while," Armbrewster said, as Old Miss Shirley, the bartender, shuffled towards them to take their order.

No one was certain of Old Miss Shirley's exact age, not even Shirley herself, but everyone was certain she was old. Her hair was gunmetal gray and rolled in finger waves. Her face was seamed with deep lines. She was born a slave on the Hopsewee Plantation in South Carolina near the banks of the North Santee River. After The Great War, she left the smell of sharecropping and pluff mud when she fell in love with Arthur "Boogaloo" Bailey, a trumpet player from Lick Skillet, Tennessee. She followed Boogaloo to Saint Louis, then Chicago, and finally Buffalo. He joined Local 533 and became Buffalo's greatest horn man. But Boogaloo, who suffered from both lame back and lumbago caused by Lick Skillet sharecropping, wandered off one morning in a freak Fourth of July snowstorm, searching for Doctor Foley's Pain Relief Medicine and was never seen again.

Old Miss Shirley, old even then, kept bartending at The Colored Musicians Club after Boogaloo disappeared, deciding the club would be the first place he'd visit if he ever returned. When the door to the speakeasy would open, Old Miss Shirley would turn to see if her Boogaloo had finally come home.

"Hello, handsomes," Miss Shirley said. "What are you thirsty for?"

Armbrewster gave their order and before Miss Shirley could shuffle off to get their drinks, Striker asked if she'd seen Lefty.

"Yesterday I surely did. Haven't seen him today, though," she said, turning when the door opened. Pando staggered in looking pleased with himself.

"The Gypsy said he came here to meet a man with a very small chin," Barrett said.

Old Miss Shirley nodded, turning back to them, her mouth curling downward in disappointment. "Hardly a chin at all. That man smelled like horse, too."

"What kind of horse?" Striker asked and tried to imagine a chinless man astride the white stallion, but the wonder horse bucked him off every time.

"How am I supposed to know what kind of damn horse? Smelling ain't seeing, but I could smell it on him from across the bar," Miss Shirley said. "Lefty could smell it, too. Kept trying to get away from him but that chin man kept pulling him close. Wasn't long before they was arguing."

"What were they arguing about?" Barrett asked.

"A ring," Old Miss Shirley said.

"You mean two rings," Slattery said.

The lines and creases in the old lady's face deepened. "If I meant two rings, I would've said two rings. That's what they was arguing about. Lefty was supposed to bring that little chin man *two* rings, but he only brought one."

"Are you sure?" Barrett asked.

"Sure I'm sure. I heard them."

"But it must have been loud in here," Striker said, trying to picture the scene as if he'd written it. "All these people talking and the band playing. Are you sure you heard right, Miss Shirley?"

"Listen, Writer Man, I may be old, but my hearing is young. Besides, I saw the ring and there was only one."

"You saw it?" Barrett asked.

"Sure. It was Slattery's ring. The one with all them diamonds that he always wears. I'd know it anywhere. It was a pretty damn thing but there was only one of them. That's a fact. And once that man with the very small chin learned that fact, he was *mad*. I mean, gun-pulling mad. They left with that chinless man's revolver stuck in Lefty's ribs. I don't know if we'll ever see that Greek boy again."

The door opened. Old Miss Shirley swiveled to see The Undertaker and Joey Maranto walk in and not her beloved Boogaloo. Maranto carried an oversized violin case.

"Did you hear where they were going, Miss Shirley?" Striker asked.

"I guess to fetch the other ring," she said, looking past The Undertaker, hoping there was somebody else coming up the stairs behind him. The door closed. The old woman sighed. "I best get your drinks. Other peoples are waiting."

"Do you remember anything else about The Man with the Very Small Chin, Miss Shirley?" Barrett asked. "Anything at all?"

"His name. Cavendish," she said, and shuffled away. "Butch Cavendish."

"Cavendish," Barrett repeated.

"Never heard of him," Striker said.

"Why are you trying to find Lefty?" Armbrewster asked.

"Long story," Striker said, as Pando joined them, hiccupping.

There wasn't a special barstool for him at The Colored Musicians Club, so Pando climbed on a regular stool then onto the bar, swinging his legs around so he sat facing the stage. "Did you order my whisky?" he asked, between hiccups.

"Miss Shirley's getting it," Striker said, and the pinsetter checked his watch and frowned.

"You don't think Lefty's the one who smacked you over the head, do you?" Barrett asked.

"No. Lefty would pick my pocket clean if he had a chance, but he'd never hurt anyone. He must've bought them off the guy who sapped me or was trying to sell them for him. But if the rings are separated, it makes finding them twice as hard. Got any ideas?"

"Oh," Barrett said, his voice soft and weak as if his radio voice had fled him. Striker and Armbrewster followed their friend's gaze across the speakeasy to a blonde woman with an angelic face wearing a red dress, the scoop neckline and capped sleeves laced in white. The hem stopped at her knee, fishtailing as she walked, flashing stocking and hope.

"Oh," Striker said.

"Oh," Armbrewster agreed, adjusting his glasses for a better look.

"Look at the cans on that tomato!" Pando said, pointing at Celestina. Barrett pushed down his arm.

"Who is she?" Striker asked, as Miss Shirley brought their drinks.

Barrett grabbed his ginger ale and downed half of it as if extinguishing something smoldering inside him. "My mother's nurse."

"From the nut house?" Pando asked, holding his whisky like a lost love rediscovered. "You can lock me up with her anytime," he said, and yapped like a Pekinese.

Barrett elbowed him, nearly knocking him over. Pando spilled part of his drink. "Say, watch it," the pinsetter said, sucking his cuff where the whisky had spilled.

"Go talk to her," Striker said, nudging Barrett in her direction. "Before someone else does."

"Right," Barrett whispered. "Yes." He finished his ginger ale and set off towards Celestina.

"Barrett!" Striker called. "Radio voice!"

Barrett nodded and cleared his throat. He popped a Pine Brothers Glycerin Throat Drop into his mouth. Celestina saw Barrett walking toward her, squeezing past couples, turning his shoulder to cut through the crowd, his face awash with dread and desire. She smiled at him not just with her lips but with eyes that seemed greener and cheeks that dimpled and glowed. Striker turned to say something to Armbrewster and noticed that Old Miss Shirley was leaning over the bar talking with Don Stefano. They turned toward him. Old Miss Shirley pointed at him, her finger bent and arthritic. The Don said something out of the corner of his mouth to Maranto, who nodded and started toward Striker.

Striker reached in his pocket and pulled out his smokes. He shook a Lucky free then raised the pack to his mouth, pulling the cigarette out with his lips. Before he could fish matches from his pocket, Armbrewster flicked his Zippo. Striker bent to the flame. He peeked in Maranto's direction and saw the gunsel almost next to him, a smirk curling his lip.

"We meet again, *friend*," Maranto said, squaring his shoulders in front of Striker, still holding the oversized violin case. "And no Slattery to protect you this time. Just your little gargoyle there," he said, raising his chin to point at Pando, still dangling his legs over the bar. "Take off, Ichabod," he said, to Armbrewster.

Armbrewster looked at Maranto, then the violin case before grabbing his drink and rising from the barstool. He crossed to the stage in a few lanky strides, pulling the drumsticks from his back pocket. He lowered the stool behind the drums, sat behind the kit, and tapped the cymbals, signaling the other musicians that it was time to play.

"What do you want, Maranto?" Striker asked, blowing smoke towards the tin ceiling and noticing the light fixture overhead was dangling by its wires. "Don't you have someone else to bother?"

"No, it's your lucky day. I hear you're asking about Lefty and a man with a very small chin."

"Why do you care?"

"I care because Don Stefano cares and that means you should care. You follow?"

Striker watched Don Stefano cut a cigar end with a stiletto. A man named Ivory was sitting next to The Don. He stood and stretched, his bald head nodding in rhythm with Armbrewster's taps, and made his way to the upright piano. He struck a single key, complimenting the cymbals. He hit the same key again.

"Why does Don Stefano care about Lefty?" Striker asked.

"That's nothing *you* should care about," Maranto said. "Why are *you* looking for Lefty?"

"He's an old friend. I wanted to catch up." The skin where The Gypsy spat pulsed.

"You know where he is?"

"If I knew where he was, I wouldn't have asked Miss Shirley."

"Don't get smart, friend. There's enough wise guys in this joint as it is."

Pando set his whisky next to him on the bar and pulled a harmonica from his pocket. He cupped it in his hands and played along with the piano and drums.

"All I know," Striker said, "is that Lefty is with a man with a very small chin."

"Cavendish."

"Who is he?" Striker asked, as the man to the right of him placed his case on the bar, unsnapped it, and pulled out a clarinet.

"Muscle from out west. Not sure why he's in town. He didn't stop by the funeral parlor and let his intentions be known to The Don like he should've."

"Maybe he doesn't like funeral parlors."

"Nobody likes funeral parlors, but we all end up in one. Some sooner than later, if you catch my meaning. Tell me what you know about this ring they were fighting about."

"I know what Miss Shirley told me."

"She says it's Slattery's."

"That's what she said."

"Tell me, friend. Are you looking for Lefty or Cavendish or the ring?"

"Like I said, I'm looking for Lefty. He's an old pal." His cheek burned as if sizzling. Striker pressed his beer mug against his face to cool the singed skin.

Maranto jabbed Striker in the shoulder when he spoke. "If you find Lefty, you call the funeral parlor right away. If you don't and I hear about it, I'm showing you Don Stefano's oven. Up close. Got it?"

"I got it," Striker said, pulling his beer away from his face and resting it on the bar.

"Don't forget."

"Say," Pando said, lowering the harmonica and nodding at the oversized violin case. "Are you going to play that thing or carry it around all night?"

Maranto smiled, as he backed away. "I might play, Little Man. If the right audience shows up."

The stage was full, and the musicians went to work: Armbrewster whisked the snare drum with brushes and the drum whispered back; Ivory's fingers sailed up and down the keyboard, his head bright with perspiration. Scaredy-Cat Floyd, who suffered from stage fright, blew his clarinet with his eyes squeezed shut, pretending he was playing to an empty room. Boom-Boom Bennett fingered the stand-up bass, a toothpick in the corner of his mouth bouncing with the beat. King Charlemagne wailed the sax, his dinner jacket on, his bow tie crisp, his cummerbund razor straight, as if he was still playing for the society crowd at The Buffalo Club. Pando's harmonica was drowned out by the band, but he kept playing, his cheeks puffing and hollowing as if money had been promised. Notes and chords braided together, wrapping themselves around hips until they swayed, feet until they tapped, souls until they soared.

Sharp notes sliced through the tin ceiling and were carried away by the wind. People walking by paused when they heard the joyful noise and decided they needed to get out of the cold, or that they needed a nightcap, or that they didn't want to go home quite yet. They filed up the stairs to The Colored Musicians Club in pairs and in groups and one at a time, the door opening and closing so often that Old Miss Shirley hurt her neck twisting to see if the rhythm and horns had lured Boogaloo Bailey back home.

Chairs and tables were pushed aside to make room for dancers. The floor was too crowded to swing, so Barrett held Celestina close, his right hand in the middle of her back, her chest against his as their feet slid forward and back, back and forward. Barrett, that whisper of a man, was built like a dancer with slender lines that bowed and bent without effort. Celestina mirrored his movements, her own slender lines bowing and bending in harmony with his. When space allowed, Barrett spun her, her red dress swirling, her smile brighter than any light in the club. They turned, and quarter turned, dipped and glided as if they'd been partners all their lives, perhaps even in a lifetime or two before this one. Barrett could smell perfume on her neck and shampoo in her hair. He breathed her in until he tasted berries and jasmine and endless April mornings.

Striker, rubbing the burn on his cheek, watched Barrett and Celestina dance, never imagining his friend possessed such rhythm. He suspected holding Celestina made all the difference. Striker wasn't the only one staring. Don Stefano also stood gape-mouthed, refusing to blink, not wanting to miss a millisecond. Heat flushed from scalp to sole as if he was seated in front of his oven. His arms hung lifeless by his sides. A Cuban cigar was wedged between his middle and forefinger, its gray ash falling to the planked floor, done in by its own dead weight. He thought of all the northern Italian women he'd ever seen, all the angels and goddesses sculpted from Carrara marble. None were as beautiful as Celestina. As he watched her hips shimmy and her legs kick, his heart, as black as it was, danced the *Tarantella Siciliana* in his chest, whirling and twirling in sextuple meter until he was left breathless and light-headed. Even a man like Don Stefano was capable of love.

When the song ended, Barrett and Celestina clapped, and their fingers laced together on their own. They made their way to the bar, both sensing something miraculous had begun. Striker applauded when they approached. A Lucky clamped between his lips, he squinted through rising smoke.

"You two are great together," he said. "You should enter contests."

"Fran, I want you to meet Celestina," Barrett said, still holding her hand. "Celestina, this is Fran Striker. He's going to be a famous writer someday."

"Pleased to meet you," she said, her smile making Striker squint even more.

Don Stefano and Maranto had wandered over and stood unnoticed next to the trio. The Don spoke before Striker could answer.

"Celestina?" he asked. "That's Italian."

"Why, yes," she answered. "My family came over from Carrara."

The Undertaker's heart danced again. He took a step closer, studying her features for future dreams. They were opposites of each other in every way: his hair was black, hers blonde; his eyes were lifeless, hers like emeralds; his skin was olive, her complexion a rich cream he wanted to drink in.

"Your name means 'heavenly'," The Undertaker said.

"I was named after my *nonna*."

The door opened, and Old Miss Shirley gasped. "It's him."

Barrett, Striker, The Undertaker, and Maranto all looked to the door. And there, in the doorway, to everyone's surprise, stood not Boogaloo Bailey, but The Man with the Very Small Chin. He wore a black duster that brushed below his knee. His eyes locked on The Don's. With a jerky, hurried motion, Maranto threw his oversized violin case on the bar, knocking over what was left of Pando's whisky.

"Hey!" Pando said, lowering his harmonica. "You owe me a drink, pal."

Maranto flipped up the latches and opened the case, revealing a Tommy gun without the magazine in place. He pulled out the gun and slapped the magazine home. Barrett saw two things: the machine gun and Celestina. He didn't want the two anywhere near each other.

"NO!" he yelled, his voice exploding by Joey Maranto's ear like a detonating bomb.

Bottles and glasses shelved behind Miss Shirley rattled. Pando lost his balance and toppled backward off the bar to the wide-planked floor below, his harmonica flying behind him. Ivory's fingers stopped sailing up and down the keyboard and were left hovering above the piano. Armbrewster's brushes quit brushing and the snare drum refused to answer. Boom-Boom's bass no longer boomed. King Charlemagne lowered his sax. Scaredy-Cat Floyd opened his eyes. The light fixture suspended above the stage swayed. The only noise left in The Colored Musicians Club was the startled Joey Maranto, fumbling, bumbling, and bobbling the Tommy gun—The Chopper, The Annihilator, The Chicago Typewriter—until it flew from his hands, bounced off the bar, and clattered at Old Miss Shirley's tired old feet.

Maranto spun around, his face twisted with anger. "You sonofabitch!" he yelled, and threw a punch at Barrett. But Barrett, that whisper of a man, that secret dancer, swayed towards Celestina, slipping the punch, then he tossed one of his own.

Barrett's roundhouse was not very good. He hadn't thrown a punch since his tenth birthday when his mother was taken to the asylum. After she'd been led away, young Barrett pounded the lopsided cake she'd baked, his tears soaking the crumbs and frosting. He threw his punch at Maranto as blindly and wildly as he had then. It lacked the crispness and technique of a Slattery jab, but it landed nonetheless, catching Joey Maranto, The Buffalo Mosquito, square on the nose. Joey was still a bleeder.

Twin red ribbons exploded from both nostrils, gushing out at an alarming rate. Blood charged over his lips, down his chin onto his starched white shirt and double-breasted pinstripe, ruining both. Blood dripped on his black-and-white wingtips, staining the stitches crimson. But The Mosquito, accustomed to blocking punches with his face and hemorrhaging copious amounts of blood from his days in the ring, shook off the haymaker and grabbed Barrett by the lapels, lifting him to his toes.

"You're a dead man," he hissed, baring blood-stained teeth and bubbling saliva.

"Forget him!" The Undertaker yelled, throwing away his cigar as he started toward the exit. "He's getting away!"

Maranto shoved Barrett and pointed at him. "You're dead!" he said, then chased after his boss.

"Come on!" Striker yelled, following the gangsters. "They may lead us to Lefty!"

Barrett and Celestina hurried behind Striker still holding hands.

Behind the bar, Old Miss Shirley bent down and picked up the Tommy gun. She cradled it in her arms, an arthritic finger curled around the trigger, and scanned the crowd for other troublemakers. Pando the Pinsetter stood up, rubbing the back of his head, certain someone had pushed him. The club was quiet except for footsteps thudding down the stairs and engines roaring away. Silent seconds passed before Armbrewster's brushes and the snare drum resumed their conversation. Ivory nodded his shiny head and his fingers set sail. Boom-Boom's bass boomed once more. Scaredy-Cat Floyd shut his eyes tighter, King Charlemagne adjusted his bow tie, and then they both began to blow. Dancers reached for each other, and all was the way it was supposed to be at The Colored Musicians Club.

EPISODE 8

Danger At Swan Lake

The Nash struggled to keep up with Don Stefano's twelve cylinder, one hundred seventy-five horsepower Silver Arrow, the automobile with a posse under the hood. *Black Beauty* shook as it rounded corners as if all four tires and perhaps the spare were about to roll in different directions. Rocker arms, pushrods and camshaft all clattered and clanged, threatening to turn to shrapnel. Inside the car, Striker, Celestina, and Barrett were crammed in the front seat being jostled and jolted as they bounced over potholes, trolley tracks, and snow covered mysteries. Barrett, behind the wheel, was oblivious to the clattering and clanging, the jostling and jolting, the bouncing and bumping, aware only of Celestina pressed against his side. She squealed when the Nash skidded or jerked as if she was at the Crystal Beach Amusement Park riding The Cyclone with both arms raised. Striker sat in the passenger seat and braced his arms against the dash, wincing each time his head and cheek were jarred.

"This is an adventure!" Celestina yelled above the laboring engine. "Don't lose him!"

And Barrett didn't. The Silver Arrow pulled far ahead, its taillights distant pinpricks, but Barrett kept them in sight as he pressed the accelerator to the floorboard. The white stallion, still free from the railyard, burst from a side street as if leading a charging army.

"Look, Johnny!" Celestina cried. "It's so beautiful. Where did it come from?"

"The railyard," Striker mumbled, mesmerized by the stallion. The steed was more impressive than Jerry had described—grander, more muscular, regal. He wished he'd brought his Kodak with him. He'd snap a photo and tape it to his typewriter and stare until he could envision a worthy rider.

Barrett took his eyes off the road to watch the champion's effortless stride, galloping as if it could run from generation to generation. As he watched the horse's rippling muscles, its hooves glinting silver in streetlight, an old black man carrying a dented trumpet stepped from the curb.

"Johnny!" Celestina yelled.

Barrett's eyes cut to the road. He jerked the wheel, swerving around the man, leaving a dime's distance between fender and hip. The car fishtailed and spun as Barrett fought for traction. He skidded down West Delavan still following The Undertaker while the stallion continued racing down Main, never breaking stride. The avenue was deserted, and naturally quiet with Forest Lawn Cemetery bordering it to the north.

"He's turning!" Celestina said, as the Silver Arrow, its headlights like far-off stars, made a right far ahead of them.

"Christ," Barrett said. "He's going into the cemetery."

"They'll spot our headlights if you follow him," Striker said. "Better park on the street."

"We're *walking* through the cemetery?" Barrett asked.

"We have to. They may be heading to Lefty. We got to find him."

"This is so much fun!" Celestina said. "It's like a radio show and we're the stars."

Barrett pulled to the curb near the cemetery entrance and killed the engine. The trio climbed from the Nash. Darkness oozed through the cemetery's fence, the iron finials sharpened to arrowheads. The wind had died, and fat, wet flakes, the kind that cling to eyelashes and cover tire tracks, fell to the ground. Celestina hooked her arm around Barrett's and rested her other hand on his bicep as they stared into Forest Lawn. He flexed his whisper of a muscle and she squeezed it.

"Shouldn't the gates be closed at night?" she asked, staring at the open entranceway crowned with ornate wrought iron, the pattern curling to filigree.

"They're supposed to be," Barrett said. "Danek locks them at sundown, at least he used to."

"Come on," said Striker, following the tracks. "Before somebody comes back and closes them."

"I've never been in a graveyard at night," Celestina said.

"I have," Barrett said. "Lots of times. Mother would take me on the third Saturday of every month at midnight."

"How did you get in?" Striker asked. The vastness of the cemetery opened before them, a burial ground of rolling hills, spring-fed lakes, and ten thousand trees, a forest in the heart of the city.

"The gates were always shut but never locked," Barrett said, hunching to the cold. "Danek must've unlocked them for us."

"What would you do here at midnight, Johnny?" Celestina asked, holding on to Barrett a bit tighter on the pretense of trying not to fall.

"On the anniversary of a person's death, we'd put flowers on their graves. But only the neglected ones, the ones no one visited. Some went back before the Civil War when the cemetery first opened. All this was Mother's idea, of course."

"You'd wander around until you found a headstone with that day's date?" Striker asked. He wanted to light a Lucky but decided the flame would give them away. "It must've taken all night."

"Well, no. This is the spooky part. There'd be a candle burning on top of a marker when we got here. That would be the first one we'd visit."

"Who lit the candle?" Celestina asked. "Danek?"

"He must've. Mother always says he knows where all the bodies are. We'd put flowers on that grave and before we could finish a prayer, another candle would be lit, and we'd head to it. We'd do that all night, chasing candles, until we didn't see any more. That's how we knew when we were done."

They marched forward, the snow soft beneath their feet as they followed the Silver Arrow's tracks. There's no quieter place than a cemetery on a windless winter night. The fallen snow muffled what shouldn't need muffling—tombs, vaults, crypts. There was no breeze to carry long-ago voices or unanswered prayers. Few visit the dead when it's cold and never at night when darkness swallows everything.

The moon snuck from clouds, illuminating the cemetery road. The new light cast shadows of skeletal trees, their bare branches like brittle arms. Striker had never seen anything as lonesome as graves drifted with snow, as if the dead had been buried twice.

A giant Indian, Chief Red Jacket, loomed above them. He held a tomahawk in his left hand. His right arm pointed west, the direction the Silver Arrow had gone. The statue's patina glowed green in the moonlight as if the great Seneca leader might come to life and leap from his base. Fronting the monument were the headstones of other Senecas: Deerfoot, Jish-Ja-Ca, and Ke-Mo Sah-Be, all former runners and scouts for General Grant. Striker thought of Tom and Huck and Injun Joe and swore he felt the icy fingers of grave robbers at his throat.

Guilt jabbed him as he pictured Janet lying in bed and editing his *Tom Sawyer* script while she waited up. He should be home snuggled next to her, reviewing her edits, discussing her changes. He wrote so quickly he needed her to fill in all he'd left out in his race to finish. More guilt crept in as he wondered who had read his boys their bedtime story. Maybe his father had, holding a delicate book in his rough hands, using different voices for the characters. If his father had read to the boys, was his mother left alone with only a neighbor to watch over her? He should have been at her bedside holding her hand, telling her stories, not traipsing among the dead.

Snow fell faster, the flakes fatter and filling the tire tracks quicker than the three could walk. The moon ducked behind clouds and Forest Lawn was as black as grief.

"We're never going to find them if this keeps up," Celestina said, leaning into Barrett. "The tracks will be gone."

"I know where they went," Barrett said, as the road curved in the direction Red Jacket pointed.

"Where?" Striker asked.

"Swan Lake. Danek's cabin. It's the only thing out this way— except graves."

"Do you think you can find it again?" Striker asked, slipping on a patch of ice.

Barrett nodded. "After we put flowers on the graves, I'd play outside while mother went inside to…visit. I remember it pretty well. It's straight ahead and off to the left before the creek."

"We'll follow you," Striker said.

The three ventured past Celtic crosses and towering obelisks, up slippery inclines and down deep valleys. They whispered names chiseled in granite to pass the time—*Wagner, Selgoe, Silas Henry Fish*— and stared at statues of soldiers and cherubs and everything in between. They lingered by family mausoleums with stained glass windows, debating if the ornate gates and heavy doors were meant to keep the dead within or the living out.

"Look at that one!" Celestina pointed to a bell-roofed memorial supported by massive columns. Marble parents stood grieving over their son propped on his deathbed, his eyes closed, holding a bible.

"The Blocher monument," Barrett said. "Mother told me the story. They were millionaires and the son, Nelson, had fallen in love with their maid, Maggie. The parents didn't approve and drove her away. Nelson searched for her but became sick and died calling her name. The parents felt guilty about what they'd done and built that monument for him, importing the marble from Carrara. The family is buried beneath the floor. They say the angel hovering above the deathbed resembles Maggie."

"You should write about them, Fran," Celestina said, pressing closer against Barrett. "It's so romantic."

"It might make a good radio play," Striker said. "The brokenhearted hero wandering alone across the country looking for his lost love. The ladies would tune in for that."

"They sure would," Celestina said.

The trio pressed on, leaving the marble Blochers behind. Snow swirled around their ankles as the wind awoke, erasing their footprints. The road bent once more, and Swan Lake came into view. Its frozen waters encircled a small, tear-shaped islet in the southwest corner where the Scajaquada Creek fed into it. There were no graves on the cay, at least none visible from shore. The tiny island was wooded with oaks and maples, birches and beeches, unchanged since Jish-Ja-Ca and Ke-Mo Sah-Be had fished and camped there. In a small clearing stood a one-room shack made of planks. Smoke rose from its chimney. The uneven yellow light of flickering candles glowed from windows. The three friends crouched, hoping the shadows hid them.

"Look," Striker whispered, pointing to the Silver Arrow and a black Packard Roadster parked on the side of the cemetery road.

"I don't see anybody," Barrett said. "They must be in the cabin."

"Is there a bridge?" Striker asked.

"No," Barrett said, his voice wavering, as memories slithered from forgotten places. "Danek canoes back and forth until the lake freezes, then walks across it."

"I guess we walk across then."

"Wait," Celestina said. "The sign." *Thin Ice.*

Something squeezed Barrett's heart. "There should be two ropes. One for coming and one for going," he said, his voice faint. He rose a bit from his haunches and searched. "Yes, there. Past the sign. One rope is tied off near the cabin and the other is anchored on this end. You hold onto them when you're crossing in case you fall through."

"Jesus," Striker said, craving a cigarette more than ever.

"I hated walking across the ice when I was a kid," Barrett said. "I still hate it. I swore I'd never do it again."

"I'll go first," Celestina offered. "I'm the lightest."

"Maybe you should wait here," Barrett said.

"And miss all the fun? Try and stop me."

Celestina stood and sprinted to the shoreline before Barrett could grab her. She picked up the rope and smiled over her shoulder before stepping on the ice. She toed the spot in front of her, testing for weak patches. Her head tilted to the side as she listened for cracking before taking the next step. Behind her, Barrett forgot to breathe. He clasped Striker's shoulder and watched as she took one cautious step after another.

"Careful," he whispered, each time she advanced. "Careful."

Striker's eyes shifted from Celestina to the cabin's door then windows, fearing Don Stefano or The Man with the Very Small Chin would spot her. Would Maranto start shooting? Had anyone ever been murdered in a cemetery? Striker saw someone pass in front of the window and thought he heard yelling coming from the shack, but the door remained shut. There was no gunfire.

Celestina kept her head down, watching each gentle footfall, searching for fissures that never appeared. When she stepped on the far bank, she spun and waved before squatting in the gloom.

"Thank God," Striker said.

Barrett released his steaming breath. "I guess it's my turn," he said, giving Striker's shoulder one last squeeze before standing and heading to shore.

"Be careful," Striker whispered, but Barrett didn't hear him. With each step, the years rolled further back until he was again ten and afraid to walk the ice. He saw his mother on the far shore, Danek by her side, both calling to him, telling him it was safe. Now, like then, Barrett froze as solid as the lake. Ankle joints locked. Calves cramped and hardened. Quadriceps contracted. Hips calcified until it was as if he was made of Carrara marble from waist to toe. His arms and hands trembled despite the sweat trickling down his sides. The ginger ale in his stomach soured. He swallowed to keep it down. He pawed at his collar—there wasn't enough air in Forest Lawn for his lungs—and remembered all those times Danek had to cross the ice to fetch him, not bothering to hold the rope. He would gather Boy Barrett in his arms, his weight as dead as a corpse, and say: 'God put the firewood there for you, Johnny. But you have to gather it yourself.' Barrett repeated the line aloud, willing his legs forward.

"What are you waiting for?" Striker whispered. "Why are you talking about firewood?"

Then, across the water, Celestina rose. She didn't call or wave. She stood for him to see her and when he did, he was snatched from the past, leaving his younger self behind. Oxygen pumped into his lungs. His ankles unlocked. His marble legs returned to muscle. He grabbed the rope, stepped on the lake, and pulled himself hand-over-hand across the ice, never once taking his eyes off Celestina. Her arms were open as he stepped on solid ground in front of her.

Striker shoved an unlit Lucky between his lips and scampered to the brim. He was the heaviest of the three. If the ice had weakened, if it were to give way, he knew it would be beneath his feet. He grabbed the rope and gave it a tug, making sure it was secure. The marks from Barrett's shoes were visible across the surface and he wondered if he should follow them, if they guaranteed a safe path. But what if that was the wrong thing to do? What if the ice there was ready to buckle? Perhaps he should move a few feet over, try his luck there. Maybe the ice was thicker off to the side…or maybe it was thinner. Striker bit down on the unlit cigarette, tossed the rope aside, and sprinted across, arms whirling to keep balance, until he flopped ashore at his friend's feet as if he had stolen second base.

"Graceful," Celestina giggled.

The Lucky, bent from the fall, was still wedged between his lips when Striker stood and brushed the snow from his knees. "If Lefty's still alive, I'm going to kill him for making us go through all this."

"Keep your voice down," Barrett said. "Danek hears like a hound."

"Come on," Celestina said, taking Barrett's hand.

Striker took one last smokeless inhale of his ruined cigarette before tossing it in the snow and following them. As they neared the shack, the three dropped to their knees and crawled to the window, snow soaking through pant legs and Celestina's stockings. Like jack-o-lanterns, the trio rose to peer through the window, their eyes above the sill.

Striker had imagined what he'd see through the glass: The Man with the Very Small Chin tied to a chair, an eye swollen closed, blood streaming from bridge and brow. Maranto would be working him over like he was training on the heavy bag, The Mosquito best when his opponent couldn't hit back. Lefty would be there, too, sprawled in the corner, as dead as a Blocher, the blood pooled beneath him. The Don would be supervising.

Striker wasn't prepared to see Maranto and The Man with the Very Small Chin, seated at a wobbling table eating fried chicken, Maranto's jacket and Cavendish's duster slung over the backs of their chairs, their shoulder holsters exposed. Cavendish's were empty while Maranto's held a pair of .38s. Maranto's shirt was bloodstained from Barrett's punch. Cotton was crammed in his nostrils, as if he'd inhaled tiny rabbits. Don Stefano was seated at the table head still wearing his overcoat and gloves, a plate of untouched breasts and Cavendish's pistols before him. Danek stood at the Majestic wood-burning stove pushing chicken around a sputtering pan. An apron hung from his hips dusted with baking flour and grave dirt. Striker heard him say the secret was buttermilk. Lefty was nowhere to be seen.

"Enough with the chicken," The Undertaker said. Maranto and Cavendish lowered their drumsticks, the diamond ring on Cavendish's right pinky catching candlelight.

"You expect me to believe you were just passing through town?" The Undertaker asked.

Cavendish nodded, still chewing. "I'm not looking for trouble here. I came to visit my uncle." He raised his small chin, bright with chicken grease, to point at Danek. "Rode in a horsecar all the way from Abilene before I picked up that Packard. Damn horses were trying to kick me the whole trip, especially this big white one. Smelled like hell in there."

"But you had trouble with Lefty," The Undertaker said. "You killed him."

"He tried to stiff me. Now he's a stiff."

"I needed him alive. You've hurt my business. You cost me money."

"I didn't know any of that. I didn't mean no disrespect. He promised me two rings. Only delivered one. And he didn't lower the price neither. I didn't like that much and slapped him around a little. Then he starts about how his wife will put a gypsy curse on me and all the misery she'll bring into my life—sickness, pain, deformity. Said he'd put a curse on me, too. Half the time he was talking in English, the other times in Greek. I didn't know what he was saying but I wasn't taking no chances with Greek or gypsy curses. And what the hell is a *Malaka* anyway?"

Striker's cheek, now scarred, flared. He scooped a handful of snow and rubbed it.

"So, you shot him," Don Stefano said.

"Just once."

"Once through the heart is usually enough."

"That's what I've found," Cavendish agreed.

"And no one knows you're here in Buffalo?"

"Only Uncle Danek. A few have seen me around—some midget,

that old bartender at the colored club, a drunk boxer took a swing at me at the railroad yard and fell over. That's about it. Oh, and Lefty, but he ain't gonna say nothing."

"Since you owe me, you need to repay me, or your uncle's fried chicken will be your last meal."

"Whatever you say, Mr. Magaddino. I want to make things right. I don't want no trouble. Tell me what needs to be done or who needs to be done, I'll do it."

"So, you're an assassin."

"I prefer 'hired gun.'"

The Undertaker thought for a moment, then reached into his overcoat and brought out a newspaper. He shook it open and pushed the front page of the *Evening Times* across the table to The Man with the Very Small Chin.

Cavendish wiped his hands on his pant legs and picked up the paper. "*Horses Escape From Freight Car,*" he read.

"The other article. Next to the horses. About the president."

"Roosevelt's coming to town. Big deal. I ain't political."

"I want him dead," The Undertaker said. "Two through the heart."

Cavendish whistled. "Hold on a second. Killing the president-elect seems like a steep price for offing a Greek." He pushed the *Times* back to The Undertaker. "Greeks aren't worth that much."

Don Stefano nodded at Joey, who adjusted the blood-soaked cotton in his nose, pulled one of the .38s from his holsters. He pressed it against Cavendish's very small chin.

"This is my town," The Undertaker said. "I set the prices. This is the price for hurting my business."

"If I kill Roosevelt, I'm as good as dead. They'll have every G-Man in the country after me. This bleeder here should just pull the trigger now and save me the trouble."

Maranto pulled the hammer back with his thumb, the sound as loud as a coffin nail driven home.

"I told you. This is my town. I will protect you, hide you until things cool down, then get you to Castellammare del Golfo where you will live out your days like a king."

"Castellammare del Golfo? Where's that? Mexico?"

"Sicily."

The Man with the Very Small Chin stared.

"Italy," The Don said.

Cavendish shook his head. "All this for killing a lousy Greek." Striker, Barrett, and Celestina slid below the window.

"What do we do?" Barrett mouthed.

"We got to think of something," Striker answered. The three bent their heads together and whispered, throwing out ideas and rejecting them, coming up with nothing.

From inside the shack, they heard chair legs scraping and voices mingling.

"…best chicken I ever had."

"…take some with you."

"Not a word of any of this, Danek."

The shack's door opened, and light seeped from the cabin. Barrett, Striker, and Celestina pressed their backs against the wall hoping the planks would absorb them. The Undertaker, Maranto, and Cavendish emerged, each complaining about the wind as they trudged toward the lake.

"Mind the ice," Danek called from the doorway.

The Undertaker raised his arm without turning, indicating he'd heard the warning but didn't care. The gangsters crossed Swan Lake in single file, with Cavendish in the lead followed by Maranto and Don Stefano, their grips loose on the rope as if there wasn't a chance in the universe they'd fall through. They made it to the other side without a slip. Seconds passed then engines fired—first the Packard, then the Silver Arrow—shattering the silence.

"We should go," Striker said, as the cars disappeared around the bend.

The friends crawled to the lake without exchanging a word. Celestina was the first to cross, her steps sure and unquestioning, her fingers curled around the rope. When she was safe, Striker stood. "See you on the other side," he said to Barrett.

He slipped an unlit Lucky between his lips for luck and hurried on the lake. The rope felt cold and heavy when he dug it from the snow. Sprinting across without holding the lifeline had been foolish. He was determined to be more careful on this return trip. His grip was firm and his first step sure as he stepped from the bank. Don Stefano's path was visible to the far shore, and Striker followed it, deciding that if the ice could hold the mobster, it could surely hold him.

Though Barrett crouched behind and Celestina stood in front onshore, he felt alone as he crossed the ice. Headstones and markers dropped from the periphery. Danek's cabin was forgotten. Fear tremored through him with each step. What was he doing on this lake? Why was he chasing gangsters and assassins in the middle of the night? What would happen to his family if the ice gave way?

He thought of his father and the night of the Ingleside fire, the way he always did when he needed courage. The Lieutenant had told him that he'd wanted to run, to leave the women and children to their fiery fate, but how could he have lived with himself if he'd done that? His father had swallowed his fear, gulping it down whole, and raced into the building alone. He led a group to safety and the gathering crowd had cheered as if he'd rounded the bases. But there were others still trapped inside.

He re-entered the engulfed building to find them, emerging the second time carrying babies and laying them safely in the grass. Mothers and nurses yelled out names of those still missing, driving the coughing and hacking Lieutenant, his red eyes streaming, back into the enflamed house.

The erring stood watching their home burn. The crowd began to murmur then pray, some crying loudly, as the minutes passed. The

Lieutenant had been inside too long. His luck must have melted in the inferno. Ceilings must have collapsed, or floors given way beneath him. He and the others were surely lost. Windows exploded from the heat, billowing black smoke and showering glass. But then The Lieutenant burst from the doorway, leading the remaining group to safety. Two unconscious women were slung over his shoulders as he staggered into fresh air.

Striker gripped the rope tighter, pushing his panic aside, determined to be like his father. He took a heavy step forward. The frozen surface felt soft and clingy as if it was grabbing his soles. He fought the urge to drop the rope and run. He looked up to see how much farther he had to go and saw Celestina ahead.

She was the last thing he saw before falling through the ice.

(MUSICAL INTERLUDE...AGITATO)

Striker clung to the rope beneath the ice, his fingers numbing through his gloves, his body shocked by the cold. Soaked clothes weighed him down as if something deep in the lake was tugging his ankles. He thrashed hoping for buoyancy, his left shoe coming free and sinking. Cold penetrated his long johns and seeped through pores. Organs slowed toward arrest. His chest burned from holding his breath. Soon he'd gasp, and glacial water would fill his lungs.

His kicking slowed. He tried to relax, to conserve energy or, perhaps, he was surrendering, realizing it was useless to fight the inevitable. It was black under water. He couldn't tell if his eyes were open or closed. He lost feeling in his fingers, his grip loosening.

When would they find his body? Spring? Who would take care of his family? Anyone? Would his father have to bury his wife and son in the same year?

His last thoughts were of Janet. Images appeared like conjured ghosts—Janet dancing in the Lafayette High School gym, her face on their wedding day as he lifted her veil, Janet bent over his manuscripts, editing them, making him a better writer. The sum of these memories weighed more than ballast and anchor. Frozen fingers slipped from hemp. He slid downward, certain all was about to end.

Then his collar was grabbed. He shot toward the opening, pulled by the power of a magnificent white stallion, by the spirits of Deerfoot, Jish-Ja-Ca, and Ke-Mo Sah-Be, by the strong arm of Danek the Polish Gravedigger, who yanked Striker out of Swan Lake and onto the ice like a beached salmon. Sputtering water, he was lifted again, and his arms were thrown over Danek's and Barrett's shoulders.

"To the cabin," Danek ordered, his voice loud enough to shatter ice, to drift snow, to wake Chief Red Jacket and the entire Blocher family. Striker skimmed across the frozen lake once more, the cabin growing larger by the second. His breathing was quick and shallow. The shivering bordered on convulsions. He tried to speak, the words coming one unintelligible syllable at a time. Celestina hushed him.

Danek kicked open the cabin door. The Majestic wood-burning stove kept the shack cozy, but Striker felt as if he was still outside. His teeth clattered like his manic typing. The room smelled of fried chicken, gun oil, and Genuine Philco Furniture Polish. The finest piece of furniture in the shack, a Philco Radiogram, stood in the corner tuned to WEBR'S *Classical Music Hour*. They were playing Rossini's The William Tell Overture.

"Get those wet clothes off him," Danek said, his voice deep, resonant, much too large for both he and Rossini to occupy the same space. He ducked from under Striker's arm and turned off the radio.

Barrett pulled off Striker's topcoat and dropped it to the floor, the mackinaw splattering on the planks. Striker wiggled off his suit coat and let it fall. He tried to unknot his necktie, but his fingers were unresponsive. Celestina stepped forward and undid the Windsor. She pulled the tie from his collar then worked the buttons on his shirt. He didn't notice his pants and long johns being peeled away.

Danek threw a heavy blanket around him "Sit by the stove," he ordered, his voice carrying a hint of Krakow, a hint of cannon. He pointed at Celestina. "*You* tell *me* what the hell you were doing on my lake."

The nurse went mute. She stared first at Danek, then Barrett, and back again. It was as if she was looking at the same person at different stages of life. The two men shared the same delicate features—the high cheekbones, the thin nose, the trimmed mustache. Danek's hands gestured as he spoke as well, but his were thick and calloused from a lifetime of labor. They did not float. And while Barrett's hairline was receding, the gravedigger was bald, the remaining gray hair wreathing his scalp. There was a hardness to him, a ropey strength that knotted his arms and corded his neck. Here stood a man who could do any job no matter how difficult or illegal.

"Well?" Danek asked. He poured coffee from a dented aluminum pot, the handle Bakelite and chipped. Striker accepted the mug with quivering hands, spilling on the blanket when he raised the cup to his trembling lips. Celestina had dragged a chair from the table and sat next to him, her gaze still alternating between Barrett and the gravedigger.

Danek followed her gaping to Barrett. "Oh," he said, looking at Barrett dead-on for the first time, his stunned expression a copy of Celestina's. "It's you."

Barrett stood as frozen as Striker as his past collided with the present like stars colliding in heaven. The impact created bursts of heat that rose within him. Everything became clear. The haunting question from his fatherless childhood was answered in an instant.

"Hello," Barrett said. "It's been a while."

Danek nodded, his words shy. "Since your mother left us. But I've heard you," he said, pointing to the Radiogram. It's woodgrain was rich and lustrous as if the cabinet were polished each night. "I only listen to WEBR."

"He writes the shows," Barrett said, gesturing to Striker.

Danek nodded to Striker then shifted his attention to Celestina, who introduced herself.

"So, who's going to tell me why you're all here?" Danek asked.

Barrett cleared his throat. "We were looking for Lefty Mavrakis. We thought those men would lead us to him."

Danek poured a cup of coffee for himself and sat at the table. He pushed aside Cavendish's plate of chicken bones, the wings and legs sucked clean. "Why were you looking for Lefty?"

"He has diamond rings that don't belong to him," Barrett said. "Well, maybe one of them. That chinless man was wearing the other. We want them back."

Danek sipped his coffee then explained, "My sister's son from Texas."

Barrett mulled this over. He had an entire chinless bloodline that he knew nothing about. This disturbed him. He worried about having future chinless children.

Danek set his coffee down as if it were bitter, which it was. "You won't find Lefty. No one will."

"So we heard," Celestina said. "Your nephew killed him."

"My god, what else did you hear?" He rubbed his bald pate. "You shouldn't have come here."

"Are you with them?" Barrett demanded. "The Undertaker, Maranto, your nephew—are you one of *them*? Are you going to help kill the president?"

"My job is to bury bodies."

"What do we do?" Celestina asked.

Danek rose. "As soon as he's thawed, you go home. You forget all this. You heard nothing out here but the wind."

"We have to go to the police," Striker said, his voice defrosting. He pulled the scratchy blanket tighter around his shoulders. "We have to tell them about Roosevelt."

"Then you'll end up ashes in The Undertaker's oven or buried out here in unmarked graves. You can't trust the police. They all work for The Don. You're alone on this. Be smart."

"We can trust my dad. He'll know what to do. But what about the ring?" Striker asked. "Will you help us get it back from your nephew?"

"He's not the type of man who gives things back. You'll have to cut his finger off if you want that ring."

"Cut it off? I'm just a writer."

"You'll think of something. You need to leave. He'll be back soon."

Celestina helped Striker to his feet, but Barrett remained motionless. "You never asked about my mother."

"How is the poor soul?" Danek asked, his Polish accent growing pronounced.

"Locked away. Do you ever think of her? In all these years, did you think of her once?"

"More than you'll ever know."

"Did you love her at all? Why didn't you marry her?"

"We should leave," Celestina said. "It's been a long night." She bent to gather Striker's clothes. "These are soaked. He can't wear them."

"He can borrow some of mine," Danek said, crossing to the other side of the room. He brushed at his eyes when his back was turned.

"Don't walk away. I need answers. You owe me that."

Danek rummaged through a child's casket at the foot of his cot used to store clothing. He straightened holding duck cloth overalls and a yellowish union suit, once white. "You need to ask your mother these questions. She has your answers."

"My mother is mad. She has been since I was ten."

"Not always," Danek said. "Sometimes she's as sane as you and me."

Striker, still wrapped in a blanket, shivered as Barrett drove from Forest Lawn.

"What do we do about the president?" Celestina asked. "We can't let them kill him."

"I'll talk to my dad," Striker said, looking out on the deserted sidewalks and empty streets as if they were all alone in the world. "He'll help us."

"Who's your dad? A copper?"

"The Lieutenant," Barrett said.

"Lieutenant Striker. Of course," Celestina said. "He's always in the paper for solving some crime or receiving some medal. Wasn't he the one who ran into The Ingleside Home For Reclaiming The Erring and saved all those unwed mothers?"

"He never talks about it. If you bring it up, his face goes ash, and he changes the subject."

"My roommate knows him. She's a nurse at Millard Fillmore Hospital. Lydia says he's a real sweetheart the way he dotes on your mother when he brings her in."

"He has lunch every day at The New Genesee. Let's meet there and tell him what we know."

"I work tomorrow. You boys go," Celestina said.

Barrett dropped Striker off on Granger Place. He crawled into bed still wearing borrowed clothes. He slept on his back, not turning or dreaming, exhausted from his adventures at Swan Lake. He didn't hear Jerry leave to shovel rails or the milkman placing bottles in the milk box. As night lightened to dawn, Striker felt a heaviness on his chest. He grew uncomfortable under the blankets and his breathing became labored. His face was wet, and he struggled to wake. He thrashed from side-to-side, the weight on his chest heavy. Guttural noises escaped as he battled sleep and myocardial infarction. He could hear panting. The Undertaker and Danek would soon have an additional burial. With a gasp—perhaps his last—he exploded to the surface again. His eyes slammed open.

The Angel of Death was not hovering near the ceiling. Lefty Mavrakis was not there to escort him into clouds and light. Striker stared into the long face, hanging wrinkles, and sad eyes of a fifty-pound basset hound sitting on his chest.

"Jesus!" Striker yelled. The dog howled.

Janet laughed next to him. "Say hello to King."

"Where the hell did he come from?" Striker asked, pushing the dog off him. King licked his mouth. "He almost gave me a heart attack."

"The boys found him on our walk last night. He was practically frozen, poor thing. We had to bring him home. He would have died." Janet pulled King to her. The hound nestled in the blankets between them as if he'd lived there forever. "Bobby named him. I don't know where he came up with King."

"Who does he belong to?" Striker asked, his heart beating like a jazz drummer setting tempo. He studied the dog's piebald muzzle and black mask that extended around his eyes to his pendulous ears.

"I think us. The boys love him. We all do."

"Janet, no." King placed a paw on Striker's leg. Striker pushed it off. "Absolutely not."

"Why? You love dogs. You've always said that every child should have a dog. We talked about this."

"We talked about this *before* the market crashed. Before Jerry moved in and my grandparents moved in and your parents moved in. Everything's changed. We can't afford another mouth to feed. King probably eats like a horse."

King lowered his head and raised his eyes as if his feelings had been hurt. Janet smoothed the covers around her then scratched the dog's head. "Well, actually, Fran, we're going to have another mouth to feed besides King's."

"Who's moving in now? Not your Uncle Louie. Please tell me it's not Uncle Louie. That guy's a crepe hanger. He ruins every holiday. His glass isn't half empty, it's leaking. He's miserable, morose. That's what I'll call him—Uncle Morose." King crawled back onto Striker's chest.

"It's not Uncle Louie, Fran. I have a feeling it's going to be a girl this time."

"What do you mean?"

"Congratulations." She leaned over the dog and kissed him.

Striker knew what she meant. He hoped he was wrong. "Are you sure?" He craved a cigarette, a shot of rye, the ability to disappear. King nuzzled his throat, his nose damp.

"Well, I'm not certain it's going to be a girl, only hoping. She'll be here in early summer if Dr. Farcash did the math right."

"June or July then," he said, picturing the calendar, counting days, his life becoming a series of debits.

"I know it's going to be hard, Fran. The timing isn't the best and money's tight. But we always talked about having a girl. We'll just have to cut back on things."

He wanted to point out that, like the dog on his sternum, they'd talked about more children *before* the Depression. He searched the nightstand for cigarettes, finding none.

"We each have our own plan," she continued. "This is part of ours."

Striker heard a stirring from across the hall. "The boys will be up soon."

"Let's tell everyone at breakfast."

Everyone. Ten mouths to feed now, soon to be eleven. They'd surpassed a baseball lineup. Come July they'd be able to field a football team. His WEBR paycheck would be stretched to tearing.

"I'll start the eggs," Janet said, putting on her robe. "Come help me."

"I'll be down in a bit. I need to do something in my office first."

"Don't be long, Fran," she said, "We never see you anymore. The boys miss you. I miss you."

"I'll just be a few minutes."

King hopped from the bed and trailed after her, his nails clicking on the hardwood. The weight, however, didn't leave Striker's chest. An invisible basset hound took King's place and grew—sixty pounds, eighty, one hundred—making it impossible to move or breathe, like he was trapped beneath the ice again. Except he wasn't cold. He was perspiring, the sweat rolling from his sideburns. He kicked off blankets.

A baby meant doctor and hospital bills. A baby *girl* meant no hand-me-downs from Bobby or Donny. She'd need new dresses and shoes and bonnets and coats. Janet would insist on dance and piano lessons. Hell, they'll need a damn piano. How much do those cost? Could he get one at a pawn shop?

26 Granger Place shrank. The walls shifted inward, the ceilings dropped, but Striker remained the same size. He rolled out of bed not bothering to change into his own clothes. He climbed the attic stairs where his Remington Sixteen awaited him. He needed to make money.

Striker opened the file cabinet and flipped through his radio scripts—*Adventureland, Adventures In The Air, Behind The Headlines.* He'd steal Phillips Lord's idea and send scripts across the country. Time was against him. He had until summer to pad his bank account, if banks still existed come July. *Campus Nights, Clippings, Crimson Fang.*

Soliciting stations in smaller cities—Cleveland, Pittsburgh, Detroit—made the most sense. They might not be as staffed with writers as the bigger stations in New York or Chicago. Program directors in those markets might be hungry for scripts and fresh talent.

Striker pulled the *Dr. Dragonette* folder and set it on top of the wooden cabinet. Who doesn't like mysterious Asians? He continued leafing through his manuscripts—*Drums of Kali, The Falcon, The Ghost Ship.* The *Hank and Honey* file was thick with episodes. *The Courier Express* had called the program new and original, describing it as a 'situational comedy,' perhaps the first of its kind to be aired anywhere. Striker would include the *Express'* article in the cover letter to the radio stations. The country needed to laugh.

Limelight of Purple, Love, The Mad Hatter, the story of a gentle, muscular man who turns leopard-like when angry or seeing blood, a *Dr. Jekyll and Mr. Hyde* tale with a feline twist. The Buffalo audience had loved it. Fan mail from listeners had poured in praising the show, asking questions about The Mad Hatter, suggesting storylines. He'd include snippets from those letters as well. *Matinee Players, Warner Lester—Manhunter, Mort Manor.*

He yanked *Warner Lester* from the cabinet and pushed the drawer shut with his elbow. Barrett's voice wafted from Swan Lake: *God put firewood there for you, but you have to gather it yourself.* Striker gathered the *Warner Lester, Dr. Dragonette,* and the *Hank and Honey* scripts and took them to his desk. He'd send these three out in the world, see if there was any interest. He needed to make money.

A pack of Lucky's rested on a stack of unopened bills. Striker shook a smoke free, ignoring the envelopes marked *Second Notice.* He lit the cigarette, and inhaled to clear his mind. He reached in a desk drawer for carbon paper. If he struck the keys hard enough, perhaps he could make three copies at a time.

Downstairs the rest of the family—Bobby and Donny, his grandparents, the in-laws—woke to the sound of Striker pounding The Remington harder than they'd ever heard before. The typing grew faster, louder, desperate.

EPISODE 9

Trendle's Path Revealed

Trendle paced his office carrying the Big Chief writing tablet, waiting for Campbell to arrive. There was a lightness in his step, a giddyap to his gait. His nose was swollen. He had no choice but to breathe through his mouth. As he paced from window to door and back, he sounded like *The Flying Dutchman* or *Iron Duke* or some other great steam engine chugging at a decent clip. Once he'd regained consciousness after being punched in the nose, he hadn't slept at all. There were the police to deal with—statements to be made, descriptions to be given, stolen items to be itemized. Then the reporters showed up with their flashbulbs popping and their pencils scratching, eyeing Adelaide's peach robe. The sun was rising when the last gumshoe and ink slinger had left, but by then he was too excited about the masked man to sleep. Adelaide forced him to go to Grace Hospital and have his nose pushed into place. When they returned, he showered and dressed in a dark blue suit he believed to be slimming and drove to the radio station feeling like a happier man.

When he heard Allan Campbell's voice in the hallway, he yelled for him to come to his office. Campbell came right away still wearing his coat and holding his fedora by the brim. "Good morning, boss," he said, smoothing his hair.

Trendle was peering out the window at the forming soup line. Campbell gasped when Trendle faced him.

"Boss! Your nose! Your eyes! What happened?"

"I was robbed," he answered, beaming. "By a masked man at gunpoint. Well, *gunpoints*. He had two enormous guns."

"My God. Are you all right?" Campbell asked, taking a step closer to study his discolored eyes.

"I'm fine. Except for my nose." He touched the bridge with fingertips.

"What did he rob?"

"My wallet, my watch. Then he forced his way home with me and cleaned out all my cash and Adelaide's jewelry."

"He didn't hurt Adelaide, did he?"

"No, shook the old girl up a bit then punched me in the nose."

"That's good. About Adelaide, I mean. Not about your nose. I'm sure the police will catch this guy."

"He might be in jail already. I hope to get all my money and jewelry back by noon," Trendle said, turning his wrist to consult a watch that was no longer there. "It was Sutton, that sound man you hired. He robbed me. I gave the police his flophouse address."

"Sutton! How do you know it was him? You said the robber wore a mask."

Trendle hooked his thumbs in his belt loops and rocked back on his heels like a fat sleuth about to reveal who done it. "Oh, it was him all right. I knew it was that scarecrow right away. I recognized his voice and those boney arms and yellow teeth. He always wears the same clothes and that coat that's two sizes too big. It was easy to figure out."

"I think those are all the clothes he owns, boss."

"Well, he'll own a striped uniform soon enough," he said, smiling at his own joke.

"You seem to be in good spirits for someone who was robbed and got his nose broken."

"The whole affair was an inspiration. Have a seat, Campbell, and look at this." He handed him the writing tablet.

Campbell set his fedora on Trendle's desk, pressed his recalcitrant hair in place, then sat. He opened the tablet and studied Trendle's sketches.

"What's this?" he asked.

"The hero for our new radio show."

"I don't think we can have a hero who's an outlaw, boss."

Trendle grinned and slapped his stomach as if he had consumed a delicious side of beef. "But he's *not* an outlaw, Campbell. Everyone *thinks* he's an outlaw."

"Because he wears a mask."

"Exactly!" Trendle boomed, his smile so wide it was as if his face had stretched, transforming his two shiners into a mask of his own.

"Who is he?"

"A cowboy. Everybody likes cowboys."

"A cowboy who wears a mask?"

"Yes."

"And why does he wear a mask?"

"To hide his identity."

"But he's not an outlaw?"

"Of course not. He *is* the law."

"Then why is he hiding his identity?"

"He has a past."

"I see," Campbell said, scratching his head.

"He helps people, Campbell. He helps the downtrodden, like the unwashed who'll be tuning in every week. They'll identify with him and those he saves. Listenership will soar. Advertising money will leap into our pockets."

Campbell shut his eyes and smoothed his hair from crown to nape trying to piece it together. "A masked, crime-fighting cowboy who helps the downtrodden and has a past. People think he's an outlaw but he's really not." He opened his eyes. "What kind of past does he have?"

"I have no idea. Maybe he killed a man. Or maybe people think *he's* been killed, and he wants to keep it that way. Regardless, he's a man alone, yet always fighting on the side of justice."

"Alone?"

"Completely! No wife. No children. Not even a friend. Well, maybe one friend. He can't talk to his horse the entire time. It's radio, after all."

"This masked cowboy idea sounds pretty good, boss."

"I know it does! And all thanks to Sutton, may he rot in jail."

Campbell flipped the tablet's pages to look at Trendle's other ideas. The remaining sheets were blank.

"What else do we know about this hero?"

"Nothing."

Campbell shut the notebook. "Any story ideas or other characters?"

"That's all I have, Allan. You need to hire writers to fill in the blanks. Find the best ones, not hacks selling pencils on street corners. Spare no expense."

Campbell's eyebrows shot to the ceiling. "Really?"

"Of course not. Don't be a damn fool. Hire the best writers for the least amount of money. If they've lost their homes, tell them they can sleep in the storage room to sweeten the pot. There's heat back there, isn't there?"

"Some."

"They'll be grateful. Find them fast, Campbell. I want a pilot script as soon as possible."

"Right away, boss," Campbell said, and stood. He placed the Big Chief tablet on the desk and reached for his fedora.

"Oh, and Campbell?"

"Yes, boss?"

"Don't hire any more armed robbers."

Adelaide passed Campbell in the doorway, entering her husband's office in a swirl of sable and Sous le Vent. A cigarette holder with a hand-painted swan swimming toward the ash was snug between her lips. "Adelaide! What a surprise. What brings you here?" Trendle asked, rushing to kiss her cheek.

"I came to bring you home. You promised you weren't going to work today and snuck off while I was sleeping. You should be resting after last night."

"I'm fine. You worry too much. Can Campbell get you anything?"

"Yes, your hat and coat. You look terrible."

"I've never felt better. I feel inspired."

"Inspired? Are you drinking Dr. Foley's this early in the day? It's not medicine, George. It won't cure shiners."

"I haven't had a drop," he said, hoping she couldn't smell the chloroform on his breath. "That masked ruffian knocked an idea into my head."

"Has he been arrested? I want my jewelry back. I feel naked without it," she said, touching her throat normally encircled with diamonds or jade.

"I expect to hear from the police at any minute," he said, once again checking his bare wrist.

"Good. Let's go home and wait for their call."

"Adelaide, I have work to do."

"Can't it wait?"

Trendle reached for his tablet. He opened the notebook to his sketch and handed it to her.

"You drew the man who robbed us?"

"No, it's the new radio hero I'm working on. Isn't he marvelous?"

"He doesn't look like a hero at all, George. He looks like the man who punched you in the nose."

"It's just a rough sketch, dear. To get the juices flowing."

"Hand me that pencil." Adelaide sat behind her husband's desk. She placed her cigarette holder in the ashtray and pulled off her leather gloves. Trendle peered over her shoulder. "Heroes need to be handsome, George," she said, sketching. "Yours looks like he hasn't eaten in days.

He needs a strong chin, like this. The kind that can take a punch. And broad shoulders to carry everyone's burdens. Oh, and he must be tall, someone we all look up to. And if he's going to wear that silly mask, he should have kind eyes to melt women's hearts and so children aren't afraid. Like this."

"Well, yes. That's a much better sketch. Very masculine. But, dear, it's radio, not motion pictures. No one will see his broad shoulders."

"Why can't it be movies? If he's a hit on radio, why can't he be a hit in theaters? Think big, George, beyond WXYZ. Think about the children."

"Children can't buy advertising."

"No, but if kids love him, their parents will buy them things. Lots of things. Masks and toy guns. Cowboy hats and holsters. Books and magazines. Oatmeal. They'll buy anything if his picture is on it. You could make a fortune from this if you're smart and own the rights. Of course, this masked man has to be popular. He has to be a hit, a sensation. You won't make a dime if he's a flop."

Trendle picked up the tablet. "I was only thinking about advertising and sponsors, not other revenue. But you're right. If he's a success, we can make this masked man into a *product,* can't we? Something to sell like Ivory soap or Coca Cola."

"Exactly," she said, pulling on her gloves then reaching for her cigarette holder. "Make him bigger than radio, George. Make him… an annuity."

"An annuity," Trendle repeated.

"Somebody must create him first. Bring him to life. Give him bad guys to catch and adventures to have. Someone needs to write his story, George."

EPISODE 10

Betrayal!

Stefano Magaddino stood in Building I's Dayroom, behind smirking onanists, holding a clutch of white roses. His hair was oiled, and he wore a black suit with red pinstripes. A rosebud matching the bouquet was pinned to his lapel. The Don had had Maranto spit-shine his wingtips to mirrors.

Celestina entered the Dayroom arm in arm in with Delores, her head resting on the nurse's shoulder. The Don sucked in his breath when he saw her. She appeared to be gliding across the floor, her shoes hidden by her long nurse's skirt. His heart once again danced in his chest. He sang her name like a lullaby so quietly the catatonics cocked an ear.

"Mr. Magaddino, what are you doing here?" she asked. Delores raised her head and hissed.

"Please, call me Stefano. These are for you," he said, thrusting the flowers toward her.

"They're lovely," she said, but didn't reach for them.

"White roses are hard to get this time of year, but I found some for you." The Don took a step closer, still offering the bouquet.

"I'm flattered, Mr. Magaddino, but I can't accept them. I already have a beau." The roses shook in The Undertaker's hand. Delores cackled, startling the easily startled who had begun to gather.

The Don struggled to keep his voice even. He was not a man accustomed to rejection. "Do you mean that skinny little man who punched Joey?" he asked, tilting his head toward Joey Maranto, The Buffalo Torpedo, who stood to the side and held his boss' overcoat and hat. Both eyes were blackened.

"Johnny was protecting me," Celestina said. "I'm sorry your man was hurt, and thank you again for the flowers, but if you'll excuse me, I must get Miss Barrett back to her bed."

"But the roses," The Don said.

Mrs. Pottebaum emerged from the shadow like a gray mist. "I'll take those," she said. "I'll put them in a vase by the front desk in case she changes her mind."

The Don let the receptionist take the bouquet as he watched Celestina leave. Delores spun her head and stuck out her tongue. The Undertaker thought of some of the men he'd killed in his rise to power—Salvatore and Antonio Giannola, Johnny Vitale, several Buccelato brothers—then of John Barrett.

The New Genesee Restaurant was located on Genesee Street near The Gypsy's house. Tamis, also known as 'The Greek' in a neighborhood filled with Greeks, was a mere dishwasher at the restaurant fresh off the boat from Piraeus when he won The New Genesee in an all-night barbudi game.

While Tamis was a pretty good dishwasher and excellent at throwing dice, his English wasn't strong. Since most of his first customers were first cousins or those claiming to be first cousins, conversing with them and taking their orders was not a problem. Buying supplies from Gerhard Lang's Meats & Provisions—*The Home of Pure Food*—was a bigger challenge. Tamis knew only a handful of English obscenities and was forced to make animal noises over the phone—mooing, clucking, oinking—when placing a meat order. Until Tamis learned the language, Old Man

Lang would deliver not the purest food to him, but the oldest meat on the verge of spoiling. Selling questionable meat to The Greek, who was unable to complain except for stringing together a few obscenities, made better business sense for Lang than throwing anything out.

As Tamis' vocabulary and his ability to complain improved, so did the food. The New Genesee became a success. At any time of day, the wooden tables and lunch counter were filled not just with Greeks but also sailors on shore leave (or those who had jumped ship), fallen women resting sore assets, and prize fighters still drunk or punch-drunk from the previous night. They, along with midgets, radio actors, jazz cats, and the occasional dog thief, made up Tamis' unusual usual crowd. Missing lately, of course, had been Lefty Mavrakis, a regular at The New Genesee who'd been known to drift from table to table asking diners if they wanted to buy a fine watch, a diamond necklace, perhaps a collie.

As the sun climbed to its highest point around noon, Barrett walked down the bright side of Genesee Street whistling "All of Me." A thick scarf, crocheted by his mother as part of her therapy, was wound around his neck as if concealing mysteries. He smiled at those he met and tipped his hat to passing ladies. Meeting Striker at The New Genesee to discuss assassination should have darkened his mood, but thoughts of Celestina put a tune on his lips and a jig to his gait. He never made it to the restaurant.

A young man in a black suit, silent as a pall bearer, sprang from a doorway, grabbed Barrett's scarf, and choked him with it. Barrett clawed at his throat. His eyes bulged as the scarf was drawn tighter, lifting him backward on his heels. The soundless pall bearer dragged the radio actor, who weighed but a whisper, toward the street and into the back of the Silver Arrow. The baby-faced kidnapper piled in after Barrett and the Pierce Arrow roared away. This all occurred in a blink of a gypsy's eye. Witnesses, who recognized both the car and the pall bearer, convinced themselves they had seen nothing and went about their business.

Striker turned the corner onto Genesee Street as the Pierce Arrow pulled away, unaware that Barrett lay bound on the backseat. He stopped at the post office and mailed copies of his radio scripts to WHK in Cleveland, KDKA in Pittsburgh, and WXYZ in Detroit, offering them to each station for six dollars an episode. He kissed the envelopes for luck before handing them to the postmaster, dreaming of new income and dwindling debts. After he mailed his radio plays, he hurried to The New Genesee to meet Barrett and his father.

He passed The Gypsy's house. The red porch light was extinguished, signaling that the working girls were not yet working. He touched his face and heat rose where Mirela had spat. It was the only warmth he felt. He wore his heaviest sweater, the thickest corduroys, the warmest socks, but shivered as if he was still struggling in icy waters.

The bell tinkled above the restaurant door when he entered. The smell of brewing coffee, cigarette smoke, and frying ham greeted him. The counter stools were filled with the lunch crowd's first wave. The Lieutenant sat at his usual corner table facing the door. A bowl of untouched *avgolemeno* soup cooled in front of him. He studied the faces that entered the restaurant, comparing them to memorized mugshots. He waved when he saw his son in the doorway.

The Lieutenant's smile faded as Striker approached. "What happened to your face? You look like Capone."

"The Gypsy spat on me."

"And it scarred? That's bad."

"What about you, Pops? You don't look so good either. You getting any sleep?"

The Lieutenant's eyes were red rimmed and watery, his skin pale and lined. "Some."

Striker sat across from his father. "You got to take care of yourself."

Before The Lieutenant could answer, Tamis came over carrying the typed lunch specials—*Meetloaf, Toona Fish, Creem Chiken*. The rest of the menu—including *Egg and Ham Samitch* for a dime and a *Pork Samitch* for fifteen cents—hung on a blackboard behind the counter.

"Hello, my friend," Tamis said, his English uncertain. "What drink want you?"

"Coffee, Tamis. Black."

"This is a nice surprise," The Lieutenant said, as Tamis left for the coffee urns. "I can't remember the last time we had lunch together."

" Barrett was supposed to meet me here."

"Haven't seen him."

"I can't wait for him. I got to get to the station. This is important."

"Are the kids okay?"

"Everybody's fine. It's Don Stefano."

The Lieutenant reached in his pocket and pulled out a rosary. "Don't tell me you're in trouble with him. Don't tell me you borrowed money."

"No, it's nothing like that. It's worse. He's planning to kill the president."

The Lieutenant stopped fingering the rosary. "What are you talking about?"

"There's a man with a very small chin in town. His name's Cavendish. He's the button man. He also killed Lefty Mavrakis. He's going to shoot Roosevelt when he comes to town. We've got to stop him."

"How do you know all this?"

Striker told his father about his adventures at The Colored Musicians Club and Swan Lake, explaining what he'd overheard outside Danek's cabin.

"Who else knows about this besides Barrett and Celestina?" The Lieutenant asked, his fingers again moving over the beads.

"Just you."

"You didn't tell Janet?"

"No."

"Keep it that way. Don't mention this to anyone. When and where is this assassination supposed to take place?"

"We don't know."

"Why does Don Stefano want the president dead? What's he got against a new deal?"

"We don't know that either."

The conversation paused when Tamis approached the table. He slid the coffee mug to Striker and then pointed to The Lieutenant's untouched bowl. "You no like soup?"

"It's fine, Tamis," The Lieutenant answered, smiling, his face unnatural, like a mortician's poor work.

"You got to eat. You too thin," Tamis said, before leaving to check on another customer.

The Lieutenant crossed his arms, and squeezed the rosary, the crucifix piercing his palm like a nail. "What is it that you want me to do exactly?"

"Arrest The Man with the Very Small Chin."

"On what charges? Being chinless is unfortunate, not criminal."

"Can't you arrest him for conspiracy? Treason?"

"It's your word against his. I could pick him up for questioning, but I couldn't hold him."

"Charge him with possession of stolen property then. He's got Slattery's ring."

"That may be an angle to get him off the streets. Did Slattery file a police report?"

"Slattery's missing."

"Drinking?"

"Yeah."

"I can't arrest Cavendish until he breaks the law, son."

"He *killed* Lefty. Arrest him for that."

"Are you certain Lefty's dead? You have a body? A weapon? A witness?"

"We heard Cavendish say he killed him. Isn't that good enough?"

"I need hard evidence to arrest a man, especially on a murder charge. Maybe Lefty went on the bender with Slattery."

"Pando went on the bender with Slattery, not Lefty. But Pando came back. He's fairly sober. He'll tell you Lefty wasn't with them."

"The word of an alcoholic midget isn't exactly gospel."

"Call Washington then. Let the G-men know what The Undertaker's planning. They'll know what to do."

The Lieutenant glanced at Tamis behind the counter, slicing apple pie. A cigarette dangled from The Greek's lips, the ash a half-inch long, The ash fell. He brushed it from the crust.

"I'll call the Feds," he said, unable to look at his son. "Let them investigate Cavendish. I'll work the Lefty angle and see if anything turns up."

"Thanks, Pops. I knew I could count on you."

"Listen, you're out of this now, understand? Don Stefano, Lefty, The Man with the Very Small Chin. Stay away from them. These are dangerous men. Let me take care of it. You worry about your family."

"Sure, Pops. Say, are you all right?"

"I'm fine. Why?"

"You don't seem yourself. I thought you'd be furious about FDR. I thought you'd charge out of here to arrest them faster than you charged into that burning building."

"My days of running into burning buildings are over, Fran. I was just thinking about that."

"Thinking about what?"

"Thinking maybe it's time to turn in my badge and hang up the gun. Let someone else do the saving around here."

"What are you talking about?"

"Retirement."

"*Retirement*? Weren't you just lecturing me against quitting? How there are no jobs out there? How will you live? How will you take care of Mom?"

The Lieutenant massaged his closed eyes with his fingertips. "I don't know. I'm stuck, I guess."

"Stuck? You love being a copper."

"Forget it. I'm just talking."

"You're scaring me, Pops. And Tamis was right. You look thin. Maybe you should see a doctor."

"I've got enough doctor bills."

"You're not telling me something."

The Lieutenant pulled his hands from his face and smiled, his eyes still dull. "I'm fine. Don't worry about me. Or Roosevelt. I'll take care of everything."

Striker looked at his watch. "Damn it. I got to get some writing done. Are you sure you're okay? I hate to leave you like this."

"Go on. We both got jobs to do. Coffee's on me."

Striker stood. "I'll call you later, all right? I want to find out where this retirement talk is coming from."

"I'll be home after my shift. Don't call too late. I don't want the phone waking your mother."

"Okay, Pops. Take care of yourself. Tell Barrett to meet me at the station if he comes in."

"Stay away from The Undertaker and the rest of them, son."

Striker waved as he left the restaurant, the bell above the door cheerful sounding, opposite what father and son felt. The Lieutenant stared into cold soup as if answers were floating amongst the orzo. Doing The Undertaker's bidding had made him ashamed even in his dreams. Allowing an assassination to take place would drive him to the asylum. He'd become everything he hated. He shoved the bowl aside. Soup sloshed on the table.

The bell tinkled again. He looked up when the chair was scraped back opposite him. Butch Cavendish flipped the chair around and straddled it like he'd mounted a horse. The old copper forced his back to straighten, his chest to thrust.

"You The Lieutenant?" Cavendish asked, pushing his black fedora off his forehead.

The Lieutenant nodded, trying not to stare at the smallest chin he'd ever seen.

Tamis approached their table, carrying mistyped lunch specials. Cavendish waved him away.

"What do you want?"

"Don Stefano sent me."

"You hungry? You should try the pie."

"Forget the pie. The Don wants you to do something for him."

"Haven't I done enough?"

"He wants Roosevelt's itinerary when he visits. *Exact* times. *Exact* locations. You follow?"

"How am I supposed to get that?"

"That's your problem."

"Is that it?" he asked, picking up his spoon and stirring the broth.

"He wants the security plan for guarding the president—how many men, where they're located, what kind of roscoes they're packing. You listening?"

The Lieutenant nodded, sorrow draping him. "Anything else?"

"Yeah, one more thing. He wants a Buffalo Police uniform. The whole outfit—badge, gun, belt—the works. And he wants it in my size. And not a new one neither. Something worn that will blend in, you see what I mean?"

"I see fine," The Lieutenant said.

Cavendish stood and yanked down his brim. "Do this quick."

Cavendish spun on his boot heel and left The Lieutenant alone with his soup and his misery.

Striker paused to light a cigarette as he left the restaurant, turning away from the wind and cupping the flame. When he looked up, he saw Cavendish cross the street and enter The New Genesee. Striker doubled back and peered through the front window, stunned to see the chinless man sit at his father's table. He waited for The Lieutenant to start jabbing his finger at Cavendish, accusing him of murder, theft, treason. He expected his father to stand at any moment, grab the assassin by the arm, spin him around, and handcuff him until metal bit into wrist. But his father did nothing except listen and nod.

It was Cavendish who was pointing fingers and giving orders. The Lieutenant slumped, absorbing the hoodlum's words like punches. When The Man with the Very Small Chin stood to leave, Striker hurried from the window, trying to make sense out of what he'd seen.

He rushed down Genesee, passing shops and street vendors without seeing them. Horns honked as he stepped from curbs without looking. He bumped shoulders without apologizing. People moved out of his way before he jostled packages from their arms. They were invisible to him. Everywhere he looked he only saw Cavendish standing above his father.

His cheek burst aflame so intensely the agony stopped him. He looked around to see where he was, squinting from the rising heat. He was standing in front of The Gypsy's house.

Mirela was shoveling her front walk wearing a sleeveless black dress with matching lace shawl, oblivious to the cold. She sensed his presence and turned, her décolletage deep and impressive. She dropped her shovel and slunk toward him, hips rolling, shoulders back, lips curling to a smile as if Striker was a paying customer. Her thick, black hair hadn't been combed in days. The wind blew it in all directions. Breath was invisible in the cold when she exhaled.

"You come back for more, Mr. Writer?" she purred, stopping in front of him smelling of brandy and body odor, which couldn't have been good for business. She nodded as she inspected his scar, pleased with her work, and ran her tongue over her lips, wetting them.

Striker forced himself to speak. "Have you heard from Lefty?"

"Lefty is dead," she snarled. "He died because of you and your rings."

"I know who has one of the rings."

"Who?"

"The man you told us about. The Man with the Very Small Chin. His name is Butch Cavendish."

Mirela's old eyes showed fresh sorrow. "He was here last night. I was out looking for Lefty's body. I cannot rest until he's buried properly, the gypsy way. I will not eat or bathe until he's in the ground at peace. When I returned, I was told that a chinless man had come around wanting a homely girl for the night and would pay extra for one with moles. We sent him away."

"I thought you let everybody in."

"None of my girls are homely. I had nothing in stock that he'd be interested in. He was sent to the poor man's brothel on Michigan Avenue. They have ugly girls there—Jackrabbit Jackie, Whistling Wilma, One-Leg Mary. Maybe one of them has moles. He wouldn't have set foot in my place even if we did have a homely girl. My man working the door had a bad feeling about him—that he was trouble, that his missing chin would upset the other customers. But he was wrong. Now I know he distrusted him because he was Lefty's murderer. He sensed it. If I was there, I would've known right away and taken his eyes there on the porch," she said, and spat on the ground, snow steaming and melting where the sputum landed.

"Your doorman didn't notice the diamond ring on his little finger?"

"He didn't mention anything about a ring."

"He wears it on his right hand."

"Only one?" Mirela asked, eyebrows rising.

"Lefty promised him both but then later told him he only had one to sell. They got into a fight. That's why he killed him."

"Who kills a man over a ring? I'll take his eyes and his ears. Someone already took his chin."

"Why wouldn't Lefty sell him both rings? Why hold out?"

"He broke up the pair," The Gypsy said. "That's the only explanation. The question is, did he sell the second before he was killed, or is it still around his neck?"

"Around his neck?"

"A pickpocket doesn't trust pockets, especially his own. There are too many cutpurses on Genesee Street for that. When Lefty had rings to sell, he wore them on a chain around his neck so thieves like him wouldn't dip their fingers when he was distracted. If he didn't sell the other ring before he was killed, it's still around his neck. Find his body and you'll find the other ring."

"If we find Lefty and bring him for burial, will you lift the curse from me?" Striker asked.

"If you bring his body for me to mourn, your scar will disappear, but the curse will remain forever. This I promise you. It's your rings that got my Lefty killed and for that you'll never be forgiven. You will never earn what you deserve."

"Cavendish killed him, not me."

"Don't worry about Cavendish. The curse I'll put on him will make yours look like a dead mother's blessing. Just bring Lefty home. Let his soul rest so he doesn't come back as a *mullo* and walk the earth as the undead."

"Where do I look? Where do we start?"

"Look in every cold, dark place."

"It's winter in Buffalo. The whole city's cold and dark."

"Then search everywhere. Hurry. Before Lefty comes back for vengeance."

She shoved Striker back a few steps. He watched as Mirela dragged herself up the half-shoveled walk to her home. Her shoulders shook under her black shawl. Striker wondered if gypsies could be burned by their own tears.

A horn's *Ahooga!* shattered every noise on Genesee Street. Charles Armbrewster skidded to the curb in his Model A. He cranked down the window and extended his neck through the opening. His glasses fogged. "Fran!" he called. "I've been looking all over for you! Jerry's been hurt!"

"What happened?"

"There was a riot at the railyard. I'll tell you about it on the way to the hospital."

Striker hustled to the Model A and slammed the passenger door behind him. Armbrewster gunned the Ford and back tires spun, shooting snow until the rubber caught road and lurched forward.

"What in God's name happened?" Striker asked, as Armbrewster *Ahooga-ed* a pedestrian to the curb.

"It was terrible. There's blood all over the snow. Janet called the radio station and asked me to find you. WEBR sent a reporter down. They say it's the worst riot since the railroad strike in '22."

"A snow shoveling riot?"

"Worse. A soup riot."

"I've never heard of such a thing."

They drove past The New Genesee. The Lieutenant stood in front, hunched in his great coat, looking as if he was deciding on his direction.

"The men had been promised hot soup for days and never got any," Armbrewster explained. "They were cold and hungry and tired of false promises. They had enough and rose up, turning their shovels on the railroad guards. The bulls swung back with billy clubs and brass knuckles like they always do. Some say there were gunshots. At least two are dead—a compact shoveler and Wild Bill Krenshaw."

"That goon's still around?"

"Not anymore," Armbrewster said, the interior of the Model A filling with elbows and knees as the lanky drummer worked the clutch and shifted gears. "Someone bashed in his head so badly it looked like a horse kicked it in."

"What about Jerry? How bad is he hurt?"

"I don't know," the drummer said, turning on Michigan Avenue. "Janet was heading to the hospital to find out. Your grandparents and in-laws are watching the kids. Say, how many people live with you?"

"It goes up every day."

They drove passed the poor man's brothel, a flop house turned bordello when the stock market crashed and boarders stopped boarding. Men with patched sleeves and torn boots, some of whom had just finished lunch at The New Genesee, were lined up on the porch steps awaiting dessert. Whistling Wilma opened the door to let in the customers. Striker wondered if she had moles. She stuck her forefinger and thumb in her mouth and shrilled a whistle, signaling the world that they were open for business.

"There's something else," Armbrewster said.

"About Jerry?"

"No, about work. I'm hearing rumors."

"What kind of rumors?"

Armbrewster shrugged, his boney shoulders threatening to slice through his overcoat. "Times are tough. Some people are going to lose their jobs."

Striker's scar smoldered. "Me?"

"God no, Fran. That place would fall apart without you. You write everything."

"Who then?"

"The announcers, at least that's what I'm hearing. They're going to ask you to take up the slack. Intro the shows, read the news, maybe direct. You've done all that stuff before."

"Full-time writer *and* announcer," Striker said, staring out the window as the world passed by. "Are they going to raise my salary?"

"No one gets raises during a depression, Fran. The other rumor is they're cutting the orchestra's salary. We're lucky we got work, I guess."

"Yeah," he said, touching his scar. "I feel lucky. You didn't tell Janet, did you?"

"Hell, I didn't even tell my wife. No need to worry her yet. It's all rumors at this point," Armbrewster said, but he didn't fool Striker. WEBR was a small station. It was difficult to keep secrets where rumors always grew into truths.

The Model A slowed as they crossed Main Street onto Harvard Place. A flatbed had stalled in the middle of the intersection. A copper directing traffic waved them around. The men in the back—replacement shovelers for the railroad yard—huddled close, their shoulders rounded to shield themselves from gusts. Striker wondered if they'd get soup.

Harvard Place was rutted with frozen car tracks and Armbrewster crept along as best he could. They passed a sprawling Georgian mansion, the new location for The Ingleside Home For Reclaiming The Erring. Striker patted his coat for cigarettes and Armbrewster nodded to his pack on the dash. He shook loose a fag and offered it to the orchestra leader who waved it away. Striker lit a Lucky then rolled down the window enough to toss the match into the street. He kept the window cracked and exhaled smoke into the cold as he thought of working more hours at WEBR—more hours away from family, more hours away from writing, more hours away from sending scripts to other stations, more hours working for the same money, an amount not nearly enough. His scar tingled, and he believed in curses. Armbrewster turned on Lafayette Avenue and pulled to the curb in front of Millard Fillmore Hospital.

"You coming in?" Striker asked, looking up at the pink-stucco building. Part of the Greek key bordering the roofline was covered with snow.

"Can't. I'm late for orchestra practice. Let me know how Jerry's doing."

"Will do." Striker climbed from the Model A and took a last drag off the Lucky before flicking it. It flew end-over-end and landed upright in a snowbank, the tip still burning. He trudged up the walk and through the arched doorway. Icicles hung above like sharpened teeth. The hospital was overrun with wounded rioters. The vestibule was filled with moaning, cursing men. Some sat blood-splattered on benches holding limbs bent at impossible angles while others touched injuries with tentative fingers, checking for broken bones and missing teeth. Nurses tried to hush them. A fight had rekindled between a shoveler and a railroad guard. Striker had to step aside as a copper hustled the shoveler to the door. One arm was twisted behind his back by the officer, the other dangled dislocated and useless by his side.

"You better put me in the same cell as that railroad bastard because I'm not done beating the hell out of him!" the man yelled, as the copper pushed him out on Lafayette Avenue.

The front desk was crowded with family members inquiring about loved ones, each shouting names of fathers, brothers and sons at the sobbing young nurse behind the desk who'd covered her ears with both hands. Striker knew he wouldn't learn anything from her, so he snuck past and wandered the echoing halls, opening doors and peeking inside examining rooms. After checking the ground floor, he climbed the stairs to the second floor.

"Fran! Over here!" Janet stood fifty feet away and waved, her skin waxy compared to her blue hat and cloth coat.

"Are you alright?" he asked, taking her in his arms. "You don't look well."

She managed a smile as she slumped against him. "You know me, Fran. The only woman in Buffalo who gets morning sickness in the afternoon."

"Let's sit down," he said, guiding her to a bench. He sat beside her, holding her clammy hand with both of his.

"Did you see all those men downstairs? Isn't it awful?"

"It's a madhouse. I didn't even ask about Jerry. How is he?"

"He's in surgery. His leg is bad, broken in a bunch of places. The bone was sticking through the skin. I'm not sure what they beat him with."

"Dear God."

"How's your face, Fran?" She reached for his cheek. "It looks worse. Why won't you tell me what happened?"

He winced and pulled away. "It's nothing," he said, wondering if there was a cold, dark place somewhere in the bowels of Millard Fillmore where dead patients are kept, if Lefty was among them.

"But how did you get it? The scar looks so…permanent."

He tried to think of the best way to explain that a brothel madam had cursed him. Convincing his pregnant wife that he was at a whorehouse for noble reasons might be more difficult than proving the existence of gypsy spells.

"Well, Fran?" she asked again. "How did you get it?"

Before he could answer, a surgeon called her name. Both she and Striker stood as the doctor approached, his white surgical gown brushing his ankles. He pulled off his matching cap, revealing close-cropped hair, the color of winter rain.

"How is he, doctor?" she asked.

"He came through pretty well. I'm not sure how much of a limp he'll have. He won't be working anytime soon, that's for sure, unless he can find a desk job—if they still exist. He may need another operation. It depends on how the bones set."

As Janet quizzed the doctor for details, Striker felt relief followed by a rush of demoralizing thoughts—that no more shoveling money would be coming into the household, that Jerry wouldn't be working, that doctor and surgery bills would arrive soon. He didn't need to be a radio detective to know who'd pay them.

The wind outside picked up again and a strong gust blew open a hallway window. As the doctor hurried to shut it, snow flew inside and swirled around Striker, blowing back his hair and flapping his pant legs, the wind howling like gypsy laughter.

EPISODE 11

The Miser of Motown

Clouds formed high above Detroit. Wind swirled across Lake Michigan. The cloudscape stretched and curled, revealing stars and moon then hid them again as the wisps churned into something new. Far below, Detroiters stepped from streetcars and taxis and studied the night sky, weighing the possibility of snow. They pulled mufflers close and set off for destinations and adventures known only to themselves.

Inside the Maccabees Building, George Trendle sat at his desk, sleeves rolled, tie loosened, breathing through his mouth as he read a script. Across from him, Campbell squinted at a different script, trying to make out the dialogue in the dim office. The room was lit by a desk lamp that cast murky light. Trendle was trying to save on electricity.

"More garbage," he muttered, tossing the script over his shoulder, the loose pages fluttering to the floor with the others. He pressed his palms against his eyes, the bruises beneath them a purplish black. "Can't anybody write anymore?"

"This Phillips Lord is pretty good," Campbell said, holding the script close so he could read it.

"Let me see that," Trendle said, snapping pudgy fingers.

Campbell handed him the manuscript. "He's the one I was telling you about. The guy from New York City."

"The one who writes about a hillbilly who tells stupid jokes? That's not the cowboy action series I was hoping for, Allan."

"We need a variety of shows, boss. This is a good family program. We could slot it during the dinner hour or maybe on Sundays."

"How much does he want for it?"

Campbell picked up the cover letter and angled it toward the light. "He gave a range. Two to six dollars per episode."

"Offer him a buck fifty. He doesn't need to eat steak every night. Tell him we'll buy four episodes and give it a trial run for a month."

Campbell jotted in his notebook, his wiry hair casting spikey shadows against the wall.

"What else you got?" he demanded, setting Lord's radio play on his desk.

Campbell pulled a script from the pile. "This one came today. The writer's from Buffalo. Fran Striker."

He snatched the script from Campbell. "Striker? Never heard of him. Nothing good ever came out of Buffalo except the Pierce Arrow and that should've been a Detroit car."

"This script's really good, boss. It's more what you're looking for."

He read the title aloud. "*Warner Lester—Manhunter.*"

"It's an adventure story. About a crime fighter."

"But not a cowboy."

"No."

Campbell watched Trendle's thick lips move as he read. He cracked his knuckles, waiting for a reaction.

"Say, this guy *can* write, even if he is from Buffalo. He grabs your attention from the beginning."

"I told you he was good."

"He's better than Phillips Lord. Hell, he's better than all these hacks," he said, gesturing to pages strewn on his desk and carpet.

"Should I make him an offer, boss?"

"What's his price?"

"Six."

Trendle rolled his swollen eyes. "What is it with these greedy writers? Six dollars an episode? He's as much a robber as that scarecrow Sutton, except Striker's holding a pen to my head."

"Should I offer him four? It's the best script we've seen."

Trendle took off his pince-nez, shut his eyes, and pinched the bridge of his throbbing nose. "Make it three. Ask if he's got anything else. Maybe a comedy. Something funny the ladies would like."

"You got it, boss," Campbell said, scratching in his notebook.

Trendle reset his glasses. "What about that other joker? The one living for free in the storeroom. Has he written anything yet?"

"I haven't seen a word from him."

"Get him in here."

Campbell scampered from the office and disappeared into the shadowy hallway. Trendle leaned back in his chair and hooked his thumbs in his belt. His face ached from being punched. He worked his jaw from left to right, but that intensified the pain, surpassing even his constant stomach condition. He cursed Ted Sutton, hoping he was alone in a miserable cell. He opened a desk drawer and cursed some more when he saw the empty bottle of Doctor Foley's he didn't remember finishing. The bottle must have leaked. He slammed the drawer shut, damning faulty caps and druggists who wouldn't be open at this late hour.

Campbell returned with a man whose skin was so fair it bordered translucent. His eyes were a shade bluer than his lips; he wore a woolen trench coat missing copper buttons and pocked with moth holes. He wiped his nose with the back of a fingerless glove. In his other hand, he held a single type-written page.

"Here he is, boss," Campbell said, nudging the shivering man forward with his shoulder.

"It's McGuire, isn't it?" Trendle asked.

"McGuinn, sir," the man corrected. He was not offered a seat.

"All right, McGuinn, how's the cowboy script coming?"

He handed Trendle what he had.

"Where's the rest?"

"That's it…so far."

"So far? One page? That's not very far at all, is it?"

"No sir," he said, wiping his nose again.

"You wrote one page in *three* days?" Trendle asked. "What am I paying you for?"

"You're not paying me."

"I'm letting you stay in my storeroom, aren't I? That's a form of payment. You've got a roof over your head. That's more than you had three days ago."

"There's no heat back there."

"It's colder outside." Trendle scanned the page. "This is awful."

"It's hard to write in that room. My fingers keep stiffening."

Trendle let the paper fall to his desk. "Let me explain something to you, McDuffy…"

"McGuinn," McGuinn said.

"…we're in the entertainment business. Do you know what that means? It means we're supposed to *entertain* our listeners. That's why they tune in. This," he said, picking up the sheet by a corner as if soiled, "is not entertaining. It's not even interesting. These words are dead. They lie on the page like little corpses." He crumpled the page and tossed it in the waste basket. "There. They're buried."

"I can do better, sir."

"I doubt it, but you can try over at WXYT or WJR. You're done here. Get your things and get out."

"But…"

Trendle held up his hand, halting him. "This is not a debate, McDermott. It's a *termination*. That's a big word. Four syllables.

Judging from your writing abilities, you may not know its definition. Mr. Campbell will explain it to you on your way out."

"Please, Mr. Trendle," McGuinn said, a jagged blue vein bulging at his translucent temple. "Can't I leave in the morning? It's late. The shelters and flophouses will all be filled. I have nowhere to go. It's freezing outside."

"I'm running a radio station, McCormick, not a charity house. People work here. Except *you*. I don't know what you've been doing, but you certainly haven't been writing. You've been living off my generosity."

"I was trying to keep warm. I couldn't concentrate."

"Well, you can do your concentrating outdoors. Allan, show Mr. McCullum the street."

"Yes, boss." Campbell gave the man a sympathetic smile as he ushered him from the office. As the two stepped into the hallway, Campbell squeezed McGuinn's shoulder and snuck a dollar inside his coat pocket. "Allan!" Trendle yelled.

Campbell froze, fearing Trendle had seen him. He kept his back towards his boss and waited for the screaming to pierce him.

"Wire that Striker fellow. Ask him if he can write a cowboy script."

Trendle didn't go straight home that night. The ache in his face had intensified as if the masked man had punched him again. Perhaps the doctor who had examined him overlooked some damage—a fractured perpendicular plate, a broken infraorbital foremen, perhaps a chipped anterior nasal spine. The pain had grown so great he could not concentrate. Campbell had offered to drive him home, but he'd declined and set off in his Cadillac in search of Foley's Pain Relief Medicine. As he feared, all the apothecaries were closed at this late at night. He tried Cunningham's Drugs, Kinsel Drug Store, even Barthwell Drugs & Candy over in Black Bottom to no avail. He pointed the Caddy towards Madison Street, every bump causing pain to shoot from mandible to brow and drove to the Detroit Athletic Club. The D.A.C. not only encouraged manly sports and promoted physical culture, but it also served the finest bootleg brandy this side of Windsor, Ontario. Courvoisier was no Foley's, but it would have to do.

The club, a six-story limestone mansion inspired by Roman and Florentine architecture, was built in 1915 to drive automobile industry kingpins out of the saloons on Woodward Avenue to some place befitting their wealth and place in Detroit society. Membership rolls were filled with familiar names—Ford, Nash, DuPont. Christmas galas, black-tie parties, and elaborate weddings held at the club were splashed across society pages for fender washers to read about in awe.

When Wall Street crashed, so did the D.A.C. A flood of members resigned, no longer able to afford dues. Others went delinquent on their accounts. Some jumped from ten-story office windows. Staff were let go. Debt mounted. To save the club, fees and standards were lowered and George W. Trendle became a member. He represented the "new blood," "the future of the club," and many of the original founders were not pleased.

Madison Street was deserted so Trendle parked in front of the D.A.C. instead of pulling around to its private lot. The curved wooden doors opened as he climbed the four marble steps leading to the club's grand entrance. He strode through the columned entranceway as if he'd built it from scratch.

"Good evening, sir," the doorman said, staring at Trendle's blackened eyes. "We haven't seen you in a while."

He unbuttoned his overcoat as he stepped inside. "Good evening, Howard. It has been a long time."

"It's always good to have you, sir."

The main lobby smelled of tobacco, fireplace embers, and dwindling old money. He handed the doorman his hat and coat as he took in the vacant oak-paneled room and the unoccupied upholstered chairs grouped in twos or encircling antique tables.

"Where is everybody?" he asked, hoping to strike up a conversation with an executive from General Motors or Ford. He'd even settle for billiards with a vice president from Hudson Motor Car, if there were any left.

Howard Wickison folded Tremble's coat over his arm. Wrinkles appeared like hedgerows on his forehead as he chose each word. "It has been very quiet tonight, sir. I think the weather has been keeping people home."

"Well, that's okay," he said, clapping the doorman's shoulder, "as long as they're home listening to WXYZ. We're the last word in radio, you know."

"Indeed you are, sir."

Trendle crossed the lobby to the cigar counter, ignoring the Remington sculpture on a table to his right and the roster of club members lost in The Great War on his left. He studied the cigars, some displayed in wooden boxes, others held in crystal jars or Cherrywood humidors. He chose a few and took turns holding them to his nose, breathing in Cuban soil, Nicaraguan rain, Ybor City dreams. As he snipped the end of a Cuesta-Rey, he decided to take a chance on the Reading Room for company rather than the Billiard Room or the Library. It was too late to eat in the Grill Room or Main Dining Room, and he doubted anyone would still be there, lingering over crème brulée. His face hurt too much to chew.

"Light, Mr. Trendle?" Howard asked, appearing at his side, a burning match between his fingers.

He grunted thanks and leaned into the flame, rotating the cigar and puffing to get an even burn. He straightened and blew smoke toward the coffered ceiling.

The doorman bowed his head and shook the life from the match. "A drink, sir? A single malt, perhaps?"

"Say, Howard. What gives? Are you the doorman, coat clerk, cigar counterman, *and* waiter? How many jobs do you have?"

"We're a bit understaffed tonight because of the weather and," he lowered his voice, "cutbacks."

"Ah, yes," Trendle said, the Cuesta-Rey protruding like an additional finger. "I had to let a man go myself today. Terrible times, Howard. Terrible times."

"Yes, sir."

"We're all suffering." Trendle puffed smoke from his hand-rolled cigar. "I'll take a cognac. Nothing pretentious. V.S.O.P is fine."

"Right away, sir. Will you be enjoying that in the billiard room as usual, Mr. Trendle?"

"No, the Reading Room, I think."

"Very good, sir. I'll bring your brandy promptly. I believe Mr. Clark is also in the Reading Room this evening."

"Emory Clark?"

"Yes, sir. He came in about an hour ago."

"I've been meaning to speak with old Emory," he said, as if he knew the man. He had wanted to meet Clark, the president of the First National Bank of Detroit, since losses at WXYZ had soared, but Clark was never at any club event that he attended. Trendle wondered if he was avoiding him.

"Very good, sir," Howard said, bowing his head again before hurrying off to the bar.

Trendle clamped the cigar in the corner of his mouth, folded his hands behind his back, and crossed the Main Lobby as if he was crossing his living room. He passed the grand staircase made of marble and limestone and hurried down the first-floor hallway to the Reading Room. He ignored oils by Frank Weston Benson, Herman Richir, and Carle Vanloo. As always, he stopped to admire Rolshoven's "Reclining Nude," sucking hungrily on the Cuesta-Rey. He breathed smoke and smacked lips as if he'd taken the last bite of a sweet, flaming dessert.

Empty leather chairs and smoking stands were arranged around the Reading Room. A brass and crystal chandelier was suspended from a ceiling rose; matching sconces dotted walls. The room was quiet except for the ticking mantel clock, a rustling newspaper, and crackling fireplace. A lone white-haired man sat by the hearth reading *Barron's* and smoking a pipe, a copy of *The Wall Street Journal* folded on his lap. He was older, deep into his seventies, but well-preserved, like a man who drank cod liver oil of his own volition. Emory Clark was trim and fit, a geriatric bantam in a three-piece suit. He lowered his newspaper as Trendle approached.

Trendle smiled, sweat forming above his lip. He removed the cigar from his mouth. "May I join you?"

The old man folded his newspaper and placed it on *The Journal.* He gestured to the empty chair next to him with his pipe stem and scowled.

"I'm George W. Trendle."

"Emory Clark." The old man studied Trendle's blackened eyes and swollen nose as they shook hands. "What happened to your face?"

Trendle glanced at his reflection in the mirror above the fireplace before taking his seat. He forced a chuckle, which caused his nose to hurt as he rested his cigar in the smoking stand. "I was a victim of a violent robbery, I'm afraid. A terrible experience I wouldn't wish on anyone. The robber wore a mask and threatened us with a gun. My poor wife still hasn't recovered."

"I'm sorry to hear that," Clark said, as he re-lit his pipe, filling the room with vanilla. "I hope the police caught the desperado."

"They most certainly did. It was a disgruntled employee."

"An employee? What line of work are you in? Penny arcades, isn't it? I'm in banking myself."

"Broadcasting."

Clark held the pipe inches from his mouth. "Radio?"

"I own WXYZ."

"I think I've heard of it. There can't be much money in that. Have you always been in broadcasting?"

"Oh, no. This is a new venture for me. I made my mark in theaters— The Columbia, The Hippodrome, The Madison. And investments of course." He gestured to the financial journals on Clark's lap.

"Theater and radio," Clark said. He took a thoughtful drag from his pipe. "Not exactly steel and automobiles, is it?"

Howard entered the Reading Room carrying a brandy snifter on a silver tray. He set the glass on the table next to Trendle. Emory Clark frowned at the cognac and ordered a glass of warm milk.

"These are interesting times for banking," Trendle said, toeing his way towards the conversation he'd wanted to have with the banker for months.

Clark drew on his pipe before answering. "That's one way to put it, with all the closings, holidays, and runs. My family has been in banking for three generations. We've seen recessions and depressions before. Nothing like this, of course. God willing, we'll survive this *interesting* time, too."

Trendle picked up his glass, pressed the crystal against his face, the pain vexing him more. "But the First National Bank of Detroit has always been strong. Surely, you're still investing, writing mortgages, issuing loans?"

"No one is writing mortgages these days, George. I foreclosed on eight million dollars' worth of properties last spring alone. Unemployment in the state is thirty-four percent as of today. People can't pay what they owe. Banks are failing all over Michigan. Hell, they're failing all over the country. Anyone would be foolish to write a mortgage now."

Trendle gulped brandy, his body flushed and heated. The pain in his face increased as if that masked man was still picking his shots, landing blows on his eyes, jaw, and already-broken nose.

"What about business loans, Emory? Some investment must be taking place," Trendle said, as Howard returned with Clark's milk.

The doorman crossed the room silent as a spirit, as if he'd been haunting the club's hallways for centuries. He set the milk next to Clark's chair, inquired if the gentlemen needed anything else, then disappeared as quietly as he'd arrived.

Clark scoffed, setting his pipe in the smoking stand and reaching for his milk. "Men come to me every day asking for loans for their failing businesses, wanting me to throw good money after bad. What's there to invest in these days?"

Trendle saw his chance. "Radio."

Clark's face pinched as if the warm milk had soured.

Trendle leaned forward. "People can't afford to go out for their entertainment anymore, Emory. They're staying home, listening to the radio. Comedies, dramas, symphonies, news. It's all being broadcast from dawn to midnight. Even during these bleak times, families are buying radios on installment plans. Sure, the cost of them has dropped sixty percent, but more people are listening! Half the homes have a radio in the living room now. There are six hundred stations in the country. Six hundred! The big networks are projected to make thirty-nine million dollars in advertising revenue by themselves. That doesn't even factor in what independent stations like WXYZ generate."

"Ah," Clark said. "I see." He took his pocket watch from his vest and checked the time.

"You should be investing in a fast-growing market driven by new technology, Emory. Radio!"

"WXYZ wouldn't be looking for a loan, would it?" Clark asked, snapping his watch closed.

Trendle tut-tutted, as if asking for a loan wasn't dangling on the tip of his tongue. "There's money to be made in radio, Emory."

Emory finished his milk and popped to his feet as if about to perform calisthenics. "George, there's no money to be made anywhere. Not in America. Not in Europe. Not with hula girls in Hawaii. 1933 isn't going to be a good year. It will be worse than the last, that's for certain. First National won't be investing, not in radio, not in radio stations, not in anything. We'll be closing branches and trying to keep the rest of our doors open. If radio is growing like you say, my advice is to sell before the bubble bursts and broadcasting crashes like every other industry in this country."

Trendle struggled to his feet. "Radio is going to be the next big thing, Emory. I can feel it. Stars are going to be made. *Money* is going to be made. It takes a station one hit show to put it over the top. You'll see. The dollars will be galloping in then. The smart ones will strike it rich."

Clark extended his hand. "I wish you luck, George. We all need some luck or good fortune or whatever you want to call it. I don't think Roosevelt or anyone else is going to save us anytime soon. It's all going to come down to serendipity."

Trendle shook the banker's hand. "Best of luck to you, Emory."

After the old man left, Trendle collapsed in the chair, the cabriole legs creaking under his weight. He gulped brandy and pressed the cool glass against his forehead. The pain had spread from his eyes to his bald head until his scalp seemed to smolder. Emory was wrong about the future of radio and the money that could be made in broadcasting. Trendle was certain of it, as he was certain Emory wasn't just speaking for the First National but for all banks: no one would give him a loan. No matter what costs he cut, WXYZ was losing money. Debts were accumulating faster than snow. With a loan no longer a possibility, 1933 would be a very bleak year if he didn't find that one hit program, if he didn't strike gold.

Fredric Remington's *The Horse Muster* hung on the far wall. Trendle rose from the leather chair, drawn to the oil painting though he'd seen it a hundred times before. Two cowboys, lariat-thin, wearing battered dungarees and dusty vests, were discussing a horse with a greenhorn sporting knee-high boots and jodhpurs. The horse was saddled, its head bent as if it'd been ridden hard. In the background stood other horses and other cowboys. Stables and trees framed the scene.

Trendle held his pince-nez with his forefinger and thumb and leaned closer to the Remington. The painting was so precise it was as if he could smell the cowboys' sweat and the dandy's aftershave. Brushstrokes undulated. The horse appeared to twitch, the cowboys move. Trendle blamed the brandy for vertigo. He stumbled back to his chair. From down the deserted hall, perhaps from the billiard room, or maybe from the painting itself, he heard a radio:

Old Ezra Holton was a prospector and, with his wife, had given the best years of his life in the endless search for gold in the west. Nothing but defeat had met him at every turn...

EPISODE 12

Gathering Firewood

Barrett was tied to a wobbly chair with his scarf. It was wrapped around him several times, his hands bound behind his back with the ends. Rope lashed his ankles, biting into flesh and wood. A black bandana masked his eyes. A second one gagged him. He was sweating, his face flushed with heat that seemed to be rising, as if a fire was being stoked in front of him. He'd struggled against the scarf all night and now slumped exhausted in the chair.

He heard footsteps coming downstairs, leather soles against concrete. They grew louder as they approached and stopped in front of him. Barrett held his breath, bracing for a punch, a slap, a gunshot, but he remained untouched, which frightened him more. The mask was yanked from his eyes, and Barrett was blinded from the sudden brightness emanating from the crematorium oven.

He turned his head and blinked until he was able to focus again. Don Stefano towered above him, dressed for a funeral, unaffected by the inferno raging in the oven. Sweat ran down Barrett's neck, dampening his collar. His overcoat felt leaden.

"John L. Barrett," The Undertaker said, pacing around Barrett like a larger planet orbiting a smaller one. "Unmarried. Father unknown. Mother institutionalized. Only child. No relatives this side of Ireland."

The Undertaker halted his orbit. He leaned forward, hands on knees so he was eye-level with the actor. His breath smelled of pepperoncini, his fingers like embalming fluid as they pulled the gag from Barrett's mouth. "If you were to disappear, would anybody notice?"

Barrett had been terrified countless times in his life—witnessing his mother slip in and out of sanity, being left alone in Forest Lawn Cemetery at night as a child—but he had never felt as terrified as he did at this moment. He wished for a gun or a knife, though he'd never used either. The one weapon he had, the one tool that might save him, was his voice. He cleared his throat, still scratchy, and thought of all the heroes Striker had written for him to play. His voice exploded like a howitzer.

"You're damn right people would miss me! I'm John L. Barrett, the most popular radio actor from here to New York City. I'm going to be in the pictures someday. You don't think WEBR will come looking for me? You don't think reporters will start sniffing? You don't think my fans will demand an explanation? Hell, I wouldn't be surprised if they're already searching for me after that stunt you pulled. Grabbing me on Genesee Street in broad daylight? Didn't you think there'd be witnesses who'd recognize me? Untie me while you still can."

The Undertaker straightened, unprepared for that voice to rush over him like a gale. He walked around Barrett, this time slower, as if reevaluating him from every angle. Many men, and a few dames, had been tied to the ancient oven chair. They'd all wept and begged. Bladders had failed. Nobody, however, had ever talked to Don Stefano in Barrett's tone and volume when sitting near the flames. None of this made sense to the gangster. The man's scarf weighed more than he did. Why wasn't he afraid? Why wasn't he pleading for his life?

"There's not much to you, is there?" The Undertaker asked, stopping again. He poked Barrett's shoulder and chest with his forefinger, probing for thickness. "You won't leave much ash."

Barrett threw back his head and laughed, deep and full-throated, as if being threatened with incineration was a knee-slapper. "Why would you do that? Why am I even here? Did your flunky grab the wrong guy?"

"You're here because of Celestina," he said, speaking the name as if it were holy.

Barretts stopped laughing. His smile melted in the heat. "What about her?"

The Undertaker heard his fear. He could smell it as distinctly as burning hair. Normalcy had returned to his world. "I want to marry her. I want her to give me sons," The Undertaker said.

"*What?*"

"She's as close to heaven as I'll ever get. I will make her the queen of The Queen City. The first lady of Buffalo. Everything I have will be hers," he said, gesturing around the crematorium.

"She'll never marry you. Never. Not if I have any say in it," Barrett said, yelling his words, not Striker's. They echoed off cellar walls.

The Undertaker peered into the oven, flames dancing and twisting. "Yes, I believe that's true. She wouldn't even accept my flowers because of you."

"Ha!" Barrett said, a strength surging through him that made him certain he could break his bonds. He flexed his thin biceps and expanded his pigeon chest, expecting the scarf to explode into shredded yarn and free him. He'd leap from the chair, push The Undertaker into the oven in one graceful motion, the way a hero would. His mother's scarf held him in place.

"I've heard you on the radio," The Undertaker said, turning from the fire. "That voice. Like Caruso. A voice like that should be arguing cases in court or making speeches in Congress. But what did you say? She will never marry me if you have a say in it?"

"That's right. Not if I have a damn say in it."

The Undertaker snapped his fingers. From the shadows the pall bearer, the young man who'd grabbed Barrett on Genesee Street, stepped forward.

"You've met my nephew Giovanni? He's a good boy. My oldest sister's son. She sent him from Castellammare del Golfo to apprentice with me. He's smart. Learns quick. Tell him something once and he knows it forever. But he has one weakness. Grappa. He starts drinking and soon he starts talking. Telling secrets. *My* secrets. Things about my business. It's not his fault. It's the Grappa. But he can't stop. He drinks then talks."

A flame flared in the oven. The Don took a handkerchief folded like fingers from his suitcoat pocket and dabbed his forehead. "Did you and Giovanni have a nice conversation on the ride over, John? What did you talk about? The weather? Boxing?"

"We didn't talk about anything. He didn't say a word. He wouldn't answer any of my questions."

The Undertaker waved Giovanni to his side. "This doesn't surprise me. Giovanni, open your mouth for Mr. Barrett. Show him." Giovanni leaned close to Barrett and opened his mouth, showing him straight teeth, a uvula hanging like Slattery's speedbag, and the empty space his tongue once occupied.

"He's my nephew. A good boy. I couldn't kill him, but I couldn't have him drinking grappa and telling my secrets all over town. So, I compromised. I tied him to that very chair you're sitting in and cut out his tongue. Now he can drink as much grappa as he wants. Everybody wins." He clapped his nephew on the back.

Giovanni closed his mouth, and a longing crossed his face—a longing to be back in Sicily, to see his mother again, to talk to her one last time.

"He's just a kid," Barrett said.

"And he will live to be a quiet old man."

The Undertaker tucked his handkerchief back in his pocket, smoothed it so the folded fingers lay against his chest, then pulled a stiletto from an ankle strap. He held the blade close to Barrett. Bits of tobacco and dried blood stained the blade.

"What if you lost your tongue, Mr. Barrett? What then? No more radio for you. No more big voice. No more Hollywood dreams. Men who *can* speak can't find jobs these days. Who would hire a grunter? Would you even want to live? Wouldn't it be easier to jump into the icy Niagara and go over the Falls than to live without your voice? Wouldn't you beg me to kill you?"

"Why would I lose my tongue?"

The Undertaker pressed the blade flat against Barrett's jaw. "I will cut it off if you don't end it with Celestina. Then I'll flip it in the oven, and you can listen to it sizzle while it cooks. The smell will stay with you always."

"Celestina will never marry you."

The Undertaker angled the blade, so the dagger's point pressed against Barrett's skin. "Is that your final word, Mr. Barrett?"

"You can't make someone love you."

"I can be very persuasive, very charming. I'll woo her. And I will win in the end if you're not in the picture. Kick her out of your life, John. Break her heart. Hurt her. If you don't, you'll be as quiet as Giovanni, and she won't want you anyway. She'll be embarrassed by the pitiful sounds you make."

"Do you really think a woman like Celestina will stop caring for me if I lose my tongue?"

The Undertaker pulled the blade away from Barrett's face and considered the question. "Perhaps not, but that's why we have ovens. She will be filled with grief when you disappear. I will be there to console her."

Barrett tried to think of a response, but nothing came. He was certain what The Undertaker said was more than a threat. It was a promise.

"None of that has to happen, John. You can keep your tongue, remain the big voice on radio, maybe even be a movie star someday. It's all very easy. Just give up Celestina."

"Damn you to hell, Magaddino."

The Undertaker smiled an undertaker smile, as if remembering all the tongues he'd taken. "I'm afraid I already am, but that's my concern. You have much to think about. You need to decide between your tongue and your love. I'll leave you alone with your thoughts."

He balled the bandana and crammed it back in Barrett's mouth. The Undertaker took the second bandana and re-masked his eyes. Barrett struggled to get free, but his mother's scarf was unforgiving. Leather soles scraped against concrete again as The Undertaker climbed the stairs. If Giovanni the Mute had left the room, he did so without a sound. He could have followed his uncle up the stairs, or he could have slunk back into a shadowy corner, or he could have been standing next to Barrett's chair, coveting his tongue.

Barrett fought against his bonds until he was exhausted. His head drooped forward until chin touched chest. His mind raced from one horror to another: his tongue sliced, his body burned, Don Stefano touching Celestina. He screamed in frustration, the sound absorbed by the gag. He needed to do something. How would Striker write his escape?

Barrett knew the answer. A hero would arrive, kicking in the funeral parlor door. The villains would be tossed down the cellar stairs one after the other: first Joey Maranto, then Giovanni. Don Stefano would be the last to tumble after them. The hero would follow, taking his time descending the steps, perhaps whistling a tune from another time. He'd step over the groaning gangsters, ignoring their complaints of broken bones and pleas for mercy. Maybe he'd kick their ribs for good measure or maybe he'd take Don Stefano's stiletto from his ankle strap and cut Barrett free. But Barrett knew no hero was going to save him.

No one was on their way to cut him free from the oven chair. Nobody even knew he'd been kidnapped. It would be up to him to save his tongue. An idea struck him. The chair he was tied to was old and rickety and had set in front of the oven for years. The wood must be brittle from constant exposure to the heat. It must splinter easily. His plan could not fail.

He rocked the wobbly chair from side-to-side, teetering farther each time until he tumbled over, smashing hard against the concrete floor, the impact sending a thunderbolt through his shoulder. The wooden chair didn't split. Knots didn't loosen. He was lying on his side with a pained shoulder and no idea what to do next. As he lay panting, trying to come up with another, better plan, the black bandana covering his eyes was pulled down. Giovanni the Mute was kneeling next to him, his face lit by flames. He held a finger to his lips, signaling Barrett to remain as quiet as himself. The pallbearer pulled a switchblade from his jacket. Barrett screamed into his gag. The mute yanked out the bandana then covered Barrett's mouth with his hand, muffling the actor's cries. A five-inch blade snapped free, reflecting oven light. Barrett imagined his mouth forced open, his tongue slashed. He could already feel the pain, taste the blood, see all that he loved vanishing. Barrett thrashed, trying to break free, trying to twist away from Giovanni. The Undertaker's nephew held Barrett in place by the jaw, the actor's mouth and tongue in easy access. With a flick of the wrist, the flick knife went to work.

Barrett howled. The blade cut through knots, sliced through yarn, ruined purls and stitches, undid hours of Delores' therapeutic work in seconds. The scarf loosened then fell in pieces. Giovanni sawed at the ankle rope until the hemp gave way. Barrett remained on his side, shocked that his tongue remained intact. Giovanni helped him to his feet.

"Thank you," Barrett said, rubbing the circulation back into his wrists. "Thank you."

Giovanni the Mute nodded then pointed to the far side of the basement to another set of steps that led to a door. He made a shooing gesture with his hands. Barrett lurched in that direction, his feet numb from being bound, still stunned that a hero had, in fact, showed up and rescued him. When he reached the stairs, he turned back and watched the mute pitch pieces of scarf into the oven. The flames devoured them in an instant. Giovanni grabbed his uncle's chair next and smashed it against the concrete floor as if there was nothing he hated more. He didn't stop bashing it until it had splintered. He gathered the wood that was strewn around him and fed the kindling to the fire a piece at a time until it, like the victims it once held, no longer existed.

The Airstream crossed Lake Erie's western shore. It had passed over Oklahoma, Missouri, Indiana, and Ohio swollen with red Okie dust. As it traveled over the great lake, it drank as if unquenchable, its cold air pulling up warmer lake water as fast as it could. It slowed, heavy from the moisture that mixed with the dead farm dirt it carried.

In Canada, the Alberta Clipper had grown, engorged by warm water pulled from Superior, Michigan, and Huron. It lumbered eastward, burdened by the moisture it carried. It, too, was sluggish, close to bursting. It still had to cross Lake Erie and additional water would be drawn in.

The two weather systems soldiered on, churning towards each other.

Striker carried an armload of Jerry's clothes down the stairs with King trailing behind. Janet was waiting for him in his former library. She'd pulled her parents' clothes from the shelves and piled them on the bed. He placed his brother-in-law's sweaters on a bookshelf that had once held his Zane Grey novels.

"I wish you would let me help you, Fran. I'm pregnant, not an invalid," she said, refolding her father's shirts.

"You shouldn't be going up and down stairs," he answered, gathering a load of dresses from the bed. "This shouldn't take long."

"Why don't you call John? The two of you could move Jerry's things down here in no time."

"I tried. There was no answer at his apartment. He didn't show up last night at the station. Armbrewster had to play his part."

"Charles can act?"

"No, he was terrible."

"What happened to John?"

"He was complaining about a sore throat yesterday. Maybe he's sick in bed."

"He's always complaining about a sore throat, but he's never missed a broadcast."

"I'll go by his apartment later and check on him."

"You're a good friend, Fran, and a good husband. I appreciate you moving Jerry's things. I can't imagine him trying to get to the second floor on crutches."

"Having him and your parents switch rooms makes sense," he called, on his way back to the stairs for another load, King following. "I should have thought of it."

In Jerry's room, once the guest room and now his in-laws' room, Striker set the dresses on the bed next to a tangle of hangers. He draped a dress on one and hung it in the closet. King sat near the hissing radiator and watched his every move with forlorn eyes. Striker didn't have time for shuttling clothes. He heard his Remington Sixteen calling. He was behind on this week's *Dr. Dragonette* episode and needed to re-type another batch of scripts to send to other stations.

The front doorbell rang, and King howled then barked then howled some more. He didn't leave his warm radiator spot to investigate, however. "Some protector you are," Striker said, hanging the last dress.

He pulled Jerry's shirts from the dresser and heard Janet answer the door. Her mumbled conversation was drowned out by King's barking, which continued until the front door shut.

"You have a telegram," she said, as he made his way downstairs, King a pace behind.

"From whom?"

"I don't know. Open it."

He balanced the shirts on the newel post and tore open the beige Western Union envelope. "It's from a radio station in Detroit. WXYZ. They want to buy the *Manhunter* series."

"Thank God. We can use the money."

"There's more."

"What?"

Striker read:

"PLEASE WRITE UP THREE OR FOUR WILD WEST THRILLERS (STOP) INCLUDE ALL THE HOKUM (STOP) MASKED HERO (STOP) RUSTLER (STOP) KILLER PETE (STOP) GIRL TIED TO TRACKS (STOP) TWO GUN BANK ROBBER (STOP) MASKED MAN MUST BE PURE (STOP) WILL PAY TOP DOLLAR IF GOOD (STOP) LET ME KNOW YOUR THOUGHTS (STOP) SINCERELY (STOP) GEORGE W TRENDLE (STOP) WXYZ (END)"

"Top dollar!" Janet said, reading over his shoulder.

"He's only paying three bucks for the *Manhunter* episodes."

"Every penny helps. Do you have ideas for a western series?" she asked, taking the telegram from his hand.

Striker remembered the *Covered Wagon Days* broadcast from the night he was robbed. The memory of Barrett's voice resonated so clearly it was as if he was standing a foot away:

Old Ezra Holton was a prospector and with his wife had given the best years of his life in the endless search for gold in the west. Nothing but defeat had met him at every turn. He is just returning from the assay office to find his patient and tired wife Millie waiting for him at the cabin door…

Janet looked up from the telegram. "What is it? You're as pale as a ghost. Is your head bothering you again? Your cheek?" Janet stroked the scar with the back of her fingers.

"I'll send *Covered Wagon Days*. I'll rework it."

"Don't you want to write something new?"

"I'll put the masked hero in for him. He'll be the main character. It will be brand new when I'm done with it."

"What's Episode One about again? It's been so long."

"I'm sending Episode Ten. The one about the gold mine."

"You're starting in the middle?"

He took Janet's hand from his face and kissed it. "That episode has been haunting me lately. It's odd that Trendle wants a hero that's pure."

"Odd? Why?"

He reached in his back pocket and pulled out a folded paper. "I started working on a new character the other day. I couldn't see him before, but I think I do now. I didn't know anything about him. I was trying to work it out. I didn't know who he was or what he looked like or even his occupation, but I knew what he believed. It's Trendle's masked cowboy. I'm sure it is."

"Let me see."

Janet read the list aloud:

I believe that to have a friend, a man must be one.
That all men are created equal and that everyone has within
himself the power to make this a better world.
That God put the firewood there, but that every man
must gather and light it himself.
In being prepared physically, mentally, and morally to
fight when necessary for that which is right.
That a man should make the most of what equipment he has.
That "this government, of the people, by the people,
and for the people," shall live always.

That men should live by the rule of what is
best for the greatest number.
That sooner or later... somewhere... somehow... we must settle
with the world and make payment for what we have taken.
That all things change, but the truth, and the
truth alone lives on forever.
I believe in my Creator, my country, my fellow man."

"This is beautiful, Fran. I wouldn't change a word. It's like the Ten Commandments."

"More like a creed."

"The masked man's creed?"

"I think so. It's the purity Trendle's looking for. I'm certain I wrote it for him."

The white stallion reared in his imagination and Striker knew that if Trendle's masked hero believed in this creed, he was a worthy rider of the great horse.

"Your father taught you those. I can hear his voice. *'Make the most out of what you have, son'.* And my favorite—*What these crooks don't understand is that sooner or later they got to pay for what they've done."*

"I got the firewood one from Barrett. I guess the rest *are* from Pops. Say, he didn't call here, did he? I was supposed to phone him last night but didn't get a chance."

"No, and he didn't stop by to see the boys like he usually does. Call him now, make sure your mom is all right."

"I'm worried about him. He was acting strangely yesterday, talking how he didn't want to be a copper anymore."

"Your father will never retire. They'll have to push him out the stationhouse door first."

"That's what I thought, but now I don't know."

"Call him."

"I will. But there's something else."

"What?"

"I saw him talking to a dime store-gangster named Cavendish."

"I'm sure he talks to criminals every day. It's his job."

"Not like this. It looked like Cavendish was bossing him around."

"Your father would've cracked him with his billy club if he tried that."

"That's what I was waiting for. But he didn't do anything. He just sat there taking it. He looked broken."

"There must be some mistake."

"Yeah, and I think Pops made it."

"You better call him."

He gathered the shirts from the railing and carried them to his former library. After placing them on the shelf, he picked up the candlestick telephone and dialed his parents' house. His father answered on the second ring.

"Pops."

"Hello, Fran."

"How's Mom?"

"Struggling. She's sleeping now. Can you come and sit with her? I need to pick up more medicine at Van Slyke's."

"Sure. I'll be there in twenty minutes."

"Thanks."

"Pops, I..."

The Lieutenant hung up, as if the last thing he wanted was to talk to his son. Striker cradled the handset. He thought back to their conversation at The New Genesee and Pops' reluctance to arrest Cavendish. He'd arrested suspects on far less evidence in the past. How many times had he brought Lefty in for questioning when a dog was dognapped or a pocket picked? He couldn't shake the image of The Man with the Very Small Chin standing above his father, how small Pops looked, as if he was dissolving in his chair. Something nagged at Striker. It tugged at him, but he resisted. It murmured the answer, but he ignored it. His creed whispered—*Truth Lives On Forever*—but he refused to admit what he was certain of. He tried thinking of how to revise *Covered Wagon Days* for Mr. Trendle, but all thoughts of what a hero should be had vanished.

The Lieutenant hadn't returned from the pharmacy when Striker arrived. He checked on his mother. She was restless beneath the covers, fighting through fitful dreams. The bedroom air smelled stale and fetid. He raised the window an inch, then settled at the dining room table. He pulled *Covered Wagon Days*, Episode 10, *"Danger At The Gold Mine"* from his jacket and studied the script, wondering where the masked man could be woven into the plot. The urge for a cigarette overwhelmed him, but he fought it. The smoke wouldn't be good for his mother. He chewed his pencil instead.

He chewed for twenty minutes, the sharpened point never touching the page. Sometimes when he created a new character it was as if they'd descended from the stratosphere to stand before him. He could see how they dressed, hear how they spoke, their thoughts as distinct as a radio broadcast. His fingers would fly over The Remington, the dialogue flowing like taking dictation. His body would be alive, each neuron vibrating with creation's energy. But no masked man appeared. He had no sense of who he was, where he came from, nor the slightest idea of how he'd save old Ezra Holton. The white stallion remained riderless.

When Pops returned, he nodded to his son, and headed to the bedroom, the pharmacy bag bulging with promise. "Still sleeping?" Striker asked, when he returned.

"Her breathing's shallow."

"What's the doctor say?"

"If these new medicines don't work, I'll have to take her back to Albany."

"That's a long train ride."

"Maybe too long."

"I'll go with you."

The Lieutenant unbuttoned his police greatcoat but didn't remove it. "Sit down, Pops."

"I need to get to the station."

"Did you call Washington?"

The Lieutenant's cheek muscles began to pulsate. When he spoke, he looked past Striker. "An agent's supposed to call me back."

Striker studied him hard. That nagging feeling returned. "It's been a day. No one's called yet?"

"Washington works like that."

"It's an assassination."

"I'm sure I'll hear today."

"What about Lefty?"

"No leads. No body."

"You need to pick up Cavendish."

"That's the first thing on my list."

"Good," Striker said, wanting to believe him.

The Lieutenant's gaze shifted back to his son. He nodded toward the script spread across the dining room table. "What are you working on?"

"A new hero. A mysterious, masked cowboy on the side of the law. A radio station in Detroit wants me to write it."

"There's no such thing as heroes, Fran."

"Sure there are, Pops. You saved all those women and children."

"The city pays me to do that."

"Bull. You kept going back in until you had everyone out. A lot of cops wouldn't have done that."

"Maybe I was a hero for a minute. Then came the rest of my life. It'd be better if people forgot that I was brave once."

"You're the bravest guy I know. What's gotten into you?"

"Heroes exist only on radio, Fran. Guys like you make them up. And that's okay. Maybe kids need them to look up to, even if they aren't real. Hell, maybe adults need them, too. Make your masked cowboy someone like that. Bigger than life. Impossibly good. Someone who will never let people down."

"Someone like you."

"Write him better than me, Fran."

The mantel clock struck the hour. "Can you stay until Mrs. Martenelli arrives? I don't want your mother to be alone."

"Sure, Pops. But are you all right? You don't sound yourself."

"I'm fine. Just take care of your mother."

The Lieutenant checked his sick wife, smoothing her covers and kissing her forehead before buttoning his coat and heading into the cold. Striker sat at the table listening to him descend the stairs, heavy-stepped, as if burdened by unspeakable sins. He waited a moment, then crept to the front window, pulling back the curtain as Pops stepped from the porch. The chinless man leaned against his black Packard smoking a cigarette. He tossed the butt as Pops approached. Striker waited for his father to spin Cavendish around, slap handcuffs on his wrists, and hustle him away for questioning. But he wasn't spun around. Handcuffs weren't slapped into place. Striker's father stopped in front of The Man with the Very Small Chin, who began talking fast, index finger stabbing air. The Lieutenant bowed his head. Cavendish finished by taking a step forward and driving his finger into Pop's chest precisely where the mayor had once pinned a medal. He poked him a second time for good measure before turning, climbing into the Packard and racing away. From the bedroom, his mother cried out.

EPISODE 13

Boogaloo Bailey's Strange Tale

Striker chose a stool closest to The Colored Musicians Club's entrance. After seeing Pops with Cavendish for the second time, he needed a drink. The speakeasy was nearly deserted. The musicians—Scaredy-Cat Floyd, Boom-Boom Bennett, King Charlemagne, and all the rest—were home sleeping in the loving arms of wives and girlfriends, some of them their own. Pando the Pinsetter snored in the corner, his chair tipped against the wall and balanced on back legs, while Old Miss Shirley wiped glasses behind the bar. She set her rag down and toddled to Striker. She wore high heels and a navy-blue dress with a sailor collar. A kiss of red daubed her lips. Pearls, as old as the sea, hung from her neck.

"You look pretty, Miss Shirley," Striker said. He pushed his hat farther back on his head, revealing a chewed pencil tucked behind an ear.

"Thank you, handsome. It's a special day."

"Your birthday?"

"Better than a birthday. Better than Christmas. My Boogaloo's home. He's playing here tonight."

"He's back? He's alive? When did this happen?"

"This morning. There was a rap at my backdoor. I thought it was the chicken man bringing eggs, but it was my Boogaloo standing on the porch. He was holding a dented trumpet and nothing else. No suitcase, no bedroll, no bindle. Nothing but his old horn and his older self."

"Where's he been? Why'd he leave? Where'd he come from?" Striker asked, already weighing if Boogaloo's story could be worked into a radio play. So many Americans who'd lost jobs and farms were going on the bum, disappearing from previous lives. There may be an audience for a lone drifter traveling the countryside, saving those worse off than him—a hero with a past filled with heartbreak and loss—righting wrongs and settling scores for those unable. *The Rail Rider* would make a good title.

"Didn't give him a chance to say much with all the kissing I was doing. And to be Bible honest," Miss Shirley leaned closer, "the things he told me made no sense. I don't think Boogaloo's quite right in the head. He's telling crazy stories about things that couldn't have happened. He's making things up he thinks he's remembering. Dr. Foley rotted his brain."

"He remembered you. That's what counts."

"That's right. Came right to me. He remembers you, too, handsome. Asked about you straight away."

"Me? I've never met Boogaloo. He was long gone before I started hanging around speakeasies."

"Like I said," Miss Shirley tapped her temple with her forefinger. "He ain't right. But he was sure asking about you. I told him you come in late with the radio crowd, but sometimes you sneak in before everyone else when it's quiet to write. He said he'd find you."

"I can't imagine what we'd talk about."

"You'll know soon enough, but you won't believe it. What can I get you to drink, handsome?"

Striker wanted whisky but could only afford beer. She patted his hand and teetered to the taps, while he shook his last Lucky from the pack. Nothing made sense. How did Boogaloo know his name? What business could the old trumpeter have with him? Darker questions gnawed at him. How did Pops know The Man with the Very Small Chin? What business did *they* have together? He knew what it meant when coppers stopped doing their jobs and men like Cavendish and The Undertaker started giving the orders. He'd seen it all his life when beat cops looked away as torpedoes shook down Mr. Kaplan at his deli or Tamis at his grill. It was no mystery why Voelker's or The Colored Musicians Club or The Gypsy's house had never been raided. Palms were greased. Envelopes passed. Uniform pockets bulged. But not his father's. Never his father's.

Janet had been right. It was Pops' voice he'd heard when writing his creed. He'd been raised on his father's beliefs of God, country and truth. What better values to instill in his new masked hero? How had Pops lost those ideals? Why was he taking orders from The Man with the Very Small Chin?

Sickness seeped in. The kind that shattered faith and made him realize his father wasn't the man he thought he was. This contagion touched memory and forced him to question all those boyhood talks Pops had given about justice, duty, and America. It made him wonder what else he'd lied about. It made him wonder if his father would go to jail.

The near-empty bar was quiet. He heard a distant train whistle and thought of all the men on the bum racing to catch it, escaping the shame of repossessed dreams. Hobos weren't the only escape artists. Slattery and Pando disappeared into bottles. Barrett lost himself in the roles he played, pretending to be someone else. Striker wanted to flee to his imaginary world where a masked man fights for justice and wins, where truth always prevails, where people are not only created equally but treated so. This new world would contain no shades of gray, just black masks and white stallions, good guys and bad, those seeking justice and those avoiding it. He lit his smoke, sipped from a mug Miss Shirley had set in front of him. He pulled *Covered Wagon Days,* Episode 10, from his coat pocket and re-read the script, trying to see the story with keener eyes and to escape this world of fallen fathers, presidents about to be assassinated, and bills no honest man could pay.

He wanted to be aware of nothing but the pages before him. But the words were as hard to find as Ezra Holton's gold. Working on *Covered Wagon Days* felt different than writing or rewriting other radio plays. Barrett's rebroadcast with the spectral voices made this script phantasmal, but it was more than that. He sensed that the stakes were higher than they'd been with anything he'd ever written. Each new syllable would raise the ante, and he was unable to write a single one. Every noise—Pando's snoring or the unsteady clicking of Miss Shirley's heels—distracted him. The door opened and a cold gust fluttered pages. Striker held them in place as if they were trying to flee.

Boogaloo Bailey stood in the doorway.

Miss Shirley ran around the bar as fast as her heels would allow. She threw her arms around Boogaloo's neck, covering his face with kisses. Seeing him for the second time was as miraculous as the first. Striker studied the old man, trying to imagine a younger version of him and to recall if they'd ever met. Boogaloo was hunched and round shouldered, still suffering from lumbago and lame back. His clothes hung loose and baggy with traces of red dust in the creases. A swelling pouched under his eyes as if he hadn't slept since he'd disappeared. His lips were swollen, damaged as if struck by Slattery's jab. Striker was certain he'd never seen this man before.

Boogaloo whispered something in Miss Shirley's ear, and she pointed at Striker. She kissed him one last time and hurried as much as she could to brew him tea. Boogaloo ambled toward Striker with a slowness that rivaled Miss Shirley's, as if each step was his last. He carried a dented trumpet that looked from a different age. Striker stubbed out his cigarette.

"I'm Fran Striker," he said, offering his hand when Boogaloo drew close.

"Arthur Bailey," the horn man replied, his voice dry and raspy, as if he had traveled thousands of miles without water. "Everyone calls me

Boogaloo." He shook Striker's hand with surprising strength, as if his grip could powder bones.

"Have we met before?" Striker asked, mining for a scrap of recalled conversation.

"No," the old man said, swinging on to the stool next to Striker. "Not once."

"Miss Shirley said you were asking about me." Striker sipped his beer and licked the foam from his upper lip. "Seems a bit odd. You asking about me and we've never met."

"Odd don't even begin to describe it."

Miss Shirley shuffled to them, the tea sloshing over the brim to the saucer. She set the cup in front of Boogaloo and tea spilled from saucer to bar. "You start telling him yet?"

"I'm starting now," Boogaloo answered.

Miss Shirley wiped the bar with her rag. "I'll let you get to it," she said, then rolled her eyes at Striker to remind him that Boogaloo was crazy.

As Miss Shirley lurched away, Boogaloo Bailey pulled a pint of Doctor Foley's Pain Relief Medicine from his back pocket and poured a slug into his cup. "For my back," he said, with a wink. He offered Striker a medicinal boilermaker, but Striker declined.

"This is how it all started, you know. The disappearing, I mean," Boogaloo said.

He'd woken one Fourth of July with a thirst for Doctor Foley's Pain Relief Medicine. There was none in the house, which mystified him. He'd bought a fresh bottle the night before as neighborhood children celebrated the coming Independence Day by throwing firecrackers at each other and playing tag with railroad flares. He had left the bottle sitting on the kitchen table unopened and filled to the top as Dr. Foley had intended. The next day he brewed a cup of morning tea and reached for the pain relief medicine to give his breakfast a shot of healing, but the bottle was empty. That was the first strange thing that occurred that day, the first disappearance.

At the time, Boogaloo thought Miss Shirley had spilled out his medicine. She'd been known to pour his Foley's and corn whisky in the sink. Living with a teetotaling bartender is not easy, and great rows would shake the Bailey household when Boogaloo discovered that his hard-earned liquor had been tossed away like yesterday's Christmas. None of their past fights compared to the one they had that Fourth of July. Windows rattled. Plaster cracked. Neighbors swore they heard gunshots.

To make matters worse, it had begun to snow. The temperature had dropped seventy degrees, which was unusual even for Buffalo. Fat flakes came down in a curtain. It was impossible to see across the street. Picnics were canceled. Fireworks were called off. Instead of going to parks or beaches, families huddled around fireplaces and listened to patriotic marches on the radio.

But snow and cold couldn't stop Boogaloo Bailey's quest for Dr. Foley's Pain Relief Medicine. He donned his winter coat and earflap hat and yelled to Miss Shirley that he was walking to Van Slyke's Pharmacy for some Doctor Foley's and she better not try to stop him and damn sure better not touch it when he got back. He slammed the front door to let her know he meant business. He grabbed a rusty coal shovel and cleared a path to the sidewalk, cursing the weather and Miss Shirley. If she had left his Doctor Foley's alone, he'd have been inside warm and medicated instead of outside freezing and shoveling. The streets were almost deserted. No cars drove by except for passing circus wagons rolling into town for their annual Fourth of July show. No children were sledding. Only a fool would be out in such horrible conditions. And there he was.

The trees all had leaves on them, of course, and the weight of that heavy, wet snow combined with the full foliage snapped branches. It sounded like rifle shots when they broke. The heavy snow hurt his back, growing his need for the sweet relief found in every dose of Doctor Foley's. He threw down his shovel and set off walking as best he could through snowdrifts. Branches fell all around him.

He stopped to catch his breath. A rifle shot cracked. He looked up and saw a branch as thick as a leg falling straight down and it struck him in the middle of his forehead as if someone had aimed. Boogaloo didn't see only stars. He saw planets, comets, meteors, Saturn's rings and Jupiter's moons. Birds chirped, wind blew, trains whistled. Voices spoke to him, but he couldn't tell what they were saying.

He awoke alone in a freight car heading west with a blinding headache, soaked clothes, and no idea who he was or where he was going. He had no recollection of Miss Shirley, Fourth of July snow, or falling branches. He couldn't understand why he was wearing a winter coat and a furry hat in the summer. By this time, he was chugging along somewhere in the Midwest. It had to be a hundred degrees with no snow in the immediate forecast. As he pulled off his hat and shook off his coat, he discovered a dented trumpet resting next to him and decided that he must be a musician and that the horn belonged to him. He placed it to his lips and, sure enough, he knew how to play. But that's all he knew.

Boogaloo rode west, wondering at which stop he should leap from the train. Any place was as good as another to a man with no memory. Then an idea struck him that he should make his new home in Muskogee, Oklahoma. He didn't know where this notion came from and wondered if that was home. The idea grew stronger the further west he traveled until it was almost as if a voice was repeating the town's name in rhythm with the clacking rails. It was a voice he couldn't refuse. So, he leaped from the train as it pulled into Muskogee. He asked a passerby if there was a jazz club in town and was pointed to The Corn Bread Club where he landed a job playing his dented trumpet.

He called himself Octavius Brown because he thought it sounded like a horn player's name. He thought he'd live the rest of his days in Muskogee, making what he could from playing horn. Years rushed by but not a single recollection returned to him. Nothing about Muskogee was familiar and no one recognized him as kin. But the night Striker had walked home and was robbed of Slattery's rings, Boogaloo had also walked home after the Corn Bread Club had closed. The wind had howled that night like something wounded. Red dust swirled from dead farms, and it reminded him of another time and another place walking in foul weather, but that time it had been blowing snow, not dust. He couldn't remember exactly when or where this occurred, but the remembrance was powerful, the first memory he had in years. Then he heard a rifle shot and that sounded familiar, too. He couldn't shake the feeling that he'd lived this night before in a different year, a different town, maybe a different life. His old back hurt with recalled pain.

For years he'd rented a room from the Widow Jordan, a fine, wide-hip woman who sometimes laid with him at night, but her door was shut, and her light was off on this particular evening, so he went to his room and shook off the red dust that had coated him on his walk home. He flipped on the cathedral radio by his bed and heard a deep voice proclaim, *You're listening to WEBR. We Extend Buffalo's Regards.* He didn't think it odd that WEBR's radio signal could reach Muskogee, Oklahoma all the way from Buffalo, New York because at that moment he started to remember all he'd forgotten. He was Boogaloo Bailey! Memories of The Colored Musicians Club and Miss Shirley and Fourth of July snow fought for his attention. He remembered it all as if he'd gone back and lived it again. Then he heard Barrett's voice as WEBR broadcasted *Covered Wagon Days,* Episode 10, *Danger at the Gold Mine.*

He sat on the edge of his bed covered in dust like he'd been riding herd and listened to the program with an uneasiness spreading through him, certain that something was missing from the script. It needed a bigger story, a bigger villain. It most certainly needed a bigger hero. Someone like Bass Reeves, the finest federal lawman who'd ever worn the star and who was buried right there in Muskogee. One cannot live in Muskogee, Oklahoma and not learn about Bass Reeves.

Some say his ghost still haunts the town on a pale horse. Boogaloo had heard all the stories late at night when tales were told, and the whisky jug was passed. As a runaway slave, he stole a Confederate horse and rode west to Oklahoma, like all the other fugitives, deserters, and outlaws. He lived with the Creek and Seminole, learning their ways, their languages, how to hunt and track and live off the land. And how to shoot.

As good with either hand, rifle or pistol, they say he could shoot the left hind leg off a fly from a hundred yards away. He memorized every inch of the Indian Territory until he knew it like a cook knows his kitchen. After Emancipation, Hanging Judge Parker made Bass a U.S. Deputy Marshall to hunt and capture murderers, rapists, train robbers, bank robbers, and those who placed obstructions on railroad tracks. He was a deputy marshal for over thirty years, arrested three thousand outlaws and brought in twenty of them dead all shot in self-defense. The friend and protector of regular folk, he put the law above everything, once tracking down his own son and arresting him for murder. Boogaloo had heard all the stories about his Indian partner, the black mask he sometimes wore to disguise himself, how silver dollars became his calling card. You point out which way the rustlers rode, Bass threw you a silver dollar. You brush down his big white horse at night and feed him oats in the morning, you got a silver dollar. Sometimes he'd flip them over his shoulder when he rode out of town for anybody to find. A dollar was worth a lot of money back then. It was worth a fortune now.

Bass stood for goodness and fought for what was right, and nobody outside of Pawhuska, Muskogee, or other parts of the old Indian Territory had ever heard of him. Boogaloo was certain that if Bass Reeves had been a white man, he'd have been as famous as Wyatt Earp. He was even more certain that this radio show from Buffalo, New York needed Marshal Reeves the way a trumpeter needs a trumpet. The Indomitable Marshal! The one who let no guilty man go free! That's what this radio show needed!

The western ended and the radio announcer declared, *You've been listening to Covered Wagon Days, Episode 10, "Danger At The Gold Mine", written by Fran Striker. Starring Darcy Menifee, Jonathan Bliss, James Connolly, and John L. Barrett.*

The idea of returning to Buffalo and Miss Shirley and telling this Fran Striker about Bass Reeves jolted him as if electricity had surged from that cathedral radio into his core. This new idea grew so large it pushed him out of his room, then out of the Widow Jordan's house and into the windy night. He caught the first freight train heading east, heading home.

Boogaloo sipped his tea and made a face. He signaled to Miss Shirley to bring them whisky and leave the bottle. She served them with a scowl as Striker scribbled notes about white horses, Indian sidekicks, and black masks, wondering if any of Boogaloo's story was true, not caring if it was. Boogaloo downed his first whisky then poured another.

"Let me show you something," he said, wiping his damaged lips then leaning to one side on the barstool. He burrowed a hand deep in his pocket, fishing out an 1888 Morgan head silver dollar, and slapped it on the bar in front of Striker.

"Is that one of them?" he asked, picking up the coin.

"That's what they say. I was playing in The Corn Bread Club one night and I was blowing pretty good. This was before my lips got all swollen and weak and air started leaking out the sides. But that night I was something to hear. I was hitting notes that younger men didn't even know about."

Boogaloo had another drink then lowered his voice. "Don't tell Miss Shirley, but they sold more than corn bread at The Corn Bread Club. Upstairs was the working girls. But like I said, I was blowing real good that night, and one of the old girls—Simone, this ancient Frenchie from Canada who could talk dirty in more languages than Beelzebub—leaves her paying customer and comes down to hear me play. She sashays to the stage when the set ends, her perfume arriving before she does, her face all smiling. She says she hadn't heard a trumpet like mine since she was a girl working the Buffalo cathouses. Then she asks me if I ever played Buffalo, if we ever met before, maybe at The

Gypsy's place on Genesee Street. I can't remember playing anywhere on account of that branch bashing my melon, but she did *sound* familiar, especially later that night when she was whispering unnatural things in my ear—you don't need to tell that to Miss Shirley neither, son."

"I won't," Striker said, finding his whisky and tossing it back without thinking.

Boogaloo offed another red eye before continuing, "I tell her I *might've* played Buffalo because I might've and I *could've* met her at The Gypsy's house because I could've. But I couldn't remember anything. I *do* remember her saying that that Buffalo horn player was the best she'd ever heard, and I sounded like him, maybe even better. She reached between her bosoms and hands me that silver dollar, still warm and powdery from where it's been. She tells me that coin belonged to Bass Reeves, and I needed to hang on to that dollar for luck. I don't know how she got that dollar or how she knew it was Bass', but you don't ask questions when a woman hands you bosom money."

Boogaloo Bailey reached over and took the coin from Striker and held it by the edges, admiring Lady Liberty's profile as if for the last time. "I've been carrying this ever since. No matter how hungry I got or how depressed this depression depressed me, I never ever thought about spending Bass Reeves' silver dollar. Can't say it's brought me much luck, good or bad. Maybe that's its power—keeping misery from your doorstep."

Striker read his notes and chewed his pencil. "Don't be scared," Boogaloo said. "You can't see color on radio. You put old Bass in that story of yours and he'll do the rest. He's what's missing. That whole train ride here I kept hearing that preacher voice saying, *You've been listening to Covered Wagon Days, Episode 10, "Danger At The Gold Mine," written by Fran Striker* like a song stuck in my head. I know it was you I was supposed to tell about Bass Reeves."

Boogaloo Bailey put the silver dollar on the bar and pushed it in front of Striker. "That's yours now. You're the one that needs Bass

Reeves' help. I wouldn't give away my bosom money if I didn't know *that* was true."

"I can't take this, Boogaloo. You've had it forever."

"My time's winding down. Young men need luck, not old horn players."

Striker picked up the coin, studying one side then the other, before thanking Boogaloo and dropping it in his breast pocket. Who didn't need a little luck these days? Or an extra dollar?

Boogaloo Bailey refilled their glasses. "How you gonna play if you keep drinking that devil water, Boogaloo?" Miss Shirley yelled from the end of the bar.

"Don't you worry, honey," Boogaloo said, and tossed back the Red Eye. "Tonight I'll sound like I'm blowing in Gabriel's band."

But soon the corn whisky mixed with Doctor Foley's Pain Relief Medicine and his eyes glassed over, and his swollen mouth grew slack. His body sagged as if he was seeping air. Striker asked more questions about Bass Reeves—What was his horse's name? Whatever happened to his son?—but Boogaloo never responded. The old trumpeter sat motionless except for his tongue, which snaked out every minute or so and probed his upper lip, testing for numbness, hoping for feeling.

Striker pushed his beer and whisky aside and turned over the script. He licked his pencil tip, thought for a moment, then wrote:

Throughout the entire west, in those turbulent days, circulated stories of a masked rider. A picturesque figure that performed deeds of the greatest daring…A modern Robin Hood…Seen by few, known by none. Few men dared to defy this man. And those that did…lost.

Striker read then reread what he'd written, certain that he'd gotten it right, but then no more words would come.

Word spread the great Boogaloo Bailey was back in town. Patrons filed into The Colored Musicians Club. They came alone and in pairs, in groups of all sizes. Voices and laughter, the scraping of chairs and barstools, clinking glasses and match strikes filled the speakeasy, waking Pando the Pinsetter. He settled in his chair, took in the growing crowd, and scratched his chest with both hands. He saw Striker at the bar and waved.

"Hi-yo, Striker."

Striker waved back. His tie was loosened, his jacket off, his sleeves rolled to elbows. Starch had left his shirt hours ago, giving way to wrinkles. He looked like a man who'd worked hard and accomplished much, but still only forty-six new words were on the page. He'd described the masked rider as picturesque, but he couldn't picture him. Not one deed of great daring came to mind. There was still Danger at the Gold Mine, but he had no idea how to alleviate it. As soon as he tried to enter his imaginary gun-fighting world, this world's problems hurtled toward him, freezing his pencil above the page. He tried to conjure Trendle's masked man, but images of Pops with Cavendish rose instead. Grief poured through him like bullet holes. Words that had always flowed were now dammed. He pressed fists to eyes, imploring them to see. Each time this new hero blurred into focus, The Man with the Very Small Chin would appear, and jab him away with his index finger.

Striker slammed his bite-pocked pencil onto the bar. He jerked his tie tight, shoved down his sleeves, and grappled into his jacket. He forced the script in his inside pocket, vowing not to think about it for the rest of the night, but it wouldn't let him. It was as if his imaginary world and real world were wrestling in his pocket. He pressed his palm against the outside of his suitcoat near his heart, pushing the script tighter against Bass Reeve's lucky silver dollar, trying to hold warring worlds in place.

He ordered another beer he couldn't afford and drank without pleasure. The hour grew late. Black musicians arrived carrying their instruments. They were thirsty from playing to white audiences in white clubs where they weren't allowed to drink at the bar. One-by-one they made their way to Boogaloo, who still sat next to Striker. He was alert but still drinking whisky at an alarming pace. Some musicians patted Boogaloo's back when they came over, others shook his hand, but all welcomed him home, telling the old man they couldn't wait to hear his horn.

"They're all here to see you," Striker shouted, above the crowd.

"They shouldn't have come."

"What?" Striker scooted his stool closer.

"I said they shouldn't have come," Boogaloo repeated, louder, angrier, his breath a whisky bouquet.

"Why? This is your night. Your homecoming. People have been waiting years to hear you play again. Most of us thought we'd never get the chance."

Boogaloo's chin trembled.

"What's wrong?" Striker asked.

"Nothing," he said.

"You can tell me."

He shook his head, freeing a tear.

"Maybe I can help."

His body quaked, starting at his calves, working upward as if something was boiling to the surface.

"It's going to be all right. Tell me."

Boogaloo's chest then shoulders vibrated as he battled to keep the truth inside. From across the bar, champagne popped and as the wine spilled down the bottle's neck, the truth spilled from him. "I can't play," he said, and his shaking stopped.

"Course, you can. You're Boogaloo Bailey. Best there ever was."

"Not no more. I'm not even Octavius Brown. I can't play for shit. Broke my lips in Muskogee," he said, pointing to his mouth.

"Lips can't break. They're lips."

"They do. Least mine did. Got pain in the bottom one. Can't feel nothing in the top. High notes are flat, and I can't hold them for

Christ. I play like a goddamn beginner. Look at this." Boogaloo pouted as if pressing against an imaginary mouthpiece. His lips trembled like failing muscles. "See that? They got the palsy. Weak as hell."

"What are you going to do?" Striker asked, the crowd still pouring in, fighting for spots near the stage. "Everyone's here to see you."

"That's what I've been sitting here trying to figure out."

"What'd you come up with?"

"I'm thinking of sneaking out that backdoor and disappearing again. Anybody asks, tell them I went out for some Doctor Foley's like last time. Then I'll hop a train and go somewhere where they've never heard of Boogaloo Bailey or Octavius Brown. Maybe up to Montreal to see if all them Frenchie women talk dirty. Don't know how I'll make eating money since I can't play, but I guess they got soup kitchens in Canada, too."

"You'll break Miss Shirley's heart," Striker said. "She waited all those years for you. She never gave up hope. She loves you."

"I know it. And I love that damn argumentative woman, too. That's why I've been sitting here trying to drink enough so I can forget her. Once that happens, I can leave without a guilty conscience."

But Boogaloo Bailey hadn't drunk fast enough. Boom-Boom Bennett had pushed Scaredy-Cat Floyd on stage, and Scaredy-Cat now stood at the microphone with eyes clenched, clutching the mic stand as if throttling an enemy. He introduced Boogaloo as Buffalo's best horn player, the man who put the sass in the brass, the legend who'd disappeared in the snow and was brought back by the wind. "Ladies and gentleman, the one, the only—Boogaloo Bailey!"

Hands clapped. Feet stomped. Pando the Pinsetter stuck fingers in his mouth and whistled until nearby ears ached. Beer mugs were banged against the bar as if they'd done something wrong. Charles Armbrewster held his skinny arms over his head and knocked his drumsticks together in a wooden salute. Boogaloo's name was shouted from every corner of the club, and Old Miss Shirley smiled until she looked young again. Boogaloo's tears were mistaken for ones of joy.

"You don't have to play," Striker said, grabbing the old man's elbow. "Give a little speech, tell them you're not feeling well. Tell them you're tired from traveling. Tell them anything."

A strange look brightened Boogaloo's eyes. He cocked his head as if listening intently. He nodded once, then again, his resolve growing with the swelling applause. "I got one last song in me," he said, as if repeating what had been whispered to him. "I know I do."

"Your mouth looks worse than before. All that whisky must have aggravated things. Tell them you're sorry. Tell them you're grateful. Announce your retirement."

Boogaloo stood, his head tilted away from Striker as if still listening to instructions. He waved to the crowd with a faraway look. Hands clapped louder. Feet stomped harder. Beer mugs shattered against the bar and Pando whistled like a New York Central locomotive rounding a bend. Boogaloo Bailey grabbed his horn and made his way to the stage. Hands stopped clapping long enough to pound his shoulder as he passed. Younger musicians reached out to touch his trumpet, hoping magic would rub off. Boogaloo's tears landed on his horn. His broken lips quivered.

Scaredy-Cat Floyd's eyes were wide and sparkling as he helped Boogaloo on stage. Boogaloo forced his numb mouth into a smile as the applause continued. He stood for a moment, soaking in the cheers, certain he'd never hear them again. He screwed up his courage and spoke into the microphone. "Let's see what this old horn can do."

The crowd gave one last roar then quieted as Boogaloo took a deep breath and raised his trumpet. Then he froze, turned his trumpet sideways to inspect it, and frowned. "I forgot the damn mouthpiece." The audience laughed as Boogaloo searched one pocket then the other, thinking it was part of his act, a showman's ploy to build anticipation. "All my years I never once got on stage without the mouthpiece shoved in. Could've sworn I did. Must be getting old," Boogaloo mumbled, every word picked up by the microphone. He rechecked his pockets.

Striker searched on the bar and under the stool where Boogaloo had been sitting, but the mouthpiece was nowhere to be found. Pando watched as a mouthpiece rolled towards him. It stopped at his feet. He reached for it.

"Here it is!" he cried, holding the mouthpiece so it caught the light from the ceiling fixtures.

The crowd chanted Pando's name as he made his way to the stage, still holding the mouthpiece aloft so all could look down and see. Scaredy-Cat Floyd lifted Pando by the hips, and he handed the piece to Boogaloo.

"Thank you, Little Man," he said.

But it wasn't Boogaloo's mouthpiece. Boogaloo's trumpet was tarnished and dull, while this mouthpiece was bright and polished, more gold than brass. It felt different than his own—smoother, softer, already warmed by invisible lips.

"It ain't mine, but it'll work," he said, his hands shaking. He fit the mouthpiece into the leadpipe and felt a vibration ripple through brass and brace.

Striker imagined the coming seconds: Boogaloo raising the horn, his deep breath, his lips forming incorrectly to send flat and lifeless notes into the world. The audience would gasp. Some would laugh or cough in embarrassment. A few would mutter disbelief. Maybe Boogaloo Bailey would try again, smiling apologetically as if it was a one-time mistake before creating more stillborn sounds. By morning, the whole city would know Boogaloo Bailey could no longer play, was officially washed up, a fraud, an off-key joke, another man who didn't live up to his legend.

But in reality, Boogaloo raised the horn to his swollen mouth. He took a deep breath and pressed his lips against the strange mouthpiece. Instead of his lips forming around the mouthpiece, the mouthpiece formed around his lips. It kissed them and sealed so tightly no air could escape. His cheeks puffed, and he produced one crystal note.

Then another. Then a string of notes, each one more perfectly shaped than the previous. The sounds coming from the trumpet bewitched the audience. No one whispered or clapped. No other musician joined him on stage. No drinks were poured or served or ordered. No coughs coughed. No feet shuffled. No toes tapped. The audience was as still as the Blochers and Ke-Mo Sah-Be and all the other Forest Lawn residents. Striker was the most stunned of all. How was this possible? Even the wind outside The Colored Musicians Club paused, as if no other sound was worthy of occupying the same space as what was blowing from Boogaloo's horn.

Boogaloo's eyes were squeezed tighter than Scaredy-Cat Floyd's had ever been. The old trumpet player was, in fact, terrified. He was hearing music that he'd never heard before, music that he wasn't playing. The buttons moved up and down by their own volition. The valves struck and pulled the balls of Boogaloo's fingers as needed. The mouthpiece controlled his wind, sucking air from his tired lungs sometimes long after his breath had given out. The valve casing pressed into his left palm and the finger ring hooked his pinky, ensuring the runaway horn wouldn't fly from his hands.

The rhythmic choices the trumpet made startled him in their daring. The phrasing swung harder than Slattery in his prime. The audience listened mesmerized as the trumpet lingered in the middle register, the sound brilliant, full, and rounded. Without warning, the horn sprinted up the scale, the notes so bright that eyes were shielded, so sharp that ears were covered. High notes soared to dizzying altitudes and Boogaloo fought to remain on the ground. The mouthpiece sucked more air, forcing it out of the bell as if it had stolen his final breath. The volume and vibration increased, and the heavy light fixture suspended above Boogaloo's head swayed. The music grew more piercing, and Boogaloo worried about capillaries breaking and ear drums bursting.

The trumpet played on, the pendant light now swinging like a pendulum. Loose screws fell to the stage one after the other, hitting the ground like ejected rifle casings. The canopy slid down the rod. Wires frayed until the last filament gave out and the brass light plunged from the ceiling in a firework of sparks, falling at a greater speed than gravity dictated. The milk glass globe exploded in a million shards when it struck Boogaloo's skull, white fragments of bone and glass fell around him like summer snow.

The crowd gasped.

Striker leapt from his stool.

Miss Shirley screamed then fainted, cracking her head against the bar. The wind outside swirled, clockwise then counter-clockwise, the sound turning to song. Inside, half the audience rushed to the stage while the other half sprinted to Miss Shirley, all trying to help. Pando hustled downstairs to flag down a copper while King Charlemagne yelled for an ambulance.

But it was too late—too late for coppers, too late for ambulances, and much too late for anyone to ride in and save the day. Boogaloo Bailey and Old Miss Shirley were already gone. They'd left The Colored Musicians Club together, soaring higher, pulled by Boogaloo's last held note, an F over triple-high C. They saw stars, planets, comets, and meteors and were amazed. They gathered speed, the Earth and jazz club far below. Holding hands, they hurtled past Saturn's rings, Jupiter's moons, and other wonders so beautiful they couldn't be named. Shirley and Boogaloo laughed, marveling at it all, then they brightened to kindred light as trumpets heralded their arrival.

EPISODE 14

The Bleeding Sky

The Airstream and Alberta Clipper collided above downtown Buffalo, above brothels and churches, soup kitchens and speakeasies, above the dead in Forest Lawn and the living on Genesee Street. The two systems combined into one giant phenomenon. The huge storm stalled over the city, blocking the sun. Water vapor from Superior, Michigan, and Huron mixed with Lake Erie's and was infused with vermilion Oklahoma dust. Blood-red water molecules ascended through freezing air and crystalized into a million-billion hexagons. Dendrites pushed outward like arms through sleeves, forming unique ice crystals the shade of rosebuds. The snowflakes fell as if the sky was bleeding.

Pando the Pinsetter was the first to notice the red snow. He stopped in front of The New Genesee Restaurant and held out his arm, watching flakes cover his jacket. He'd been drinking with purpose since joining Slattery on his bender but had stopped when Boogaloo and Miss Shirley died. The trumpeter's final note still rung in his ears. The sweats and shakes came and went like the moon-driven tide, but the hallucinations were something new. He thought he was imagining the red snow, just as he'd sworn he saw a white stallion galloping toward Granger Place. Sometimes he imagined the face of the man he'd killed peering at him above a snowbank, or reflected in a mirror, or staring from the far end of the bowling alley. Whisky withdrawal played tricks like that.

Sober Buffalonians, however, were wandering hatless and coatless from homes and businesses to stare at the sky or point to the crimson-dusted street, convincing Pando the hued flakes were as real as his arm. He tipped his head and stuck out his tongue, hoping the snow tasted like wine. The bitter flavor of foreclosed farms landed on his lips, and he spat it away.

"What the hell?" Striker said, coming out of The New Genesee. He held out his hand, studying the red flakes landing on his glove. Behind him, in the restaurant window, Tamis made the sign of the cross Orthodox fashion, right to left, then hurried back to the counter as if the end of days had inconveniently begun during the breakfast rush.

"Hi-yo, Striker. So, you see it, too?" Pando asked.

"Why's it red?"

"Don't know. It's like the goddamn angels slit their wrists."

"There must be a scientific explanation." Striker thought back to his chemistry days at the University of Buffalo and all he'd learned or still remembered. He ran through the periodic table and scientific equations but couldn't come up with a better hypothesis than hemorrhaging seraphs or Dr. Dragonette's diabolical weather machine.

Children abandoned meager breakfasts to throw snowballs, delighting in the snow's strange color. Cars pulled to curbs. Drivers stood on running boards and scratched their heads, their smiles wide and dumb. Church bells rang all over the city, calling parishioners to prayer, in case the apocalypse was upon them. The bell in St. John's steeple clanged across Colonial Circle. Red snow accumulated on General Bidwell's statue, giving the impression that both he and his steed had been mortally wounded.

Mirela stumbled by wearing her sleeveless black dress with the matching lace shawl, the mix of body odor and brandy strong enough now to turn heads and melt ice. She ignored Striker, but he felt his scar come to life as she neared. "What does this mean?" she muttered, wringing her hands, her eyes wilder than her hair.

A slender hobo shuffled toward Striker and Pando. He wore black high-top bowling shoes stolen from Voelker's All-Night Bowling Emporium, patched trousers held by a length of rope, and a navy pea coat with sleeves stopping short of his wrists, the skin pink from exposure. The bum's tattered hat was pulled low and a long scarf, dung-colored and mothball smelling, covered his face. He stopped in front of Striker.

"Sorry, pal," Striker said, reaching in his pocket for Luckies. "I'm a little light myself." He offered the man a cigarette.

"Fran," the hobo whispered, tugging down his scarf. "It's me."

"Barrett?"

Barrett pulled the scarf back into place. "Keep your voice down. Call me Stanley."

"Why are you dressed like that? Why do I have to call you Stanley?"

"Yeah, what the hell is going on?" Pando echoed.

"I'm in disguise. Let's get off the street before anyone spots me."

Barrett nudged Striker towards the restaurant, Pando following behind. They sat at a table away from the other diners. Barrett faced the door, his head jerking towards it each time its bell rang. Striker looked toward the door every time it opened, too, hoping it was Pops, dreading if it was.

"Where've you been?" Striker asked. "Armbrewster has been covering for you. He's terrible."

"The worst," Pando agreed.

"And Celestina's been calling the radio station. She thinks you have another girl."

Before Barrett could answer, Tamis came over to take their order. He pointed at the disguised radio actor. "If you no money, you get out."

"It's okay, Tamis," Striker said. "Stanley's with me. Three coffees to start."

Barrett wanted chamomile tea with manuka honey to soothe his throat but kept his scarf up and his mouth shut, fearing his voice would give him away. Tamis grunted, glared at him, and mumbled under his breath about bums and Malakas all the way to the coffee urns.

"You look frozen," Striker said.

"I am. I'm afraid to go home, to drive my car. I've been wandering back alleys. Last night I stayed at the YMCA. There wasn't any heat."

"Why are you doing this? What's going on?"

Barrett told Striker and Pando everything about his kidnapping from the time he was shoved in the back of Don Stefano's Pierce Arrow until Giovanni the Mute had cut him free. The conversation paused when Tamis brought their coffee. Pando pulled a bottle of Foley's and poured some in his cup, telling himself that it was medicine so he was still technically on the wagon. Barrett pulled his scarf down, sipped his coffee, then re-covered his face.

"You need to get out of town," Striker said, resuming the conversation. "Get Celestina and make a run for it."

"I'm afraid to go near her. They may be watching her apartment. I don't want to put her in danger. I need to talk to your old man."

Striker stared into his cup. "I wouldn't tell Pops anything."

"He needs to arrest them. The Don, Maranto, The Man with the Very Small Chin. The whole dirty lot of them."

Striker, a magician with words, struggled to produce any. "You can't tell Pops because I think he's working with them. I've seen Cavendish giving him orders. Twice."

"Holy shit," said Pando.

"I don't believe it," Barrett said. "Not your father. He was the last honest cop."

"He's not looking for Lefty. He didn't question Cavendish. I'm sure he never called the Feds about the assassination. Now he's taking orders from Cavendish? What else could it be?"

Barrett uncovered his face. "Jesus, both our fathers work for The Undertaker. What do we do, Fran?"

"You need to get out of town. Go on the lam. The Undertaker'll cut out your tongue if he catches you."

"And cook it in his oven," Pando added.

"I'm not leaving. You can't save Roosevelt and find Lefty by yourself. You're not some lone hero."

"You need to be on the first train headed west," Striker argued.

"What you need," Pando said, sitting back in the chair, "is a goddamn gun." He reached in his pocket, slapped a double-barrel Derringer on the table, and pushed it toward Barrett.

"Is it real?" Barrett asked, picking up the gun, which fit in his palm.

"Real as anything I see these days. Its granddaddy killed Lincoln."

"I can't believe this would kill anything. It weighs nothing."

"It'll kill all right, except when it jams."

"It jams?" Barrett asked.

"Not all the time. When it does fire, you got to be close, though. No more than seven feet away. And you only have two shots. You got to make them count. Stick it in your pocket until you need to stick it in someone's ear."

"It's not very intimidating," Striker said, who wrote about long-barrel .45's, snub-nose .38's, Tommy guns with fifty-round drums. A Derringer was a whisper of a gun.

"Christ, it doesn't need to be intimidating. Nobody'll even know you're holding it. You can outdraw Billy The Kid if it's already in your hand."

"Is it loaded?" Barrett asked.

"Sure it is. Won't shoot if it's not."

"How much do you want for it?"

Pando waved the question away. "Nothing. I got ten more like it at home and a couple more stashed at the bowling alley. And all the bullets you will ever need. Buy me a drink or two next time you see me and we'll call it even. Maybe three drinks. Four will do. Wait. Damn it. I'm not drinking no more. Buy me breakfast, I guess." He poured more Foley's into his cup, filling it to the brim.

"Thanks, Pando." He slipped the pea shooter in his pea coat then smoothed his mustache into place.

"Why do you have so many guns?" Striker asked.

Pando's eyes grew dark. He made sure no one was in earshot. "A long time ago, when I was a young pinsetter, I killed a man," Pando said, his sentence falling heavy on the table. He felt unburdened, as if he was about to float toward the ceiling. He'd never spoken those words aloud.

"So those stories are true," Barrett said, adjusting his scarf.

"What'd you hear?"

"I heard you killed a man in a card game. He was holding aces and eights," Striker said.

"I heard you killed a bartender with your bare hands when you were drunk," Barrett said.

"I hear you kills your wife," Tamis said, arriving again at their table. He made a slashing motion across his throat, then passed out breakfast menus. Today's specials: *Spinitch Omlet, Buddermilk Pankakes, Orange Jews.*

"Those are all damn lies. I didn't kill any bartenders or wives or circus clowns," Pando said, the words hard to get out. "I killed a lone ranger."

"A lone ranger," Striker repeated.

"What do you mean?" Barrett asked, his voice muffled by his muffler. "A forest ranger?"

Pando pulled at his collar, the sweats returning. "A Texas Ranger. Retired."

Striker pulled *Covered Wagon Days*, Episode 10 from his pocket, and turned pages, scratching out *Marshal* and replacing it with *Ranger.*

Pando was born and raised in Loco, Texas. He worked at The Little Loco Gaming Arcade setting pins and juggling between frames to earn extra cash. Duckpins and duckpin balls were his specialty, though he was known to juggle empty whisky bottles, as well. People liked seeing a juggling midget and would throw coins, sometimes silver dollars, in appreciation. Except the lone ranger.

No one knew the retired ranger's name or where he hailed from, but he'd come in every Tuesday to bowl by himself. He wasn't on a team and didn't want to play anyone. He spoke little and smiled less, his sunbaked face mean, cracked. It was never clear if he hated midgets, jugglers, or the combination of the two. Instead of throwing coins at Pando, the ranger threw bowling balls. As soon as the last pin fell, Pando would scamper to reset pins and each time, the lone ranger would whip a ball like he was trying to pick up a spare. Pando would dive in another lane or jump over the ball to avoid being struck. This happened between every frame, every Tuesday, every time.

One night, Pando had enough. He was setting pins and not paying attention and the ranger clipped him good, sending him flying. In a raging fury, Pando picked up the seven pin with both hands and launched it at him. It flew end-over-end like a tomahawk and hit the ranger square between the eyes, knocking him off his feet, his head striking the alley floor like melon against brick. Pando was certain he'd killed the retired lawman and ran from of The Little Loco, leaving the lone ranger for dead. He hopped the first train that came along, but three days later a railroad detective caught him in a box car and tossed him out.

Luckily, The Hozenflogen Traveling Circus had set up tents not far from the tracks and Mr. Hozenflogen hired him immediately as their former juggler had met his untimely demise by drunkenly wandering into Larry The Three-Legged Lion's cage. He did not wander out.

Pando loved performing from the first time he stepped in the ring. He loved all of it—the crowd, the applause, the smell of popcorn and greasepaint. He juggled everywhere and on everything—on The Donkey-Face Boy's shoulders, on The Elephant Lady's lap, even while riding a beautiful black stallion oddly named Silver. He stayed with the Hozenflogens for two years, traveling across the south and up and down the east coast until Mr. Hozenflogen caught him doing more than juggling on top of Mrs. Hozenflogen, a big round woman with a bigger libido.

He was thrown from the moving circus wagon as it pulled into Buffalo and landed in snow, which confused him—considering it was the Fourth of July. Pando came to a stop on Elmwood Avenue right at Old Man Voelker's feet holding his hard duckpin in one hand and Mrs. Hozenflogen's *Bustenhalter* in the other.

"*Bustenhalter?*" Striker asked, looking up from his radio script. Silver was now written as the white stallion's name.

"Brassiere, and not a small one either. I still have it. I can show you. As the circus wagon rolled away, Mr. Hozenflogen pitched all my stuff out the back yelling like a loon—no offense to your mom, Barrett."

"None taken," Barrett said, through his scarf.

"By the time that wagon got to the corner," Pando continued, "Elmwood Avenue was littered with small clothes, duckpins and bowling balls stuck in the snow. I didn't understand what Hozenflogen had been yelling about, but Old Man Voelker translated the German for me. He was screaming all the ways he was going to kill me if he ever saw me again—shoot me, stab me, feed me to Larry The Lion. Ever since then I've carried a little Roscoe on me," he said, nodding at Barrett, "in case I ever bump into Hozenflogen and he wants to make good on his threat or if that lone ranger somehow survived and tracks me down. I sure would like to bump into Mrs. Hozenflogen again, though. She was something," he said, remembering his corpulent lover's softness.

"And Voelker hired you?" Barrett asked. "You're lying in the street without a stitch of clothes, and he *hired* you?"

Pando's sweats and the shakes were subsiding. "He picked up one of the duckpins, brushed the snow from it, and asked where I was from, if I was a bowling man. I told him I was a juggler *and* a pinsetter. That impressed him. He'd never met a juggling, pinsetting midget from Loco, Texas before, like it was a rare thing. Or maybe he felt sorry for me. Either way he offered me a job and I've been setting pins at Voelker's ever since. That old man's always been good to me."

"Ever had to use it?" Barrett asked, reaching in his pocket to make sure the Derringer was still there amongst the tissues and Pine Brothers Glycerin Throat Drops.

Pando's complexion ashed. "I fired it for the first time at a man the other day."

"Who?" Barrett asked.

"I shot at The Man with the Very Small Chin."

"Cavendish!" Barrett exclaimed.

"Why?" Striker asked.

The pinsetter gave way with the pretense of drinking coffee and chugged Foley's straight from the bottle. "I'd been drinking with Slattery all night, and we were going to catch a train to meet a prostitute in Poughkeepsie."

"The one with hair like butter," Striker said, never forgetting a detail.

"Or was it Piscataway?" Pando mumbled, his eyes unwinding to a faraway stare.

"She had a sister for you," Barrett prompted.

Pando shook his head, clearing gray fog and other colored mists that clouded his brain. "Slats said she'd be perfect for me. She was on the short side and would do anything for a silver dollar. We were hurrying, but the snow was deep. I couldn't keep up. Slattery was afraid we'd miss the train. So, he carried me, but he'd been boozing and kept dropping me on my head. It was like being thrown off the circus wagon every ten feet. The wind was blowing hard the last time he dumped me. I couldn't see a goddamn thing. It was a true white-out. When the wind stopped, Slattery was gone."

"Where'd he go?"

"Jumped a train, I guess. Then this big white horse ran by."

"Silver," Striker said.

"Silver was black. This one was huge and white and running hard toward men shoveling the tracks. It headed right for this one poor bastard, and I thought for sure he was going to be trampled."

"What happened?" Barrett asked.

"The wind picked up and blinded me again. When it stopped, the horse was gone, disappeared like Slattery. I'm pretty sure it was a hallucination. Had to be."

"What about The Man with the Very Small Chin?" Striker asked. "When did you shoot at him."

"I saw him pushing Lefty ahead of him, covering him with an old-time gun the size of my leg. They stopped in front of a coal car. He spun Lefty around. They were shouting at each other. I couldn't make out what they were saying. The wind swallowed their words. Then The Man with the Very Small Chin knocked Lefty to the ground. Lefty raised his right arm and pointed his forefinger and pinky at that chinless bastard and jabbed at him three times."

"He cursed him," Striker said, his scar changing color from gray to blue to amaranth.

"I don't know what he did, but The Man with the Very Small Chin didn't like it. He took a step back then shot Lefty through the heart. One shot. Bang," Pando said, his finger and thumb forming a gun.

"That's when you shot at him?" Barrett asked.

"I was too far away, and the wind was blowing. I fired both rounds but only hit snow. You couldn't hear the shots with all that wind. The chinless man didn't even look around. He slung Lefty over his shoulder like a sack of onions and disappeared into the storm. I ran the other way as best I could through the drifts. I didn't stop until I found a speakeasy. I kept drinking after that but stopped when Boogaloo and Miss Shirley died. I'm back on the wagon for good, and I don't mean circus wagon neither," he said, and took a slug of Foley's.

"Jesus, look outside," Striker said, his voice loud enough to make all the diners turn toward the window. Behind the counter, Tamis made the sign of the cross again.

Snow was falling in a solid red veil, enveloping the restaurant, making the other side of Genesee Street impossible to see.

Barrett pulled his scarf down and stood. "The sky's bleeding."

Pando, heavy-lidded as the Foley's kicked in, belched in agreement.

"The sky is bleeding," Barrett repeated, his powerful voice faint and faraway as if being broadcast from The Buffalo State Asylum for The Insane.

"It's not blood," Striker said. "It just looks like it for some reason."

"Mother told me to see Danek when the sky bleeds."

Striker rose from his chair and stood next to his friend, both staring out the front window. "Why?"

"She said he knows where all the bodies are."

"I guess he would. That's his job."

"Cavendish killed Lefty. Danek is Cavendish's uncle."

Striker felt as if someone was shaking him awake. "If Cavendish had a body to hide…"

"…he'd go see his uncle, the gravedigger," Barrett said.

"He knows where the bodies are. He knows where Lefty is. Lefty may still have a ring. We got to talk to Danek."

"Are you sure The Lieutenant wouldn't go with us? Who knows what my father'll do?"

"Who knows what *my* father will do? It's just us. We're alone on this." Striker threw his last coins on the table for the coffees and grabbed his hat, dizzy at the thought of crossing Swan Lake again. "You coming, Pando?"

The red snow was falling sideways, the sky an open wound. "Fuck no," the pinsetter said, and nodded off, dreaming of lying again in Mrs. Hozenflogen's arms where it was safe and soft and snow was always colored white.

Barrett covered his face with the dung-colored scarf. Striker pulled up his collar, and the pair charged outside while the rest of the city took shelter. Mothers had dragged children indoors, pulling them by their ears, worrying the red snow was poisoned and forced them to take Epsom baths. The devout prayed in churches and formed lines outside confessionals, certain Judgment Day was imminent. Ragged, less religious men who had wandered into St. John's and Our Lady of Black Rock from flop houses and shelters, eyed collection boxes for easy pickings and scanned the congregation for open purses. Timid coppers, the ones who were never awarded medals, stayed back at the stationhouse drinking coffee and eating fried cakes, convinced the colored snow was dangerous.

Striker and Barrett sprinted down the deserted street, side-by-side, arms pumping, catching each other when one slipped or the other skidded. They ran towards Barrett's car, hidden in an alley the previous night. The Buffalo they dashed through had become an experimental painting: curbs, roofs, railroad tracks—all red. Sidewalks, avenues, powerlines—red, red, red. Striker, breathing hard from endless Luckies, knew the world he'd create in his next science fiction script would be as red and strange as this one. If he wrote again.

He'd hardly written a word since he saw Pops taking orders from Cavendish. It was as if heroes no longer existed. He'd stared at blank pages and blank walls and his mind remained barren. He'd taken long evening walks from one end of the city to the other waiting for wind-carried voices to reach him, but they whispered in other ears. His Remington Sixteen sat as silent as an unloaded gun. Trendle's one-line telegrams arrived each morning:

"ANY PROGRESS ON COWBOY SCRIPT? (END)"
"DO YOU HAVE PAGES TO SHARE? (END)"
"WASN'T KIDDING ABOUT TOP DOLLAR (END)."

Even now, as he ran through this vermillion dream, he hoped the masked ranger would materialize, but only Barrett was beside him.

They brushed red snow from the Nash and windshield wipers cleared the glass, leaving behind pink droplets, some intact and others dripping down as if racing. They drove through red-covered streets as if coursing through blood vessels. Barrett checked his mirrors expecting the Silver Arrow to appear behind him with Joey Maranto at the wheel, Giovanni riding silent shotgun, and The Undertaker in the back, sharpening his stiletto. No other cars were on the street.

Striker, marveling how the Nash handled corners and came to true stops, something he didn't remember it ever doing well, wished he still owned the car. He worried about Janet walking everywhere during this unforgiving winter, slipping on sidewalks, falling into streets, and cars skidding in her direction. He worried about miscarriages. Although it was still morning, the skies had darkened to dusk as the storm intensified and his mood blackened. A sense of everything ending and being replaced with something unfamiliar overtook him. He didn't know if this new chapter would be a good one for his family. His scar smarted. The city sped by in a red blur.

His thoughts drifted to Pops. Where was he right now? Sitting by his mother's side or sitting with The Undertaker? Was he at the police station getting orders from his captain or was he taking orders somewhere from Cavendish? He didn't know his father anymore and wondered if he ever had.

And still the mask man did not appear.

Forest Lawn's gates were open, and they rushed in like mourners impatient to grieve. They passed Deerfoot, Jish-Ja-Ca, and Ke-Mo Sah-Be, lying right where they'd left them. Chief Red Jacket still pointed the way, his arm never tiring, his jacket now truly red. The Blocher's white monument was peppermint streaked like a graveyard candy. The white stallion still had not been recaptured and stood atop a ruby hillock as if surveying all he owned. He reared on hind legs, froze for an instant as if he, too, was a monument, before pivoting and racing deeper into the cemetery.

The Nash rounded a bend, and Danek's cabin came into view. Cavendish's Packard was nowhere in sight. The ice was covered red, hiding any cracks or fissures. Striker eyed the warning sign.

"You don't have to cross again," Barrett said. "He's my father. I'll talk to him."

"Not alone you won't. Cars can be hidden. Anyone could be inside, even my dad."

"Stay behind, Fran. Be lookout. Honk if anyone comes."

"Forget it. We're in this together. Let's go."

Striker got out of the car and crossed in front of the hood towards Swan Lake. Memories of falling through the ice flooded him: the freezing water, the weight of his clothes, the certainty of death. He balled his fists to stop his hands' trembling. This was as close to one of Slattery's rings as he'd been since he'd been robbed. He wouldn't allow ice or fear to stop him. Barrett followed behind.

He wasn't sure what he'd do if Pops was inside. Confront him? Fight him? Beg for explanations? He'd give anything to see him standing above Danek, interrogating him about Lefty, demanding information about Cavendish, acting like himself again. Striker was sure if that happened, the world would be righted. Words would flow. Roosevelt would be saved. Red snow would turn white.

The tow line was buried. Striker had to hunt for it, kicking the snow, pushing it aside with his ankle until it was uncovered. Smoke rose from Danek's chimney, the smell of burning wood filling the red air. He hoped the gravedigger would emerge from the cabin and call out guidance—to be brave, that the ice was thickest in the middle, that he should move a little to the left—but the cabin door never opened. He picked up the rope and started across, the snow providing traction.

"I'm right behind you, Fran," Barrett said, holding the rope a few feet behind him. "I'm right here if anything happens."

Striker heard his creed—*To have a friend, a man must be one*—but it was quickly drowned out by his pulse thudding in his ears. The radio heroes he created were never afraid. They gritted their teeth, set square jaws, and charged forward, like his father had when saving those women and children. What had happened to that man?

He took a step, and the world did not give way. He placed his left heel in front of his right toe like an aerialist crossing a high wire. Had there been a tight-rope walker in The Hozenflogen Traveling Circus or had a juggling midget and three-legged lion been attraction enough? To take his mind off the ice, he imagined all the acts and oddities under Hozenflogen's big top—The-Donkey-Face Boy, The Elephant Lady, the black horse named Silver. Pando walked among them, juggling bowling pins and small firearms. Striker wondered if he'd write about it someday. Maybe it would be a juvenile novel, a murder mystery, and each circus member would have a motive. As they neared the far shore, he began to think of titles: *Murder Under The Big Top, The High Wire Mystery, Curse of The Elephant Lady.* He worried that he'd never come up with more than titles. And what if he didn't? What if stories and words had abandoned him forever? What then? WEBR would fire him. So would Trendle. How would he feed his family? Where would they live? What work existed in a depression for a writer who couldn't write?

The two radiomen stepped on the bank. Striker's chest hurt from holding his breath and the fears that tormented him. He was sweating despite the cold and again hid trembling hands in coat pockets so Barrett wouldn't see.

"Well done," Barrett whispered.

"After today, I'm never crossing that ice again."

"Me neither."

They walked to the shack, careful not to make noise, and snuck to the window. Danek was alone, shaving in front of a cracked mirror. Striker felt relief and disappointment that Pops wasn't there. He watched Danek tilt his head and reach over, pulling skin taut and stroking downward, cutting a clean, confident line with the straight razor, never once giving thought to nicking himself. The blade moved as if by its own volition, the steel an extension of his hand, dispatching lather and whiskers with glints and gleams and flicks of the wrist. The blade danced across skin. When his face was scraped smooth, he rinsed and dried the blade, folded it closed, and tucked it in his boot, a habit acquired as a street beggar in Krakow. He blotted his cheeks with a threadbare towel and didn't bother slapping on Bay Rum, Florida Water, or Dapper Dan Aftershave.

They moved to the door and Striker rapped hard on the planks. Danek swung it open. "You two again. What do you want?"

"Lefty Mavrakis," Striker said.

"He's dead."

"We want his body. We think you know where it is."

"Why do you think that?"

"My mother told me to see you when the sky bleeds," Barrett said. "She says you know where all the bodies are. This falling red snow is as close to a bleeding sky as we're going to get. We don't want all of the bodies, just Lefty's."

Danek stared at his son as if peering in a looking glass. He saw not only a younger reflection, but the absent years that lay between them. To have him standing on his doorstep again was a penny short of miraculous. "Go home. Please."

"We're not leaving until you tell us where you stashed Lefty."

"Listen to me, son. I'm trying to protect you. Forget Lefty. Forget my nephew. Forget The Undertaker. This isn't some radio show. These people will kill you if you get in their way. And when they do, I'll have to bury you both. Go home."

"Do it for me," Barrett said. "I've never asked you for anything, but I'm asking for this. Tell us where Lefty is."

Above the cemetery, the newly-formed weather system churned and chugged. The heaviest part of the storm hovered over them, blocking the sun even more as if night were falling early. Striker expected the stars and moon to appear, but the sky remained without light.

"You're determined to get yourselves killed, aren't you?" Danek asked.

"Where's the body?"

Something gave way inside Danek, the way it always does when a father can't refuse a son. "You'll need flashlights."

"We don't have any," Barrett said

"God forgive me, I do. Come inside." They followed Danek into the shack. As he opened cupboards looking for flashlights, Striker warmed his trembling hands by the Majestic wood-burning stove. The gravedigger found two nickel-plated flashlights in a kitchen drawer. He switched them on, checking battery strength.

"Where did you bury him?" Barrett asked. "Here or somewhere else?"

"The ground's frozen," he said, replacing the batteries, slamming them in like he was loading a shotgun. "I can't dig graves until it thaws. Spring is my busiest season. I'll work from sunrise to sunset to catch up and get everybody in the dirt where they belong. Until then I shovel snow."

"What do you do with the bodies in the meantime?"

"I put them in the receiving vault and hope for an early spring."

Striker stopped rubbing his hands above the stove. "That's where Lefty is?"

"That's where I left him. You can never tell what dead Greeks and gypsies might do."

"You'll take us there?" Barrett asked.

"It's in the room behind the cemetery chapel. You two go. I'll be watching over you in case my nephew comes back."

"And if he does?"

"I'll take care of him."

Striker didn't ask how. Danek handed them the flashlights and pulled his coat from one wall peg and a key ring from another. "When we get to the ice, get behind me and walk in my footprints. Put your feet exactly where I've stepped."

"How do you know where to cross?"

"I can cross anywhere. Today's not my day to die."

"You're sure of that?" Striker asked.

"Chicken bones don't lie."

"What?"

"The Gypsy read my fortune once. She played with chicken bones and saw the future. She told me when and where I'd die. Today isn't the day. Put your feet exactly where I step."

When they reached Swan Lake, they did as they were told, following in Danek's footprints, only Striker bothering with the tow line. The gravedigger took sure strides, never once hesitating or looking down. Knowing when and how he would die didn't depress him or make him count remaining days. He didn't mark a cabin wall like a prisoner ticking off time served. Instead, he went through life crossing thin ice and busy intersections without looking and without fearing men like Stefano Magaddino. The ice under him didn't crack. In fact, Striker swore it hardened each time he set his foot down, the frozen lake growing thicker and safer with each step.

When they reached the shore, Danek pointed to the Nash. "You drove here in that? The coffin won't fit."

"Lefty's in a coffin?" Barrett asked.

"You think I stack bodies like firewood until spring? A casket won't fit in that car no matter which way you turn it."

"We could take him out," Barrett suggested. "Sit him up."

"Lefty doesn't bend anymore."

"What kind of casket?" Striker asked.

"A Voelker Coupe, but he's the only one in it—for now."

"We need a hearse," Striker said.

"Where are we going to get a hearse?"

"From The Undertaker."

"I'll be burying both of you," Danek said.

"You want to steal Stefano Magaddino's hearse?" Barrett asked. "Can't we grab Slattery's ring and leave Lefty here?"

"Mirela said she'll take the scar away if we bring Lefty to her. Maybe she'll lift the curse, too."

"Gypsy curses aren't real, Fran. Let's get the ring and forget about the body."

"We need the ring *and* the body," Striker insisted.

"But do we have to steal The Undertaker's hearse?"

"He's the only one who has one."

"If The Don catches you," Danek said, "you won't have to worry about curses."

"Can't we borrow somebody's truck? There's plenty of them around that don't belong to Don Stefano."

"The cops will pull us over for sure if they see us driving a truck in a red snow storm with a homemade casket in the back."

"And they won't stop a *hearse* driving in the middle of a red snowstorm?"

"Nobody ever stops a hearse. It's bad luck."

"Do you two even know how to steal a car?" Danek asked. "How to get it started without a key?"

"We both do," Striker said.

"We do?"

"*The Falcon*, Episode Three, "Escape from Sing Sing." You played the convict who boosted the getaway car."

"That was real? That's how you really steal a car? I thought you made it up."

"Lefty showed me. I took notes for the script."

"You *wrote* about stealing a car, Fran, but you never actually *did* it. This isn't radio."

"Lefty made me practice. We went up and down Genesee Street. I must've gotten six or seven cars started. That doesn't count the ones with the keys left in the ignition. Maybe we'll get lucky, and the keys will be in the hearse. I mean, who would steal a hearse?"

"Nobody in their right mind."

"You'll both end up sharing a Voelker Coupe."

"I'll need the tools Lefty gave me. We'll have to go by the house."

"You'll need a crowbar for the casket and these," Danek pulled the key ring from his coat pocket. "If you manage to steal a hearse without getting killed, drive behind the cemetery's chapel. You'll see a double-set of cathedral doors. Those doors lead to the vault. The longest key on the ring unlocks them. Lefty's inside."

Although it was mid-morning, lights came on all over the city as the storm continued to block the sun and hemorrhage snow. The Nash traveled deserted red streets. Schools had closed. Principals feared the snow was dangerous to children, could somehow burn skin, damage eyes, and cause permanent discoloration. Many shopkeepers listened to their wives and stayed home, moving from window to window, stunned at what they saw. Banks used the weather as an excuse to declare another holiday, their holdings safe another day. The New Genesee and The Gypsy's brothel were both doing brisk business, each providing comfort in their own way. Striker blew cigarette smoke out the cracked window, taking in the city swaddled in red.

"We could go to jail, Fran," Barrett said, interrupting his thoughts. "Hearse stealing, breaking and entering, grave robbing, illegally transporting a corpse. We'll be old men by the time we're paroled. Hell, they may try pinning Lefty's murder on us, too."

"It's not breaking and entering if we have a key."

"Fine. Trespassing, then. We'll get out of prison a year early."

"Listen to you. You should be a lawyer."

"What if your father pulls us over? What happens then?"

"I don't know, but it's funny how your father is helping us, and Pops won't."

Barrett pulled down Granger Place and parked in front of Striker's house. A red snowman with stick arms and stone eyes, Bobby and Donny's greatest creation, stood sentry in the middle of the lawn. Striker hurried up the front walk and King bounded toward him, barking and whining, when he stepped inside. He stopped to scratch the dog's ears before rushing up the stairs.

"Fran? Is that you?" Janet called from the kitchen.

"Yes," he answered, not stopping.

"Didn't you take off your boots? You're tracking red snow through the house," she said, following him to the attic.

"Sorry."

"Why's it red, Fran? It's so eerie."

"It's like a sign or something. A warning."

He flipped on the light, then climbed the last flight to his office.

"Milo Mazza was here."

He pulled open a wooden file cabinet and flipped through scripts, searching for *The Falcon* folder. "Who?"

"Milo Mazza," she said, entering his office, winded from the climb. "The furnace man."

"What did he want?"

"The boiler was making an awful clanging noise. I thought it was going to explode."

"Did he fix it?"

"The bill's on the kitchen table."

He wanted to ask how much Milo Mazza charged for coming out in a red snowstorm but decided it didn't matter. Milo's bill would be placed on his desk with the others and wait its turn to be paid. He hoped Trendle would really pay top dollar for a western. He'd settle for middle dollar. Any dollar. Of course, he'd never receive any money if he couldn't write.

"We need to talk about Christmas, too, Fran."

He shut the cabinet drawer, *The Falcon* folder under his arm. "Christmas? That was weeks ago."

"We put too much on credit. The bills are starting to come in."

"From where?"

"Everywhere. You spoiled the boys."

Striker managed something like a smile. "Dollar down, dollar when they catch us."

"This isn't funny, Fran. It's a lot."

"Put the bills on my desk. I'll take care of them."

"We can't just keep putting them on your desk. We need to *pay* them. Remember your creed? Sooner or later, we have to settle up."

His anger simmered, first toward Hoover and Wall Street, and then at the bills he had and the ones on their way. Mostly he was angry at the emptiness in his wallet.

"I'm scared, Fran. Our savings is almost gone. We've already sold the car. Mr. Flickenger told me I can only pay with cash now. How are we going to feed everyone?"

"I'm working on that cowboy script for Trendle. He promised top dollar, remember?"

"Is it done? We need money right away."

Striker turned away from her. "It's coming together."

"What if I got a job, Fran? To help out. In case Mr. Trendle doesn't like the script. I can work until the baby comes."

"Where? Doing what? There are no jobs."

"Mr. Flickenger heard a rumor that Don Stefano is looking for someone to cook and clean for him, maybe help out at the funeral parlor. I could do that."

"You're not working for The Undertaker, too."

"Too?"

"Never mind."

"We need the money, Fran. You know we do."

"Not from him we don't."

"Money is money.

"Let's talk about it later. Barrett's waiting for me," he said, and pulled Lefty's lock-picking tools from the folder.

"You're going back out in this storm? This is important. We need to talk about this."

"We will. Tonight. I promise. But first I have to run an errand with Barrett."

"You're not in trouble, are you? You've been acting so strangely lately. Is that scar changing color?"

He wanted to tell her about The Gypsy's curse, The Man with the Very Small Chin, and the hearse and corpse they were about to steal. But those were stories for a later time, after he'd resolved everything, when they could both laugh about midgets, mutes, and mobsters. She had enough to worry about for now.

"I won't be long and then I'll come straight home. I have to work on the cowboy script. Then we'll talk."

"Damn it, Fran, don't you leave."

He pocketed the lock-picking tools and sprinted for the stairs.

Magaddino's Memorial Chapel was a three-story, A-Frame house with a second-floor bay window. The funeral parlor was on the first floor, The Don lived on the upper two. The crematorium, of course, was in the basement.

Barret's scarf was pulled so high it almost covered his eyes. "I never thought I'd be back here," he said. His tongue felt awkward in his mouth, like it was searching for a hiding place.

"You don't have to stay. Drop me off around the corner. We'll meet at the cemetery chapel."

"I can't leave you here by yourself, Fran. Friends don't leave friends behind."

"It's more dangerous for your tongue if you stay here. It's better if I do this alone."

"I'll keep the engine running in case you can't get the hearse started and you have to make a run for it."

"You'll be spotted in two minutes. The Undertaker owns most of the houses and apartments on the street. His crew lives up and down the block and keeps watch. It's the safest neighborhood in the city. It's better if you head back."

"How are you going to get away if everyone's watching?"

"Nobody'll think twice about a hearse pulling out of a funeral parlor. Let me out over there in the shadows."

The Nash coasted to an inky spot in the mouth of an alley. The two men shook hands and Striker slipped from the car. Barrett took Pando's Derringer and placed it on the seat next to him before driving back towards Forest Lawn.

Striker cut down the alley, his footsteps smothered by snow. He peered around the corner, thankful for the mid-morning darkness. A Ford funeral coach was parked in front of a one-car garage. Three other cars were lined next to the limousine, including the chinless man's Packard. The other two must belong to Giovanni the Mute and Joey Maranto. How many other mobsters were inside checking windows and keeping watch? At least his father's police cruiser wasn't parked amongst them.

He hopped a fence to get into the funeral parlor's backyard. The chain-link was rickety and made noise as he grabbed it, the toes of his boots finding purchase in the diamond openings. He scaled it quickly, hoping he hadn't made too much racket, and took cover behind the hearse. His footprints would give him away if anyone peered out the window. He wished it would storm harder and fill his tracks.

The Ford was mounded with snow, as if red frosting had been spread from headlight to taillight. The other cars, especially the Packard, had less accumulation. Striker wondered if this meant they'd be leaving soon. He'd have to hurry. He moved around the hearse, clearing snow from the windshield and windows with his hands as best he could. The passenger door was unlocked, and he scooted in, easing the door almost closed but not pulling it shut, fearing it would sound like a pistol being cocked in the red stillness.

He'd hoped he'd find the key dangling from the ignition or under the floor mat or above the visor, but he wasn't that lucky. He lay across the bench seat, trying to keep his head down, and unwrapped Lefty's lock-picking tools. His fingers were cold and stiff from brushing windows; he blew into cupped hands. After feeling returned, he inserted the tension wrench into the keyhole and then eased in the pick. It'd been two years since *The Falcon,* Episode 3 had aired. He'd lost what little lock-picking skill he'd once possessed. The binding pin refused to cooperate. He struggled to lift it, not remembering it ever being this difficult. Every second that passed increased his chances of being discovered. Windows would fly open. Alarms would sound. Armed men would shout threats in English and Italian and slog through red snow to grab him and drag him to the basement furnace.

Then he heard Lefty's voice, the memory so strong it was as if his mouth was by his ear: *Keep the tension on, Malaka. That's it. Work it under. Push it up. Tension. Tension. Now jiggle. Lift. Lift. Hurry!*

Everything slowed for Striker—his breathing, his fear, time. Lefty's voice calmed him as he maneuvered the pick and wrench. He closed his eyes, working by touch, imaging the tools doing what Lefty whispered.

A second-floor window was thrown open. "Hey! Get away from there! Someone's stealing the hearse!"

Hurry, Malaka. Hurry. Push it to the shear line. Push!

The funeral parlor's backdoor swung open, smacking against the house, and there was more shouting and curses.

You're almost there. Lift, Malaka. Lift!"

Striker felt the pin give. The ignition unlocked and rotated. He punched the starter button on the floor with the bottom of his fist and the engine turned over.

Bravo, Malaka!

He rolled on his back as Joey Maranto peered through the passenger window holding a gun, his eyes a purplish black. Striker bent his knees to his chest and kicked out as hard as he could. The almost-shut door flew open, struck Maranto in the chin, and knocked him to the ground, the gun firing before falling to the red snow. Blood flowed from the new gash like he'd blocked another jab with his jaw.

Striker swung behind the wheel and threw the Ford in reverse, scraping the length of the Packard with his front fender. Maranto rolled to his knees, searching for his lost gat as Striker put the funeral coach in gear and pressed the accelerator to the mat. The Man with the Very Small Chin ran from the house waving an antique .45 but had to dive into a red snowdrift to avoid being run over. The hearse fishtailed down the driveway, the open passenger door flapping like a single-winged bird attempting flight. He thought he heard gunshots, but it was only thunder.

Niagara Street was unplowed, and Striker drove through it like parting the Red Sea. He'd forgotten to clear the snow from his side mirror and rolled down the window to brush it clean. When he did, he saw the Packard in the reflection. Maranto was leaning out the passenger window, his wounded chin blossoming red. This time it wasn't thunder.

It wasn't Striker's idea to serpentine. He hit a patch of ice and skidded left, over-corrected his steering and skidded right, then swung back left again. Most of the bullets missed their mark, but some sung their way into metal. The hearse fishtailed from curb-to-curb as he fought for control. Panic didn't set in until he saw the flatbed carrying red-covered railroad shovelers driving towards him. He stomped the brake pedal.

The Ford's backend gave way and the hearse spun, the flatbed's horn blaring as it bore down. The funeral coach spun two or three times before it came to a stop facing the oncoming Packard. He could see Maranto reloading. The flatbed roared by, the shovelers' faces wind-burned and terrified as they clung to the truck.

Striker floored the accelerator, the back wheels spinning and shooting red snow like sparks until they gripped. The hearse swayed, then lurched forward at an angle until it straightened and drove head-on towards the Packard. He didn't notice Maranto leaning out the window again, gripping his wrist, trying to steady his aim. He only saw Cavendish behind the wheel, his eyes growing wider than his jaw as the hearse barreled towards him.

Maranto fired twice, exploding headlights into tinkling glass. Striker never wavered. The distance between the Packard and the hearse shrank at a murderous rate. Blood dripped from Maranto's chin as he aimed the barrel at Striker's forehead. The Mosquito smiled.

But The Man with the Very Small Chin did not. He lost his nerve and jerked the wheel to the right. The Packard veered from the hearse, jumped the curb, and smashed into the Sin Will Find You Evangelical Temple, shattering the storefront window with *Holler For Jesus* painted on the glass.

Striker lit a Lucky and drove to the cemetery as if late for Lefty's funeral.

Forest Lawn's winding roads had drifted to varying heights of red. The hearse struggled to make it through, becoming mired by Red Jacket's statue. Striker rocked the funeral coach back and forth, alternating from Reverse to Drive, until the Ford broke free. It plowed forward, spinning its tires in spots, until it made its way behind the chapel where Barrett waited inside *Black Beauty*. Striker backed the hearse to the double-cathedral doors and left the engine running. The white stallion, still free, galloped by, a blur of white against a red backdrop.

"Jesus, they shot at you?" Barrett asked, exiting the Nash and inspecting the hearse. Bullets had pierced the rear door, back window, and the front grill.

"That's the last time I'm stealing a hearse," Striker said, watching the horse disappear around the chapel.

He pulled Danek's keys from his pocket and selected the longest. Barrett opened the Nash's trunk and retrieved a crowbar.

Forest Lawn's chapel occupied the middle portion of a single-story, sandstone building with arched doorways and green-painted window frames. The building had been expanded this year and the Family Room and crematorium had been added to the right of the chapel while the columbarium had been added to the left. Jerry had worked on the project, unloading heavy stone from truck beds for a dollar a day. Barrett trained the flashlight on the door lock and Striker pushed in the key.

"Have you seen Danek?" he asked, opening the creaking door.

"He's behind some tombstone keeping watch. He'll freeze to death if he's not careful."

"Today's not his day to die," Striker said, and led the way into the vault.

There was not much difference in temperature inside the vault than out. Striker could feel cold concrete through his brogans. The walls were lined with metal doors hung on heavy hinges. Barrett played his light across them all. Striker pulled open the first door. Wooden biers ran the length of each wall and held caskets awaiting the thaw. They went down the line, opening doors, searching for one of Voelker's coffins.

"This is creepy," Striker said. "I never knew places like this existed."

They split up, each taking a side, opening vault doors. Striker found The Voelker Coupe behind the seventh door on the left. It was the only coffin in the chamber.

"In here," he called, his voice echoing off concrete.

Barrett joined him, their flashlight beams roaming over Lefty's coffin.

"Old Man Voelker does nice work," Barrett said, admiring the finish.

"Do you want to open it?"

Barrett handed Striker the crowbar. "You're the one who lost the rings."

Barrett held both flashlights while Striker pried the lid. Nails protested their extraction by screeching. When the last gave way, he dropped the crowbar and it clattered off concrete. He lifted the top. There lay Lefty, his once-white shirt stained reddish brown with blood, his tie still pulled tight to his collar, his face bruised. Striker's scar pulsed like a heartbeat.

"Jesus," he said, propping the lid against the bier. "Poor Lefty."

"Should we clean him up before we take him to Mirela?"

"How?"

"I don't know."

"Let's get the ring and get him out of here."

Striker didn't want to touch Lefty's corpse. He wanted to be home, telling stories to his boys about wizards and warlocks to explain the red snow, or working in his attic office, trying to write what he now thought of as The Lone Ranger script. He wanted to be anywhere except in a cold tomb about to rob a dead man.

"Jesus, hurry up, Fran. I don't want to get snowbound in a receiving vault, for chrissakes."

"He's the deadest guy I've ever seen."

"The longer you wait, the deader he's going to get."

Lefty's tie had stiffened from coagulated blood and was difficult to unknot. Striker yanked until he was able to pull it down enough to unbutton the collar. Around Lefty's neck hung a gold chain, but his thermal undershirt stuck to his chest. The congealed blood had grown adhesive, and he couldn't work the chain free. Striker peeled the shirt away with a ripping sound he hoped was tearing cotton and not skin. He jerked the chain loose and dangling from the end was Slattery's ring. The seven circular diamonds sparkled in his flashlight's beam like rediscovered stars.

"Thank God," he said, unclasping the chain and sliding the ring free.

"Let's go," Barrett said, grabbing the coffin lid and setting it back in place. They didn't bother to re-nail it.

They each grabbed one end of The Voelker Coupe and lifted it from the bier, both wishing they had more pall bearers. Old Man Voelker took pride in his work and used heavy wood, never skimping on thickness. Their arms strained, locked elbows ached, sweating fingers lost grip. They dropped Lefty once while still inside the vault and again outside, the red snow cushioning the fall. They left the casket on the ground while Barret opened the hearse's bullet-riddled loading door. The funeral coach was upholstered in white velvet, the exact color snow was supposed to be, torn in places from .45 slugs. Striker lit a cigarette, and he and Barrett heaved the wet, cracked casket into the back, sliding it into place, and slamming the rear door closed. They locked the vault and climbed into the Ford. Striker put the coach in gear. Never had there been a hearse driver so eager to get to a brothel.

Streetlights glowed, the snow around them a brighter red. Barrett led the two-car funeral procession through the empty streets, the hearse following in the Nash's tire tracks. Houses looked locked for the night, though it wasn't even noon. Yellow ribbons of lamplight seeped through curtain gaps. The excitement of hearse and corpse stealing, of being chased and shot at, had worn off, and Striker grew drowsy behind the wheel, lulled by the tires' hum. They hadn't secured the casket and each time the hearse braked or accelerated the coffin slid forward or back, bumping the rear door or Striker's seat, keeping him from nodding off. When the hearse hit a snow-filled pothole, The Voelker Coupe's lid bounced open. Striker rolled down the window, hoping the cold would keep him awake.

The Gypsy's porch light glowed as red as the snow, letting everyone know that it was business as usual on Genesee Street despite the storm. The Nash and hearse pulled around and parked by the backdoor. No one answered when Striker knocked. They had to walk to the front. A boy, no older than twelve, shoveled the walk, starting at the porch steps and working his way to the street. When he reached the curb, the steps would be covered again, and he'd start over, like a shoveling Sisyphus. The Gypsy must have promised the boy something more salacious than two bits for keeping the brothel's path cleared during a red snowstorm. He was doing a thorough job, his edges true, the walk cleared to the pavement.

The whorehouse was as busy as payday. Every couch, settee, and over-stuffed chair was filled with waiting sailors, soldiers, railroad detectives, and long-standing members of the Fraternal Orders of Moose, Elk and Eagle. Mirela's customers were certain the unnaturally colored storm was ushering in doom, and this was their last chance at something like love. An old man sat hunched at the upright piano looking despondent and playing "Happy Days Are Here Again," his cracked yellow fingernails clicking against keys. Outside the air was filled with red, but The Gypsy's living room was gray with cigarette smoke. Cannabis wafted from the corner where jazz cats huddled.

Striker asked the doorman for Mirela. He pointed to a table in the parlor where she sat alone, a bottle of bootleg Remy Martin and a plate of chicken bones before her. Her hair stood as if she'd been electrocuted. The sleeveless black dress worn for days was stained and torn, the lace shawl missing. She arranged the bones on the plate, moving a tibia here and a radius there. Next, she snapped a wishbone in half without wishing, and laid the two pieces on opposite sides of the cloth, the shorter half closest to her. Her lips moved in silent incantation as she separated the seven pairs of ribs, pulling them apart one-by-one, taking care not to break them. She arranged them across the perimeter, framing the other bones, as if the ribs were once again offering protection. Leaning forward, she studied them, looking through clinging bits of meat and skin to answers hidden in marrow.

Barrett and Striker could smell The Gypsy before they entered the parlor, her body odor so sharp they could taste it. When Striker called to her, her name reached her distorted and muffled. He called to her again and she began the long swim to the surface. She raised her head with great effort, as if the weight of her disheveled hair was too much to bear. Striker's cheek ignited when they locked eyes.

"You," she said.

"We found Lefty."

"Liar."

He reached in his pocket and placed Slattery's ring next to the Remy. "It was on a gold chain around his neck like you said."

She stared at the ring as if it were the silver bullet that had pierced Lefty's heart. She would not touch it. "Where is he?"

"In a hearse parked out back," Barrett said.

"You brought him to me?" she asked, tears mixing with sorrow in her eyes.

"Should we carry him in?" Striker asked. "We could use a few more men to help us."

Mirela signaled the doorman, who pushed through the crowd, not caring if he bumped shoulders or spilled drinks. He bent down, and The Gypsy whispered instructions in his ear. Without a word, he straightened, marched to the living room, and picked out the sturdiest soldier, sailor, Elk, and Moose to act as pall bearers, promising them a discount on the lasciviousness of their choice. They disappeared to the back of the house and returned a few minutes later, smiling and stomping red snow from their boots, anxious to take advantage of discounted pricing. The doorman was the last to return and nodded to The Gypsy.

"I must go to my Lefty," she said, standing and spilling brandy and bones on the oriental rug, as if they were no longer needed.

"Wait," Striker said. "My scar. You promised."

"A gypsy never lies except when they do," she said.

She placed her hand over his scar and cupped his face with such tenderness he wanted to weep. He shut his eyes as her fingertips traced every bump and ridge of damaged tissue. His face warmed wherever she caressed, as if soothing bathwaters cascaded down his skin. Centuries of healing and miracles and maternal love washed over him, cleansing everything in its path. Striker's entire body felt safe and held by heavenly arms. A deep peace calmed him. He felt what only can be described as bliss. Until Mirela slapped him. Hard.

His head snapped to the side, the smack so loud the old man stopped playing the piano. Elks and Eagles turned toward the sound, but the Moose, already upstairs rutting, were too preoccupied to notice.

"It's gone!" Barrett said.

Striker's felt his stinging face, the skin as smooth and unblemished as a newborn's. Mirela, her work done, started for the back of the house where her husband's corpse awaited. Striker caught her wrist.

"What about the curse?"

"The curse," The Gypsy said, jerking free, "stays until you die."

EPISODE 15

Shootout!

Striker needed a bigger house. In addition to Janet and the boys, his in-laws, his grandparents, King the bassett hound, and, Jerry, who had been discharged early from the hospital, Barrett had moved into 26 Granger Place in an attempt to hide his tongue from The Undertaker. Living with the Strikers was better than his other options: sleeping another night at the poorly heated YMCA or asking Celestina to hide him on the asylum ward for the less-inflicted.

It was an easy choice to make. He and Striker sat in the living room listening to WEBR and George Armbrewster stumbling through his lines as Dr. Dragonette.

"He doesn't even sound Asian," Barrett said.

"Asian? He doesn't even sound literate. I don't think he can read."

"What did he say?" Barrett asked, leaning closer to the Crosley. "What was that last word?"

Striker covered his face with his hands, each mangled piece of dialogue like an assault on one of his children. "It wasn't a word, at least not an English one. He's inventing his own language."

"Sponsors are going to drop us."

"We need to smuggle you in and out of the station without being seen or we're all going to be out of jobs soon."

Then there was silence. Dead air.

"Oh, God. He lost his place," Barrett said.

"He mixed up the script pages again."

They listened as the other actors—James Connolly and Darcy Menifee—tried to improvise through the scene. "Cut to commercial," Striker pleaded. And they did. Papers were rustled, and then James Connolly read a thirty-second spot for Larkin's Ironing Wax, *Guaranteed To Keep Flat-Irons Clean And Smooth.*

The commercial ended and *Dr. Dragonette* resumed, but Armbrewster was racked with a coughing fit, the kind that irritated throats and tore the glottis wider. The orchestra broke into "Brother, Can You Spare A Dime?," the coughing still audible above the song.

"Shut it off," Barrett said. "If I listen another second, I'll jump out the window."

"We're on the first floor."

"Then I'll go up to your office and jump out the attic. Shut it off."

Striker switched off the Crosley and unfolded *The Evening Times.* He handed The City section to Barrett and kept the front page, the headline reading *Red Snow!* Below was a picture of the white stallion running past dark drifts, but it was the right ribbon column that caught his attention: *Roosevelt To Speak At Music Hall.*

"No."

"What?" Barrett asked.

Striker read aloud: "President-elect Franklin D. Roosevelt will be greeted at a mass meeting at the Elmwood Music Hall tomorrow night that will afford this region its only opportunity to see him prior to his inauguration. This extemporaneous address will be the first in a tour across the state, concluding at his home in Hyde Park. Sharing the stage with Mr. Roosevelt will be a party of about fifty, including Mrs. Roosevelt, local Democratic and Erie County leaders, and distinguished figures in Western New York democracy."

"So, Cavendish will try to kill him tomorrow," Barrett said, letting the paper fall to his feet. "What else does it say?"

"Erie County Democrats were imparting finishing touches for the Roosevelt welcome which will start at 5:30 tomorrow afternoon at the Central Terminal upon his arrival."

"Cavendish could try and shoot him there."

Striker continued, "Erie County's salute to the president-elect will open with a motor parade from the Central Terminal to the Hotel Statler, the streets lighted by flares, the route being Broadway to Main Street then to Delaware Avenue and the hotel."

"Roosevelt won't be in a convertible, will he? It's got to be four miles from the train station to the Statler. He could get shot anywhere on the way."

"It'll be cold and dark by 5:30. He'll be bundled inside a limousine."

"Does it give more of his itinerary?"

Striker scanned the article. "Dinner at The Statler hosted by Lieutenant Governor Herbert H. Lehman and then Roosevelt will leave for the music hall. He speaks at seven-thirty."

"Cavendish will make his move either at the train station, hotel, or at the hall."

"They assassinated McKinley here. We can't let them kill Roosevelt, too. Buffalo will be known as the city where presidents go to die."

"Let's talk to your father again, Fran. He won't let anything happen to the president."

Striker set the paper aside, clasped his hands and bent forward as if grieving. "We can't trust him. We can't risk it. It's up to us to stop Cavendish."

"How are we going to do that, Fran? We might not even get close to the Statler or the hall. Those places are going to be mobbed."

"Let me think," he said, his fingers finding their way to where The Gypsy's scar had once branded him. He stroked smooth skin until he smiled. "We'll get as close as any member of the press. We work for WEBR."

"We're not the press, Fran. I'm an actor and you're a writer. There's a difference."

"Hell, the boss'll be happy we want to do it. Everybody's pulling double-duty at the station since they fired all those people, like Armbrewster filling in for you instead of hiring a real actor. We've both done reporting and announcing before. They'll let us. We'll get press passes and walk right in. Then we look for a man with a very small chin."

"How do we stop Cavendish if we find him?" Barrett said, pulling the Derringer from his pocket. "I'm armed like a midget."

"Yes, but pound-for-pound, inch-for-inch, Pando's the best armed midget in Western New York. We'll borrow all his guns."

Janet waited for Fran to come to bed. She was propped on pillows, arms crossed, her book unopened on her lap. King snored next to her. She heard creaking risers as Striker climbed the stairs, the boys' bedroom door opening and closing as he checked on them, the wind singing its siren song. The hall light was doused. Floorboards squeaked as he entered their bedroom. "You're still up?" he asked.

"We haven't had a chance to talk with Barrett here."

"Thanks for letting him stay."

"Hopefully they fix the heat in his apartment soon. This house is getting crowded."

"Too crowded," Striker said.

"How did the writing go? I didn't hear any typing."

"The Ranger script's coming along," he said, turning to drape his cardigan over the back of a chair, avoiding her gaze.

"That's good. We need the money. The Nagys' on the corner had their furniture repossessed today. Couch, radio, everything."

"Dear god," he said, sitting heavy on the edge of the bed.

"And I ran into Colleen Wall at Kaplan's. She was trying to sell a necklace. I think it was her mother's. She asked if I've seen Lefty."

He leaned forward, resting his forearms on his thighs.

"What are we going to do, Fran?"

"I'll type up another batch of scripts. I'll mail them to stations in Cincinnati, Saint Louis, Muncie. They're good scripts. Somebody'll bite."

"What do we do in the meantime?"

"I'll keep writing. Maybe short stories. Magazines are still paying."

"That takes time. We need money now. I'm going to talk to Don Stefano. Maybe he still needs somebody to clean."

"He kills people, Janet."

"Well, he's not going to kill the cleaning lady, for God's sake."

"How do you know? What if you see something you shouldn't see or hear something you shouldn't hear? He wouldn't think twice about giving you a ride in a Voelker Coupe."

"Now you're being dramatic. Half those stories about him probably aren't even true. Real life isn't like *Dr. Dragonette*, Fran."

"He's worse. He's real."

"We need money. It'll only be until the baby comes. Maybe by then these other radio stations will be buying your scripts. Maybe this Lone Ranger will turn into something."

"If you want to work, fine. Just not for The Undertaker."

"Then for who? He's the only one hiring. He's the only one who has money. I'm not in any condition to shovel railroad tracks."

"I'll think of someone."

"Well, you better think fast because we're almost broke."

The next afternoon, as the sun was setting, Striker and Barrett set off for the train station with press passes tucked in hatbands and pockets full of Pando's Derringers. When they arrived, all the parking spaces near the depot were filled, some with jalopies with patched tires and others with new Fleetwoods and Lincoln Roadsters, their lines so elegant poor men ran their hands along fenders, touching what they could never have. Barrett was forced to park *Black Beauty* blocks away on Fillmore Avenue. He and Striker trudged through the red drifts up Paderewski Drive alongside couples with children on their shoulders or towed on Flexible Flyers. Every light in the New York Central's office tower was ablaze as if hope was arriving on the *20th Century Limited*.

When the Central Terminal had opened three years earlier, a few months before Wall Street crashed, two thousand people had crammed into the grand concourse for the inauguration. They cheered when the first train, *The Empire State Express*, departed for New York City. As Striker yelled "WEBR! Coming through!" and pushed his way into the terminal, he guessed as many people had come tonight. How many innocent people would be killed by stray bullets if The Man with the Very Small Chin started shooting in this crowd and police and G-Men shot back? How many times would the midget's Derringers be fired?

A brass band struck up My Country Tis of Thee near the baggage check. "We'll never find Cavendish in this mob," Striker yelled. "Let's split up."

"What do I do if I find him?"

"Stop him. Tackle him. Create a scene so the cops rush over and arrest both of you," he said, but Barrett, that whisper of a man, had never tackled anyone. He smoothed his mustache and pictured himself on The Allendale's silver screen dressed as The Lone Ranger, wrestling Cavendish to the ground. He could almost hear the applause.

The friends shook hands, wished each other luck, and headed in opposite directions: Barrett towards the stuffed bison pedestaled at one end of the concourse, Striker towards the four-sided brass clock at the other. Striker kept his right hand in his pocket, gripping one of the Derringers, its small size providing little confidence.

The throng's two thousand voices blended into a single din over patriotic trombones. Necks craned, people rose on tiptoes hoping to spot Roosevelt or his wife. Striker pushed through all of them. He ignored the women and scanned male faces as fast as he could, gauging the size of their jaws. The chins he inspected were strong, jutting, bearded, or cleft. Cavendish's missing mandible wasn't among them. Striker grew more impatient and jostled people aside, moving from one to the next, ignoring the complaints of the shoved.

The New York Central Railroad advertised on WEBR. Barrett would often read their tagline: *The 20th Century Limited, you can set your watch by it*. Striker heard those words as if he was standing in the The Gold Room watching a broadcast. He checked the terminal's brass clock. At precisely 5:30, The Limited rolled into the station, its whistle blasting FDR's arrival. Roosevelt's car was the last on the train but would be the first to deboard. The crowd knew this and pressed forward. The police pushed back. Striker climbed on a long bench for a better view. He raced from one end to the other, turning in all directions, jumping as high as he could. Cavendish was nowhere to be found.

He imagined the scene: Police and Secret Servicemen would part the crowd. Roosevelt would walk into the concourse stiff-legged, his limbs locked in braces. Eleanor would support him on one side, maybe his son Jimmy on the other. He'd smile, wave, the cigarette holder forever between his teeth. The band would play something rousing, perhaps Sousa. The crowd would cheer and whistle with fingers stuck in mouths. Then, as FDR neared, an arm would extend clutching a revolver, the arm of Leon Czolgosz, of Gavrilo Princip, of Butch Cavendish. Shots would be fired. Three? Four?

Roosevelt would fall, the world's course forever changed. Women would scream. Men would shout and draw weapons. Others would be mortally wounded by ricocheted bullets. The crowd would panic and surge for exits. Children would topple from parents' shoulders. Women would be trampled. Casualties would rise. Later that day in

Washington D.C. or Detroit, Texas, Cactus Jack Garner would be elevated from vice president-elect to the thirty-third president-elect of the United States, all because Fran Striker couldn't find a man with a very small chin. Striker tore off his hat and beat it against his thigh.

"Fran! Fran!" Barrett yelled, his lithe frame slipping between bodies where only a fingernail could pass. It wasn't until he was by the bench that he got his attention.

"I talked to a porter-friend of mine," Barrett said. "Roosevelt changed plans. He isn't coming up to the concourse. He has a special armored Pierce Arrow waiting for him down by the tracks. Let's get to the Statler!"

Striker leapt from the bench, landed on a screaming woman's foot, and ducked when her husband swung at him. He struggled to keep up with Barrett, who dipped and pivoted through the masses as if dancing across the grand concourse with Celestina in his arms.

They ran through the black night and red snow all the way to Fillmore Avenue. Barrett started the Nash, the presidential motorcade already snaking toward Broadway. Police cars led the way, sirens wailing, followed by dark sedans, darker limousines, and a Pierce Arrow with a pair of American flags jutting from the grille. Sputtering flares illuminating the presidential route were stuck in snowbanks, reminiscent of that wintry Fourth of July when Boogaloo Bailey had set out for Van Slyke's Pharmacy and Pando the Pinsetter had been thrown naked from the back of a circus wagon.

People lined the sidewalks to watch Roosevelt pass. Children waved. Old doughboys dressed in their A.E.F. uniforms saluted. Residents of Buffalo's Hooverville stared, their expressions forlorn. The Pierce Arrow's windows were fogged—perhaps Eleanor was a mouth breather, too—and it was difficult to tell if FDR was waving back at the children or clearing the glass with his hand.

While Barrett drove, Striker pulled a half dozen Derringers from his pockets, rechecking each gun to make sure it was loaded. He hoped his hands trembled from cold and not cowardice. As he returned the two-shooters to coat pockets and pants pockets and vest pockets, he wondered how many guns Cavendish carried, how many men he'd killed, and if soon they'd be exchanging hot lead.

The Statler Hotel rose above Niagara Square across from Buffalo's newly built city hall. William McKinley's monument, a white obelisk guarded by sculpted lions, stood between. What did Roosevelt think when he drove past a memorial to an assassinated president? Did he worry he'd be next? Did he sense a chinless man was stalking him? Did he reach for Eleanor's hand, as cold as it might be, for comfort? Striker was well-aware of the dead president's shrine as he and Barrett skidded by, a white warning of what could happen if they didn't stop Cavendish.

Ellsworth Statler's Buffalo hotel was the grandest in his chain and had lodged the rich and infamous—Lindbergh, Babe Ruth, Al Capone. Velvet ropes cordoned off the walk leading to the Delaware Avenue entrance, the hotel's name etched in black marble above the door. The crowd was packed three-deep unaware FDR had been taken inside through an employee entrance where no one could see his leg braces and wheelchair. The crowd remained, however, and grew larger long after Roosevelt's arrival time passed. Many of them had nowhere to go. Standing in the cold outside The Statler was as fine a place as any if you were homeless.

Striker and Barrett parked blocks away and ducked under the gold ropes, flashing their press passes to every copper who gave them hard looks. They pushed into the hotel's vestibule, the marble floors and fountains quarried from Botticino, Italy, Carrera's jealous sister city. Crystal chandeliers suspended from high ceilings shone as brightly as high noon as Striker and Barrett fought their way forward. The vestibule was large, stretching the length of the building. The foyer was much smaller than The Central Terminal's Grand Concourse, however. The crowd pressed closer together, making it harder to wade through.

"They must be having dinner in there," Striker shouted in Barrett's ear, and pointed to The Statler's Golden Ballroom.

The double doors were propped open, providing a glimpse of life untouched by the Depression. Crystal chandeliers, identical to the ones in the vestibule, dangled above like expensive earrings. Gold leaf accentuated crown molding, balcony railings, and Corinthian pillars, giving the impression that the ballroom was, indeed, golden. Round, linen-covered tables were set for ten, the silverware gleaming from chandelier light. "Let's see if we can get in," Barrett said, holding his press pass aloft as if it would somehow part the sea of people in front of them.

And the sea did part, not for Barrett and Striker but for The Lieutenant, who stood with arms crossed, blocking their way. "Pops," Striker said. He took in the blue uniform and silver badge, things he had seen his father wear all his life. The sight of them today seared him with anger.

"What are you boys doing here?"

Barrett waved his press pass. "Working. We Extend Buffalo's Regards. We're covering Roosevelt for the radio station."

"What are *you* doing here, Pops?"

"Working, of course."

"For who?"

It was The Lieutenant's turn to take in his son's burning eyes, jutted jaw, creased brow. His anger confused him. "What kind of question is that?"

"The kind that gets asked when Cavendish comes to your house, and you don't arrest him." Hundreds of voices mingled in the vestibule. Laughter pealed from each corner. Flashbulbs popped as local dignitaries arrived, shaking hands, and smoking cigars. But in the small circle around father and son, silence reigned.

"You saw that."

"From the front window." The Lieutenant's eyes darted away from Striker as if his corneas would burn if they lingered.

"Why was he there, Pops? Why did I see you with him at The New Genesee before that?"

"You spying on me now, Francis? Following me around to see who I talk to?"

"It looked like he was giving you orders."

"You don't know what you saw."

"I know I didn't see you handcuff Cavendish. I'm guessing you didn't ask him about Lefty either. Smart money says you never called The Feds about the assassination. What gives, Pops?"

The Lieutenant's eyes were restless and roaming, never settling on one face and never returning to meet his son's gaze. They landed on a gilded mirror, his reflection unrecognizable. "You boys shouldn't be here. You're not working. You're trying to play hero. I told you before, Francis. There are no heroes."

"You're wrong, Pop. There are heroes. Everyday heroes. The ones you never hear about on the radio. The ones who fight for what's right. Maybe they don't wear masks or carry guns or get their picture in *The Courier*, but they're out there. And sometimes those ordinary Joes find themselves in a situation bigger than they are and they surprise the world. They dive in and pull the drowning man from the lake or run into that burning building and save women and children. And don't give me that baloney that you were just doing your job. I saw the way you lived your life. You can be that man again, Pop. Help us."

"It's too late for me."

"It's never too late."

"How do you know?"

"Because in there, somewhere, is a piece of you The Undertaker hasn't touched. A piece from when you were a good copper and fought guys like Don Stefano and Butch Cavendish and didn't think twice about it. A part leftover from when you ran inside the Ingleside Home

For Reclaiming The Erring and saved all those women and children from burning. A bit of who you've always been."

Tears welled in The Lieutenant's eyes. He wiped his nose on the back of his hand. He remembered the smoke and flames, the heat hotter than any oven, and the screams of unwed mothers and illegitimate babies that still haunted him. Lately he'd worn the medal he was awarded heavy on his heart, the decoration pierced through skin and beating muscle. The weight of it reminded him of how far he'd fallen since then.

"I remember being so proud of you when I was a kid," Striker continued. "There goes my Pops, I'd say. Every Bruno, clout, and gangster would scatter when they saw you coming. Everyone felt safer when you were around. You can be that man again, Pops. You don't belong in Don Stefano's pocket. You can help us."

Striker's words struck him like a flurry of Slattery punches, each combination finding their mark. The speech had wobbled him, his legs jellied and untrustworthy. He leaned forward, grabbing his boy's shoulder for support. The Lieutenant's strength returned in heartbeats, as if he was recapturing a bit of his former self by touching his son. His spine straightened. He swallowed hard, summoning words and courage and a hint of what he'd once been. "Cavendish isn't here," he whispered.

"Where is he?" Barrett boomed, his voice louder than a dozen lieutenants, maybe two dozen, the sound fluttering wall tapestries and rattling crystal.

"At the music hall."

"Thank you," Striker said, squeezing Pops' upper arm.

Striker and Barrett pivoted toward the door, time too precious to waste. They had ground to cover, a great man to save. Striker felt the weight of Pando's Derringers and The Lone Ranger's Creed fluttered to him: "...*man should make the most of what equipment he has.*"

"He's dressed as a Buffalo copper!" The Lieutenant yelled. Heat engulfed him as soon as he'd spoken, as if he was again back in Ingleside. He struggled for air, expecting to see black smoke pouring into The

Statler like it had at all those years ago. His lungs screamed. His throat burned. He tore at his collar and clawed at buttons, as if trying to get to something better beneath his uniform.

The Elmwood Music Hall was originally built as an armory and the barracks of the 74th New York Volunteer Infantry Regiment, part of Major General Daniel Sickle's famed Excelsior Brigade that saw action in Fredericksburg, Chancellorsville, and Gettysburg. The cavernous drill shed, "The Old Barn," had exposed steel trusses, poor heat, and uncomfortable folding chairs nicknamed 'jackknives' that often folded while in use. The acoustics challenged the sharpest ear.

Depending on where one sat, the sound might be garbled, echoed, or absorbed into yellow brick. The Old Barn's best feature was its size, seating three thousand between floor and balcony, easily accommodating audiences for visiting philharmonics, Enrico Caruso, and several Jimmy Slattery fights, the quality of the matches dependent on the degree of his sobriety. Teddy Roosevelt had spoken there and now his fifth cousin would take the podium to lay out his vision for the troubled country.

Men, who earlier in the day had stood around garbage-can fires on Elmwood Avenue so they wouldn't freeze, were unfolding rows of jackknife chairs, pushing brooms, and hanging red, white and blue bunting from the balcony, happy to be out of the cold and working. The Buffalo officers who guarded the entrance they came to frowned at Striker and Barrett's press passes but let them in. County sheriffs leaned against the stage watching sweepers. Dark-suited G-Men hid in the shadows watching everyone else. As far as Striker could tell, all the law enforcement officers from all agencies flaunted fully-developed chins.

Roosevelt was at least an hour from arriving and the crowd forming lines outside the Elmwood Avenue and Virginia Street entrances were not yet allowed inside. Without the crowds to fight, it was easier to search for Cavendish. They split up with Striker heading toward the stage and Barrett toward the back of the hall. Striker worked his way down one side of the Old Barn and up the other, studying every Buffalo police officer he saw. Some he recognized from The New Genesee, others from speakeasies. He knew who was quick with the billy club and which ones took bribes. There were many he didn't recognize from different precincts and different parts of the city. They all had something in common, however: none of them was The Man with the Very Small Chin.

Striker and Barrett met halfway around the armory, Barrett having the same poor luck. They made two more circuits around the drill shed and not even the cops with the weakest chins resembled Cavendish. They searched balconies, broom closets, and bathrooms but there was no trace of Roosevelt's would-be assassin.

"What if The Lieutenant lied to us?" Barrett asked. "What if Cavendish is back at The Statler?"

Striker placed both hands over his stomach, as if he'd taken a Slattery blow to the gut. "I should've known he'd pull something like that. One of us should have stayed at the hotel."

They continued to walk in circles around the hall, peering into the same faces and searching the same broom closets until doors opened and the crowd poured in. The hall filled with a cacophony of three thousand voices, six thousand shuffling feet, a dozen jackknife chairs collapsing as people sat down. Pipes, cigars, and cigarettes were lit, and a blue haze swirled toward buttresses. Flasks appeared, the owners tippling with a wink, knowing FDR would soon make imbibing legal again. Striker stood by the Elmwood Avenue entrance, checking faces as they entered. Barrett watched the Virginia Street door. Cold air blew in with the crowd, making the drafty Old Barn draftier.

Barrett recognized the face immediately. His heart accelerated faster than Don Stefano's Silver Arrow. His hands and legs grew shaky. He popped a Pine Brothers Glycerin Throat Drop to fight sudden dryness. It took two or three hard swallows before he could speak.

"Celestina!" he called, his voice louder than any weapon that had ever been fired by the 74th New York Volunteers. Steel trusses shook, sending dust floating down like indoor snow. People near Barrett ducked or winced or protected their ears. Cops reached for their sidearms, certain a weapon, perhaps a field cannon, had been fired. Celestina spotted Barrett and a blush rose from throat to cheekbones. Barrett shielded his eyes when she smiled. She waved and floated to him, the crowd stunned by the couple's sound and light. Patrolmen pulled their hands from holsters.

Then she was in his arms, kissing his face, repeating his name, telling him she had missed him to tears. And he was returning her kisses, whispering that he saw her in his dreams.

A breath caught in her flushed throat and she pushed him an arm's length away. "You shouldn't be here!" she said, holding tight to his elbows. "What if Don Stefano or one of his men sees you? You should be hiding."

"*You* shouldn't be here! It's dangerous. There might be shooting."

"I know. That's why I came! We have to stop Cavendish."

Barrett pulled her close. When he opened his eyes, dizzy from her perfume and her body against his, he scanned the crowd to see if anyone was watching.

"Here," he said, pulling one of Pando's Derringers from his pocket, keeping it hidden between them. "Put this in your purse. You might need it."

"Keep it," she said, turning her hip so it pressed his thigh. He could feel the pistol in her coat pocket. "I brought my own."

"You know how to shoot?"

"Daddy taught me. You never know what's going to happen in this town."

Barrett hugged her again and whispered, "Cavendish is disguised as a Buffalo copper, but The Undertaker may have more men here. Don't trust anybody except me and Striker."

"Where is Fran?"

"Watching the door on the other side. Let's find him," he said, and strode off with his shoulders back and head high, already pretending to be The Lone Ranger.

Striker had left his post by the Elmwood entrance. Only civilians had entered since the door had been unlocked, not a chinless copper among them. If Cavendish was here, he must already be inside. He imagined how he'd write the assassination scene and placed himself in the killer's mind. Cavendish would need to be close to the stage to have a clear shot, but he needed to escape as well. The podium's front and sides were too risky. Good citizens might leap from jackknifing chairs, the seats snapping closed behind them, and shove Cavendish to the ground even while the gunshots still rang. There would be less people behind the stage. It would give him a chance to flee. Striker headed that way, the going slow now that the hall had filled.

Above the crowd's bobbing heads, Striker spotted a Buffalo patrolman angling toward the rostrum. His back was to him, his chin out of view, but something was off—his pace was too fast, his overcoat too large. He walked ramrod straight. Fingers fluttered at his side, as if itching to reach for a gun. Striker palmed the Derringers in his pockets. With a flick of his thumbs, he cocked two pistols and pushed his way after him.

When the ill-dressed officer turned his head, Striker saw that his profile was interrupted at the jawline, the contour incomplete. Striker had hoped when danger arrived he'd act as calm and in control as his imagined heroes—but this wasn't radio. His heart pounded like a thousand hooves. Sweat coated his palms. The Derringers grew slippery in his grip.

Then another feeling—euphoria—more potent than a barrel of Dr. Foley's Pain Relief Medicine, washed over him: Pops hadn't lied. Striker hurried to catch up with Cavendish, the drafty Old Barn hot as if it had been set ablaze. People blocked him as they milled around or sprawled at his feet as folding chairs folded beneath them. Striker forced his way around the upright and leapt over the prone, hurrying after Cavendish who'd disappeared around the dais.

By the time he'd fought through the jubilant Democrats and arrived backstage, Cavendish had disappeared. The corridor was less crowded than the main hall, as he'd suspected. Only police and G-Men were in sight. A curving concrete hallway branched in either direction.

Striker looked to his left then right, but it seemed as if only officers with the strongest jaws had been assigned to this area. He closed his eyes and concentrated, hoping he could hear Cavendish's heels clicking, but too many feet shuffled, too many throats cleared, too much of the crowd's clamoring spilled into the rear passageway.

He chose the left hallway, uncertain if Cavendish had gone in that direction but certain he needed to do something. He didn't get far. A beefy copper stepped in front of him, his sweating face full and round.

"That's close enough, bub."

"Press," he answered, pointing to the pass tucked in his hatband. "WEBR."

"I don't care if you're Walter Winchell. No reporters or photographers are allowed to see Roosevelt enter or leave the building."

"Why?" he asked, peering over the copper's shoulder. More uniformed police and dark-suited G-men were clustered near the hall's rear entrance, checking the time, synchronizing watches, awaiting Roosevelt's arrival.

"Because of his chair, genius. Now back the way you came," he said, giving Striker a shove.

Striker had no choice but to follow the corridor to his right. He passed cops leaning against walls, looking bored as if they were working security at a past-prime Slattery fight. The further down the hallway he went, the more deserted it became. A set of footfalls echoed. The acoustics were unreliable. It was impossible to tell how far ahead they were. Striker stopped to listen, holding his breath, but sound continued to mislead. He thought he heard two sets of footsteps, the second pair matching pace with the first. Then the second set sped up, the footfalls mixing with indistinguishable voices, replaced by grunts and groans of two men scuffling. Striker yanked out Derringers and raced down the hall, every part of his body alive and jumping.

He rounded a curve and saw Danek and his nephew rolling on the ground, their faces contorted with rage and desperation. Cavendish's upper body was rigid and unyielding. He'd been pinned but held his uncle's wrists. Danek was strong from years of digging graves and carrying caskets containing multiple bodies. His right hand broke free, and he punched his nephew where his chin was supposed to be, his ropey arm a piston delivering blow after blow. Striker aimed the pistols but the two grappled as one and he was afraid of shooting Danek by mistake.

Danek stopped punching the very small chin and was now holding his nephew's wrist, trying to prevent him from drawing his gun. But Cavendish, despite having never dug a grave or carried a Voelker Coupe, was able to pull his hand loose and draw his pistol. The gravedigger reached in his boot for his straight razor. He flicked it open, but he had made the age-old mistake of bringing a knife to a gunfight. Cavendish pressed the revolver against his uncle's abdomen and pulled the trigger, the gunshot absorbed by flesh and organs and yellow brick walls. Danek slashed at Cavendish's gun hand.

The blade cut through flesh and finger, the razor honed sharper than any szczerbiec or karabela ever forged. "No!" Striker yelled, firing both Derringers twice, their discharge drowned by the cheering crowd enthralled by a fire-and-brimstone speech delivered by an up-and-coming politician from Kenmore. But Striker was more than seven feet away and all four bullets missed their mark, swerving from Cavendish as if deflected by a gust of cruel fate.

The chinless man bucked off his dying uncle and struggled to his side, moving stiffly He aimed his gun at Striker. The blast knocked the writer off his feet, his chest above his heart exploding in pain. His head banged off the cement floor and he skyrocketed, blasting through armory roof and dark night clouds, soaring past Saturn's rings and Jupiter's moons, launching past stars, planets, comets, and meteors until he saw blinding kindred light and had to look away. A single trumpet played for all the heavenly bodies, the notes as clean and pure as if Gabriel had blown them. The last held note, an F over triple-high C, struck Striker at his core. The weight of it pushed him back the way he had come, reversing his course past meteors and stars. He hurtled again by Jupiter and Saturn, through dark night clouds and armory roof until he was back on the music hall floor, the left side of his chest aching as if kicked by the great white stallion. He reached for the pain, expecting to feel blood and torn flesh but all he felt was Bass Reeve's silver dollar in his shirt pocket, dented from deflecting the bullet, and leaving Lady Liberty's profile imprinted on his heart.

By the time his head cleared, Cavendish had disappeared. He crawled to Danek, who groaned and gurgled on his back, his shirt soaked as red as any snowdrift outside. The light was dimming in the gravedigger's eyes.

"The Gypsy was right," he whispered, blood bubbling on his lips, his eyelids closing. "Today was the day."

The hallway felt empty and cavernous, as if something important had been lost and nothing could take its place. Striker hung his head in the vacuum of Danek's death. It was then that he noticed Cavendish's severed pinky lying next to the gravedigger, still adorned with Slattery's ring. The finger felt soft and still alive, the amputated end sliced cleanly by the razor. The ring slid off without a fight, the gunslinger's blood greasing the way. Striker dropped it in his coat pocket.

Two sets of footsteps echoed toward him, their pace hurried but not running. It made sense that Cavendish had an accomplice, maybe Joey Mosquito, The Buffalo Torpedo or Giovanni the Mute, but why would they come back? For the ring? For the finger? To make sure he was as dead as Danek? Or maybe Cavendish had realized that The Don had sent him on a fool's errand and was aborting the assassination, retracing his steps down the hallway, searching for a way out. Striker would be ready when they rounded the curve. He tossed aside Cavendish's finger, almost weightless without the ring, and stood, wincing from pain. It felt as if his breastbone had been broken, his sternum smashed, the back of his head throbbing almost as much as it had the night of his mugging. He dug out two more Derringers and held one in each shaking hand.

Striker inched forward until he was seven feet from the corner and cocked the revolvers. Barrett and Celestina rounded the curve, stopping when they saw the Derringers pointed at them.

"Oh," Barrett said, when he saw his father.

Both he and Celestina rushed toward the gravedigger. The nurse crouched down, checking Danek's pulse. She looked up at Barrett and shook her head.

Striker stood next to his friend. "He was a good man, John. He was trying to stop Cavendish."

"He looks peaceful," Barrett said, and he did. Although Danek had met a violent death, his face was not twisted in pain or agony, shock or fear. The weathered lines around his eyes and mouth from a lifetime of digging outdoors had been smoothed away, a calmness taking their place. The resemblance to Barrett was even stronger.

"We'll have to tell Delores," Celestina said.

Barrett heard gentle weeping. It floated between the asylum's bars and iron screens down Elmwood Avenue, passed Bidwell Flowers, Kaplan's Delicatessen, and all the other shops. It fluttered by empty storefronts and full flophouses. The weeping glided by homes and apartments, the families inside huddled around radios. It skated through motorcades and police lines, old yellow brick and bloody avunculicide, until only Barrett and his father could hear it. "She knows," he said, and Striker and Celestina believed him.

In the distance, sirens from FDR's escorts wailed and grew closer. Striker checked his watch: 7:15.

"It's Roosevelt," he said. "He's coming."

"They won't let us by the backdoor. Let's head to the stage," Barrett said, taking a last look at his father, the intensity of his grief surprising him.

They ran down the hall with Barrett and Celestina leading the way. Striker, slowed by his painful chest and aching head, fell farther behind. On the ground, he noticed blood drops. He imagined Cavendish running with his shooting hand elevated, perhaps wrapped in a black bandana, hoping to stem the hemorrhaging from his missing finger. The blood trail stopped at a utility closet.

Barrett and Celestina had rounded another bend and were already out of sight. Striker called to them, but their footsteps faded away. He jerked open the closet door, guns at the ready, but the closet was empty. An iron ladder was bolted to the wall and led up a shaft the size of an enlarged chimney. Fresh blood wet each rung. *Roof Access* was stenciled in paint adjacent to the ladder.

Striker pocketed the Derringers and began to climb. The shaft was dim, lit by caged lightbulbs creating long shadows interrupted by daubs of yellow light. The chest pain intensified each time he pulled himself upward. Tears filled his eyes and he blinked them away, staring only at the next rung. His hands were slick from Cavendish's blood mixing with his sweat. He concentrated on his grip, amazed that a chinless man could climb a ladder with nine fingers. Each rung was covered in more blood than the last, as if the hemorrhaging increased the higher he climbed. If Cavendish lost consciousness and fell, he'd knock Striker from his ladder perch as he hurtled past, and they'd both tumble to their deaths.

The higher he rose, the quieter it became. He was ascending above the clapping crowd, the podium-pounding speaker, the jackknifing chairs far below. His overcoat was bulky, making it difficult to scale the ladder. He wished he had left it behind. How much further to the roof? Was he halfway there? A quarter? He stopped to rest, hoping to quell the ache in his chest. Clutching the ladder with his left hand, he wiped the right across his coat to dry it. He heaved himself up another rung, but the smooth iron was greasy with assassin blood. One foot slid off then the other. He stifled a cry, fearing the sound would race up the shaft to Cavendish with him dangling like a bullseye.

His feet kicked to regain purchase. A kneecap smashed against side rail. Hanging by his arms, the chest pain was sharp and sudden as if he'd been shot again. This time there was no lucky silver dollar to save him. His arms aching and his grip about to fail, the toe of one shoe found a rung, then so did the other. He wrapped his arms around the ladder, hugging it with his forehead pressed against cold steel. His heart bucked like an unbroken bronco. He refused to look down to see how far he might have fallen.

After a moment, he resumed his ascent, climbing slower now as he worried about his finger and foot placement, not daring to risk another slip. Cold air rushed down the shaft. Sirens grew louder. He looked up for the first time. The hatchway to the roof was open, the shaft's murkiness blending with the night.

Striker climbed faster, praying his hands and feet stayed on rungs, but slowed as he neared the top. He stopped. He took off his hat and raised it above the hatchway, expecting it to be blasted from his hand. When no shots were fired, he placed the fedora back on his head and peered over the hatch. Cavendish stood by the roof's edge, facing away from the ladder and shaking off his oversized greatcoat. Strapped to his back along his spine was a Winchester lever-action rifle, its barrel pointing downward. Striker scanned the rest of the roof for Joey Mosquito or Giovanni the Mute, but The Man with the Very Small Chin was alone. As he raised a little higher above the hatchway, he noticed how close the buildings were to each other. He imagined

Cavendish shooting Roosevelt as he got out of his car or situated in his wheelchair, an easy target in either case.

How many shots could be fired from a repeating rifle? How many times would he be hit? As FDR lay dying on the sidewalk, his blood turning the snow redder, Cavendish would drop the Winchester and leap from rooftop to rooftop until he found a fire escape. Once on the street, he'd blend with all the other police until he could slip away to a waiting car.

Striker swung his leg over the hatch and onto the roof. The Derringers were out and cocked as if by sorcery. The red snow muffled his footsteps as he approached the chinless killer. The air was filled with sirens, honking horns, clarinets and trumpets as Roosevelt's motorcade arrived. Cavendish had the rifle unstrapped from his back, loaded, and was aiming it over the side.

"Drop it," Striker said, when he was steps away, trying to sound like a hero and not like a man who only wrote about them.

Cavendish whirled around, and Striker fired one of the Derringers as he continued walking toward him. The bullet struck Cavendish's shoulder, spinning him. The rifle flew from his hands and over the side, landing on FDR's bulletproof Pierce Arrow below. Cops and G-Men looked toward the roof. Weapons were drawn. Fingers pointed. Officers ran inside. Roosevelt was pushed back into the car when Striker fired the second Derringer, shooting Cavendish in the knee. The chinless man crumpled to the ground, howling in pain, and reached for his holster. But Striker, who had never stopped walking forward, cocked the Derringers again as he stood above him.

"Don't even try it," he said, certain he delivered the line exactly like Barrett would have on the radio.

Maybe it was Striker's tone, or the two revolvers aimed at his eyes, or the onset of circulatory shock, but Cavendish's hand froze near his holster. Seconds passed, as if he was weighing his chances, then he raised his arm in the air, surrendering, his right sleeve soaked in blood from his missing pinky. His other arm hung limp at his side, his shoulder wounded. He looked down at his shattered knee then back to Striker, his face ghostly.

"You," he said. "A writer, of all damn things."

"That's right. A writer. Now ease that roscoe from the holster and toss it away." The failed assassin did as he was told.

Striker kept his revolvers trained on Cavendish while he waited for police to climb the shaft. He was glad the chinless man was still alive to face justice. Maybe Bass Reeves had killed twenty men in self-defense, but Striker knew The Lone Ranger would never shoot to kill. And, as sudden as a bullet, he knew everything about the masked man: his past, why he wore his mask, and how he would save Ezra Holton's gold mine. It was as if his muse had found him on the rooftop and had murmured secrets in his ear that heroes really do exist. The need to write gripped him so completely, he could feel The Remington Sixteen's keys beneath his fingers, hear its hammers striking paper, see words appear before him like newly formed stars.

Snow began to fall. The flakes were white.

EPISODE 16

Fortune Calls...Collect

George Trendle thought his heart was attacking him. His mouth breathing came in gasps. Sweat dampened his silk smoking jacket. Something squeezed his chest. He removed his pince-nez and rubbed his eyes, making sure what he'd read was neither spectral nor the product of cerebral hypoxia.

"George?" his wife asked, lowering the front page of the *Detroit Free Press*, its headline blaring *Red Snow Blankets Buffalo*. "Are you all right?"

"Adelaide," he moaned, as if it was the last word he'd ever speak.

They were sitting in matching wingback chairs by their fireplace, a wine decanter and large bowl of nuts between them, fifteen stories removed from the out-of-luck, out-of-work, out-of-timers who fleshed out the bread lines below. The wind howled and the snow blew, but their drapes were shut tight as if nothing beyond their windows were their concern.

"What is it?" she asked, going to him. She felt his forehead. "Are you ill? Is it your stomach again? Was it something you ate?" she asked, which could have been any number of things.

They had dined that evening at The Detroit Athletic Club and he'd consumed two champagne cocktails with aged French cheese before dinner, grilled sea scallops paired with a glass of Gavi as an appetizer, beef consommé accompanied by a full-bodied Claret, a shaved radish medley, kneaded calf medallions, Lyonnaise potatoes, glazed carrots, several more glasses of Claret, a fruit Pavlova, most of Adelaide's chocolate ice cream, and now decanted Port and a half pound of salted almonds to aid his digestion by the home fire.

"Water," he croaked, and she hurried to the kitchen and returned with a tall glass and a cloth to wipe his face. He drank the water until it was gone.

"Better?" she asked, taking the glass.

"Yes," he said, his mouth breathing returning to a more rhythmic wheeze.

"What was it? Did you have some kind of spell?"

"This script," he said, raising the manuscript to show her. "I've heard it before. Not exactly this version but an earlier draft."

"On what station?"

"Not on the radio. At the club."

"I love when they put on skits. They're always so funny, especially when the men dress like women."

"There was no skit. Nobody performed anything, but I *heard* the words."

"It wasn't on the radio, and it wasn't performed, but you heard it? I don't understand."

"I was looking at the Remington in The Reading Room—you know the one I mean—when I heard this script being performed like it was broadcasted from…somewhere. I sat and listened to it and was enthralled. It was wonderful. When it ended, it was like I'd woken up. I wandered through the club looking for the radio. I wanted to talk about the show with whomever had been listening to it, to see if they thought it was as good as I did."

"And did they?"

"I couldn't find anybody. The place was deserted. Howard the

Doorman said I was the only one left in the club and no radio had been playing."

"So, you imagined it? You heard voices?"

"I don't know what I heard."

"I'm calling Dr. Wolcott."

"I don't need a doctor."

"Lie on the couch while I call," she said, and hurried from the room.

"Don't call Wolcott," he yelled after her. "Call Campbell, for chrissakes. Tell him to get over here right away."

Trendle didn't lie on the couch. He remained seated in his chair rereading the script titled *The Lone Ranger,* Episode 1, "Danger At The Gold Mine." The manuscript had arrived Special Delivery from Buffalo as he was leaving WXYZ. He'd folded the manila envelope, jammed it in his overcoat, and hadn't had a chance to read it until now. Striker's first words had leapt from the page and grabbed his heart, reminding him that he'd heard this episode before, and it'd been magical.

Adelaide murmured into the hallway phone. Bits of one-sided conversation reached Trendle in his wingback chair: *Distressed. Overworked. Addled.*

"I'm not addled!" he yelled, scooping a handful of almonds. "Call Campbell!"

When Campbell arrived, Trendle was being examined by Dr. Wolcott, a tall physician who bore a striking resemblance to a ginger-haired Abraham Lincoln. Trendle had removed his smoking jacket and had rolled his sleeve, the blood pressure cuff tight around his bicep.

"What's wrong, boss?" Campbell asked, still wearing his hat and coat. "Are you all right?"

"He's hearing voices," Adelaide answered. "Cowboy voices."

"His blood pressure is high," Dr. Wolcott announced, straightening after reading the gauge.

"Of course, it's high, you ninny. Something great is about to happen to me."

"Does this spell have anything to do with the robbery, doctor?" Adelaide asked. "Maybe he was concussed. Maybe that's why he's hearing voices. That masked brute punched him awfully hard."

"For heaven's sake, Adelaide. I don't have a concussion. I'm excited about the script."

"What script, boss?"

"The Lone Ranger script. It's there on the table next to the nuts."

"Lone Ranger?" Campbell asked, picking up the manuscript.

"That Striker fellow sent it. He's a genius, I tell you. We need to get him on our payroll. We need to get him to Detroit."

Campbell sat in Adelaide's chair and read the masked man's first adventure. Trendle watched for his reaction as Wolcott placed the stethoscope on his chest, searching for a heart.

"He was complaining of chest pains before you arrived," Adelaide said.

"Elevated heart rate but a strong, steady beat. No evidence of myocardial infarction," Wolcott declared. "Perhaps he ate something that disagreed with him."

"I can't imagine what," Trendle said. "I ate the usual tonight."

"Boss," Campbell said, lowering the script, "this is what you've been waiting for. The masked man, his mighty horse, silver bullets—it's all here."

"Not all of it. Keep reading. I have revision ideas I want to talk over with you before I run them by Striker."

"Can't that wait until tomorrow, George?" Adelaide asked. "You should rest."

Wolcott pulled the stethoscope from his ears. "She's right, George. Listen to your wife. Sleep is what you need. I think you're exhausted."

"Sleep is *not* what I need," Trendle argued, slapping his paunch. "Fran Striker is what I need! I'm calling him tomorrow!"

Striker slept that night with King sprawled between him and Janet. No dreams visited. He didn't relive the rooftop gunfight with Cavendish nor wake to jot a story into his nightstand notebook. Danek's funeral wasn't replayed like a misty Movietone newsreel. Cigarette cravings didn't rouse him. Not once did he get up to check on the boys or to see if Jerry needed anything. When morning skies lightened into smears of pink and purple, he wasn't awakened by his jangling alarm clock or the bell in St. John's steeple tolling the hour. He was jarred from sleep by the phone ringing downstairs—two long rings then two short. Both Janet and King raised their heads.

"Who's calling this early?" she asked.

Striker grunted a reply as the ringing stopped. He flipped the pillow and tried to push King closer to Janet with his leg. The hound was unmovable. Jerry shouted his name, letting everyone know the early morning call was for him.

"Who could it be?" Janet asked. "The station?"

Striker kicked off the covers and got out of bed, the hardwood floors cold beneath his feet. He shrugged on his robe, found his slippers (the left one slightly chewed by King), and grabbed his pack of Luckies from the nightstand. King rolled on his back, claiming Striker's side of the bed as his own. Jerry called him again.

"Coming," Striker answered, his voice rough from sleep and yesterday's smokes. He tied his robe as he descended the stairs and shook a Lucky Strike free, realizing when he had it between his lips that he'd forgotten matches.

Barrett still hadn't returned to his apartment. With Cavendish and The Undertaker's gang behind bars, it was safe to return, but he didn't want to give up feeling like he was part of a family, like he was part of something bigger than himself, a feeling he hadn't enjoyed since he was ten. The blankets were pulled to his eyes, which were open but unfocused. Striker waved a silent greeting as he passed.

Jerry was propped in bed on pillows in the former library, a plaster cast encasing his left leg from toes to hip. Crutches leaned against the wall. He held the candlestick phone in both hands, the mouthpiece pressed to his chest.

"It's a collect call from a George W. Trendle," he said. "From Detroit. It sounds important."

Striker took the phone, sat on the bed next to his brother-in-law, and accepted the charges.

Barrett shut his eyes and pulled the blankets over his head, wanting to drift back to sleep. He didn't remember what he'd been dreaming when the phone had jarred him awake, except that it had been pleasant and rich with Celestina's laughter.

He smiled under the woolen covers as he tried to will both sleep and the beautiful nurse to return to him. Striker's phone conversation was ignored then forgotten. Barrett straddled sleep and consciousness, unaware of how long Striker talked or when the mumbling from the library stopped. He was floating beneath the covers, about to kiss Celestina when he felt a tapping on his leg and the blankets pulled from his face. Striker was above him, unlit cigarettes behind both ears.

"That was the owner of WXYZ on the phone," he said, words rushing together. "In Detroit. He loved *The Lone Ranger* script I sent him. He has some ideas I need to add but wants to make it his lead show—get a sponsor for it, advertise it, really push it. He says he thinks it could be something special!"

"Great," Barrett said, reaching for the blankets.

Striker stopped him. "There's more! He wants this first episode to be perfect. We talked about revisions, and he wants to premier it here in Buffalo as a test run before debuting it in Detroit. He's even coming down for the broadcast and to meet me. John, you need to play The Lone Ranger. You're the only one who has the voice for it. When I was writing his part, it was *your* voice I heard in my head. You *are* The Lone Ranger!"

"Sure. Let's talk at breakfast," he said, rolling over.

"He says we're going to be rich, John. He says whoever plays The Lone Ranger is going to be a star. And not just on radio. Movies, John! Hollywood! Just like you always wanted! Trendle has big plans for The Ranger. This is our break. I can pay off all these damn bills, maybe even the house. You and Celestina could move to Detroit and then California. Just imagine it!"

Barrett sat up, awake enough to let his imagination run as wild as Striker's. "The movies? Hollywood? Do you think it's possible, Fran?" he asked, already envisioning tuxedos and spats, Celestina in evening gowns, his hands wet from Grauman Chinese Theater cement. He saw his name lit up on movie marquees and splashed across lobby posters. He saw everything he'd ever wanted.

"Trendle thinks so. I need to start on his revision ideas while they're still fresh in my mind."

He took the stairs two at a time all the way to his office, each riser groaning at the early hour, leaving Barrett awake yet lost in dreams of what could be. Striker rolled a sheet of paper into The Remington Sixteen and pounded the keyboard, his fingers moving so fast it was as if his typewriter had grown spurs.

EPISODE 17

The Lone Ranger

The day *The Lone Ranger* premiered in Buffalo all storm clouds had passed. The sky was a brilliant blue, the sun bright and hopeful. The temperature had risen and the fat, wet flakes that had fallen earlier clung to tree limbs and sugared rooftops. When mothers opened curtains and children peeked through drapes, the scene that greeted them was so full of beauty and magic, it was as if Christmas had come a second time. The wind was nowhere to be found.

Striker had spent the afternoon building snowmen with the boys and drinking hot chocolate as he told stories by the fire. He now stood under the brass clock at the Central Terminal waiting for Trendle to arrive on the 5:10 from Detroit. A leather satchel was slung over his shoulder containing the revised Lone Ranger script as well as four other Lone Ranger episodes he'd written. Flattened cigarette butts were scattered by his feet. He chain-smoked another. Something rattled through him, a feeling reminiscent of when his children were born and he'd realized his world was poised to change in wondrous ways.

A portly man wearing a camel coat and carrying a silver-knobbed walking stick approached and he knew it was Trendle. He looked like a man who bought and sold things, the type of person who read the business section first. Striker had so many story ideas swirling in his head—The Lone Ranger, a crime fighter named The Green Hornet, a Mountie and his dog having adventures in the Yukon. Walking toward him was a man who could take all those ideas and turn them into radio shows, movies, books, money. Opportunity was calling, and it wore cashmere.

"Fran?" the man asked, pulling off a lambskin glove. "I'm George Trendle."

"It's a pleasure to meet you after all the telegrams and phone calls."

"Indeed it is. And this is Allan Campbell, my right-hand man," he said, turning to Campbell, who was indeed standing on his right side and carrying all the luggage. He didn't have a free hand to shake so he nodded and smiled.

"We're all set for the broadcast tonight," Striker said, as they headed to the exit. "I made the cast run through the script three times. They're ready."

"And who is playing The Ranger?" Trendle asked, his breath smelling of alcohol and chloroform.

"A fantastic actor named John Barrett. When he delivers his lines, you *see* The Lone Ranger. He was made for this part. I've never heard him perform as well as he has in rehearsals. Audiences are going to love him."

"Excellent. And what about the revisions we talked about and the development of The Ranger's character?"

Striker slid the satchel off his shoulder and handed it to Trendle. "Here's the latest version of tonight's episode plus four new ones."

"*Four?* You've been busy," Trendle said. "I'm impressed."

"It's been good to stay home and write. It's been chaotic around here lately."

"Yes, you made all the papers foiling that assassination attempt. Well done, even though I was a Hoover man myself. We can use that, you know."

"Use what?"

"Your heroism to promote The Ranger series. 'A Story of A Hero Written By A Hero.' What do you think, Campbell?"

"I like it, boss."

"I do, too. Write it down," Trendle said, and Campbell smiled and nodded as he readjusted his grip on the luggage.

"Did you want to go to the hotel and drop your bags?" Striker asked. "Freshen up?"

"No, let's head to the radio station. By the way, I wanted to talk to you about the opening and closing music."

"Our orchestra leader, Charles Armbrewster, was still working that out. We tried different pieces during the run-throughs, but nothing seemed quite right."

"I don't care what you use as long as it's in the public domain. No sense in paying some Tin Pan Alley huckster for something I can get for free."

"I'll check in with Charles when we get to the station. He must have come up with something by now."

When they arrived at WEBR, Trendle and Campbell commandeered Striker's office to read through the new Lone Ranger scripts. Striker wasn't invited to join and left to pace the radio station halls, smoking one Lucky after another. He saw Armbrewster through the Music Library window, a room lined with shelves of 78 RPM records and stacks of sheet music. As he opened the door, he heard trumpets, piccolos and flutes.

"What do you think?" Armbrewster asked, turning down the volume. "Rossini. 'The William Tell Overture'."

"It's perfect."

"You know the best part? It's so old it's in the public domain. It won't cost us a penny to use. Isn't that great?"

"It was meant to be."

Striker stopped in The Gold Room next and watched *The Polish Dance Hour* musicians perform the Zgaga Polka until the accordions annoyed him. He made his way towards his office. The door was still closed.

Barrett and the other actors were in an adjacent conference room reading through The Ranger script, which was unusual, especially since Striker had already made them rehearse three times. With most broadcasts, they were lucky to have the finished script ten minutes before they went live, but this Lone Ranger was not a typical broadcast. They'd never premiered a series for another station before. Strangers from out of town had never come in to observe their performance. And Striker, the man who'd saved Roosevelt, had never wandered through the studio wearing such a stricken look, his complexion the same shade as the ash dangling from his cig. Even the air felt different, as if something invisible was gliding through WEBR, swirling around the microphones, waiting for the *On Air* sign to illuminate before touching them all.

As *The Polish Dance Hour* came to an end, James Connolly took his place in front of the floor mic and read the news: two striking miners killed in Illinois, a farm relief bill introduced in Congress, the gas station at Grant Street and Bird robbed of thirty-five dollars. The actors filed into The Gold Room, holding scripts, exchanging smiles and shy glances as if setting out together on a first date. Campbell and Trendle stood in back, a step inside the door. Trendle breathed faster and louder through his mouth. Connolly was wrapping up the day's events. Striker took the director's spot in the booth.

At the bottom of the hour, he pointed to Armbrewster, who dropped the needle on a 78—the WEBR Players hadn't had time to rehearse "The William Tell Overture." Rossini filled the studio then the city, galloping its way through speakers, into kitchens and living rooms. Striker pointed to Jonathan Bliss, who was announcing as well as reprising his role as sheriff from the original *Covered Wagon Days* script.

Throughout the entire west, in those turbulent days, circulated stories of a masked rider. A picturesque figure that performed deeds of the greatest daring…A modern Robin Hood…Seen by few, known by none. Few men dared to defy this man. And those that did…lost. As Bliss read the lines, his voice grew deeper. The golden draperies glowed more golden. Heads in kitchens turned. Ears pricked in living rooms. Everyone leaned a little closer to their radios.

Striker pointed to Darcy Menifee and it all began. Living room couches, chairs, and footstools disappeared. Kitchen tables, stoves, and ice boxes vanished. In their place rose Old Ezra Holton's cabin, his gold mine, and when Barrett read his first line, The Lone Ranger appeared in their homes for the first time. They heard his breathtaking voice, saw the broad shoulders, the fast guns, the black mask. Mothers stopped darning socks. Fathers lowered *The Evening Times.* Children flinched when shots rang out and The Ranger's bullets struck wrist and shoulder bones. Time did not stand still during the broadcast. It traveled backward from Depression to Old West. Struggling families listened with wide eyes and open mouths as Ezra Holton, a struggling prospector, was about to be swindled out of what he'd earned. Sheriff Curry couldn't stop Arizona Pete. No one could.

Except The Lone Ranger.

The coconut shells clapped in The Gold Room sounded like thundering hooves in Buffalo homes as they announced The Ranger's arrival. Listeners saw the white stallion's rippling muscles, flowing mane, silver shoes. They looked at each other in astonishment when they learned that the bullet dug out of Arizona Pete's shoulder was silver as well. They wondered, who was this masked man? Where did he come from? Why doesn't he shoot to kill?

Families didn't speak during the program. They listened with mouths agape as The Lone Ranger saved Ezra from being hanged, as Silver kicked apart a chimney to reveal hidden documents proving Ezra's claim. No one said a word as The Lone Ranger rode off without waiting for thanks or reward. He just tossed a silver bullet over his shoulder as if flipping a lucky coin.

After Ezra's claim had been returned and Arizona Pete and his partner had been led away by Sheriff Curry, Striker again pointed to Jonathan Bliss: *Tonight you have met the most picturesque figure in the entire west. From out of nowhere he rides his fiery white horse. Taking the lawless country by storm. Taking the law into his own hands if necessary. Defying the crooks and bad men. Living alone, riding hard, and shooting straight...We will be hearing from this masked man again...This Lone Ranger. He is riding like the wind to bring help to someone who needs help, and retribution to one who needs punishment.*

Striker pointed to Armbrewster and Rossini filled the city from the Central Terminal to the Statler Hotel. Trombones rattled the bars at the Buffalo State Asylum for The Insane and the drums and cymbals woke illegitimate babies at the rebuilt Ingleside Home For Reclaiming The Erring. Bassoons and French horns drowned out Scaredy-Cat Floyd, Boom-Boom Bennett, and Kid Charlemagne at The Colored Musicians Club while piccolos, flutes and oboes bounced off the Blocher monument and Danek's empty cabin at Forest Lawn. Even Don Stefano, huddled alone in a federal prison cell, heard the work of Gioachino Antonio Rossini, a fellow Italian, and wiped a tear.

Stunned families turned off their radios and looked at each other with hopeful eyes. There was someone out there helping those who needed it? Someone who righted wrongs? Who brought the guilty to justice? Maybe the crooked cops and the railroad bulls and those who had crashed the stock market would be made to answer for their crimes. Maybe houses and farms would be un-foreclosed and repossessed furniture returned. Maybe believing in this Lone Ranger and all he stood for would carry them through this depression. They blinked and shook their heads and searched the floor, hoping that tossed silver bullet had landed in their lives and rolled toward their feet.

Striker pressed the *Off Air* button and the studio erupted in cheers. Actors hugged and praised each other's performances. Trendle and Campbell shook hands, as if they had accomplished something.

Striker tilted his head and released all the smoke he'd held in his lungs. He stared at the ceiling, imagining that all the stories and characters he'd ever write were above him, beyond the ceiling and roof, floating amongst the stars waiting to find him.

Then Barrett was dragging him out of the booth to the others, who pumped his hand and smacked his back. Darcy Menifee kissed his cheek, leaving lip prints. James Connolly opened champagne, the popping cork a gunshot, and poured into outstretched coffee cups. Charles Armbrewster left The Gold Room to retrieve his flask hidden in the Music Library. When he returned, he announced that the switchboard was lighting up with calls about The Ranger.

"You did it, Fran!" Barrett boomed. "That script is magical!"

"You were otherworldly, John! You *are* The Lone Ranger!"

"We're going to be famous, Fran! Rich! Hollywood!"

"That was fantastic, boys!" Trendle said, throwing a beefy arm over Barrett's shoulder, the weight of it causing him to slouch. "We got a real winner on our hands. Those other Ranger scripts you wrote might even be better than this one, Fran. I'm not sure which one we should premiere in Detroit."

"I have so many ideas swirling around about The Ranger, Mr. Trendle. I'd like to talk to you about them."

"Why don't we go to your office and let these kids celebrate? There's something I want to discuss with you, as well."

Trendle, Striker, and Campbell crammed into Striker's broom-closet office. Campbell shut the door and the room seemed even smaller. Noise from the celebrating actors seeped under the door and through the keyhole.

"Have a seat," Trendle said, like the office was his. Striker sat on the only chair, the other two men towering above him. He couldn't keep still. His leg bounced. Fingers drummed against thighs. Heat zipped through him like he'd downed a shot of bootleg whisky. Striker felt like a ten-year-old who'd heard The Lone Ranger for the first time.

"I wasn't kidding, Fran. I think The Lone Ranger *is* a winner. He's special. I think you're special, too. I know talent when I see it, and you have it in spades." Trendle pulled out a bottle of Dr. Foley's and offered some to Striker. He declined. He was already drunk without tasting a drop. A vibration buzzed through him. He fought the urge to leap from his chair and Lindy Hop, Carolina Shag, then Big Apple all the way home to Janet where they would Balboa like newlyweds until the moon set and the sun rose.

"Thank you, Mr. Trendle," he managed to say, the vibration within him shaking his voice.

"I have such confidence in you, Fran, that I want to offer you a contract."

"A contract?"

Trendle snapped his pudgy fingers and Campbell handed him a document which he then handed to Striker. "The largest contract I've ever offered to any writer."

"The largest?" he said, reading the agreement. The number wasn't staggering, but he could start paying the second notices stacked on his desk. He could support the family who'd moved in with him and maybe another set of grandparents or cousins who might need a home. He could help with his mother's medical bills. There wouldn't be much left after all the dresses and dance lessons and bonnets his baby daughter would need, but it was more than he had now. It was a start. It was an answer to a prayer.

His leg bounced faster. His fingers drummed like Armbrewster hitting the skins. The vibration within rattled bones. The actors broke into a rousing version of "Happy Days Are Here Again," as if Roosevelt had rolled in to celebrate with them. Another champagne bottle popped open.

"Of course, we would need you to move to Detroit and work exclusively for WXYZ."

"I'd have to leave Buffalo?"

"It would make revising and collaboration much easier if we were all in the same town," Campbell said. "You'll be able to work closely with the actors and directors and other writers this way. No more long-distance calls and telegrams."

"I'll have to talk that over with my wife."

"Of course, of course," Trendle said, waving the Foley's. Pain relief medicine sloshed on Striker's shoes.

"So, Barrett will be moving to Detroit as well?"

"Barrett?" Trendle asked.

"The actor who played The Lone Ranger tonight."

"Oh, no. He's not coming."

The urge to dance, the vibration within him, the feeling of intoxication, all left him as suddenly as a Gypsy slap. "Why? You heard his voice. It's magnificent. He *is* The Lone Ranger."

"His voice's one-of-a-kind, but look at him," Trendle said, opening the office door.

Celestina had arrived, and Barrett was dancing with her. He held her in his thin arms. She wore her highest heels and was taller than him.

"He has a big voice but he's a little man," Trendle said. "The Lone Ranger needs to be broad shouldered, strong, as powerful as the horse he rides."

"It's *radio*," Striker said, getting up to shut the door so Barrett wouldn't overhear. "No one will see how tall he is. He'll *sound* big, that's what counts."

"But it's *not* just radio, Fran. You need to start thinking bigger. It's public appearances at schools and department stores. It's riding Silver in Fourth of July parades and county fairs. It's pictures in newspapers and magazines and features in newsreels. The Ranger'll be doing those, plus things we haven't even imagined yet."

"You could hire another actor to do appearances."

"No one else has a voice like his. People would know the difference. Kids can spot a phony a mile away. But it's more than having The

Lone Ranger visit churches and Boy Scout troops. It's movies, Fran! Hollywood! That's the goal! That's where the money is! Barrett is perfect for radio, but The Lone Ranger is going to be bigger than radio, bigger than all of us. I can feel it. We'll hire some strapping Michigander to play him. Someone who sounds and *looks* like a leading man."

"I don't feel good about this, Mr. Trendle. We're a team. I promised Barrett. He thinks he's going to be The Lone Ranger. This was supposed to be his big break, too. I don't feel good about this at all."

"You know what will make you feel good, Fran? You know what will make your *wife* feel good, besides that fat salary I offered you? I'll *guarantee* that you'll always have a job with me for as long as this depression lasts. I'll put it in writing. It doesn't matter if the hard times last three years or thirty, you'll never have to worry about losing your position as long as I'm in charge. How's *that* for security? People are getting thrown out of work and out of their homes by the hundreds, by the thousands, and you'll never have that concern. You'll be able to sleep soundly knowing you'll always have a paycheck if I'm able to write one."

Campbell cleared his throat, catching Trendle's attention, and handed him another document. "Of course," Trendle said, "like in any good relationship there has to be give and take. One side can't always be giving, and the other side can't always be taking. That's not fair."

"Of course not," Striker said, his thoughts swirling and dissipating like cigarette smoke.

"So," Trendle said, handing him the second document, "it's important that you contribute something to this partnership, as well."

Striker read aloud, "I, Francis Hamilton Striker, of the City of Buffalo, in consideration of the sum of ten dollars, do hereby sell, assign, and transfer all existing and future manuscripts of which I am the author entitled *The Lone Ranger* to George Washington Trendle, of the City of Detroit…"

WEBR grew as silent as Forest Lawn.

Singing and laughter from the other side of the door stopped. The words Striker read filled the little office, cramming every nook, cranny, and corner like a dirge. No one spoke. Trendle breathed silently through his nose. The document Striker held didn't rustle. He felt as if he was back on the ladder at The Elmwood Music Hall, hundreds of feet in the air, his grip giving way as he tumbled into a screamless fall.

Two quick knocks rapped, startling the three men. Barrett opened the door, his face flushed from champagne and dancing. "We're out of booze, Fran. We're moving the party to Voelker's. You gotta come, too."

"Yeah, sure. I'm right behind you."

"You're invited, too, Mr. Trendle. We're all in this together now," Barrett said, and shut the door before Trendle could answer.

Striker re-read the document. "You want to buy the rights to *The Lone Ranger?*"

"There has to be give and take, Fran."

"For *ten* dollars?"

"Think of the salary, Fran. The security. Your family."

And he did. He thought of Janet, Bobby, Donny, the baby on the way. He thought of his grandparents and his in-laws and Jerry's and Pops' medical bills. He thought of Janet's grandparents and all the widowed aunts and older uncles who might need help surviving this depression. He thought of Christmas bills, and furnace bills, and second notices. He even thought of King the bassett hound. He thought of everyone, in fact, but himself.

Then, as if The Lone Ranger were standing by him reciting his creed, he heard the words that were both true and sometimes heartbreaking—that men should live by the rule of what is best for the greatest number.

And The Gypsy laughed.

EPISODE 18

Slattery Returns

The night was crisp and clear, the sky a blanket of polished diamonds. Striker trudged through the falling snow. There wasn't a breath of wind. A cigarette burned between his lips, the tobacco harsh and bitter. He smoked it anyway. His copies of the signed documents were folded inside his breast pocket above the bruise left by Bass Reeve's silver dollar. It felt as if two bricks were pressed against his heart, forcing it to earn each beat. One contract gave him and his family security. The other, he was sure, would give him a lifetime of regrets. Trendle had made it clear that the two could not exist without each other.

Selling the rights to The Lone Ranger felt wrong, like he'd abandoned his child on a rich man's doorstep. But did it matter? What if The Ranger series was like *Ghost Ship* or *Drums of Kali* or *The Falcon*, shows he'd written that had run their course after ten or twenty episodes, then were replaced by others and forgotten? What if there were no Lone Ranger books or movies or toys? What if ten dollars was a cheap price to pay for providing for his family?

Then again, what if *The Lone Ranger* was as successful as Trendle had imagined? What if it was *more* successful? How could he tell Barrett he would never play the masked man again?

Voelker's bowling sign seemed greener against the cloudless backdrop, the neon buzzing like a thousand hornets. Striker thought of turning around and walking home, confessing it all to Janet, but he needed to talk to Barrett first. He deserved better than hearing it from Trendle or, worse, Campbell. Striker was the one who had to tell him the untellable.

He knocked three times on the side door, paused, then knuckled a final rap. The peephole flipped open. "What do you want?"

"To bowl a few frames."

The peephole snapped shut and deadbolts slid free. The door opened enough for him to turn sideways and enter the speakeasy before slamming shut behind him. The deadbolts locked into place. He unbuttoned his overcoat and outstretched his arms, but Little John Liddle made no move to pat him down.

"You ain't been around lately," the bouncer said.

"I've been busy. How you doing tonight, Little John?"

"Not aces. I've been looking for you."

Little John Liddle's face twisted as if a great struggle were taking place beneath the skin, a wrestling match between right and wrong. His expression contorted, the battle intensifying. The scar that cleaved his sloping forehead deepened as if he were about to split open.

"I've been looking for you for a long time," he said, and his right hand crept inside his suitcoat and stayed there, the wrestling match with his conscious entering the second of three falls.

Striker flushed as if he were tied in front of The Undertaker's oven. The world shifted, and realization slapped him hard, harder than when The Gypsy had smacked his scar away. He was certain Little John Liddle was about to pull an automatic from his jacket and aim it at his heart. He saw everything galloping away: his family, The Lone Ranger, Detroit, his salary. Never once had he thought that Little John Liddle worked for Stefano Magaddino—until now. Even from his cold cell, The Don was pulling strings, tying loose ends, eliminating witnesses.

"I'm sorry," the bouncer said, and great tears spilled down his cheeks, landing on his unpolished wingtips.

"John, don't," Striker said, but the bouncer's arm was already moving. Striker wished he still had a Pando Derringer and wondered if he could've outdrawn him. He braced for bullets, hoping they wouldn't hurt too much. Janet's and his sons' faces danced around him. He wanted to hold them one last time. Characters he hadn't written yet—Tonto, Dan Reid, Britt Reid, Tom Quest, Sergeant Preston and his dog King—crowded into the speakeasy's vestibule, their lives in the balance as much as his. Radios across the city went silent, as if they, too, were waiting to see what happened next.

Little John Liddle yanked his arm from his coat, but he wasn't holding a pistol or an automatic. He held a fistful of cash and offered it to Striker.

"I'm sorry," he repeated.

Tonto gave the signal and young Tom Quest, the Mountie and his dog, and the Reids disappeared into the aether, awaiting the time when Striker needed them. Radios in Buffalo resumed broadcasting.

"What's this?" Striker asked.

"It's all of it. I didn't keep none."

"All of what, Little John? You don't owe me anything."

The bouncer nodded his head violently. "I do. I do. I never should have done it."

"What are you talking about?"

"She made me. That voice in my head. She kept whispering for me to do it. She wouldn't stop. I didn't want to. I always liked you. You never caused no trouble in here, but She made me."

"Made you do what, Little John?"

"Smack your head and steal them rings."

"*You* stole them?"

"She made me. I saw Slats give you them when I was making my rounds inside. They looked so pretty. That's when She started telling me to do it. To knock you over the head with my gat and swipe them. She wouldn't stop."

"Where'd the money come from?" Striker asked, taking the cash and counting it.

"I sold them to Lefty. The next day I felt bad about what I done. I tried to find him and buy the rings, but I couldn't find him nowhere. She was mad that I wanted to give them back and kept yelling at me until my brain hurt."

"Lefty's dead, Little John. That's why you couldn't find him."

The bouncer's eyes grew wider than Bass Reeves' silver dollars. "I didn't kill him, did I? I don't remember Her telling me to do that."

"The Man with the Very Small Chin shot him," Striker said, and finished counting. Lefty had paid Little John a quarter of what the rings were worth. He held the money out to him. "This isn't mine."

Little John Liddle took two steps back and raised his arms as if about to stop a freight train. "No, no, no. If I keep it, She'll be after me to get more the same way—by clobbering people. She keeps telling me how easy it was, how I could be a rich man and go to The Gypsy's house every night and lay with pretty girls."

"Maybe we should give the money to Slats if he comes back. They were his rings you stole."

"He'll drink it away," the bouncer said. "You keep it."

Three hard knocks, a pause, and then a final knock came from the door. Little John Liddle flipped the peep hole open, but no one was there. He turned back to Striker. "The money's yours. Take it so I can sleep."

Three more knocks, another pause, a final rap. The bouncer opened the mail slot but again saw nobody.

"Jesus Christ," a voice said, from the other side. "Down here. It's Pando, you moron."

"What do you want?"

"To bowl a few frames. Now open the goddamn door."

Little John slid back the deadbolts and let Pando into the speakeasy. "You got to leave your little gun with me."

"I know the drill," Pando said, pulling a Derringer from his pocket. "It's not like I don't come here every night, for chrissakes. Oh, hi-yo, Striker. I didn't see you standing behind this knucklehead."

"I've been looking for you, Pando."

Pando wiped his forehead with his forearm, still sweating his way through withdrawal. "You need to borrow my guns again?"

"No, this is yours," Striker said, and held out the money.

"Mine?" Pando asked, taking the cash. "Why?"

"Your reward for saving Roosevelt. If it wasn't for your Derringers, I never would've stopped The Man with the Very Small Chin. That money came from FDR himself. He wanted you to have it."

"I'll be damned. Now I wish I'd voted for him. Open the door, Little John. I'm buying tonight," he said, and all thoughts of remaining on the wagon were forgotten.

Little John let Pando inside and shook his head at Striker, still holding the door open. "You and your stories." Striker shrugged and fished out another Lucky.

"No hard feelings?" Little John asked, sticking out his hand.

"None," Striker answered, the bouncer's mitt devouring his when he shook it.

"I hope stealing Slattery's rings didn't cause you no trouble."

"Nothing to write about."

When Striker stepped into the bar, everybody cheered. The band played better, women's perfume smelled more alluring, the beer thrust at him felt colder, but none of it made him feel better. Trendle's documents anchored him in place. Barrett waved from the dancefloor as he twirled Celestina, and Striker sunk another foot. Never had a few sheets of paper weighed so much.

Armbrewster gestured to an empty stool next to him. Before Striker could reach it, another cheer erupted. He turned as Slattery entered the speakeasy dragging one damaged leg, looking as if he'd gone another fifteen rounds with Maxie Rosenbloom and the outcome had been the same. His left eye was swollen shut and a mouse puffed beneath the right. His lip was cut, his Irish grin was even more crooked as if his face had been punched out of alignment. He held up his arms and pumped the air with bruised fists, like he'd won something.

"What do you say, Shakespeare?" he asked, when the applause stopped.

"I say I'm glad to see you. How you feeling?"

"Hungry. I'm hoping Old Man Voelker'll cook me some schnitzel. Can't remember the last time I ate."

"When did you get back?"

"Can't remember that either. It was a hell of a bender. I woke up about a half hour ago at The Gypsy's house. She threw me out when I told her I was out of money. She's a tough one."

"You have no idea."

"Say, you got my rings?"

"Of course," Striker said, taking them off the chain around his neck and handing them over. He, like Lefty, no longer trusted pockets.

Slattery slipped them on and, once again, the one hundred thirty-five-day champion had diamonds on his fingers but no dollars in his wallet.

"Did I miss anything while I was gone?"

Striker thought of the stolen rings, The Man with the Very Small Chin, Lefty's murder, The Gypsy's curse, the adventures at Swan Lake, Boogaloo Bailey's return and sudden departure, red snow, Danek's death, saving FDR, and creating The Lone Ranger. He knew it was someone else's story to tell. He was too tired.

"Pando'll fill you in. He's buying," he said, pointing to the pinsetter on his special stool, sitting as tall as any man in the place.

"Pando *buying*? Things *have* changed. Talk to you later, Shakespeare," he said, and limped his way over to bum a drink and order schnitzel.

Striker stood on the edge of the beginning, taking it all in. He would miss this place with Hans pouring illegal drinks and the sawdust in Old Man Voelker's hair. He'd miss The Colored Musicians Club and all the jazz cats making magic on stage. He'd miss Tamis at The New Genesee and Armbrewster and all the actors at WEBR. He'd miss Slattery and Pando haunting speakeasies and borrowing beer money. He'd miss every part of the city from Genesee Street to Elmwood Avenue and every direction in between. Most of all he'd miss Barrett. But he didn't know that would start tonight and last a lifetime.

He struck a match and lit a Lucky, but the flame wasn't bright enough to reveal the future. He couldn't see the seven hundred Lone Ranger radio scripts, the eighteen Ranger novels, and dozen more young-adult books that he would write. He couldn't make out The Green Hornet or Sergeant Preston or Tom Quest. At least not yet. The flaring match didn't shine on the millions Trendle would make off the masked man or his claims in interviews and closing credits that it was he, not Striker, who'd created him.

It was too dark in Voelker's to know that Trendle would honor their agreement and pay his salary throughout The Depression, only firing him once in the '40s when he'd ask for a raise but hiring him back when sponsors complained. The match had been extinguished long before it could show Barrett, that whisper of a man, shoving him aside and storming away from radio and their friendship. He'd marry Celestina and become a lawyer. Instead of using his voice to play heroes on the air or in Hollywood, he'd use it to be a hero in the courtroom, defending the innocent and those who needed help. The only argument he wouldn't win would be the one he was about to have.

Striker didn't see any of this. Instead, he saw everyone gathered together for one final time, their arms tossed over each other's shoulders, their glasses raised, their singing and laughter like hoofbeats thundering from the past, echoing forever.

(MUSIC FINALE)

Author's Note

Novels are never written in a vacuum, and there are always people who help turn an idea into something you can hold. As always, I need to thank Carla Damron, Dartinia Hull, Beth Uznis Johnson, and Ashley Warlick for revision suggestions, a text thread that has run for over ten years, and free jars of moonshine. Fred Leebron deserves a special thanks for all his support and for believing in *Yesteryear* when no one else did. I can't thank Andrew Gifford at the mighty SFWP enough for taking a chance on me twice and for his tireless support for all his authors. Adam Sirgany has my deepest gratitude for editing *Yesteryear*. He made it a better book, and I will miss our Sunday afternoon Zoom calls.

While *Yesteryear* is based on a true story and historical characters, I shaped certain elements for convenience and to fit the narrative timeline. For instance, I relocated Stefano Magaddino's funeral parlor from Niagara Street in Niagara Falls, New York to Niagara Street in Buffalo. I described The Colored Musicians Club's present location, but it didn't relocate to 145 Broadway until 1934, a year after the events described in *Yesteryear*. 1934 was also the year Striker signed the contract with Trendle not 1933. Chalk up all other historical inaccuracies to poetic license.

Research provided me with a great excuse to buy more books. All the works listed in the bibliography were invaluable and provided rich details for me to weave throughout the story. *His Typewriter Grew Spurs* by Fran Striker, Jr. was especially helpful. The Striker family donated Fran's papers to the State University of New York at Buffalo, and going through those cartons was both an education and a joy. I'm grateful to the UB Special Collections librarians for all their help.

As for the magical elements in the novel, those are all true and occurred as written.

—SGE

Bibliography

Bickel, Mary E. 1971. *Geo. W. Trendle, Creator and Producer Of: The Lone Ranger, the Green Hornet, Sgt. Preston of the Yukon, the American Agent, and Other Successes.* New York: Exposition Press.

Bisco, Jack. "Buffalo's Lone Ranger: The Prolific Fran Striker Wrote the Book on Early Radio," *Western New York Heritage* vol 7. no. 4 (Winter 2015).

Blake, Rich. 2015. *Slats: The Legend and Life of Jimmy Slattery.* Buffalo, NY: No Frills Buffalo.

Burton, Arthur T. 2008. *Black Gun, Silver Star: The Life and Legend of Frontier Marshal Bass Reeves.* Lincoln, Neb.: University Of Nebraska Press; Chesham.

Corr, Jack "Lone Ranger Author Taking us on 1 Last Ride." n.d. Chicago Tribune. Accessed January 11, 2023. https://www.chicagotribune.com/news/ct-xpm-1986-02-19-8601130429-story.html.

French, Jack. 1998. "The Miser of Motown: George W. Trendle." Www.cobbles.com. Accessed January 11, 2023. https://www.cobbles.com/simpp_archive/linkbackups/george-trendle_miser.htm.

Grams, Martin. 2015. "Martin Grams: Myth Debunked: Bass Reeves Was NOT the Lone Ranger." Martin Grams. April 2, 2015. http://martingrams.blogspot.com/2015/04/myth-debunked-bass-reeves-was-not-lone.html.

Hudson, Mike. 2008. *Mob Boss: A Biography in Blood.* Niagara Falls, N.Y.: Power City Press.

Maltin, Leonard. 1997. *The Great American Broadcast.* E P Dutton.

Michaels, Albert L, Richard O Reisem, and Bette A Rupp. 1996. *Forest Lawn Cemetery*. Buffalo, NY: Forest Lawn Heritage Foundation.

Marcou, Dan. 2013. "Police History: Was U.S. Marshal Bass Reeves the Real Lone Ranger?" Police1. August 26, 2013. https://www. police1.com/police-heroes/articles/police-history-was-us-marshal-bass-reeves-the-real-lone-ranger-zpapufnIejg5PgTJ/.

Osgood, Dick. 1981. *Wyxie Wonderland*. Bowling Green, Ohio: Bowling Green University Popular Press.

Rizzo, Michael F. 2012. *Gangsters and Organized Crime in Buffalo: History, Hits and Headquarters*. Charleston, SC: History Press.

Rothel, David. 2013. *Who Was That Masked Man? The Story of The Lone Ranger*. Nashville, TN. Riverwood Press.

Striker, Francis. 1929-1986. *Francis Hamilton Striker Papers*. Buffalo, NY: SUNY Buffalo Archive and Manuscript Collections.

Striker Jr., Fran. 1983. *His Typewriter Grew Spurs… A Biography of Fran Striker—Writer: Documenting the Lone Ranger's Ride on the Radiowaves of the World*. Runnemede, NJ: Fran Striker, Jr.

Voyles, Kenneth H, and John A Bluth. 2001. *The Detroit Athletic Club, 1887-2001*. Arcadia Publishing.

Warner, Jennifer. 2012. *The Lone Ranger*. BookCaps Study Guides.

About the Author

Stephen G. Eoannou is the author of the award-winning short story collection, *Muscle Cars*, and the novel *Rook*. He holds an MFA from Queens University of Charlotte and an MA from Miami University. His work has been awarded an Honor Certificate from The Society of Children's Book Writers and Illustrators and won the Best Short Screenplay Award at the 36th Starz Denver Film Festival. Eoannou lives and writes in his hometown of Buffalo, New York, the setting and inspiration for *Yesteryear*. Find him online at sgeoannou.com and on Twitter @StephenGEoannou.

Also from Stephen G. Eoannou

"These stories will transport you. Enjoy the ride."
— K. L. Cook, Author of *Love Songs for the Quarantined*
   and *Last Call*

"Part Richard Russo, part Bruce Springsteen, part OTB parlors
and Cutlass Supremes, Eoannou's debut collection is all—all—
heart. A fine first collection, and I look forward to the next."
— Brett Lott, author of *Jewel*, an Oprah Book Club Selection.

"*Muscle Cars* is a magnificent debut."
— Ashley Warlick, author of *Seek The Living* and *The Summer
   After June*

About Santa Fe Writers Project

SFWP is an independent press founded in 1998 that embraces a mission of
artistic preservation, recognizing exciting new authors, and bringing out of
print work back to the shelves.

  @santafewritersproject | @SFWP | sfwp.com